House of Shadows

House of Shadows is Pamela Hartshorne's fourth novel to explore the haunting relationship between the past and the present. An historian as well as an award-winning romance writer, she lives in York, and continues to draw inspiration from her PhD research to write about the 16th century, in fact and in fiction. *Time's Echo*, her first novel written under her real name, was shortlisted for awards on both sides of the Atlantic.

You can find out more about Pamela here:
www.pamelahartshorne.com
facebook.com/PamelaHartshorneAuthor
@PamHartshorne

By Pamela Hartshorne

Time's Echo

The Memory of Midnight

The Edge of Dark

House of Shadows

Praise for Pamela Hartshorne

'What a terrific novel. I really enjoyed it and became
deeply involved in the lives of the two heroines'
Elizabeth Buchan

'If you love history, romance and ghosts, you'll love this'
Deborah Swift

'A superbly haunting time-tripping story'
Peterborough Telegraph

'Fast-moving and atmospheric, it's an involving read'
Choice

'I read the last page and was left wanting more.
That's how good the story is . . . her characters are
strong, and her plot is excellent. Great stuff'
Shropshire Star

'Hartshorne weaves her own bit of
magic with this bewitching tale'
Northern Echo

'A rattling good read'
York Press

'A fantastic page-turner, filled with twists and turns and a
great cast of characters . . . perfect for fans of Tudor fiction
such as Philippa Gregory, and of course fans of time-slip
fiction such as that of Barbara Erskine'
Lisa Reads Books

PAMELA HARTSHORNE

House of Shadows

PAN BOOKS

First published 2015 by Macmillan

This paperback edition first published 2016 by Pan Books
an imprint of Pan Macmillan
20 New Wharf Road, London N1 9RR
Associated companies throughout the world
www.panmacmillan.com

ISBN 978-1-4472-4958-0

1 3 5 7 9 8 6 4 2

A CIP catalogue record for this book is available from the British Library.

Typeset by Ellipsis Digital Limited, Glasgow
Printed and bound by CPI Group (UK) Ltd, Croydon, CR0 4YY

Visit www.panmacmillan.com to read more about all our books
and to buy them. You will also find features, author interviews and
news of any author events, and you can sign up for e-newsletters
so that you're always first to hear about our new releases.

House of Shadows

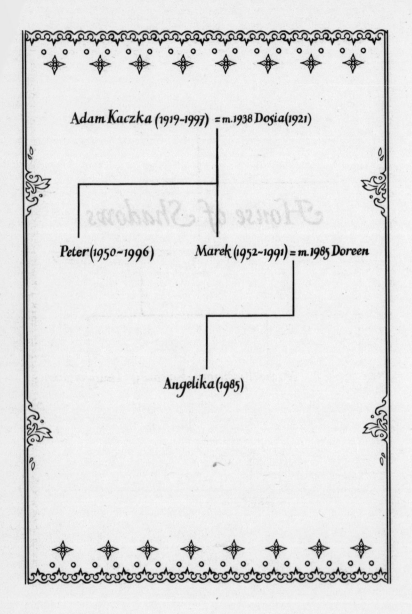

Adam Kaczka (1919–1997) = m.1938 Dosia (1921)

Peter (1950–1996)   Marek (1952–1991) = m.1985 Doreen

Angelika (1985)

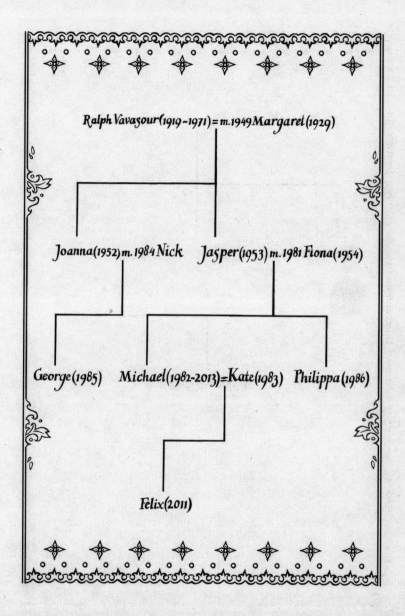

Ralph Vavasour (1919–1971) = m.1949 Margaret (1929)

Joanna (1952) m.1984 Nick   Jasper (1953) m.1981 Fiona (1954)

George (1985)   Michael (1982-2013) = Kate (1983)   Philippa (1986)

Felix (2011)

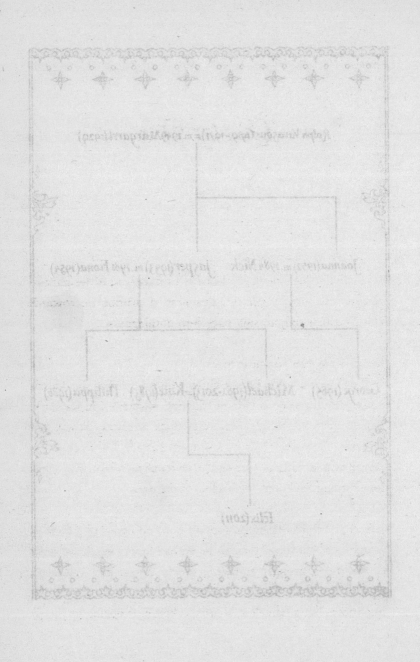

Chapter One

What's your first memory? Mine is of darkness, of weightlessness, of waiting. A stir of awareness, a drifting up towards consciousness only to sink back into nothingness.

'Kate? Kate, can you hear me?'

I can hear a voice. I don't know who Kate is, but she doesn't answer. Perhaps she is like me, floating, suspended in the dark. It feels peaceful, this blankness. A thick, cushiony absence of sensation. Whenever I drift close to its surface, the blackness is jagged with shards of pain and a clamouring terror that sends me scuttling back into the shelter of the dark.

It is later, I think. There's a sound I don't recognize: a lazy hiss, a long sigh, but too regular to be human. In my head, the sense of waiting is stronger, spiralling slowly at first into insistence, and then urgency. There is something I need to do, something important, but a nameless, shapeless horror is licking its lips at the edges of my consciousness, and I'm afraid. I know I must wake up, I must remember, but I can't, I *won't*. It's safer to stay hidden in the dark.

Fragments.

'How long can she go on like this?' A voice, fretful.

'She's breathing on her own now. The doctors say we just have to wait.' A different voice. Calm, cold. No way of telling if the voices belong to a man or a woman. They come to me from a great distance, distorted by the depths of my unconsciousness.

'It would have been better if she'd died.' Bitterly.

'Don't say that.' A pause. 'Not here.'

It could be a dream. Does that mean I am asleep? I think I must be.

A sensation of not being alone, a hand cool against my wrist, and dread, stabbing out of nowhere. Someone bending over me. I can feel the press of a body, feel breath on my cheek, and a whispering in my ear, rank with malice.

'You were supposed to die.'

It is quick, so quick I may be imagining it, but I'm sure of the relief that floods through me when the fingers slide from my arm and whoever it is straightens.

'Oh, nurse, how is she doing today?'

That may be a dream, too. I hope it is. I hope I am dreaming.

*

Remember. You must remember. The thought struggles through the dark and the fear and a white glare of pain, but it is like putting a shoulder to a stiff door. I strain to open my mind, but when I force a crack all I can see is terror swooping towards me and I try to scream but I can't open my mouth. I can't breathe. I can't move. *I can't move!*

'I think she might be coming round.'

Brisk footsteps, competent fingers at my wrist. 'I'm just going to give you something for the pain, Kate.'

A prick, lightning quick, and then a plummet back into the blissful blankness.

There are huge weights on my eyelids and a relentless, unnatural noise is nagging me awake. Beep, beep, beep, beep. With a huge effort, I manage to open my eyes. I see a wall, flat and bright and somehow strange, and something about it makes my mind throb with alarm. I hurt all over and my mouth is so dry I can't swallow.

My eyes drop from the wall to a sheet. It is white and smooth. A bed. I am in a bed. At last something that makes sense.

But I can't move. I try to lift an arm, to twitch a toe, but my body won't respond. An invisible beast has me pinned to the bed, and my heart panics like a trapped bird, battering frantically in my chest, as I let my eyes close.

'Good God! Fiona! She just opened her eyes!' An urgent rustle, like paper being hastily discarded.

'Are you sure?'

A body leaning over me. I smell fine wool, dogs, a reassuringly familiar hint of leather. 'Get the nurse! Kate? Kate, can you hear me?'

'Jasper, stand back. Let the nurse see.'

A pause, and then an authoritative hand is laid on my wrist. 'Kate? Can you open your eyes?'

I don't know who Kate is, but the voice is clearly speaking to me. I force my lids open to see a woman dressed in a blue tunic. The colour hurts my eyes and there is a wrongness to her clothes that I can't identify.

'Where . . . ?' There is something blocking my throat, a pipe of some sort that makes me gag, and the woman squeezes my hand kindly.

'Don't try to speak, Kate. You've had an accident, and you're in hospital, but we're looking after you and you're going to be fine.' She smiles at me. 'Would you like to see your family while I call the doctor?'

She steps back to reveal a man with frayed features and a weak mouth. There is a faint twitch under his right eye. Beside him is a woman. Her hair is an elegant ash blonde, and neatly combed. It's difficult for me to judge how old they are. In their fifties, maybe? The man's fair hair is faded, and it flops over his forehead. Once he must have been very attractive, but now he looks worn, blurred, as if the edges of him have been rubbed out.

I don't recognize either of them.

My eyes dart back to the nurse. I want to say, *They're not my family*, but I can't speak past the tube in my throat.

'Hello, Kate,' says the man, trying a jovial smile that doesn't quite work. 'What a fright you gave us!'

'Jasper!' the woman says with a warning look. 'There's no need for that now.' She is a handsome woman, but her eyes are cool. 'We're very glad to see you awake, Kate,' she says.

I try to shake my head, but all I can do is shift it slightly against the pillow. There is so much that is wrong, I can't take it in. They are strange people, in strange clothes, speaking in strange voices. And why do they keep calling me Kate? My name isn't Kate. It is . . .

I don't know, I realize. I don't know who I am. Horror yawns around me and I close my eyes in desperation.

'Don't worry if she doesn't know you at first,' the nurse says over me. 'It's quite common for patients to be confused when they first regain consciousness, and it may take some time for her memory to return. It's best to let her come round slowly, but it's very good news that she's out of the coma. We'll call you if there's any change overnight, of course, but let her sleep now.'

They have taken the tube out of my throat. It hurts to talk, but I have had a drink through a straw and I feel properly awake for the first time.

Now I am lying propped up in the bed, attached by a bewildering number of wires to various machines. My eyes are skittering around the room. I don't recognize anything. There is something profoundly wrong about this world, with its pale, painted walls and its pervasive smell that is both pungent and curiously blank at the same time. The windows are covered by strange slatted hangings, and they seem to open into another room rather than onto a street or a garden. I can't see the sky. The light is unnatural, constant. I have no sense of time. Is it morning, or evening? There is no way of telling.

Sounds are subdued in here. I strain my ears for something familiar – a laugh, a dog barking, a child crying – but there is nothing I recognize, just lowered voices, the faint squeak of shoes outside the door, and the slow, painful thud of my heart, while in my head, terror roars. I don't dare turn my mind, don't dare face the dull dread that looms out of the dense, impenetrable shadows where my memory should be. I have tried to remember, but it is like groping blindly through fog: impressions of shock, of the sudden, sickening sensation of falling, tumbling horrifyingly through the air. A figure is there, but the harder I try to make out its face, the more it recedes.

I don't know who I am or where I am. I know only that I am alone and I am frightened.

I'm in a different room. I don't know how or why I came to be here. The bed is the same, high and narrow and curtainless, but there is a window with great glass panes and this time it looks outside, which is a relief, although all I can see is sky. The clouds are a pale, mottled grey and the light seems peculiar, although I can't put my finger on why.

Two women are standing by the bed. One is dressed in the same harsh blue as the woman who told me not to try to speak. *Nurse.* The word floats into my mind and I clutch at it. She is a nurse. I'm not sure how I know this, but I do, and I know what a nurse does. She cares for the sick.

The other woman wears a white coat. She has smooth skin, brown as a nut, and her hair is black and shiny. She is looking at a board in her hand, but as if sensing my gaze, she looks up and offers a brief smile.

'I'm Dr Ramnaya, Kate. How are you feeling?'

I think about it. I feel as if I have been beaten all over with cudgels. My head booms and throbs, and there is a relentless pain in my leg, but worse than that is not understanding where I am or who I am. 'Afraid,' I say. My tongue is so thick and unwieldy in my mouth that I can barely form the word, but she seems to understand.

'You're quite safe now,' she says.

'Have I had the sickness?'

'You've had a very nasty fall,' she tells me.

Falling. Tumbling awkwardly, terrifyingly. My legs over my head. My arms flailing. My heavy skirts dragging me down, down, down. The scream blocked in my throat.

Dr Ramnaya is lifting my eyelids and shining a light into my eyes. Can she see my confusion, my fear? 'Can you remember what happened?' she asks me.

I moisten my lips and try to speak again. 'Don't remember anything,' I manage with difficulty.

'It's quite normal to lose your memory after a traumatic brain injury,' Dr Ramnaya says as she steps back. 'You've fractured three ribs and your left femur – the bone in your thigh – has been badly broken. We've pinned that with an intramedullary

7

nail, and stabilized your fractured pelvis with an internal plate. But we were initially more concerned about the fracture to your skull. Given that you fell over thirty metres, you're very lucky to be alive at all,' she tells me. 'Fortunately, it seems that the branches of a tree broke your fall, but you were in a coma for almost a week, and retrograde amnesia is quite common in these circumstances.'

I can't make sense of what she is saying through the pounding in my head. I understand 'tree', 'fall', 'week', but the other words are tumbling and jarring around my brain as I try to work out what they mean. My confusion must show in my face, because Dr Ramnaya tries again.

'You may forget who you are and incidents in your life, and you probably don't remember much about being in the intensive care unit where you were taken at first, or being transferred to this hospital when your condition became more stable, but you'll retain general information about the world – how to speak, how to ride a bicycle, that kind of thing.'

What is a bicycle? But I am too confused to interrupt her.

'You might also remember facts, but not the names of the people closest to you.' Her fine brows draw together as she registers that I am struggling to follow her. 'For instance, you probably know what the Queen is called?'

She looks at me encouragingly, and I search my mind desperately, pushing aside all the words that are clamouring for an explanation. There must be something in there. And sure enough, as I probe the darkness, a name rises to the surface.

'Elizabeth,' I say slowly, and relief spills through me as I see her nod. Thank God, I have remembered something.

'See?' she says. 'Your other memories may take more time to come back, but you should regain most of them eventually, and until then, try not to force it. The more you try, the less likely you are to remember, so let's concentrate on your physical condition for now.

'In the meantime, you're in good hands,' she tells me briskly. 'You've been moved to a private hospital near York so that your family can visit you more easily. Although they're able to care for you, they've explained that the house is very old and can't be adapted, so you'll need to be able to get up and down stairs before you can go home. Lord and Lady Vavasour have been very concerned.'

Vavasour. The name chimes within me, and Dr Ramnaya must see my expression change, because she glances at the nurse.

'That means something to you?'

Already the feeling of recognition, the certainty that I am on the brink of remembering something important, is fading. 'No, it's gone,' I say, frustrated in spite of what she has said about not trying too hard to remember.

'Well, it's not surprising that you recognize the name,' she says. 'It's your name. Kate Vavasour.'

No. It is the only thing I am instantly sure of: that is not my name. 'I'm not Kate,' I whisper. It is all I know. *I am not Kate.*

'Try not to worry about it,' the nurse says, squeezing my

hand. 'Give it time, and you'll start to remember who you are, but for now, let's concentrate on getting you better.'

The couple who were here when I woke up before come back. I remember his floppy hair and the tic under his eye, her controlled smile. It feels good to be able to remember something, even if it is only since I woke up in hospital. Very gradually, the whirling confusion is settling, and a corner of my mind has cleared, just as Dr Ramnaya said it would. I do know what a bicycle is, of course I do. I know what a hospital is, too, and a stethoscope, and a television, and when they tell me that I'm in York I can picture the city perfectly. I understand what 'amnesia' means, and the nurses' blue tunics and trousers no longer look unutterably strange. I can recognize that my visitor's jumper is cashmere, and that he wears green cords and a navy Guernsey with a checked shirt and tie.

But I still don't know who I am.

I have tried and tried, but all I remember is fear and a drumming sense of urgency. There is something I have to do, someone I have to find. I must remember, but I can't. I cling onto the things that I do know, because if I try to think about anything else, my mind simply closes down in desperation.

My visitors sit in the uncomfortable-looking chairs that are provided on one side of the bed. They tell me that they are Jasper and Fiona, Lord and Lady Vavasour, my parents-in-law. They say that I was married to their son, Michael, but that he died almost three years ago. Everything about Fiona is cool – her hair is pale, her jumper an icy blue, the pearls at her throat a gleaming ivory – but when she talks about her son, her hands close tightly around the arms of her chair and her knuckles show white.

I am a widow, they say. I live with them now at Askerby Hall.

No! I want to protest. *No, my husband is not dead. He cannot be! I would know, I would feel it.* But when I try to conjure up an image of him, there is nothing, just the rushing darkness in my head, and that frightens me more than anything. How could I have forgotten my dearest dear, my heart?

My throat closes and I turn my face away from the grief in their eyes. I should weep, but how can I cry for someone I cannot remember?

'But you have a son,' Fiona says, and my pulse leaps with a recognition that lifts me off the pillow, careless of the pain in my ribs.

My son! Yes, yes, I have a son! Of course.

And it comes back to me, the terror, not for myself but for him. I don't know why, but I have been terribly afraid for him. 'He is safe?' I ask urgently.

'Of course he is safe.' Impatience feathers Fiona's voice as I crumple back against the pillows, the relief so sharp that I close my eyes at the sting of tears.

'Thank God,' I say, my eyes squeezed shut still, my fingers tight on the sheet, and I let out a shuddery breath. 'Thank God.' I have not realized until now why I have been so afraid, but of course it has been for my son. I open my eyes after a moment, when I am sure that I am not going to cry. Something tells me that Fiona will despise tears. 'Can I see him?'

'We didn't want to upset him by bringing him in,' Jasper says apologetically. 'You're still a bit . . . bashed up.'

'We thought seeing you like this would distress him.' Fiona is cooler.

'We brought you a photo, though.' Jasper produces a picture and puts it into my hands. 'This is bound to jog your memory. There's Felix.'

I stare at the image of a small boy of about three, fair-haired, blue-eyed, with an alert, mischievous expression and an engaging smile. An endearing child, for certain, but not mine. I know it in my bones, and my heart hollows with dread.

I shake my head. 'No,' I say. 'That's not my son.' I can't remember his name, but I know it isn't him. I *know* it. I let the photo drop onto the blanket and look from Fiona to Jasper, these people who claim to be my family but who show me a child who is not mine. 'Please, you have to tell me. Where is *my* son?'

Chapter Two

'Oh, for heaven's sake!'

'Gently, old thing.' Jasper tries to lay a calming hand on Fiona's arm, but she brushes it aside. 'The doctor said we have to be patient.'

'Haven't we been patient enough with her?' Fiona's voice cracks and she presses her fingers to her forehead, fighting for control. 'Dear God, if we have to go through all that again . . .'

There is a long pause.

'All what?' I say at last, looking from one to the other. 'What have I done?'

Jasper forces a smile. 'Nothing. Everybody's upset. We've been very worried about you, Kate, you must understand that.'

'Why do you keep calling me Kate?' In spite of myself, my voice is shaking. 'It's not my name.'

Fiona presses her lips so tightly together that they almost disappear, but she has herself under control once more. She lifts her head, exchanges a glance with Jasper. 'You're confused,' she says coldly. 'The doctors said you would be for a while. Thank heavens we didn't bring Felix in,' she adds to Jasper. 'It would have been hard enough for him to see his mother in this state without her refusing to recognize him as well!'

There is a tight band around my head, digging cruel fingers into my brain, and exhaustion crashes over me. 'I'm sorry,' I say, too tired to argue, and I'm relieved when the nurse comes in and says they must leave me to rest.

A clinical psychologist comes to assess me. He is a stocky man with a receding hairline and shrewd eyes behind his glasses. He introduces himself as Oliver Raine, and says I can call him Oliver. He asks if I remember him as he sits down in one of the visitors' chairs.

'I don't remember anything,' I say, plucking fretfully at the sheet. There's a thumping behind my right eye, a counterbalance to the nagging pain in my left leg. I have had my daily physiotherapy session earlier and I am aching and uncomfortable, and increasingly frustrated about my inability to remember my own name. It is infuriating and I can't get past the conviction that the Vavasours are keeping my son from me.

Remember, remember, you've got to remember. The words tick endlessly, fruitlessly, around in my head.

'Have I met you before?' I ask Oliver, and he nods.

'I came to see you when you were first moved here, but I'm not surprised that you've forgotten. Some short-term memory impairment is quite normal following a brain injury like yours, and it can take some time to recover.'

'How long?' The sense of urgency is exhausting me, but the more I try to recall what it is I have to do, the blanker my mind becomes. 'It's awful,' I tell him, embarrassed by the tremble in my voice. 'I don't even know my own name.'

'We only realize how much we rely on our memory to function normally when we lose it.' Oliver's expression is sympathetic. 'The brain is very complex, and when things go wrong the consequences can be profound, as I'm sure the doctors treating you have already explained. In your case, you remember how to use the television remote and speak English, but nothing about yourself. You've got a memory retrieval problem. It's as if your brain is a library where all sorts of useful information is stored, and it's been shoogled up and scattered by the injury to your brain. So where before you could go straight to the shelf which had the information you wanted, now you can't find anything.'

'I can't even see the shelves,' I say morosely.

'But you are starting to remember again, aren't you? The nurses tell me that you recognize them now.'

'That's true.' I haven't thought of that as a positive sign before. 'And I remember Dr Ramnaya, and that Fiona and Jasper have been to see me.'

Oliver nods his encouragement. 'So your memory is working on storing new information, it just can't get at anything that was stored before your accident.'

My accident. I finger the wedding ring that looks so odd on my hand. 'Oliver,' I say abruptly. 'What happened to me?'

'Hasn't anybody told you?' He sits back in his chair,

steepling his fingers as he regards me with a thoughtful expression.

'Not really. A fall, they said.'

'You fell from the roof of Askerby Hall.'

A rushing in my ears. My stomach tilts as if I'm standing on the edge of a vertiginous drop, horror grabs at my throat, and then I'm tumbling into an abyss, my heavy skirts hampering my fall, making me twist and lurch awkwardly.

I suck in a stuttery breath and will my thundering heart to calm as I press my palms into the hospital blanket. I am safe, I tell myself. I am not falling.

'What . . . what was I doing on the roof?'

'Nobody knows.'

I think about the Vavasours, Fiona pressing her fingers to her forehead. *Haven't we been patient enough with her?*

'They think I jumped, don't they?'

'Did you?'

No! The voice is loud in my head. I don't remember, but I *know.* 'No, I wouldn't leave my son!' My mouth works shamefully, and it is a struggle to keep my voice steady. 'Why won't they let me see him?'

'He's fine,' says Oliver. 'He's safe, he's well.' He pauses. 'Lady Vavasour says you don't recognize his picture.'

'Because it's not my son.' I press my fists to my temples. I can sense my child in the murky shadows of my mind. He's just there, but when I try to reach for him, to pull him free and see his face, it sends his image drifting further into the distance. 'Where is he? Why can't I remember?' I ask despairingly.

'Perhaps you're trying too hard.' Oliver shifts in his chair and leans forward. 'Let's try something. Close your eyes.'

I'm glad of the chance to hide the sheen of tears. Behind my eyelids I see a blurry pattern of light. 'Are you going to hypnotize me?'

'Nothing so elaborate,' says Oliver. 'I just want you to think about whether you know what it means to be happy.'

'Yes,' I say without hesitation.

'Can you imagine yourself feeling happy?'

'Yes,' I say again, more slowly, delighted as the blur behind my eyelids clears and an unmistakable picture forms in my mind.

'Good.' Oliver's voice is low and tranquil. 'When you think about yourself being happy, what are you doing?'

'I'm riding my mare.' I can feel the bunch and slide of the horse's powerful muscles, smell the leather of the saddle and the reins in my gloved hands.

'Where are you?'

'On the moors.' My eyes are closed, but I can picture it so clearly it must be a memory. The sky over the moorland is a vast blue arch, broken only by a few blotches of clouds, as if dabbed there by an indifferent painter. The air is crisp and clear, and laced with the sweet smell of the heather where the skylarks dart. I can hear the thud of my mare's hooves on the dusty track, the plaintive bleat of a sheep in the distance.

'Is there anyone with you?' Oliver's voice seems to come from another world.

'Yes.' In my mind, the breeze snatches at my hat as we

gallop and I lift a hand to hold it to my head, laughing as I turn to— but the image vanishes, swallowed up in the blank, black emptiness of my memory, and my throat closes with despair. I need to know who was there beside me. It was someone I love, someone who laughed with me. I am sure of it.

I put a hand over my mouth to stop it wobbling.

'I can't remember,' I say.

'But you remember something, don't you?' Oliver is encouraging. 'That's good. Askerby is right on the edge of the moors, so that makes sense. The Vavasours never mentioned anything about you riding, but I know they have quite a stable there, and perhaps when you get home, the horses will trigger your memory.'

'Perhaps,' I say dolefully. I am desolate at the loss of my companion, if only in my memory. It makes me realize how lonely I am. The only people who have been to see me are the Vavasours. Don't I have any friends? Any family of my own?

'Who am I?' I ask Oliver.

He studies me over his steepled fingers. 'It may not feel right to you at the moment, but your name *is* Kate. You're thirty-three. You married Michael Vavasour in London, and you have a son, Felix, who's four. Since Michael's death, you and Felix have been living with the Vavasours at Askerby Hall.'

'What about my own family? Do I have parents? Brothers and sisters?'

'As far as I know, you're an only child. Your parents are both alive,' Oliver tells me. 'They're aid workers, and I understand they're in Somalia at the moment. They're working in a very remote part of the country, and may not even know about your accident yet. Lord Vavasour has been making efforts to contact them, but it's not easy.'

It doesn't sound as if I am close to my parents, but how can I know?

I wish I could tell Oliver that's not really what I want to know, anyway. I want to ask him what I'm like. Am I kind? Am I generous? Am I bitter or needy or sweet or strong? But what can he say? He doesn't know me.

Apparently I am the kind of person who would jump off a roof and not even have the decency to kill herself. Memory shimmers then, of a voice while I was lying in the dark: *It would have been better if she'd died.*

And another: *You were supposed to die.*

But they might not be real memories. I might have made them up. I can't be sure.

What do I feel about myself? My eyes drift to the window. I know I yearn to be outside, that I work stubbornly through the pain of the physiotherapy because I long to walk again, to leave this place that feels so wrong. I think of that moment of happiness I remembered, riding over the moorland, breathing lungfuls of sweet air, laughing. There was someone beside me, someone I loved, I know that, someone who loved me. Was it Michael? I turn the wedding ring on my finger. It doesn't feel right, but Oliver tells me that my name is Kate, that my son is safe, that my husband is dead. I should believe him. Why would he lie to me? Why would any of them lie to me?

'Do you want to try closing your eyes again?' Oliver asks gently, and I nod.

I lean back against the pillows and shut my eyes, watch the kaleidoscope of lights revolve blurrily behind my lids.

'Don't think about it,' he says. 'Just tell me the first thing you remember.'

I open my mouth to tell him about waking up in hospital when, unbidden, a different image swims to the surface.

'My mother,' I say slowly, without opening my eyes. 'I remember my mother. It's not really a proper memory. It's more of an impression.' Desperation. Fear. Lowered voices in the hall below. *Madness*: the word jagged in the air.

'I was very small,' I say. 'Four, perhaps. Maybe five. My mother was in a dark room. It was very hot, and her hands were tied to the bedposts. She was screaming and pulling at the ties, begging me to save her.'

I falter, remembering my distress. Of all the things I need to recall, why does it have to be this? The babe had died, I remember that. My brother. I remember scrabbling frantically at the ties that bound my mother to the bed, and how she screamed and screamed. Her mouth was wide open, her eyes staring, her skin sheened with sweat.

Disquieted, I open my eyes. 'She had just had a baby. Why would she have been screaming for help? She kept saying that they wanted to kill her.' I shiver, remembering the anguish in her voice, the horror in her eyes.

'It sounds as if she might have been suffering from postpartum psychosis,' says Oliver, tapping his fingers thoughtfully under his bottom lip.

'What, and they tied her to a bed? What kind of treatment is that?'

'You were only small. Perhaps she wasn't really tied down.'

'She was! I remember it really clearly!' I look at my hands as if I can still feel my little fingers tugging urgently at the knots of linen.

'Memory is a very complex process,' Oliver says carefully. 'We don't really understand how it works. We might think we remember an event in great detail, but numerous studies have demonstrated that even the clearest memory is often largely invention. We conflate memories of different occasions, and subconsciously edit our behaviour. We take scenes from a book we've read or a movie we've seen and unwittingly incorporate them into our memories. So when you remember your mother being tied to a bed, for instance, it might be that you remember her being hurt in some way, and you've bound that up with a memory of struggling to undo a knot on another occasion. It's unlikely that she really was tied to a bed.'

He stops and studies my face. 'Or perhaps you're project-ing your own feelings of helplessness about being injured,' he suggests. 'You might feel trapped in this bed just as you're imagining your mother being trapped. Do you think that might be possible?'

I scowl. 'So what you're saying is that even if I do manage to remember something, I can't trust my own memory? I might as well make it all up!'

'It's not that bad,' he says, smiling. 'Think of your memory as a muscle. The more you use it, the stronger it will become. You don't need to remember every detail of every day, after all, even if you could. All you want at first is to recognize people and places and events. We all need a sense of the past in order to operate properly – we need to know who we are, and why we think and act the way we do. Memories give us a context,' he says. 'In a very real way, they make us who we are.

'You need to remember, Kate,' he says, 'but be prepared. As you've already discovered, not all memories are good ones, and there may be some things you'll wish had stayed forgotten.'

You were supposed to die. Perhaps Oliver is right. Perhaps it's better not to remember everything.

They say it's April. I can't tell from the blank rectangle of sky which is all that I can see through the window. I spend long hours looking at the light and longing to breathe fresh air. I hate the feeling of being confined. It makes me breathless and panicky, and the memory of my mother tied to the bed squirms darkly at the back of my mind. Only the thought that she is strong enough to go from terrified madness to working in Somalia stops me from screaming myself. If she can survive that, then I can survive lying here, my head aching with the effort of battering at the blankness inside it.

I concentrate on getting stronger. I set my teeth at the pain and make myself do every exercise Mary, my physiotherapist, prescribes. She sets me goals. First I have to stand using a Zimmer frame, and then using crutches. My ambitions are limited to getting from the bed to the chair, and then from the chair to the bathroom. When I ask how long it will be before I can ride again, Mary tuts. 'One step at a time,' she says. 'We need to get you walking properly first.'

Every goal seems insurmountable at first, but Dr Ramnaya is pleased with my progress. 'Carry on like this and we'll be able to let you go home soon,' she says after a month has passed.

Which would be better news if I could remember where home was.

More Vavasours arrive, taking it in turns to visit. Strangers who tell me that I know them well. My sister-in-law. Michael's cousin. His aunt Joanna, with a strong resemblance to Jasper, down to the nervous tic under the eye and the suggestion of weakness around the mouth.

Michael's sister is called Philippa. She is moody and resentful, but her barbed conversation is a welcome change from the relentless cheeriness of the nurses. She's in her late twenties, I'd say, but when I ask her what she does, she just shrugs. 'Not much.'

It turns out that I have married into a wealthy family. The Vavasours own large tracts of the North Yorkshire moors. I live at Askerby Hall, a fine example of an Elizabethan house that is open to the public between Easter and the end of October. Visitors pay handsomely to gawp at its dramatic long gallery and moulded ceilings. They shuffle through the beautifully preserved rooms with their panelled walls and portraits and marvel that this is a house that has belonged to the same family for over four hundred years.

'The house is gorgeous,' one of the nurses tells me. 'I used to dream about living there and being a grand lady.' She winks at me. She is a bosomy woman with curly hair and a round, good-humoured face. I know all the nurses now and Sandra is one of my favourites. She adores my parents-in-law ('They are so lovely, aren't they?') and treats them like visiting royalty. I half expect her to curtsey whenever they are in the room.

Fiona and Jasper respond with a graciousness born of centuries of privilege. Something about the way they smile and take Sandra's wide-eyed admiration as their due sets my teeth on edge. I wonder if I always felt that way about them. They visit me regularly, but there is no warmth in the way Fiona presses her cool cheek against mine, and although they are always correct, I don't sense any affection. They are doing their duty, but they don't care.

According to Sandra, Askerby Hall is so unspoilt and such a perfect example of a grand Tudor house that it is often used as a location for historical dramas. 'Last year, they had a whole lot of Americans came over from Hollywood making a movie. One of them comedy horror films,' she explains, popping a thermometer in my mouth and straightening my sheets with her quick hands. 'Not my kind of thing,' she says, 'but I'll go and see it when it comes out, just to see Askerby.'

The gardens at Askerby are famous, too. There is a knot garden and a maze and a beautiful walled area. There is woodland and parkland and a river, where various events and activities are organized to draw in the public: adventure play-grounds and hawking displays and re-enactments. 'We had a season ticket when the kids were little,' Sandra says as she whips out the thermometer and makes a note on the chart that sits on the end of my bed. 'They loved it. We couldn't get our Dave off the rope ladders.

'You're ever so lucky,' she goes on, and then looks at me lying in my hospital bed, my leg in a cast, a bandage around my head, my face still battered. 'Well, maybe not right now,' she amends with her comfortable laugh, 'but just wait until you get home! Once you clap eyes on Askerby again, you'll never want to leave.'

Chapter Three

Michael's cousin, George, comes to see me two or three times. George manages the vast Askerby estate. He's a surprisingly shy, solid man with what I am already recognizing as the Vavasour good looks: a clear-cut jaw, guinea-gold hair and eyes that are a distinctive dark shade of blue.

George doesn't do small talk, and he has trouble meeting my eyes. It's obvious that the hospital and my injuries make him uneasy. The silences are painful until I realize that all I need to do is to ask him about the estate and his expression lightens. He can talk for hours about sheep or shooting, about dips and animal feeds and raising pheasants. He doesn't like the town. He's not actually wearing muddy wellies, but you can tell that he would be more comfortable if he was. He loves Askerby, that is clear.

'He's really passionate about the place,' I say to Philippa, whose turn it is to visit the next day. 'Will he inherit eventually?'

'George?' She gives me a funny look. 'Of course not. When Pa dies, Felix will be the next Lord Vavasour.'

Felix. The little boy they insist is mine. I avoid Philippa's eyes, just as George avoids mine. 'It doesn't seem very fair.'

She shrugs. 'That's just the way it is. The title has been passed down the male line since the fifteenth century. George isn't even a true Vavasour,' she says. 'Joanna changed his name by deed poll. His real name is Wilson or Brown, something depressingly ordinary, anyway.'

Philippa tells me Joanna, Jasper's sister, had a brief rebellion over thirty years ago and married against her parents' wishes. 'It was a disaster, of course,' Philippa says. 'Her husband dumped her when George was still a baby, and she slunk back to Askerby. Luckily George looks like a Vavasour. Now everybody pretends that he always has been.'

Michael's sister is slumped in the chair next to mine, picking at her nails. She has missed out on the Vavasour gold hair, but her eyes are the same deep blue, and she could be beautiful were it not for the discontented twist of her mouth. Every day I try to learn something new about the family I am apparently part of, and I know now that Philippa runs the stables at Askerby. Like George, I always get the sense that she is itching to get back to the country.

'I can't imagine Joanna as a rebel,' I say. I hoard all the information I can get, storing it away in my empty memory, where it rattles around without a context. Joanna makes the occasional dutiful visit but I don't have a real sense of her yet. The tweedy skirts, waxed jacket and cut-glass accent create a barrier between her and the rest of the world, a slippery surface which repels any attempt to find out what she really thinks or feels.

I've been trying to work out the family arrangements in my head. 'So you all live together at the Hall? You and George and Jasper and Fiona and Joanna?'

'And Granny,' says Philippa. 'She's eighty-seven now and the drive in from Askerby is too much for her, but she still rules the roost at home.'

It sounds an odd set-up to me. 'I live there, too?'

'Since Michael died.'

'But that was a couple of years ago, wasn't it?'

'You've remembered?' she says in surprise, but I shake my head.

'No, your father told me.'

'Oh.' For a moment there is a distant look in her eyes. 'It's more like three now. It's hard to believe,' she says. 'Michael was the only one of us who got away, and even he had to come back to Askerby in the end.'

'Got away?' It's an odd phrase for her to choose, I think. 'You make it sound like an escape.'

'I think it was for Michael. He was different. He wasn't interested in hunting or shooting or farming. All he cared about was books.' Philippa sounds baffled. 'After he graduated, he got a job with a small publishing house, earning peanuts, but he loved London. That's where he met you.' She looks at me. 'Do you really not remember him?'

What does she think? That I am pretending? 'No,' I say. 'I don't remember anything.'

'Weird,' says Philippa.

That's one word for it, I suppose. 'Why am I living at Askerby if Michael loved London so much?'

'Money,' she says succinctly. 'Felix was only a baby when Michael first fell ill. You didn't have any money, Michael couldn't work, your parents live in some godforsaken part of Africa . . . You had to nurse Michael and look after Felix. Nobody blamed you for admitting that you couldn't manage on your own.'

'But Michael's dead now,' I point out. 'I must be able to work.'

'Sure, but you don't exactly earn big bucks as a graphic designer, and Michael didn't have anything to leave you. All the Vavasour money is tied up in the estate. You've still got Felix to look after, and frankly, you were a mess after Michael died. You didn't have the energy to resist Ma and Pa, who are determined for Felix to grow up at Askerby. He is the next Lord Vavasour, after all. They don't want him growing up in some council flat, which is all you'd be able to offer him.'

'So I have thought about moving out?'

Philippa lifts a shoulder, uninterested. 'You were talking about it before the Great Leap.' That's what she calls my fall. She's the only one who acknowledges what happened; even though I can't believe that I jumped, I prefer her frankness to the careful way the others avoid the subject.

'Of course,' she says, with a nod at the cast on my leg, 'you won't be going anywhere now.'

It is like trying to put together a jigsaw with only a handful of blurry pieces. Lying in my hospital bed at night, I pick over the conversations I have with Philippa and the other Vavasours for clues about my life: I am a freelance graphic designer, I don't earn much money; I live with my parents-in-law, I'm a widow. I loved my husband, I'm suicidal. The Vavasours tolerate me for the sake of Felix, the boy they say is my son, but they don't love me. I don't think they even like me very much. Nobody will come right out and say it, but I get the feeling they think I am highly strung and over-imaginative at best. In one corner I set my memory of my mother screaming in the dark. It seems to have nothing to do with the fact that I have parents working in Somalia. I can't put any of it together.

There are facts and there is what I feel, and they don't seem to be connected. I exist in a strange limbo, my memories pitiful scraps teased out of the murk – a mad mother and a ride across the moors – but when I mention the latter to Philippa, she stares at me.

'*You? Riding?* You'd rather stick pins in your eyes than get on a horse!'

'What?' I gape back at her. This is the one good thing I remember, how at home I felt in the saddle, that exhilarating ride through the heather under the vast arch of the sky.

'You hate horses,' Philippa says. 'Michael used to tease you about it, but you said you'd been attacked by one once, and you were quite happy to admire them from the other side of a fence.'

'But . . .' I fall silent, remembering what Oliver Raine told me about memories. Maybe I was remembering a scene in a film, like he said, but you don't remember smells from a film, do you? You don't remember the feel of the reins through your gloves or the fluid power of the horse beneath you.

Too often there is a disjunction between what they tell me is true and what I know but cannot remember. Sometimes at night I lie sleepless in the bed, and I'm aware of the dull ache of bruised and broken bones, of a cracked skull, but it doesn't feel like my body at all. I'm there but not there at the same time.

When I do sleep, I find myself running, blindfolded by the dark and panicky, twisting frantically between the clamour of voices in my head that call me this way and that but never show themselves. They are voices I know, people I am desperate to find, but when I wake and try to recall the exact timbre of a voice, a familiar rhythm of speech, all I am left with is confusion and desperation.

There's a membrane stretched across my mind, spongy and opaque. I can sense the memories trapped behind it, scratching and scraping for a way out, and I probe constantly, as if at a sore tooth, testing and prodding, in the hope that one day I will break through and my life will spill out. I can't bear not knowing anything about myself, but I am afraid, too. I keep thinking about what Oliver said: *There may be some things you'll wish had stayed forgotten.*

Still, I keep straining to remember. Every now and then

there's a fluttery, frantic sense in my head, like a trapped moth beating its wings against cupped hands, and I feel sure that a memory is very close, but it's gone before I can grasp it.

The first memory comes without warning. I am dozing, my face turned towards the window. It's bright outside, and the light beats against my eyelids. It's reminding me of something . . .

I stir, frowning a little, and turn my head the other way. I open my eyes and see a young woman sitting by my bed, her head bent over *Country Life*, and out of nowhere terror jolts through me. I must gasp, because she looks up quickly in concern.

'Oh, Kate, I'm so sorry! Did I give you a fright?'

Already that nameless dread is evaporating and I feel foolish. 'Just a bad dream,' I manage. I must have been sleeping. I didn't hear her come in. My mouth is very dry and she obviously hears the hoarseness in my voice because she tosses the magazine on the bed and jumps up.

'Would you like a drink? The nurse said you might be thirsty when you woke up.'

'Thanks.'

I sip gratefully at the water then lie back against the pillows to watch her as she bustles around, setting the beaker back on the bedside table, tidying away the magazine. She seems familiar, and my heart lifts at the thought that I might at last be recognizing somebody.

'You haven't been to see me before, have you?'

'I went to the hospital a couple of times when you were in

a coma,' she says. 'We tried to take it in turns to sit with you and talk to you in the hope that we'd get through eventually, but this is the first chance I've had to come and see you since you've been awake.' She smiles at me as she sits back in the chair. 'You're looking so much better, Kate.'

I have given up protesting that Kate is not my name.

She folds her skirt around her knees as she speaks, and it comes to me in a flash. 'Judith!' I laugh with relief. 'Oh, thank God I've remembered someth—' I break off at her expression of dismay and my heart plummets. 'You're not Judith?'

She shakes her head and I can see the pity in her eyes. 'I'm Angie.'

'Oh. Sorry. Whoops.' I try to laugh it off but it feels awkward. For a moment, I was so *sure*. 'I suppose they've told you that I've lost my memory?'

'They did, and it must be awful for you.' Her voice is warm with sympathy. 'I'm so sorry, Kate. It's a terrible thing to happen, but the main thing is that you're going to be okay.'

She is neat and pretty with a heart-shaped face. Her hair swings in a brown bob and her eyes are a friendly brown instead of the Vavasour blue, but there is something naggingly familiar about her all the same.

'Are you a Vavasour?' I ask.

'Me? No!' Something flickers in her face, but it is gone so quickly that I barely have time to register it before she is laughing. 'I'm Angie Kaczka. I work at Askerby.'

'Was part of your job visiting me when I was in a coma?'

'Of course not! We're friends.'

Friends. The word warms me. That is what I have been missing, I think. I smile back at her a little tremulously.

'You do seem familiar.'

'So I should hope,' she says with mock sternness. 'We've spent a lot of time together over the past couple of years.'

'Really?'

'After Michael died . . .' Angie hesitates, picking her words. 'It was a tough time for you. You've never been that close to Michael's family,' she says delicately and I nod, unsurprised. That much I have already gathered.

'I must have been glad to have had you to talk to.'

'We went through a few boxes of tissues,' she acknowledges with a faint smile. 'Not to mention a few bottles of Chardonnay!'

I smile back at her gratefully. 'It sounds like you're a good friend. Thanks, Angie.'

She waves that aside. 'We got on well right from the start, even though we're quite different.'

'In what way?' I ask curiously. At last, someone who can give me a sense of what I'm like.

'Well . . .' Angie settles into her chair, thinking. 'You grew up in Africa, and I've never left Askerby. You're very independent and . . . I don't know . . . unconventional, I suppose, and I love all the Vavasour traditions. You're clever and arty, and I'm very practical.' She shakes her head and laughs. 'Now I come to think of it, I can't understand how we ever got to be friends at all! But I always loved spending time with you and of course I adore Felix. He's the dearest little boy.'

She glances at me, suddenly uncertain. 'Is it true you don't remember him?'

I look away from the reproach in her eyes. I know what she's thinking. What kind of mother doesn't recognize her own child? What kind of mother could turn aside from Felix with his mischievous smile and be absolutely certain that he is not her son, that there is another child somewhere that she loves unconditionally, if only she could remember him.

'I'm afraid so.'

'I just can't believe it,' Angie says. She twists her hands together. 'I just *can't*. You used to be so close until—'

'Until what?' I ask when she breaks off.

Angie looks uncomfortable. 'I'm not sure I should say anything,' she says awkwardly, and I struggle further up against my pillows.

'Please, Angie. I need to know what happened.'

'Look, you mustn't worry about it, Kate. It's just that you haven't really been yourself these last few months. I mean, obviously you've been grieving for Michael, but there's been something else going on, too. You were acting a bit strangely.'

'Strangely? How?'

'I don't know.' Angie shifts in her chair, clearly wishing she hadn't started this. 'Distracted, I guess. Sometimes it was like you just weren't there. And you got obsessed with the family history. It was like you were more interested in the past than in Felix. But none of us ever dreamt you were depressed or that you would . . . you know . . .'

'Jump off a roof?'

She looks distressed. 'I can't believe you'd do that to Felix.'

I can't believe I jumped either. I squirm a little at the sickening twist of guilt I always feel when people talk to me about Felix.

'How is he?' It should have been the first question I asked, I know.

'He's fine. I've moved into the Hall so I can be there at night, and I look after him most of the time. Philippa's with him today, as I had to come into York. You mustn't worry about him. We're taking good care of him.'

'I'm sure you are, but what about your job? What exactly do you do at Askerby, anyway?'

'Oh, a little bit of everything,' she says. 'I help out whenever I'm needed. A bit of this, a bit of that. I help George in the estate office, and Lady Fiona when she has charity events to organize. I run errands for the whole family. There's a cook and a housekeeper, of course, but there are always little jobs that need doing.'

I wonder why the Vavasours can't run their own errands, but I don't say so. 'It sounds like you're indispensable,' I say instead.

'I wouldn't say that.' But she looks pleased. 'I like to think they know they can rely on me for anything. There was no question about me moving into the Hall to look after Felix. All the Vavasours know that he's more important than any estate business.'

'Do you live far away?'

'Just at the Lodge with my grandmother, but if Felix wakes in the night at the moment, he likes me to be there.'

'Still, it's a big ask for you to give up your whole life for him.'

'I don't mind. I love Felix,' she says. 'He's so sweet.' She sighs a little. 'You're *so* lucky to have him, Kate.'

You don't deserve him. She doesn't say it aloud, but the words hang in the air all the same.

'*Any*way . . .' She summons a bright smile. 'I'm sure you'll get your memory back soon and it will be fine, but I've got to say I'll miss Felix. We've been having a lovely time together.'

'You obviously love children.'

'Yes, I do, but Felix is special.' Her smile is a little crooked. 'I wish I could have a little boy like him.'

I feel horribly guilty again that Angie so clearly loves my child more than I do.

'Would you like children of your own?'

'I'd love them.' Her eyes darken. 'I'm an only child, and I always yearned to be part of an extended family like the Vavasours. I used to wish I could be like Michael and Philippa and George, all growing up together at the Hall . . . I'd love to give my children an idyllic childhood like that,' she says wistfully. 'But . . . well, it's hard, living in the country. There aren't that many men at Askerby. The young guys tend to leave.'

'You could leave, too,' I suggest. It seems obvious to me, if she wants children that much, but Angie is clearly astounded by the idea.

'Leave Askerby?' She stares at me. 'But it's my home.'

'You could make a home somewhere else.'

'Easy for you to say. You grew up moving from country to country. You don't understand what it's like to be from somewhere, to be part of it.'

I can't argue with that. I don't.

'Askerby's home for me,' Angie says. 'I'd die if I had to leave.' She says it without melodrama, as if it is a simple fact. 'It's where I belong,' she says.

'How does someone called . . . Kash-ca?' I look at her to see if I have pronounced her surname correctly and she nods, smiling. 'How do you end up belonging at Askerby? I may have lost my memory, but I know that's not a Yorkshire name!'

'No.' She laughs as if relieved at the change of subject. 'My grandparents escaped from Poland in 1938, and came to live at the Lodge at Askerby in 1950. Babcia – Gran – is ninety-five and still there. She brought me up there after my father died, so Askerby is home to me.' She stops and gives her head a little shake. 'Sorry, it's just so strange having to explain to you what you already know.'

'It does make conversation awkward,' I agree with a sigh. 'All I can do is ask questions.' I'm hungry for more glimpses of my life before this nothingness. 'What did I use to do all day? Please tell me I don't sit around waiting for you to run errands for me!'

Angie laughs. 'No, you're very self-sufficient.'

'Do I work? Someone – Philippa, I think – told me I was a graphic designer, but I can't remember anything about it.'

'You haven't done much of that since you and Michael

moved to Askerby. It was difficult when Michael was so ill. Felix was a baby, and you'd had to leave all your contacts back in London, and then Michael died . . .' She pulls a face. 'You were a bit lost for a while,' she says. 'But we've been building a new Visitor Centre at Askerby, and George suggested you could help with the displays, so you'd started working on that.'

I'm glad to think I wasn't completely idle. 'What sort of displays?'

'About the history of Askerby, mainly. You were researching the family history, finding pictures and letters and stuff like that. You seemed much happier with something to do, but then . . .' She hesitates. 'Well, that's when you started to get obsessed about the history and everything, before, you know.'

Before I started behaving 'strangely', presumably.

'George still feels really guilty about it,' Angie says, and I look at her in astonishment.

'Why?'

'He thinks that if he'd never encouraged you to look into the history, you'd never have gone up the tower in the first place.'

I'm silent for a moment. Putting together displays sounds a very innocuous activity to me. I don't see how it could have led me to throw myself off a roof.

'That's nonsense,' I say.

'That's what I tell him,' Angie says eagerly. 'It's not his fault.'

'Of course it's not his fault.'

'I wish you'd tell him that. I know he feels bad about it.'

I try to imagine myself happily researching in a library. It doesn't feel right. Wasn't I bored? 'What happened about the displays?'

'You never got around to putting them together. We've got a whole room in the new Visitor Centre waiting for an exhibition. I've offered to do what I can, but obviously with looking after Felix . . .'

'Perhaps I could get back to it when I'm out of hospital,' I say, without really thinking about it, but her face lights up.

'That would be great. I liked it when you were thinking about the displays and feeling involved with Askerby. We used to have a good time whenever you came down to the estate office,' Angie tells me with a nostalgic smile. 'If George was out, we'd have a cup of tea and a good old natter. I miss those days.'

I picture myself gossiping with Angie. That's a bit easier to do. 'What did we natter about?'

'Ooh . . . I don't know. Anything and everything.' Angie flutters her hands vaguely. 'A bit of gossip . . . Lady Margaret's latest put-down . . .'

'Who's Lady Margaret?'

The brown eyes open wide. 'Golly, you really have lost your memory! Lady Margaret is Lord Vavasour's mother, and she's quite a character. In her day she was a great society beauty, but now she's definitely the matriarch of the family, and she believes in speaking her mind. You and she had some . . . differences of opinion,' she finishes delicately.

'Really?' I'm pleased to think that I'm able to stand up for myself. I feel so blank that I've been afraid I must be very boring.

'Oh, yes.' She lowers her voice confidentially. 'I think the Vavasours were a bit shocked when Michael brought you home.'

'Shocked?' Better and better. 'Why, what did I do?'

'Let's just say, you weren't how they imagined the future Lady Vavasour,' Angie says. 'You were a bit bohemian for them.'

From what I've seen of Fiona and Jasper, I can imagine bohemian didn't go down well with them.

'I suppose they were hoping for a nice "gel" with a head-band and pearls?'

'Well, someone who belonged in the country at least. You don't even ride.'

My pleasure at the thought of shocking the Vavasours fades. Another person who claims that I don't ride when it is the one thing I remember doing.

'Oh, you mustn't think they're not fond of you,' she says hastily, seeing my frown. 'They're used to you now. You have to remember that Askerby is a very traditional place, and it's important to keep those traditions going. Lord and Lady Vava-sour do a marvellous job,' she assures me. 'They're really the heart of the community, and they do fantastic work for charity.'

Retrieving *Country Life* from the bedside table, she flicks through the glossy pages. 'They hosted a ball in the long gallery in aid of various local charities.' She finds the page she wants and folds the magazine back so that I can see. 'Look, they gave us a whole page of pictures,' she says proudly.

I examine photographs of groups of strangers smiling at the camera against a backdrop of wood panelling, which is all that can be seen of the long gallery. The women are in evening dresses, the men in black tie. They all look extraordinarily alike. The young women have long hair, the older ones have their hair elegantly cut like Fiona's. Is this really my world? The names underneath don't mean anything to me.

'Oh, there's Philippa!' I exclaim, for something to say. She looks as if she wished that she were riding instead, and I don't blame her. A thought occurs to me, and I glance at Angie. 'I wasn't there, was I?'

Faint colour tinges her cheeks. 'No, you were in hospital. We did wonder about cancelling, but it was for such a good cause . . .'

'I think I'd rather have been in a coma,' I say, and Angie looks shocked at first and then she laughs.

'Oh, Kate, you're still the same!'

I turn my attention back to the magazine. 'Is that George? He brushes up nicely, doesn't he?'

Angie doesn't say anything, but I sense her stiffen slightly, and I get the feeling I have put my foot in it somehow. She said there were no available men at Askerby, but of course there is one single man. There's George.

I slide a look at her. Her face gives nothing away, but I can't help wondering what she really feels for him.

'Were you there?' I ask her.

'Oh, yes.'

'I hope you had a nice dress,' I say lightly.

'I was behind the scenes,' Angie says. 'It was a busy night. I had to liaise with the caterers and the band, and the security . . . there was no time for dancing!' She rolls her eyes humorously. She doesn't seem to mind that the Vavasours get all the glitter and the glory, and she is hidden away.

'It sounds to me as if you're the one who does all the "fantastic" work for charity, not Fiona and Jasper,' I say, disgruntled on her behalf, but Angie frowns.

'Nobody's going to pay money to meet *me*, are they? You've never been able to accept how things work, Kate,' she tuts. 'I'm happy to do anything I can. The ball was great publicity for Askerby,' she says, 'and that's what matters.'

There's a glow in her face when she talks about Askerby. I wonder if the Vavasours appreciate her devotion.

'Anyway, I haven't really asked how you're feeling.' Angie's expression sobers and she leans forward.

'I'm okay,' I tell her. 'Physically, at least. The doctors say I can leave soon. But mentally . . .' I wonder how to explain how lost I feel without a memory. 'It's like I'm floating in a great, empty bubble, and I've got nothing to hold onto.'

Angie takes my hand and squeezes it. Her grip is strong and reassuring. 'Hold onto me,' she says.

Chapter Four

All at once, I am close to tears. It's only now that I realize how lonely I have been, and how badly I need a friend. I feel a connection with her that I can't explain.

'Angie,' I begin impulsively, wanting to tell her how much her visit has meant to me, but her phone beeps just then and with an apologetic grimace, she pulls it out to glance at the message. 'Is that the time? I must go, I'm afraid,' she sighs. 'I promised to pick up some dry-cleaning for Lady Margaret, and they'll be closed if I don't get a move on.'

'Will you come again?' I ask almost shyly as she gets to her feet. 'If you've got time,' I add.

'Of course I will, especially now that I know you're on the mend.' She puts *Country Life* back on the bedside table. 'I'll leave you this to read, but is there anything else you'd like me to bring next time?'

I feel that I would prefer a book to a magazine, but it seems rude to say so. Besides, I don't know what I like to read.

'Could you bring some photos? Of the house maybe? Or anything you think might jog my memory?'

Angie knocks her knuckles against her head. 'Why didn't we think of that before? It's a brilliant idea. I'll see what I can dig out. You just concentrate on getting better until then. And don't worry about Felix. I'll look after him for you.'

I don't know if it is the mention of Felix that brings the familiar stab of guilt, but she bends forward to kiss me on the cheek and as she speaks the dread swoops out of my memory and flaps in my face so horrifyingly close that I cannot help flinching back.

'Oh, I'm sorry,' she says, contrite. 'I forgot how sore you must still be. Did I hurt you?'

My pulse is hammering high in my throat, but the fear has vanished as quickly as it came. I'm left feeling uneasy and exposed, which is ridiculous. My ribs punish my sudden move-ment with a savage throbbing. That must have been all it was.

'No.' I clear my throat. 'No, I'm fine. It was just . . . a twinge.' I'm sorry she's going, but suddenly I am exhausted. I summon a smile. 'Thank you for coming, Angie.'

When she has gone, I lie back on the pillows. I don't want to think about the terror that lurks in the darkness of my memory, waiting to ambush me when I am least prepared. Dis-quiet prickles over my skin at the thought of it. *Remember, remember*: the urgent whisper is back in my head, so loud that I press the heels of my hands to my ears. I'm afraid to remem-ber. I don't want to remember, not right now.

I think determinedly about Angie instead. I like her warm

smile and the sparkle in her eyes, the droll faces she pulls, so it makes sense that I liked that about her before. Besides, there is something comfortingly familiar about her. I can't put my finger on it, but we really are friends, of that I am sure.

It feels good to have a friend, I think, closing my eyes, and I remember thinking the same the day I first met Judith. The memory has sneaked into my head without me realizing it and suddenly it is there, fully formed and so vivid that my eyes fly open in something like shock.

When Oliver Raine puts his head round the door a few minutes later, I don't even wait for him to sit down. 'I've remembered something about my childhood!' I tell him excitedly, not tired any more. 'I remember the day Judith arrived at Crabbersett!'

'Excellent.' Oliver settles into the chair Angie has just vacated. 'Is Crabbersett where you grew up?'

I nod. 'I lived there with my aunt and uncle.'

Even as I say the words, unease prickles my excitement. Why would I have been living with my uncle and aunt rather than my parents? And didn't Angie just tell me that I grew up in Africa? But I shake the feeling aside. I am too happy to have a real memory at last to start doubting it.

'Tell me about Crabbersett,' says Oliver.

'It is a fine manor,' I assure him. 'There's a stone gatehouse and a courtyard lined with stables and outhouses and barns, and when I lived there it was always busy with folks to-ing and fro-ing. I dare say it still is.'

Absorbed in my memory, I don't register Oliver's puzzled expression. I can see the Manor so clearly in my mind, it is hard to believe that I could ever have forgotten it. The grey stone mellow on that late-summer afternoon, the dimness of the hall. It was harvest time, and any servants that could be spared were helping to scythe and stack the corn while the good weather lasted. My aunt wanted me to sit and sew with her, but I hated sewing. I was too impatient, and I pricked my fingers and bled over the fine linen and then my aunt would scold me. Besides, it was a fine day, and the thought of sitting still on a stool made me dizzy. I slipped out after the meal and hid in the stables, my favourite place in the world. The stable boys were all at the harvest, and I had the place to myself.

My uncle had a horse he called Prince, I tell Oliver. I can see him now: liquid, intelligent eyes, powerful haunches and long, whiskery lips that were soft as velvet against my palm when I fed him a treat. They said he was dangerous, but I wasn't frightened of him. I longed to ride him. It would be like riding the wind, but even I was not brave enough to defy my uncle.

I scratched Prince's neck and then found my own pony, Doll, who whickered a greeting. I gave them each an apple I had filched from the barrel, and then scrambled up the ladder to the hayloft. I liked it up there, where I could pretend that I ruled my own kingdom. In the hayloft I was queen, like our lady Elizabeth, and I could make my own rules. Children could do whatever they liked in my land. There was no sewing, no stern lectures, no endless praying. In my land, nobody cared if you ran or shouted or laughed too loud.

The air smelt of warm hay and apples. I was hot in my skirts, and a piece of straw was caught in my bodice. It tickled uncomfortably through my shift, and I dug around to pull it free, wriggling against the confines of the lacings. One of the stable cats had had her kittens in the corner of the loft. They mewed and squirmed, and spat a little as I picked one up and gently stroked its head with my finger.

Down in the yard, the dogs had started barking, and there was a shouted exchange at the gatehouse. I set the kitten carefully back with the others and crept over to the edge of the loft in time to see the carter pull up his horses in the yard. They blew through their noses and shifted their great hooves on the cobbles while he called to them.

The cart was laden with sacks and parcels and a barrel. Salt fish, no doubt. I wrinkled my nose.

And perched next to the carter, a small girl.

I knew who she was. I'd heard my uncle and aunt talk of my aunt's cousin who had disgraced herself by marrying a steward. Now she was dead, and the steward long gone. Her child was an orphan, and my uncle had decided to send for her to Crabbersett to be company for me.

'And mayhap Judith will teach Isabel to be less unruly,' my uncle had grunted.

The carter jumped down and turned to lift the girl roughly to the ground as he shouted to the maid to fetch her mistress.

I eyed Judith curiously. She was eight or so, I judged, about a year older than me, but age was about all we had in common. Where I was lanky and plain, with a tangle of red hair that made my aunt despair, Judith was small and plump and pretty. Her fair hair was braided neatly down her back, and she stood meekly with her hands folded in her apron as she waited for my aunt to arrive.

I felt sorry for her. I had only a hazy memory of my father by then, and the last time I'd seen my mother she had been strapped screaming to the bed. They had scooped me up as I struggled to unfasten the knots and carried me away, howling.

The next time I went upstairs, the chamber was empty. My mother was gone, and nobody would tell me where she was, but I saw the maids crossing themselves and whispering uneasily about 'a sin' and 'madness'. The sickness took my father soon after, or so I was told. Much of that time was a blur, but I do remember how overwhelmed I felt when I arrived at Crabbersett for the first time.

My uncle had fetched me himself, and I had had a maid with me, but I knew how Judith must feel. I had been bewildered and lost at first, too. At least I had had Lawrence, my cousin, who was older than me and a boy besides, but he had condescended to let me tag along with him in his games sometimes. Lawrence had been sent into service with Lord Vavasour six months since, though, and I missed him. It had been lonely with just my uncle and my aunt, who were kind enough, but my aunt Marion especially liked to stand on her dignity, and she scolded me endlessly for playing with the stable boys and kitchen brats.

I leant out of the hayloft as far as I dared. Judith looked as scared as I had been. She needed a friend, too. We would be like sisters, I decided, wiggling my hand to catch her attention. When she looked up at last and saw me, her eyes widened and her rosebud mouth dropped into an 'O', but I laid a finger to my lips and she closed it obediently. I grinned at her, and after a moment she smiled back before bending her head once more. She was just in time as my aunt swept out to greet the new arrival, stopping only to exchange a sharp word with the carter, who was anxious to unload and be on his way.

'Judith?' she said, not unkindly, and Judith nodded without raising her head. 'I am your cousin Marion. Welcome to Crabbersett, child. You will be company for your cousin Isabel. I had hoped she would be here to greet you, but no, that girl is never where she is supposed to be!'

I ducked quickly back into the hayloft before my aunt could catch sight of me. I wanted to meet Judith without her stern eyes on us, and I turned back to the kittens, well pleased. I was sure Judith and I were going to be friends, and at seven, a friend was all that I could want.

It wasn't long before Judith reappeared, clearly having been sent to look for me. She stepped cautiously into the courtyard, where the barrels and bundles unloaded by the carter were still piled up, waiting for the servants to return from the harvest.

Wriggling forward on my stomach, I beckoned to her from the hayloft.

'Come up,' I said, pointing to the stable door below me. 'There's a ladder in the stable.'

She looked doubtful but disappeared out of sight. I brushed the hay off my skirts and went over to the hole in the loft floor where the ladder was propped. I could see her sidling past the horses in the stable. They shifted nervously in response, putting back their ears and rolling their eyes as they stamped and snorted, and Prince reared up and kicked the wall of his stall as she crept past.

Judith flinched. 'Take care not to show them you are afraid,' I told her from my position above. 'They can feel your fear.'

'Cousin Marion bids you come back to the house,' she said, her face upturned to mine.

'Come up and see the kittens first,' I said. 'See, there's the ladder.'

'I do not think I should. Cousin Marion would not like it.'

'Do not think of my aunt,' I assured her. 'She will not expect you to find me immediately.'

Judith hesitated, eyeing the ladder. It was rough hewn, but sturdy enough. 'It doesn't look safe.'

'You will not fall,' I promised. 'Come up one rung at a time. I will help you.'

She bit her lip but took hold of the ladder, and with my encouragement hauled herself up rung by rung.

I beamed at her as her head appeared through the hole in the floor at last, and I held out a hand to help her up into the hayloft.

'Welcome,' I said, smiling. 'I am Isabel.'

'I am Isabel,' I repeat jubilantly to Oliver when I have finished telling him everything I remember. 'You *see*? I knew Kate wasn't my real name! I *knew* it!' I am shaky with relief at having remembered who I am at last. It's hard to explain how untethered I have felt not knowing, and now a blessed certainty

seeps through me. Now I can connect the fragments swirling around in my head and start to put myself together again.

Oliver seems less excited at my breakthrough. 'You were using Kate before the accident,' he reminds me.

'My name is Isabel,' I insist, setting my jaw stubbornly.

Still he doesn't seem convinced. He scratches his cheek. 'Does anything strike you as strange about that memory?' he asks after a moment, and I can tell he is picking his words with care.

'Strange?' Disquiet pricks the bubble of my elation. 'What do you mean?'

'You said your parents were dead,' Oliver points out.

I have forgotten that in the excitement of the memory. 'Well . . . maybe I was making that up,' I offer a little lamely. 'Maybe I was cross with my parents for sending me to stay with my aunt and uncle, and I was punishing them. Kids do that sometimes, don't they? They don't want to admit that something is true, so they invent a different story to explain what's happening.'

'And not just children,' Oliver agrees. 'It's called confabulation. Creating a story that the mind can accept.'

'There you go.'

'It's interesting that you mention Crabbersett, too. It's a tiny village not that far from Harrogate. Given your lack of memory, your parents-in-law told me something of your background, and they mentioned that you spent most of your childhood overseas or with your grandmother in the south. In fact, one of their reservations about Michael's marriage was that you had never been to Yorkshire. If you haven't gathered yet, they're a very proud Yorkshire family,' he adds with a ghost of a smile.

The sense of unease is growing, elbowing aside my giddy excitement and setting up fine vibrations at the back of my skull, like a distant warning shrill.

'What are you trying to say? Do you think I'm lying?' In spite of myself, my voice rises.

'Of course I don't think you're lying.' Oliver tries to calm me. 'I think you believe that you've remembered a scene from your childhood, but how do you explain the goods being delivered by a horse and cart or the servants harvesting? You said you were wearing a bodice, too – would you really have been wearing one of those in the eighties?'

My face freezes as his words hit me like stones. Perhaps it is odd, but this is the first time the strangeness of it has occurred to me. As I remember the scene, it was all perfectly normal. I didn't even think about the cart with its barrels of salt fish, or what I was wearing, but now . . .

I picture again my aunt bustling out of the front door. Her hair was covered by a French hood, her sleeves were puffed and ended in small ruffs that echoed the stiff linen collar at her throat. Her skirts were stiff but not extravagantly wide, and protected from the dust and mud of the courtyard by the guards at the hem. She had seemed to me dressed quite as usual, just as my own bodice, laced tightly over my smock and pinned to my long skirts, was just what I took for granted.

They were clothes worn by Tudor ladies, I realize now, and

nothing like those Philippa or Fiona wear, or those I saw in the magazine Angie left for me.

'Kate? Are you all right?' Oliver has been watching my face and I wonder in a detached, distant way whether I have gone white. A sense that something is badly out of kilter is churning in the pit of my stomach and sending belches of a fluttery, panicky feeling through me.

It was a *memory*. I hold onto that thought. How could it be anything else when I can picture it so clearly? I can still smell the hay and the horses, still feel that tickle of straw stuck in my bodice. And Judith, with her pale gold hair and that rosebud mouth flattened with determination as she took hold of the ladder. She had been *real*. Surely she had been real?

I know what Oliver is going to say. I'm not remembering at all, but recycling a scene from a film I've seen, a book I've read. But it doesn't feel like that. I was there. I know I was.

But then I think about the clothes, the carter, the way I've been told that my parents are not dead but working somewhere in Africa, and the world tilts and sways again. I could swear I had remembered an incident from my own childhood, but I must be wrong. I must have taken a story I have seen or read somewhere and made it my own.

What other explanation could there be?

Chapter Five

'You don't look so good today.' Angie pulls down her mouth in sympathy as she studies me.

'I'm okay.' I shift in the bed, suppressing a wince as my broken ribs protest. In truth, I am feeling wretched. The doctors aren't unduly concerned, but everything is hurting at once and a vicious headache is stabbing in my skull. It feels as if I have climbed a mountain only to slither down to the rocks and gravel at the bottom again.

It's been like this ever since I remembered Judith and Crabbersett. I can't get the memory out of my mind. It circles endlessly, twisting and flickering, taunting me with its clarity. At one level, I know Oliver Raine is right and that it can't be a real memory, but at the same time the truth of it pulses along my veins with every beat of my heart: I am Isabel, I was there. It is now that does not make sense, not then.

Remember. You must remember. The need is still jangling in my head. I *have* remembered, I want to say, but it is not the right memory, or it is only part of it. There's something else I have to do, something to do with my son. Not the one whose photo they have shown me, but my real son, the son I can't picture but whose absence is a constant chill shivering in my belly. Lying in this bed in the half-darkness that is a hospital night, I stare up at the ceiling while foreboding steals through me. I am afraid. I don't know why, or of what, but I am, and I can't tell anyone because I *can't remember*.

At night especially, when there is no one to distract me, no physios to manipulate my limbs, no nurses to take my blood pressure or tick off charts, no Vavasours making their duty visits, I realize that I am trapped as effectively as my mother was when she was bound to that bed. In my memory, her face is blank, but I can recall everything else in viciously clear detail: the taut tendons in her neck as they stretched in a scream, the raw red scrapes at her wrists where she struggled against the bindings, the madness in her wildly rolling eyes, the stench of piss and fear. All night long the images bombarded me, zooming around at the back of my mind until one or other would dive to the front, streaking through my memory of Judith and the hayloft, and jar me awake to find my skin clammy with sweat.

'I didn't have a good night,' I tell Angie when she looks unconvinced by my automatic 'okay'.

'Poor you,' she says. 'Do you want me to come back another time?'

Her eyes are a warm, bright brown, her nose is pert, and there's a tiny dimple by her mouth when she smiles. Her hair swings shinily to her jaw. She looks clean and wholesome and blessedly normal, and such a contrast to the murky confusion churning in my head that I want to grab onto her, to anchor myself to her cheerful competence.

'No, no, stay.' I squeeze a smile past the pounding in my head. 'I could do with the distraction, honestly. But only if you've got the time,' I add, seeing the briefcase that she's carrying.

'I've been to the printer,' she says, settling herself in the nearest chair. 'We need some new leaflets for the summer season, so it was a good excuse to come to York and see you at the same time.' She's pin neat again today in a houndstooth skirt and a short-sleeved jumper in a buttery yellow that makes her skin glow. I don't know, but I get the feeling I'm a scruffier dresser.

Angie smiles at me as she pats the briefcase on her lap. 'Lord and Lady Vavasour know where I am and they can get hold of me if they need me, but they were very insistent that I spend some time with you. They know we're friends. And George told me to take the whole afternoon if I needed. Felix is with Lady Vavasour, so he's in good hands,' she assures me.

As always when Felix's name comes up, I shift uneasily, letting Angie think my involuntary grimace is just a twinge of pain.

'They've taken the dogs for a walk,' Angie chatters on, oblivious to my discomfort. 'Felix loves doing that with his granny. He adores the dogs, doesn't he?' Clearly she has forgotten that I don't know anything about my son. 'He's had a bit of a sniffle the last few days, but he's fine now – you know how quickly kids bounce back! – and we had no trouble getting him to gobble up his lunch today. I asked Jo – the cook,' she adds in belated recognition of my memory loss, 'if she'd make him macaroni cheese as a treat as it's his favourite and he's been so good lately.'

I realize my hands are tight on the arms of the chair and I force myself to relax my fingers as I manage a strained smile.

'I'm glad he's behaving,' I say, while inside a voice is screaming: *Don't tell me about Felix! Tell me where my son is!*

'He's an absolute poppet,' Angie says, her expression soft. 'Of course, he can be a bit naughty sometimes, but I don't let him get away with it. Children need boundaries, I think, so I'm a *teeny* bit firmer than you sometimes, but I honestly think it makes him feel safer,' she explains earnestly, 'especially since everything has been so unsettled. Oh, you mustn't think I'm too strict with him,' she hurries on, clearly misunderstanding my discomfort. 'We have lots of cuddles, too. Felix knows he's loved.'

Just not by his mother, obviously.

A pain is jabbing behind my eyes. 'Did you bring any photos?' I ask, desperate to change the subject.

'I did.' Angie pulls out an iPad and sets the briefcase back on the floor. 'George and Felix and I spent *ages* choosing a selection for you.' The dimple appears by her mouth. 'We had a lovely time. I love looking through old photographs, don't you?'

I don't know. Do I? I don't say that, though.

After a bit of fiddling around to set up a slideshow, Angie hands the iPad to me. 'Here you go.'

How is it that I remember exactly how to use an iPad but not my own child? I stroke my fingers across the screen to bring up one picture after another. The first photo is of a grand house, and something in me jumps at the sight of it, a tiny jolt that has zipped through me and gone before I can decide whether it is recognition or fear.

Angie doesn't notice. 'That's Askerby Hall,' she says reverently as she cranes her head to see what I'm looking at. 'It's beautiful, isn't it?'

I don't answer immediately. I study the photo. It's a professional shot, taken from a plane or a balloon, I'd guess, and showing the Hall set back behind a courtyard framed by a handsome gatehouse and other brick buildings, and against a backdrop of gardens and woods, with the moors looming bleak and brown beyond.

The house itself is built of mellow brick. It stands four storeys high and is harmoniously balanced with five bay windows on either side of a great door and a higher hexagonal tower at each end, behind which two wings stretch to form a giant, square 'C'. A chill trembles through my heart as my eyes rest on the tower on the right. I don't want to ask Angie, but I am sure that this is where I fell.

The pounding in my head has become a sharp, stabbing pain, making me half close my eyes and squint at the screen. Yes, Askerby Hall is beautiful, but its beauty strikes me as vaguely repellent. The facade is too perfectly balanced, too symmetrical between those two towers, and a slyness seems to lurk behind the black sheen of its windows.

I shake myself. I'm being fanciful, but there is something about the house that is catching at me. Emotions are blowing through me like a tumble of leaves in a breeze, twisting and turning, skittering out of my grasp before I can tell if they are joy or grief, shock or familiarity, love or horror. My stomach hollows, and I can feel my blood beating thick and slow, thudding in my ears.

'I honestly think it's the most beautiful house in England,' Angie says. 'I love living there.'

I force my attention from the picture. 'I thought you said you lived at the Lodge with your grandmother?'

Just for a moment her pretty face freezes before the dimple pops out again. 'I do. I'm just at the Hall until you're well enough to look after Felix yourself.'

'What about your grandmother?'

'Oh, she's fine,' Angie says with a careless wave of her hand. 'She knows Felix is the priority, and it's not as if she's been abandoned,' she adds, registering my doubtful expression. 'Felix and I pop in and see her every day.'

'You've got a lot on,' I say dubiously. 'Felix, your grandmother, and presumably trying to do your job, too.'

'I told you, the Vavasours understand, and it's brilliant for me. I can't think of anything I'd rather do than be with Felix.' She leans towards me, her eyes twinkling disarmingly. 'To be honest with you, I've always wanted to live at the Hall. I never told anyone this before, but when I was little I used to pretend that I was Lady Vavasour,' she confesses. 'Babcia had a pair of court shoes with heels that I thought were the last word in sophistication. When I was little, I used to borrow them and a string of beads, and stand in front of the mirror practising shaking hands and saying, "How do you do?".' She puts on a gracious voice that is, in fact, remarkably like Fiona's. '"Thank you so much for coming." "It's been so nice to meet you."' She pulls a face, and I'm not sure whether the embarrassment is real or feigned. 'You must *promise* not to tell, though,' she says, rolling her eyes. 'I'd just *die* if any of the Vavasours knew!'

'You were just a little girl,' I say. I can picture her tottering over to the mirror in her grandmother's shoes so clearly that I wonder if I did the same when I was small. Although from the little I've gleaned about my mother, she doesn't sound like the type of woman to wear heels.

'Still,' Angie says. 'It's our secret. Promise?'

'Cross my heart and hope to die,' I agree, and out of nowhere a cold breath on my neck makes me shiver.

'Honestly, Kate, I'm so happy at the moment,' Angie tells me. 'I get a little frisson just waking up in the Hall every morning. They've given me a *huge* bedroom next to Felix. It's amazing! There's no cooking or cleaning, and Lord and Lady Vavasour have been so kind and appreciative. They've made me really welcome.'

I wrinkle my nose. 'I'm not sure I'd want to eat breakfast with my bosses every day.'

'Oh, I don't eat with the family. Felix and I have our meals in the little dining room by the kitchen – but, of course, you

61

don't remember it!' She pulls a face. 'It suits me perfectly, anyway. I'm on hand if anybody wants me, and I don't have to trek down to the estate office to see George—' A faint wash of colour warms her cheeks. 'I mean, to see if he wants me to do anything,' she amends.

Tactfully, I hide my smile and look away to give her time for that tell-tale blush to fade. My suspicion that Angie is in love with George has deepened. Frankly, I don't understand why she doesn't object to being shunted off to the servants' quarters, but she is clearly loving it. In fact, it would probably suit Angie very well if I stayed in hospital forever, I think wryly. I even open my mouth to tease her about it, but it seems ungracious after all she is doing for me.

'Well, as long as you really don't mind,' I say instead.

'Of course I don't.' She beams at me. 'What are friends for? It's really disappointing you don't recognize the Hall, though. George and I had a little bet about it, and now I'll have to tell him he won.'

She pretends to pout, but her mouth curves when she says his name. Yep, I think to myself, she's definitely in love with George. I can't quite get his appeal myself, but each to her own. I just hope he has some feelings for her, too. George is so stolid that it's hard to tell what he feels about anything. He clearly doesn't care enough about Angie to insist that she eats with the family instead of being banished below stairs, but then, what do I know?

Nothing. I know nothing.

With an inner sigh I turn my attention back to the iPad.

'Maybe some family pictures will jog your memory?' Angie leans across me to move the slideshow on, and once again I find myself hissing in a breath and shrinking back into my chair. Angie can't help but notice. 'Don't worry,' she says cheerfully, 'I'm being very careful not to knock you this time!'

'Sorry,' I mutter.

'Ah, bless. It doesn't matter at all. Now, what about this one?' she asks as a photo of a young family appears on the screen. The man is attractive with a thin, intelligent face and the Vavasour hair gleaming gold and ruffled by the wind. His smile is warm and he is holding a baby who is reaching for its mother, a slight, vivid woman with straight, dark hair blowing about her face. She's not exactly pretty, but her expression is lively and there's an offbeat charm about her. She's wearing a beret and laughing back at the baby. It's a charming picture. They're on a beach somewhere. You can just make out the sea behind, and the photo seems to sparkle with ozone and happiness.

'Who are these?' I ask, interested. They look more fun than the Vavasours I have encountered so far.

There is a pause. 'That's Michael and Felix,' Angie says, pointing at them. Her finger moves to the woman. 'And that's you.'

A roaring in my ears, and my hands tighten on the iPad to steady myself against the rushing sensation that threatens to unbalance me. *Me.* I stare at the picture, confounded. That's not how I imagined myself at all. I thought I was tall and lanky with a tumble of thick, dark red hair. The woman in the photo was never a curly redhead, that much is clear. I want to say to Angie, *Are you sure?* but I stop myself just in time. Of course she's sure.

My entrails are looping and twisting alarmingly. I'm glad I'm sitting down; I'm sure my knees wouldn't support me otherwise.

'I thought you'd be sure to recognize that one,' says Angie, disappointed. 'It's the one you keep beside your bed. We were very careful taking it out of its frame so that we could scan it in.'

'No, I . . . No,' I say. I feel as if I should apologize. I clear my throat. 'Michael looks nice,' I say weakly.

'Oh, Michael was *lovely*,' she agrees. 'Lord and Lady Vavasour were devastated when he insisted on going to London rather than staying to learn how to run the estate, but Michael couldn't wait to leave. I don't know why.' She sounds baffled. 'He never used his title, and I don't think he would have come back at all if he hadn't been so ill. I suspect the Vavasours blamed you for a while, but I don't think that's fair. Michael always said he wouldn't play lord of the manor.'

I file that information away, still looking at the picture. I study the faces, longing for a spark of recognition, but I might as well be looking at a picture in a magazine.

'They look happy,' I say wistfully.

'You were,' says Angie, and there is a thread of something I can't identify in her voice. 'You were the perfect family.'

The perfect family. And now Michael is dead and I am in

hospital and Felix, the baby reaching so confidently for his mother in the picture, is alone. Not so perfect any more.

'Keep looking,' Angie says after a moment. 'You never know what will make a memory click.'

Obediently, I stroke the screen, bringing up one picture after another. There's George and Jasper in waxed jackets, guns under their arms, black Labradors quivering with eagerness at their knees. Fiona looking gracious. Philippa on a horse. I pause when I see the horse, conscious of a faint tug, but as soon as I try to reel it in, it slips away. More photos of Michael: as a little boy in his school uniform, a gangly adolescent looking up warily from reading ('Michael always had his head in a book,' Angie says, uncomprehending), and a sad one of him looking terribly ill with the woman – me – beside him, the baby on her lap and a Christmas tree in the background. She is smiling but you can see what an effort it is. Michael has diminished, and he is pale and insubstantial against the festive background. You can almost see him receding from his family in spite of the hand she has placed on his knee as if to hold him with her.

There are more pictures of Felix, of course, too, at different stages, but none of them means anything to me. I touch his face on the screen, guilt uncurling in my belly, and very aware of Angie watching me. I feel desperately sorry for him. He is a dear little boy, I can see that, and he needs his mother, but he is not the child I am longing for.

I have asked Fiona and Jasper if they will bring Felix to see me, hoping that if I can see him for myself I will realize that he is my child and shake this terrible conviction that my son, the son I cannot picture or name but whose existence feels so real to me, is in danger.

But Fiona doesn't think that is a good idea. 'You look terrible,' she said when I raised the question. 'Felix would be frightened. He's perfectly happy with Angie. We don't think there's any need to get in another nanny.'

When I asked Fiona if Felix needed a nanny at all, she was quite sharp.

'Please don't make a fuss about this, Kate. We don't want one of your rants right now.'

I'm somebody who rants? The idea pleases me, I have to admit. It's good to know that at normal times I have opinions, that I can be difficult. I am not just someone who sits passively, remembering nothing, knowing nothing.

'You're in hospital,' Fiona reminded me unnecessarily, 'and somebody needs to look after Felix. Angie offered and she's clearly devoted to him.' I would quite like to ask why, between them, Felix's aunt and grandparents can't look after him, but I decide that would be unwise. I am very aware that for now I am dependent on the Vavasours. Until I remember who I am and how to work, I have nowhere else to go.

'Wait until you get home,' Fiona decided. 'It would be better for Felix to see you again on familiar territory.'

Now, the more I examine the photos of Felix, the more distant he seems. 'I'm sorry,' I say helplessly, aware of Angie's expectant gaze on my face. I can feel how protective she is of Felix. It's almost as if she is his mother and I am the stranger, and I wonder what Felix himself feels. Does he miss me, or has he already transferred all his affections to Angie?

Swallowing, I move on to the next picture. To my relief, it's not of Felix this time. Instead, his mother – I keep having to remind myself that she is me – is standing in front of the Hall. I can see part of the carved arch over the massive oak door in the background, and a needle-fine sense of recognition darts through me. Do I remember the door, or do I just remember seeing a photo of it? It's impossible to tell.

In the photo, I'm holding a little wire-haired terrier, and laughing as it tries to lick my cheek. I'm right about being scruffy: I'm wearing jeans and a baggy jumper. I like the look of the terrier. It is white with brown patches and a very black nose. 'Is that my dog?'

'That's Pippin,' Angie says. 'I think she was one of the family dogs, but she adopted you when Michael was dying, and now she follows you around everywhere.'

Funny, I haven't thought of myself as a dog person. I can only remember my little pony, Doll, and my uncle's fine horse.

Except that apparently I am afraid of horses and have never ridden in my life.

'There are always masses of dogs around at Askerby,' Angie is saying, oblivious to the unease that tickles at the back of my neck like a cold finger. 'George has a black Lab he takes everywhere, and Lord and Lady Vavasour have three more, as well as Pippin.'

She wants me to move on. She flicks through a few more photos of Fiona and Jasper at various events, smiling fondly at each, before she comes to a black-and-white studio portrait of a beautiful young woman with an extravagantly long neck and sweeping shoulders. A cloud of dark hair frames her face. Huge, dewy eyes gaze into the middle distance, and her glossily lipsticked mouth is parted in a semi-smile.

'Wow, who's this?'

'Lady Margaret, as she was in her heyday. Technically she's Dowager Lady Vavasour, but on the estate we always call her Lady Margaret. The portrait is always on display in the Hall, so we wondered if you might remember it.'

'I don't think so. She looks like a movie star, doesn't she? Rita Hayworth or Vivien Leigh.'

Those names spring easily to my lips. It isn't fair that I can remember them instead of something useful, like what I need to do to ease the panicky flutter in my belly.

'I know what you mean,' Angie says, 'but I advise you not to use the word "movies" in front of Lady Margaret. According to her, "movie" is a "ghastly Americanism". We had a terrible time last year when the film crew from Hollywood were shooting on location at the Hall and they would keep referring to their "movie",' she goes on, only to clap a hand over her mouth. 'Oh.'

'What?'

'Nothing,' she says hurriedly. 'I mean, I've just remembered something I need to do. It doesn't matter. Look, here's Lady Margaret now.' She seems a little flustered as she moves the screen on once more.

The contrast between glowing youth and old age is almost

shocking, but even now, Margaret is a striking woman. Her dark hair is an elegant silver, and though her eyes are sunken and her skin covered in a delicate veil of fine lines, her bone structure remains unblurred. You can still see the high cheekbones, the aristocratic nose, the unyielding jaw, but that dewy gaze has become a cold, quelling stare.

'Nothing?' Angie asks. She sighs. 'I can't imagine forgetting Lady Margaret once you've met her,' she says when I shake my head.

'She looks . . . formidable,' I say.

'Oh, she's *marvellous*. You'd never believe that she's in her late eighties. She still does such a lot for charity, while my grandmother just sits in a chair now.'

I hope I'm imagining the faintly dismissive note in Angie's voice as a photo of another elderly woman appears on the screen. 'Is this your grandmother?'

'Yes. I included it as you used to spend quite a lot of time with Babcia. You were very good to her,' Angie adds with an indifferent glance at the screen.

Angie's grandmother is clearly much older than Margaret, and no, she hasn't worn as well, but I suspect she has worked a lot harder than Margaret all her life, too. In the photo, she's sitting in a high-backed armchair, looking frail. I can see her scalp through the fine hair, and the hands that rest on her lap are blotched with dark spots, but she is smiling at the camera.

'She's got a sweet smile. What's her name?' I ask. 'I don't call her Babcia, do I?'

'No, that's a Polish version of "Granny". Her name's Dosia,

spelt D-O-S-I-A but pronounced Do-sha,' Angie tells me. 'Not that she would care if you did call her Babcia.' Angie wrinkles her nose. 'I'm afraid she's getting quite confused now. She probably wouldn't know you if you went to see her.'

I sigh and let my hands fall on the iPad. They settle just like Dosia's in the photograph. 'Well, that makes two of us,' I say.

Chapter Six

It is easy to lose track of time here. I know my room intimately now. I know exactly how the light angles through the windows and moves around the room, and how the pattern on the inoffensive beige curtains changes depending on how far back the nurses push them when they open them in the morning. I know the bland prints on the walls off by heart: one is a seascape, a blurry blend of blues and pinks and greys, and blobs that are meant to be figures walking along a beach, and the other is a cafe scene in what I am sure is meant to be Paris. I spend a lot of time wondering how my brain can retain an idea of Paris, but not the most important things in my life: my child, my husband, my parents, my name.

My name is Isabel. Secretly, quietly, I say it to myself every day.

The days have a routine of their own: constant checks of my temperature and pulse and an endless round of cups of tea and meals delivered on a tray. For all this is a private hospital, the crockery is still thick and practical, the cups and saucers an unpleasant shade of pink. Steel covers sit over plates of tepid food which all smells and tastes the same. The meals and checks are interspersed with visits from doctors who prod and peer and from Mary, the physiotherapist, with whom I gradually explore the world beyond my room. The day I walk as far as the nurses' station with the aid of a stick is a red-letter day. The nurses bring me a special cake to have with tea to celebrate.

It is six weeks before I am able to manage steps. Mary says that when I can walk up and down the stairs to the next floor, I can go home. Home to a place I cannot remember at all. I long to leave this blank, bland room, but there is a part of me that dreads it, too. It will be like stepping into the unknown, into a world where the only memories I have to guide me apparently do not belong to me at all.

I am desperate to remember something of my life as Kate, something that will help me navigate the days ahead. Is it since losing my memory that I have understood that we can only move forward if we know where we have come from, or is that something I have known all along? As it is, I fear that I will be groping through the dark, feeling my way cautiously, step by step, unable to recognize the normal cues that might remind me where I went wrong before.

On the last night in the hospital, I can't sleep. The visitors have gone home and all is quiet, or as quiet as a hospital ever gets. The lights are dimmed in the corridors and the constant background hum of machines and squeaky footsteps on the lino floors is so familiar to me by now that I hardly hear it at all.

I am watching television with the sound turned down. Some police drama is on, but I am not really following the story. On the screen, there is shouting and hands are slammed onto desks, cars are driven with grim urgency. Nothing that could possibly connect with the memory that jumps into my head without warning, so clear and intense that I cannot believe I have forgotten it until now. One minute I am staring vacantly at a police car speeding along a dark street, and the next I am remembering how I peered through the squint at Crabbersett to see what was happening in the great hall.

'Isabel!' Judith tugged at my sleeve. 'Come away. We shouldn't be here.'

I ignored her. My uncle had a small, secret closet off his chamber. It was forbidden to us, and perhaps because of that, it was my favourite room in the house. I'm afraid I was ever contrary that way.

One wall had a grille over a window looking down into the chapel that meant he could listen to the service without troubling himself to dress, like the rest of the household. Even better, to my mind, was the little clover-shaped squint carved into the other wall. You could peer down into the great hall and see who was coming and going without anyone knowing you were there at all.

I put my eye back to the squint. 'The Vavasours are here,' I whispered for Judith's benefit. 'They are dressed very fine. That is my cousin Lawrence, there in the blue doublet.' I drew back so that Judith could see, but she only wrung her hands.

'We should go before anyone finds us.'

'Oh, pooh, they are all downstairs gawking at our grand visitors.' For days now all the talk had been of my Lord and Lady Vavasour and how they were coming to Crabbersett.

And why.

It was Judith who had told me, when we lay in bed one night. 'I heard your uncle and aunt talking,' she had whispered. 'They think to make a match for you with Edmund Vavasour.'

'But I do not want to be married!' Scrambling up, I pushed the hair out of my face in dismay. A bar of moonlight fell through the casement window and turned Judith's golden hair to silver.

Since she had climbed into the hayloft ten years earlier we had never been apart. Judith was the dear friend I had always wanted, even though we were as day to night, as sunshine to storm. Where I was gangly and plain and untidy, Judith was small and neat and fair. I was restless and unruly, and she was so quiet that oftentimes folk forgot she was there at all and spoke unguardedly; she learnt all manner of things that maids like us were not supposed to know.

My aunt Marion approved greatly of Judith, who sewed a neat seam, unlike my own careless, looping stitches, and was diligent about her prayers, while I fidgeted and cast longing glances at the door. I teased Judith that she was like a cat, twitching her paws at the first sign of wet. I could not understand how she could prefer to stay inside rather than be out, and she could not understand the pleasure of riding over the moor, face lifted to the wind, while the skylarks darted above the heather.

For all our differences, we fitted together like fingers in gloves. We knew each other inside out. In summer, we chased butterflies around the garden, and caught them between our cupped hands for the pleasure of letting them go. We lay in the orchard and spat cherry stones to see who could send them further. In winter we skated on the frozen pond, holding each other up, shrieking and laughing while the cold stung our cheeks.

Every night I brushed Judith's hair until it gleamed gold, and she did her best to tame my wild curls. Together, we puzzled over ciphering. Judith untangled the silk threads in my needle case and unpicked my seams, and I sang loudly to disguise the fact that she was an indifferent player on the virginals.

When Judith fell ill with the pox, I sat holding her hand while she burned with fever, and refused to be separated from her. No sooner did her fever break than I caught it. We shared even the pox. Afterwards, Judith was barely blemished – a single pockmark on her temple – but I was left with a scatter of marks high on my cheeks that my aunt bemoaned forever after, though it seemed to me that they could have been much worse and I cared little for my appearance anyway.

'You do not need to,' said Judith, who was always groomed to a nicety. 'You are an heiress, while I have only my face to recommend me.'

That was true, although my fortune did not spare me regular beatings as a child. My aunt despaired of taming me. 'What am I to do with Isabel?' she would lament. 'How will we ever find a husband for her when she will not sit still for two moments together but must hop around like a flea?'

Why could I not be more like Judith? was her constant complaint. Judith told me not to mind her. I had my fortune and needed nothing else. A few pockmarks would not deter a suitor with an eye to my dowry, she told me, and so it proved.

The night when Judith told me that my uncle and aunt were discussing my marriage, I was restless and uneasy. I had known, of course, that it would happen one day, but it had always seemed a prospect that belonged to the distant future, not to *now*. I did not want to move away. I loved Crabbersett, the Manor with its bustling household, and the village where I knew everyone from Ellen the goose girl to Sir Thomas Hunter the priest.

I still took an apple to Doll, long outgrown; but in her place I had a spirited grey mare with lovely liquid, dark eyes. I called her Blanche. Blanche had a heart as big as the sky, and I rode her every day I could. I hated to be confined. I knew every beck, every wood, every dip and hollow of the high moors where the sheep grazed in the summer and where the dour shepherds would greet me with a nod. It was my home and I trembled at the thought of leaving it all behind to be married and bear children.

For that would be my lot, I knew. Marriage was for the procreation of children. What use was a barren wife? And whenever I thought of childbirth, I couldn't help but think of my mother, delivered of a dead babe, bound to the bed, her eyes bulging and rolling like a terrified horse, the whites glistening with madness in the stifling darkness.

Judith's news sent my thoughts scattering in alarm. I hugged my knees to my chest and watched the moonlight fall in a lovely silver strip across the bed we shared.

'I do not want to be wed,' I said again.

Judith clicked her tongue. 'Of course you must marry, Isabel. What else is there for you?'

Outside, I heard the throaty hoot of an owl. I imagined it taking flight in the darkness, its wings rustling in the air as it soared and swooped in search of its prey.

'I wish I didn't have a fortune!' I said childishly. 'I wish I could live in the woods and forage for my food. I wish I could fly and be bound to no man.'

'Isabel!' Judith pulled herself up against the bolster and shook her head at me. 'You should not say such things.'

'Why not? They are true!'

Judith sighed. 'You must take care, you especially.' She lowered her voice. 'If they heard you, people who do not know you, they would say that you are mad.'

Mad like my mother.

'Your aunt worries enough about you as it is,' Judith said.

I did not want to talk about madness. I tried to make light of it. 'She worries that I cannot sing or cast accounts!'

'It is more than that.' The moonlight caught Judith's eyes, and I had the disconcerting impression that they were blank and silver as pennies. 'We know what you are like,' she said in her soft voice, 'and we love you for it, but others do not understand. They think it strange that you are not content to ride in a coach but must be out in all weathers and wear breeches underneath your skirts to ride astride.'

'I am learning husbandry, as my aunt wishes.' I hated the defensive note that crept into my voice. 'I cannot inspect cattle or crops well from a coach.'

'Oh, Isabel, you know what I mean,' sighed Judith. 'You do not like the things a lady should. You do not do or say the things a lady should.' She hesitated. 'Your aunt fears that you are too like your mother. She told her chaplain that her passions ran strong, just as yours do. And I fear for you too,' Judith said. 'You must not say that you want to live in a wood, or fly, even in jest. You do not want to give people the excuse to remember how your mother died. You know what folk are like. "Like mother, like daughter", they will say.'

I knew she was only trying to help me, but I didn't want to hear it. I fixed my eyes on the moonlight pouring through the window. My mouth was set in a stubborn line, I am sure, and I was determined to keep silent, but I had never been able to stay sullen for long and besides, the idea of an imminent marriage was barrelling through my defences, and as I sat there, something inside me began to crumble.

'Judith.' I broke the silence in a whisper. 'I am afraid.'

'Come, can this really be you?' Judith sounded shocked. 'Isabel, who fears nothing, who jumps every beck and out-stares every snorting stallion? Isabel the boldest and bravest of wenches?'

I swallowed. I knew that she was trying to tease me into a

smile, but I couldn't. 'I fear this,' I said, low. I rested my fore-head on my knees and told her the truth that I had hidden for so long. 'I fear that I will indeed go mad like my mother. I fear they will shut me in a room if I have to give birth and I will not be able to breathe. I fear they will tie me to the bed as they did her, and that I will lose my reason as she did.'

I am afraid.

The words shiver in the darkness as I lie in the hospital bed, a faint but vibrating echo from the past, and I am afraid again, afraid of what remembering them means. For this is not a film I have seen, it is not a book I have read. That fear was real. It was inside me, a fist clenched tight, just as it is now. The pulse beats rapidly in my throat, as it did then. I can still feel the fine-ness of the linen smock pressed into my face where I leant my head on my knees. The chamber smelt musty, faintly smoky, and a quill from one of the feathers in the mattress was poking through the sheet and digging into my bottom. I did not invent that. I remember it. *I remember.*

On the television, the drama is still playing out. There is running, a chase through a warehouse. Someone has a gun. I blink at the scene without understanding what I'm seeing. My mind is far away.

It doesn't make sense. It is impossible for me to be remem-bering an evening that belongs centuries ago, I understand this, but at the same time I know that the memory is real. I don't want to remember any more now, but it is as if a door has been unlocked in my mind, and now that it has swung open I cannot close it again.

Judith stroked my hair very gently. 'I know,' she crooned. 'I know you are fearful.'

'It isn't fair,' I said. I lifted my head and blinked back the tears burning behind my eyes. I preferred to be angry and resentful than afraid. 'When I marry, I will have to leave everything that is dear to me. I will be wed to a man who can take my fortune as his own and do what he likes with me. I will have a child and they will shut me up in a room and bank up the fires, and then they will be surprised that I run mad!'

My voice rose until Judith shushed me. 'Hush now,' she said, her hand still stroking my hair comfortingly. 'It is our lot to marry if we are fortunate. What else is there for us, after all?'

'How will I bear it without you?' I said miserably.

'You will have to charm your husband so that he will do whatever you ask, and then you may send for me as your companion,' she suggested, and I brightened. I had not thought of that.

'Do you think I may?'

'You will need to be kind to your husband,' said Judith, 'and then you may do whatever you will.'

Chapter Seven

Judith had given me some hope, but when I looked through the squint that day, I was far from reconciled to the idea of marriage. I remember peering down into the hall, where I could see my uncle, bowing deeply to a florid man in a sumptuous fur-trimmed gown and a splendid velvet hat. Beside him, my aunt curtseyed a little awkwardly; I could tell that her knees were paining her.

'Anyone would think the Queen's majesty herself had come to call,' I whispered, determined not to be impressed.

Who were these Vavasours after all? Judith knew, of course. They had been merchants in York once, but thanks to their fortune and some shrewd marriages were now connected to the greatest families in Yorkshire and could count some of the courtiers close to the Queen as their allies. According to Judith, they owned land throughout the county, but their family estate was at Askerby, past Helmsley, where Lord Vavasour had knocked down the old manor and built himself a fine new hall in the latest fashion. 'They say it has glass in every window,' Judith had said.

I could scarce believe that such a family would be interested in me, but Judith insisted that it was so. 'Your uncle hopes to make an alliance with Lord Vavasour,' she said. 'And you are part of it. Why else did your aunt tell you to wear your best gown?'

I tugged irritably at the constriction of the stomacher, which was so tightly laced I could hardly breathe. Between that and the stiff hoops of the farthingale, it was awkward to bend. I had already endured a painful half-hour while Judith combed out the tangles in my unruly hair, which never would lie straight, no matter how tightly she tried to bind my curls.

Under my aunt's direction, I had been carefully dressed. 'Like a joint of meat to tempt a buyer,' I had muttered to Judith. My skirts were a vivid green, embroidered in gold, and my sleeves were outrageously puffed. The starched ruff kept my chin tilted high and a gold chain hung at my waist. Oh, I was very fine, and I hated it. I could not wait to get back into my old skirts and escape outside.

Two young men stood behind Lord Vavasour. One of them was my cousin Lawrence, who I scarce recognized. He had grown into a man since I last saw him. Beside him stood another youth, swaggering in his patterned Venetians and pinked doublet. His collar was crisp and white, and a short cloak was swung dashingly over his shoulder.

'That must be Edmund, Lord Vavasour's heir,' said Judith, who had crept forward in spite of her fear and was craning her head to look. I made room beside me so that she could see. 'He is comely,' she whispered as Edmund bowed and flashed a smile that had my aunt bridling with pleasure, and there was an odd note in her voice that I did not recognize.

They think to make a match for you with Edmund Vavasour.

My stomach felt hollow. It could not be true. They could not really be going to marry me to this posturing fool who looked as if he feared to splash his stockings with mud.

'What a popinjay!' I curled my lip at him.

'Oh, Isabel!' Judith chided. 'He could be old and gouty and fat, but instead he is young and fair and wealthy. He has kin with influence, and look, good teeth too. What more do you want?'

'I want him to smile less,' I said sourly.

I did not want to impress Edmund Vavasour with his arrogant swagger. I was not interested in his teeth or his fine house. But I knew that I would have little choice in the matter. My fortune could not sit idly when it could be traded for men's profit, and me with it.

I started to complain about it, but Judith put a finger to her lips. 'Shh!' she hushed me. 'They are talking about you.'

'What? What are they saying?'

'Your aunt is saying that she will send for you to join them. Quick, we mustn't be found in here,' said Judith, in a flurry to be gone. 'You know we are forbidden. You will be beaten if your uncle hears that you were here.'

She didn't fear beating herself – my aunt knew well that she was never responsible for any of the trouble I led her into – but she was always trying to save me from the rod.

'He won't beat me today if he wants to show me off to the Vavasours,' I said, but I followed Judith as she scurried back to the parlour, where we were supposed to be quietly embroidering a coverlet.

Scarcely had we picked up our needles than Agnes, one of the maidservants, appeared and said that my aunt had sent for me to attend her in the great hall.

I cast aside my embroidery and jumped to my feet. 'Come, let us go, Judith.'

Agnes looked askance at Judith. 'My mistress just sent for you,' she pointed out to me.

I'd noticed the servants did not care overmuch for Judith, and it always puzzled me.

'I am too close to them,' Judith had said with typical serenity once when I commented on it. 'They know I am dependent on your aunt and uncle's charity. Were it not for that, I would be a servant for hire as they are.'

'Of course she means for Judith to come too,' I insisted, overruling Agnes.

So Judith followed me down the stairs and into the great hall, which all at once seemed crowded with Lord Vavasour's great retinue. Dogs milled around, snapping and snarling at each other until they were broken apart with a curse or a boot, and servants squeezed through the press of people with jugs of wine.

'Ah, here is my niece.' My uncle was all smiles as he presented me to Lord Vavasour. I sketched a curtsey. I did not see why I should rub my nose in the rushes for him.

Lord Vavasour looked at me assessingly, as he would eye up a prize heifer. He did not seem impressed. His only response was a grunt before he crooked a finger. This was the signal for his son to step forward, all dazzling in his fine clothes.

I could have predicted that Edmund would make an extravagant bow, and so it was. There was no need for such a display. It made me feel that he was mocking me. His face was perfectly straight, but I was sure when he lifted his gaze to mine that he was laughing. He had very dark, very blue eyes, so blue that it was unsettling, and all at once I was very aware of my lanky frame, of the pockmarks on my cheeks and the hair that sprang from its pins. I was furious with myself for caring when I had never cared before, and I stuck my nose in the air. That only seemed to amuse him more.

There was no pretence that a bargain was not being struck with my person – or rather, my fortune – at the centre of the discussion. I was placed next to Edmund at the end of the top table when we sat down to dine. He was annoyingly attentive, helping me to custard and some salad of hard eggs, a fritter, a slice of gingerbread. He studied every dish to pick out the plumpest roasted lark, or the most delicate slice of veal baked with raisins and dates and seasoned with saffron and cloves. He made sure that I had some sauce with it, and I tasted the sharpness of the vinegar, the sweetness of the sugar, cut through with pungent ginger. He carved me a slice of venison pie with his own knife. Such condescension.

I accepted his attentions coldly, wishing he'd stop piling food onto my plate. Normally I had a hearty appetite, and the cook had made my favourite dish of capon stewed with prunes, but between my tight lacings and Edmund's presence, it was impossible to enjoy my meal that day. The meat stuck around my mouth and I had trouble chewing. I was too aware of his glinting blue gaze, of the warmth of his body beside mine.

Judith was seated at a lower table. Whenever I caught her eye, she nodded encouragingly at me; I knew I was supposed to smile and flutter my eyelashes at Edmund, but I couldn't do it. Whenever he spoke, I heard a ripple of laughter in his voice, like sunlight on a stream, unmistakable but impossible to pin down and say: *There it is*. Whatever it was, it made me tongue-tied and stiff, I who was normally so fiery and quick to retort. It made me furious that I should be so discomfited.

As soon as the meal was over, my uncle and Lord Vavasour withdrew to my uncle's closet, where no doubt they would get down to the true business of the day, bargaining over my fortune. As the servants began to clear the tables, I slipped away before my aunt could catch my eye. Judith was less skilled at escape, and I saw my aunt beckon to her as I backed out of the door and almost knocked over the little maid, Peg, who was labouring under a pile of trenchers.

'Leave those!' I seized her arm and she goggled at me. 'Come and unpin me. I cannot manage alone.'

With Peg's help, I unpinned my sleeves, and breathed a sigh of relief as the stomacher was loosened. I wriggled out of the farthingale hoops and left my skirts in a heap as I pulled on the pair of breeches I used for riding and tied them at the waist. I wore them under a kirtle with a modest padded roll which gave my skirts some shape but at least made it possible to ride.

There was still no sign of Judith so I slipped with Peg down the stairs to the kitchen, where the cook sighed and shook his head at me but let me go. In a faded blue kirtle and a plain collar, nobody would take me for the heiress with her fashionable farthingale and extravagant ruff. Or so I hoped.

As always when I was in turmoil, I headed for the stables, and there Judith found me, mindlessly grooming my uncle's magnificent stallion. Genet was a successor to Prince, even bigger, even blacker and with an even trickier temper, but I forgave him his moodiness for his speed and grace.

Judith edged into the stable. 'Your aunt is asking for you,' she said, eyeing Genet warily.

'Tell her you cannot find me.' I was surly at the knowledge that I had behaved badly. 'I have had enough of doing the pretty to that mincing fool Edmund Vavasour. Did you see his stockings with their embroidered clocks?' I asked her. 'Does he think he is at court?'

I sneered because it was easier to think of him with contempt than to remember how ugly and awkward I must have appeared. I imagined him whispering to his father that he would not marry me, no, not for a thousand of my fortunes, and I told myself I was glad of it, because I certainly did not want to marry *him*.

'I dare say he was carried here in a litter so that he did not have to get his shoes dirty,' I said to Judith.

'Why, Mistress Isabel, I do believe you have taken me in dislike!'

Judith squeaked with alarm, and I sucked in my breath as Edmund's head appeared around the side of the stall. He must move like a cat through the straw. I hadn't heard him approach at all.

'You know what they say,' I reminded him when I had my breath back. 'Eavesdroppers never do hear good of themselves.'

'You do me wrong,' he protested. His face was as straight as ever, but his eyes danced. 'I am perfectly able to ride, you know. It is not my fault that it is a fine day and there is no mud to splash my stockings.'

I eyed him resentfully, disliking the way he made me feel foolish and jittery. 'You came on a fat pony, perhaps? It wouldn't do to fall off and crush your silks!' I knew I was being unforgivably rude, but I couldn't help myself, and Edmund only laughed.

'I don't think my Bale would like to be called a pony,' he said. 'He is as mettlesome as that beast you're hiding behind.'

'I am not hiding!' The accusation stung and I stepped forward boldly. 'Don't come near,' I warned as Edmund made to enter the stall.

Judith gasped at his bravery. 'Indeed, sir, you should not go in. The horse is dangerous!'

'He is not dangerous.' I corrected her with a dagger look. 'He does not care for strangers, that is all.'

'He will not mind me.'

Edmund's confidence grated on me, and I half hoped that

Genet would punish him for his insolence. Instead I had to watch incredulously as the horse lowered his head and let Edmund scratch his cheek and murmur a greeting.

When Genet blew softly into his hand, as docile as the motherless lambs that were brought into the shed at lambing time, I could only watch with my mouth a-cock, half outraged, half impressed in spite of myself.

'Well!'

At that, Edmund looked up from whispering in Genet's ear and grinned at me. All at once he looked like a boy, not an intimidatingly elegant young man, and I found myself smiling back at him.

'I have never seen him do that before,' I confessed. 'Do you have some magic in you?'

'No magic,' he said. 'It is all in the hands, and in the voice.' The words were innocent enough, but he made them sound disturbing. Something in his smile set heat squirming in my belly, sent it flooding into my cheeks, and I made myself look away.

'Let me see your horse,' I said.

'Certainly,' said Edmund. 'He is very well-mannered.'

I thought I heard a faint stress on that 'he', which I guessed was directed at me, but I decided to ignore it. I followed Edmund to the end of the stable, where a magnificent horse, easily as big as Genet, was tethered. He greeted his master with a whicker and bent his head graciously to me.

'Oh, you are very comely indeed,' I told him, and I slid a glance at Edmund under my lashes. 'May I ride him?'

'No,' said Edmund, not even pretending to be polite. 'Well-mannered he might be, but Bale is too strong for you.'

'I ride Genet,' I lied, and he raised his brows and clicked his tongue.

'Isabel, Isabel . . .' he chided.

I lifted my chin. 'I *could* ride him! I can ride any horse,' I said. 'I will race you.'

'A race?' Challenge lit his eyes. 'I do not think you dare.'

Judith moaned. She knew how I would react to that.

'Do I not?' I asked, and my heart thrummed with excitement.

'Isabel!' Aghast, Judith looked from me to Edmund and back again. 'You must not! How can you think of it?' She wrung her hands, a bad habit of hers when she was anxious. 'If your uncle finds out you even *talked* about riding that horse . . . !'

'They will be sitting over their wine for hours yet,' said Edmund. 'They are talking politics and trying to work out where they all stand with the Scottish queen.'

'Very well then.' Afire with the challenge, I would not listen to Judith, who followed, vainly trying to persuade me to change my mind, as I ordered a stable boy to put my saddle on Genet, staring him down when he voiced a timid objection, and lead the horse out to the mounting block. 'We'll race up to the cross on the moor,' I told Edmund.

'And where might that be?'

'You need only follow me,' I said loftily. 'Genet and I will show you the way.'

Edmund laughed. 'So be it.'

The stable boys gawped as I hopped up on the mounting block and scrambled into the saddle, thrilled by my own daring. It was not a very elegant mounting, but Genet was bigger than any horse I had ridden before, and it was all I could do to get on him at all. Edmund was already mounted, his horse turning in restless circles, and Genet shifted edgily as I rearranged my skirts over my breeches and took a firm hold of the reins. I wasn't used to being so high, and Judith seemed tiny and fragile from my position atop the saddle.

'Isabel, please!' she begged. 'What if you fall?'

'I will not fall,' I said dismissively. 'I never fall.' But out of nowhere a chill ran through me, and I shivered in spite of myself.

I shook the feeling aside as I concentrated on mastering my uncle's horse. Truth to tell, I could barely control him. The feel of his powerful muscles beneath me was terrifying and exhilarating, but with Edmund's eyes on me, I assumed an expression of nonchalance and managed to guide him through the stone gateway. Judith watched, pinch-faced, her hands folded tightly in front of her stomacher.

Once through the village, we let the horses have their heads. The tracks up to the moor were dry, baked hard after nearly a month without rain, and the dust rose around us as the horses' hooves thudded on the ground. I felt as if I were flying atop the powerful horse, as if at any moment he might launch into the sky and gallop through the high, thin clouds that streaked across the blue. My blood was singing, and I laughed, reckless and unrepentant.

Even the fact that Edmund's horse nudged ahead to the cross at the very last second could not spoil my pleasure in the moment. The smell of dust and heather. The moors rolling gaunt and golden to the horizon and the huge light. Genet's flanks heaving as we slowed, his neck twitching against a fly. My thighs, cramped with the effort of staying in the saddle, my hair wild about my shoulders. And Edmund, high on his horse, laughing with me. He had lost his cap, and his hair was tousled, his eyes an intense blue that reflected the sky.

I will never forget this moment, I thought. *Never*.

Chapter Eight

But I *did* forget. Now that the memory is pouring back in a blessed rush, the relief of remembering is so intense that it catches in my throat. It is as if I am seventeen again. *Of course*, I sigh to myself. *Of course that's how it was.* How could I ever have forgotten when I had been so sure that I never would?

Edmund was as breathless as I. He brought Bale round until the two horses were side by side but facing in different directions. Now I could see the dust and sweat on his skin, the creases in his cloak, the way his ruff had turned limp and faintly grubby with his exertion. 'I like you better this way,' I told him, and he grinned.

'I only dressed like this to impress you.'

I gaped at him. 'To impress *me*?'

'You are an heiress,' he pointed out. 'My father was very clear that I needed to win your approval. How was I to know that I should have turned up in scuffed jerkin and muddy boots if I wanted to make a good impression?'

We turned the horses for home and let them walk to cool down after the wild ride. I was smiling, remembering the thrill of it, the sense of flying, of freedom. Nothing was said between Edmund and I, but I *knew*. It was as if my past was gathering, tensing itself for a leap into my future, as if from the moment I had pulled myself into the saddle my life had changed course. It seemed to me then that I had turned onto a track and found Edmund, and we would ride side by side forever.

We talked easily as we rode back through the village, past the humped cottages, squat beneath their thatch. They were dark and noisome inside, I knew, but the women called to me cheerfully as they sat in their doorways, their hands busy. Children stared at us from the dust, hens scuttled out of the way of the horses' hooves and dogs ran after us, barking and snarling. From the forge came the unmistakable sound of clanging and hammering.

I think we had both forgotten all about everyone at the Manor, but when we turned in through the stone gateway, we found my uncle and Lord Vavasour waiting for us in the yard. My uncle's face was thunderous and Lord Vavasour looked grim.

I glanced at Edmund.

'Now, what roused them from their politics, do you think?' he murmured, his blue eyes cool and faintly wary. I wondered if he would be beaten, the way I surely would. 'Did your little maid tell on you?'

'My maid?' I did not know who he meant at first. 'Oh,

Judith . . . No,' I said firmly. 'Judith is my dear friend. She is like a sister to me. She would never do anything to hurt me.'

Gradually my eyes focus on the screen, where the detectives are questioning a new suspect, but I'm not really seeing them. I'm thinking about my prickly reaction to Edmund, and the wild, forbidden thrill of riding my uncle's horse. I feel again the bunched power of Genet's muscles, the exhilaration of speed and strength and the golden, giddy sense of freedom, the heat that burned in my belly when Edmund looked at my mouth, and I realize that I am smiling.

But as the implications dawn on me, my smile retreats slowly. I didn't care for Edmund's fancy Venetians or the short cloak tossed over his shoulder, but I hadn't thought that he looked odd, any more than it had seemed strange to have to pin my sleeves to my bodice. I frown at the screen, where the male detectives wear trousers and rumpled jackets, their ties wrenched askew to indicate their frustration. Not a doublet or clocked stocking in sight. They eat burgers, not roasted lark; drink coffee, not spiced wine.

Pointing the remote at the television, I switch it off and stare at the blank screen. It reminds me of my memory, which is as dark and impenetrable, except for those few moments which wink at the edges of my mind, vivid as jewels, brilliant and impossible to ignore. Memories which I know Oliver Raine will tell me are not really memories at all.

But if they are not memories, what are they? Hallucinations? An elaborate fantasy I choose for some reason to enact in Tudor costume? They don't feel like fantasies; they are too real. The world I remember is not one created by a fevered imagination. It is grounded in the everyday details of touch and taste, of the smell of the horses, the foam at their bridles, the fine hairs glinting on the backs of Edmund's hands.

I swallow. What am I thinking? That those memories are real after all? Chewing my lip, I turn the remote over and over in my hand. I may not know much about my life now, but I know that if I start claiming somehow to remember a life from over four hundred years ago, eyebrows will be raised. There will be muttered consultations with Oliver Raine. As far as the Vavasours are concerned, I have already tried to kill myself, and although I cannot believe that is true, they will no doubt be looking for signs of another breakdown.

And if they suspect I am losing my grip on reality, what is to stop them having me sectioned? My parents are out of contact, Michael is dead, and Felix is a little boy. Who else is there to care enough to believe in me? Angie is my friend, but she is fiercely loyal to the Vavasours too. If they are worried about me, she will worry too. I don't think she would protest if they said that I needed help.

The thought of not being let out sends a wave of panic rolling through me, churning in my stomach and knotting my entrails. I have endured all these months in hospital; I cannot bear the idea that I might have to stay here. I am yearning to breathe the moorland air, to feel the wind in my face. I cannot let anyone suspect madness.

No, wait. I put a hand to my head. Madness was Isabel's

fear . . . I am getting muddled. I make myself breathe slowly in and out until my racing heart steadies, but the dread is still there. I must be very careful. I won't tell anyone what I have remembered. Judith, Edmund, my life as Isabel: I will keep them all to myself for now.

The last time I saw Oliver, he told me that being in familiar surroundings should help trigger my memory. 'I'll come out and see you at Askerby when you've had a chance to settle back into some kind of routine,' he said. 'I'll be able to assess your progress much more effectively there.'

Perhaps, I tell myself, Oliver will be right. Perhaps when I get to Askerby and see Felix in the flesh everything will fall into place and I will remember my life as Kate. Perhaps then I will understand why Edmund and Judith have sprung so fully formed into my imagination, and this desperate sense of urgency quivering at the corners of my mind will fade.

I hope so.

I have longed to leave this room, where the squeak of wheels on the meal trolley and the smell of tea have driven me to distraction, but when the moment comes, I find myself ridiculously close to tears.

Philippa brought in some clothes for me a couple of days ago: a long, Indian print skirt in muted reds and oranges, a camisole top, a chunky cardigan. I stroked the skirt wonderingly as I lay it out on the bed.

'Is this what I usually wear?'

Philippa tipped her hand carelessly from side to side. 'You're more of a jeans girl, I'd say, but we thought a skirt would be easier to put on with your leg.'

The cast is off, and I have been doing my exercises, but even with the steel pin in my leg I still can't walk without a stick.

'You should have seen Ma's face as she looked through your wardrobe.' Philippa lounged in one of the chairs, her legs hooked over the arm, and mimicked Fiona wrinkling her nose. 'She's stuck in the eighties and thinks nice girls should still be wearing twinsets and pearls and a velvet headband.'

'She must have been very disappointed when Michael brought me home,' I said, looking at the skirt. I may have lost my knowledge of fashion along with everything else, but even I can see it wouldn't work with a twinset and pearls.

'They should have known he would go for someone unsuitable,' Philippa said. 'He always said Askerby was a time warp and he didn't want to live in the past. We're always boasting of our "centuries of tradition". Michael hated that. He had a huge row with Pa once. He said if the Vavasours put as much effort into thinking about the future as they did into obsessing about preserving the past, we'd be a much healthier family, but of course, Pa couldn't have that. The whole point about Askerby is that it never changes.'

I can't work Philippa out. There's a cynical edge to everything she says, and sometimes she seems to actively dislike everyone at Askerby, but when I ask her why she doesn't leave, she says she can't be bothered. 'I get to live in a house with a cook and a whole army of cleaners, and I spend all day with horses,' she says. 'Why would I give that up to live in a poky flat, get a grotty job and do my own washing-up?'

It feels strange getting dressed, like putting on someone else's clothes, and I keep smoothing the skirt over my knees, trying to find something familiar about it. There's a mirror over the basin in the corner. I stare at my reflection for a long time. The bandages around my head have gone, and my hair is starting to grow back in a fine, dark fuzz. It is never going to grow into red curls, I can see that, but my mind refuses to accept that the woman in the mirror is really me. She looks like a refugee, thin and hollow-eyed, with a bruised, shell-shocked air. That isn't me. Where are the pockmarks on my cheeks, my big nose, the clear green eyes I know from the looking glass?

I lift a hand; the reflection lifts a hand. I stretch my lips into a ghastly smile; the reflection does the same.

It *is* me.

There is a buzzing in my head. My mind rears and bolts, like a horse faced with a hedge too high to leap, but before I can fumble my way back to the chair, Jasper has appeared in the doorway, and Fiona is smiling her cool smile behind him.

'Ready to go?'

The nurses who have lined up to say goodbye blush and bridle with pleasure when Jasper and Fiona shake hands with each of them and thank them for looking after me so well. Then it is my turn, and overwhelmed at the prospect of leaving the only place I can remember, I hug them tearfully. Fiona's smile stiffens as she watches. Clearly, overt displays of emotion are not the Vavasour way. Good manners, yes. Tears and hugs and reassuring pats, definitely not.

I don't care.

Jasper offers me a wheelchair, but I insist on walking out by myself. The stick helps, but I haven't reckoned on how long the hospital corridors are, and by the time we reach the car at last, I am exhausted and shaky. Jasper drives a mud-splashed Range Rover and he has to help me up into the front passenger seat.

It is my first glimpse of the world outside the hospital and everything is startling and strange. The roads are crowded with vehicles moving at extraordinary speeds, and I shrink back into my seat, flinching as cars and huge trucks hurtle towards us. I am convinced they must hit us, that the road isn't nearly wide enough, but they flash past in a seemingly unending stream, with a muffled whooshing noise.

I am glad when we leave the worst of the traffic behind and Jasper turns onto the quieter country lanes. It is a fickle June day, fiercely bright one minute, spattering the windscreen with a short, sharp shower the next. The greenness of the hedgerows is so intense that it hurts my eyes, and I have to keep blinking as the countryside shimmers in and out of focus.

Sensing that I am struggling, Fiona keeps up a desultory conversation with Jasper from the back seat, and I am grateful that neither of them tries to draw me in. The roads grow progressively smaller, and it is only when Jasper slows to turn into a narrow lane that he glances at me.

'We're nearly there. Does anything seem familiar yet?'

'No,' I say, but that isn't quite true. Something about the

landscape is chiming inside me. The road dips and climbs, and as we crest the rise, I see the moors spread out before me in a great golden sweep up to the sky. Patches of dark shadows race over the hillsides as clouds are blown briskly over the sun. It is like coming unexpectedly on the sea, the sea I don't remember ever seeing but which I can imagine so clearly that I must have done: the space and the glittering light and the restless movement of the waves. I feel as if I am teetering on the edge of something enormous, and I catch my breath.

'I remember this,' I say.

I remember how Edmund drew his horse to a halt at the top of the hill and turned in his saddle to wait for me.

'It is not much further,' he said.

All day the country we passed through had been hidden behind a curtain of dense, dark rain, but as we rode up the hill it eased to a drizzle and I gasped at the sight of the moors spread out ahead of me. They made the familiar hills by Crabbersett seem tame. Looking out beneath the brim of my hat, where the raindrops funnelled into a steady stream, I saw a thin shaft of golden light split the heavy black clouds in the distance from the tops of the hills. The vastness and wildness of it made me feel small, but at the same time my heart swelled at the sight of the open sweep of country. No trees or hedgerows or copses, nowhere to bind you or enclose you.

It had been a long, hard ride from Crabbersett, and it had rained all the way, crashing through the leaves and battering onto the ground in an implacable downpour that beat onto my hat until it was limp, and I was saddle sore and weary, although I would have died rather than admit it.

'How do you, wife?' Edmund asked.

I wiped the rain from my face with the back of my hand. 'I am wet,' I told him, but I was smiling. I took off my hat and laughed at the jaunty feather, which was now bent and bedraggled out of all recognition.

They had brought a coach for me, but I would have none of it. 'I do not want to be shut up in a chest on wheels,' I told Edmund, snapping at him like my aunt's old lapdog whenever anyone tried to help it. 'I will ride with you.'

'It is like to rain,' Edmund had warned.

'What do I care for a bit of rain?' I said scornfully. 'I will not melt.'

In truth, I nearly did. The rain turned the track to a quagmire and we had to pick our way slowly along the way. Edmund's escorts were hard-faced men whose eyes were never still, their hands never far from their daggers. They rode close beside us. 'There are vagabonds aplenty hereabouts,' said Edmund, matter-of-fact, when I queried the need for their presence. 'Poor wretches who have nothing to lose by attacking an unarmed party. They would not hesitate to strip you of your rings and your girdle – and worse.'

But we had made it onto Askerby land without incident.

'You would ride,' Edmund reminded me mildly.

'Aye, and as well I did,' I said. 'If you had been saddled with a wife in a coach you would have had to turn back long since.'

'True,' he agreed. 'It is fortunate I did not marry an obliging wife, after all.' He had a way of smiling that was not quite smiling, more a crinkling of the eyes and a quiver hovering around his lips. It made me warm and dissolve and shiver, all at the same time.

'Look.' He pointed down the hill. 'You can just see Askerby down there. It is not far now.'

'Not far now.' Jasper's voice jolts me back to reality. It is a strange thing, remembering, being there and not there at the same time, seeing and not seeing. Without leaving my seat, I have gone away. The road, the car, the man beside me are all curiously blank compared to the intensity of the life I have remembered. I put a hand to the back of my neck, and although one part of me knows quite well that it has not been raining, another part is startled to find that my skin is quite dry and there are no rivulets of water running cold into my collar.

All at once being enclosed in the vehicle feels threatening, unnatural. Jasper is a stranger. I want Edmund with his sort-of smile. Time feels disjointed. The road bends round to the right and heads down the hill. It twists and turns under the trees, passes over a narrow bridge.

I know where I am and that we are driving down the hill in a car, that behind me Fiona is saying something about lunch, but in my mind I am riding down the same hill in my sodden skirts, my tired horse's hooves skidding in the mud, following my husband down towards Askerby at last.

Chapter Nine

'How are you feeling?' Jasper asks. He sends me a concerned glance, and I wonder if I look as white and shaky as I feel.

'A bit strange,' I say honestly. I can't tell them the whole truth, though. They mustn't suspect for a moment that I have been lost in memories of another life altogether.

Fortunately, they don't seem to find this odd. 'The nurses warned that you might feel overwhelmed after being in hospital for so long,' Fiona says as we drive through a pretty village of grey stone houses. I can't see much. I glimpse a pub, a little school, a church with a square tower that sets something jangling in my head. 'I'm afraid you still have a long road ahead of you before you feel really well again.'

Dr Ramnaya told me this as well, but it's only now that I realize just how dependent I am going to be on the Vavasours. I am not strong enough to work, even if I could remember what I do and how I do it, so it's going to be some time before I can support myself and Felix, who everyone says is my child.

'It's very good of you to look after me,' I say, twisting a little in my seat so that I can include Fiona in my thanks. 'It's not as if I'm your daughter.'

'You're Felix's mother,' Fiona says, as if that explains everything. 'What would everyone think if we left you to manage on your own?'

At least she doesn't pretend that they care for me. What matters to them is the Vavasour reputation. They have centuries of tradition to uphold, after all.

'I meant to say –' Jasper interrupts the slightly awkward pause – 'I did manage to get in touch with your parents eventually. It was jolly hard to find them!' Jasper talks with a bluff heartiness that always seems forced, as if he is acting the part of a country landowner in some pre-war drama. 'It turns out they're working in the back of bloody beyond, and they only get to communicate with the outside world on occasional trips to their field office, but I was able to reassure them that you were out of danger and that we were taking you home.'

The only parent I remember is my mother, but the mother who was strapped to the bed screaming in her madness is not the mother who is somewhere in Africa, content to let strangers care for her daughter. Does it bother me that my parents haven't been in touch with me themselves? That I am not important enough for them to want to be by my bedside? It's hard to tell how I usually feel. I can't summon any sense of missing them, so I suspect I have been used to their absence for a long time. Their lack of interest in me is embarrassing rather than sad.

'Thank you,' I say uncomfortably. 'I'm afraid, though, that means you've been lumbered with me. I must have been such a nuisance over the last few months, and I don't think I'm going to be able to work for a while yet, as you say. I don't know when I'll be able to leave.'

'There's no question of you leaving,' Fiona says sharply. 'Felix is a Vavasour and so are you now. Askerby will always be your home.'

It sounds more like a threat than a promise.

Jasper turns the car through an imposing gateway with great pillars on either side, topped with statues of snarling lions. I don't remember them at all. On the left is the Lodge, tucked into the trees like a fairy-tale cottage. It has little windows hatched with diamond panes and quirky angles and ornately twisted chimneys. I half expect a wolf to pop its head out of one. There's a neat garden, with roses lining the path to the door, and a vegetable patch. Over the wall, I can see runner beans scrambling up wicker wigwams. The Lodge should be charming, but it's not. There's a sullenness about the lowering roof, a stillness behind the windows, and the whole house is enveloped in the shadow of the trees that seem to be creeping up around it.

'Is that where Angie lives?'

'For now,' Fiona sighs. 'We'd really like to renovate it and give it to one of the young estate workers – it's perfect for a family – but for reasons I have never understood, Jasper's father gave it to her grandparents rent free for life!'

'My father was friends with Adam Kaczka during the war,'

Jasper says with a faintly defensive edge. 'They flew Spitfires together.'

'I still don't see why he had to give them free accommodation. These people always live *forever* when that happens! Dosia must be almost a hundred now.'

'She was a sweet woman. Mother never liked us going down to the Lodge, but Joanna and I used to sneak off occasionally and play with Marek and Peter. Dosia would always have a cake or squash.' His voice warms with the reminiscence. 'She used to make ice cream in a tiny ice-cube tray and the most delicious chocolate sauce. Far better than Cook ever made.'

Fiona is unmoved by Jasper's memories. 'I'm beginning to wonder if she's *ever* going to die,' she sighs in exasperation. 'As far as I know, nothing's been done to the house since the fifties. It'll need to be gutted.'

'What about Angie?' I say. 'Won't she want to stay?'

'Thank goodness she's not covered in the agreement. It was just for as long as Dosia or Adam were alive. Adam died ages ago – not before time, I must say, he was a most unpleasant man, wasn't he, Jasper?' Fiona doesn't wait for him to answer. 'The Lodge is much too big for a single person, anyway. Angie will be much happier in a nice little house in the village.'

I'm not sure about that. I remember how Angie's face glows when she talks about Askerby, how she had looked at me without comprehension when I suggested that she move away: *I'd die if I had to leave.*

'She seems very committed to Askerby,' I say cautiously.

'I don't know what George would do without her,' Jasper offers. 'Or any of us, come to that. Angie gets us all organized.'

'Yes, she's marvellous,' Fiona agrees in her cool way. 'We should really give her a proper role here. George would like her to be his full-time assistant, I think, but the rest of us have rather come to rely on her. She's been wonderful with Felix.'

'So I gather,' I say.

'And she's the only one who can manage my mother,' Jasper says. 'Pretty little thing, too,' he adds blithely, unaware of his wife's baleful stare from the back seat.

My fingers are twisted tightly together in my lap, and I force myself to relax them as I fold my lips and stare out of the window to stop myself snapping back at them. I wonder how Angie can bear to devote her life to people who think of her as a 'pretty little thing' and refuse to give her a proper job because it'll mean they have to pick up their own dry-cleaning, people who will move her out of her home without a second thought.

We are driving up an avenue lined with beech trees. The parkland on either side is dotted with more magnificent trees, great oaks and ash and horse chestnuts heavy with candles. Cows graze peaceably, their heads in the lush grass, and I count nine horses twitching their tails under a spreading sycamore. It's a tranquil scene, but as the avenue curves round and the gatehouse comes in sight, my heart starts to pound, thudding against my ribs with a queasy mixture of anticipation, apprehension and alarm. Because here it is: Askerby Hall.

The gatehouse is topped with two hexagonal towers, mini-

ature versions of those on either end of the great house. Instinctively, I look towards the one on the right, and terror swoops
through my brain without warning, blurring my vision and
making the world shriek and spin sickeningly. I clutch onto the
leather seat with both hands while I wait for my breathing to
steady. I don't need to be told that that is where I fell.

'You must remember Askerby Hall,' says Fiona behind me.

I nod slowly, grateful when that awful feeling of vertigo
recedes almost as quickly as it came. 'Yes,' I say. My knuckles
are white where I am clinging to the seat and I make my fingers
relax, although I don't let go completely. In truth, I'm not sure
if I do remember or if I'm thinking of the photos Angie showed
me on her iPad, but it seems easiest just to say that I do. 'Yes, I
remember.'

'Well, thank goodness you've remembered *something*.'
Fiona is exasperated by my memory loss. I sometimes wonder
if she thinks I am just pretending.

Jasper drives through the gatehouse into the courtyard, and
the sound of the tyres on the gravel crunches loudly in my ears
and makes me tense. He stops the car right in front of the great
carved doorway and switches off the engine. Silence swamps
the car and for a moment none of us moves.

'Well,' Jasper says at last in a hearty voice that is too loud
for the restricted space. 'Here we are.'

I don't answer. I am looking up at Askerby Hall. The car has
been feeling claustrophobic and alien, but now that we're here,
I really don't want to get out. I can feel the house waiting for
me, watching me. The mullioned windows are dark but they

glitter silver as the sunlight sweeps across the facade only to plunge back into dullness as the wind pushes the clouds across the sun. Light, dark, light, dark. It is as if the house is trying to send a message only I can decipher, except that I have forgotten the code. Is it beckoning me in, or warning me away?

The light is the only thing that moves, the light and my painfully thumping heart. The stillness is uncanny, ominous. It is as if we have driven into an old painting and are frozen in time. Jasper and Fiona must feel it too, or surely they would say something, do something. To my horror, I feel a cry pushing into my throat and desperately I swallow it down. There's no reason to scream. We are just sitting in front of an old house.

The spell is broken as the front door opens and what seems like a whole pack of dogs swarms out. They surround the car, barking and wagging their tails. George follows them, and comes round to the passenger door. 'Settle down,' he shouts at the milling dogs, without any noticeable effect.

He opens the door and holds out a hand to help me down. 'Welcome back, Kate,' he says, and as I take his hand another memory streaks through my mind: Edmund, his face sheened with rain, smiling and holding up his hand to help me off my horse. *Welcome to Askerby, wife.* A longing for him, sharp as a spear, slices through me and I cannot help flinching, but George does not notice, or if he does, he puts it down to my injuries.

'Easy does it,' he says, and I let him help me gingerly down from the car, into the sea of dogs. There are only four of them, I realize, but they are tumbling over each other and thoroughly overexcited, rushing between Fiona and Jasper and George. A black Labrador shoves its nose in my crutch.

'Jago, stop that!' George pushes him aside with an apologetic look. 'Pippin has been pining for you,' he tells me. 'She'll be overjoyed to see you.'

'Which one is Pippin?' I ask in an effort to distract myself from memories of Edmund. Angie showed me a photo of her, I know, but all I remember is a small, scrubby terrier with bright eyes and a black nose.

George looks around vaguely. 'I thought she'd be here.' He stops as he sees what I see: a small, wiry dog crouching by the step. Her teeth are bared and she is looking straight at me. She is growling.

'Good God,' says George. 'What on earth is all that about? Stop that, Pippin.' He makes to step towards her, but I put a hand on his arm.

'Leave her,' I say. There's a drumming sense of dread beating along my veins. 'It's all too much right now.' For me as well as for the dog.

Jasper has been unloading my small bag from the car. 'Let me get rid of all these dogs,' he says. He hasn't noticed Pippin. 'They'll knock Kate over if we're not careful.'

He gives George my bag to carry and whistles for the dogs, who bound around a bit more and then rush after him through an archway into another courtyard. Pippin looks after him, then back at me. Her growl deepens. I stand very still and after a moment she bolts after Jasper.

'How strange.' George looks more upset than I am. 'Pippin adores you. Normally she won't leave you alone.'

'Everything's strange at the moment,' I say. I'm thinking of Edmund, and the first time I came to Askerby. The impossibility of it makes me stumble, and George puts an arm around me to steady me. His touch makes me cringe. *No,* I want to shout at him. *No, not you!*

'Sorry,' I mutter. 'I'm not used to being on two feet.' I look around, desperate to stand alone. If I cannot have Edmund, I do not want anyone. 'Could I have my stick?'

Fiona produces the stick the physios have given me from the back of the car. It is an unlovely thing, sturdy steel with a thick rubber base and a padded handle, but I take hold of it as if it is my only support, and to my relief, George takes his arm from my waist, although he keeps hold of my elbow. Fiona comes up on my other side. She doesn't touch me, and I'm glad about that. I think I would scream if she did.

I feel very odd, as if I am missing a skin. There is something very wrong but I'm not sure exactly what it is. I look up at the house, wondering what it is trying to tell me, and somehow my eyes are drawn to the tower again.

Falling . . . I'm falling . . . Falling out of my life and every-thing that I remember. Falling into darkness and fear. My mouth opens but I have no breath to scream. I wanted to fly, to soar as gracefully as a bird, but instead I am cumbersome, twisting and tumbling awkwardly, with a strange and terrible slowness. The ground is reaching up for me. It is going to grab me and swallow me up.

Nausea roils in my belly and I falter as my mind spins darkly once more. When I drop my eyes to the ground I am surprised not to see myself crumpled there. There should be a mark, surely? A stain, or an indentation. Something to show where 'then' ended and 'now' began. But it can't have been here, I realize after a moment. Dr Ramnaya said a tree broke my fall, so I must have landed somewhere on the other side of the tower.

George's gaze has followed mine to the tower as I stop. There is an awkward pause.

'Let's go inside,' says Fiona smoothly from behind us. 'Kate needs to rest.'

I let them steer me up the steps, into the great hall, where Philippa is waiting, slouched against a massive oak table. 'You made it back, then?' she says.

'Thank goodness we're closed today,' Fiona says. 'Otherwise we'd have had to take her round the back to avoid being gawped at by tourists.' She looks around the hall as if imagining it crowded with people in shorts and T-shirts, all tipping their heads back to admire the intricately carved plaster ceiling or pausing reverently in front of the portraits hanging on the panelled walls. It is a room meant to impress, to intimidate, and it does.

'Yes, we wouldn't want anyone to witness an emotional Vavasour family reunion, would we?' says Philippa, straightening.

I am not listening to them properly. I'm trying to put my finger on why the hall feels not quite right. I know I remember it, but the memory is elusive. It flits in and out of my mind like a moth looking for a way out of a room, and I can't fix it in one place.

'Have you changed things around since I've been in hospital?'

Philippa gives a snort of laughter. 'Change? That's a good one. We don't do change at Askerby. "Centuries of unbroken tradition", that's our tag line. I don't think anything's changed here since the seventeenth century.'

'You do exaggerate, Philippa,' Fiona says, running a hand through her ash-blonde hair and barely tousling it. 'Electricity, plumbing, the Internet . . . We have to have a website and a Facebook page and someone to tweet for us, whatever that means, not to mention hordes of tourists swarming all over the place in summer.' She sighs. 'Sometimes it feels like *everything* has changed. It's so important to hold onto what's special about Askerby. People expect it of us.'

'I agree,' says George, sounding very like Jasper. 'We can move with the times on the estate, but the house needs to stay exactly as it is. What do you think, Kate?'

I don't answer. I'm looking at the huge fireplace. The flickering, frustrating memory is coalescing into an image. A fire burning and me, holding my hands out to the flames. I remember the overpowering smell of wet wool and the way the steam rose from my sodden skirts. A servant brought wine and cakes and took away my poor hat and my cloak.

Edmund, pouring the wine, handing me a goblet. I remember the taste of it, tart on my tongue, as I looked around the hall and took in its grandeur for the first time. It was built in the new fashion with a fine plaster ceiling, panelled walls hung with brilliantly coloured tapestries and a tiled floor. The magnificent staircase made my jaw drop. I was used to the narrow steps at Crabbersett, where the great hall was rude and dark and old in comparison, but I felt a pang of homesickness for it all the same.

Edmund and I had been married three days earlier. The marriage negotiations were not straightforward, for all the allure of my fortune. Edmund's father died suddenly, barely a month after Edmund and I had raced out over the moor, and that upset my uncle's calculations, which had in any case been thrown into disarray by Lord Vavasour's disgust at my unruly behaviour, as my uncle never failed to remind me.

He was furious with me for taking his horse, and deservedly so, I had to concede. I was beaten and confined to the house for weeks afterwards, allowed only to walk with Judith around the knot garden. I hated it. So many little hedges, directing you one way or the other down trammelled paths, no space to run or to ride. I fretted and fumed and kicked at the gravel, but deep down I knew that the wild, golden ride with Edmund had been worth it.

Our marriage would be delayed, but I was certain that Edmund would come back for me. My uncle was more cautious. Lord Vavasour's death meant shifting alliances. My cousin Lawrence, who had been in service with Lord Vavasour, was sent for to come home, while my uncle looked to his own interests. He was too canny to commit my fortune until he was sure of Edmund's worth.

'Edmund is young yet,' he told my aunt, while Judith sat quietly sewing. 'Let us see what he is made of before we bind up Isabel's inheritance with the Vavasours.'

When Judith told me that, I imagined my money and myself, trussed in canvas like a bolt of cloth, ready to be handed over to the highest bidder. I thought of my mother, bound to her bed, her mouth open in a soundless scream, and I shuddered.

But what choice did I have? Judith pointed out. 'You must marry,' she said. 'Else you will spend your life here, doing as your aunt tells you, being grateful for your food and board.'

That was her fate, as we both knew. She was right. And if I had to have a husband, I wanted it to be Edmund.

He was Lord Vavasour now, I reasoned. He could do what he liked. Why then did he not come for me?

Chapter Ten

My uncle grunted whenever Edmund's name came up. 'I dare say he's looking around for a more biddable bride,' he said, fixing me with an unforgiving eye.

The thought of Edmund with another bride stung like salt in a wound, but as the months passed and he did not come, I put up my chin and pretended that I did not care. I was too proud to ask Lawrence what he knew of Edmund's plans, though he must have known him as well as anyone. Nothing had been said. No promises had been made. What did I care? If he wanted a milksop maid to wife, he was welcome to her, I told Judith, who just smiled and shook her head.

So when my uncle announced out of the blue that a settlement was agreed and that Edmund would be coming to Crabbersett for the handfasting, I was furious. How dared they discuss me and hand me over like a sack of wool without even consulting me? But Judith was right: I had nowhere else to go.

Simmering with resentment, I barely sketched Edmund a

curtsey when I was summoned to the great hall, and my mouth was pressed into a line so tight my lips disappeared. I could see my aunt gesturing frantically at me to smile, but I wouldn't. Why should I smile at Edmund when clearly he cared nothing for me? We had ridden together once, but that meant nothing. He could not want me, with my snarled hair and bitten nails, with my big nose and pockmarked cheeks and fierce brows. He was interested only in my fortune, that much I understood. Why else would he want to marry me?

So I held myself aloof, and if Edmund noticed my coldness he gave no sign of it. When we were handfasted, he laid his lips on mine to seal our betrothal and I hated the way my heart kicked, hated the clutch of excitement at the base of my spine. I could not be myself with him, the way I had been when I stole my uncle's horse and rode out beside him. Instead I felt as if a layer of me rubbed off in his presence, as if he peeled me like an onion, and I was left raw and exposed.

Crabbersett was thrown into a frenzy of preparations for the wedding. My uncle's doubts about Edmund's connections were forgotten, and all the neighbours thereabouts were invited to witness his triumph in securing such an influential alliance. My aunt, too, was determined to impress.

'When will you stop growing?' she tutted, pulling my best gown out of the chest and holding it against me.

I was eighteen by then, and lanky with it, and I towered over her, careless that my skirts barely scraped my ankles. I had no interest in a wedding gown and if it had been up to me would have been married in my old blue kersey that draped easily over the saddle, and I fidgeted until my aunt snapped at me to stand still.

There was a show to be made, and besides, she loved to finger bolts of cloth and could happily talk patterns and adornments for hours. She chose for me a warm red silk to fall over a farthingale. I had slashed sleeves and a frilled collar, and Judith embroidered a stomacher with wild flowers and butterflies and bees and, right down at the point, a wasp. Even I could see that it was beautiful.

My old gown my aunt gave to Judith to furbish up as best she could. 'Can she not have a new gown for my wedding?' I asked my aunt when Judith was out of the room.

She pursed her lips. 'She will have your gown, and lucky she is to have that.'

'But it is unfair,' I protested. 'Judith loves gowns more than I do, and we are as sisters. Why should she not have what I have?'

'But you are not sisters,' said my aunt. 'Do not make the mistake of forgetting that, Isabel. You have your place in life, and Judith has hers. We have given her a home, and indeed we are happy to do so. She is a good girl, modest and dutiful, but she has bad blood and no money.

'The world is the way it is,' she said firmly. 'Do not try and fight it. Your uncle manages your fortune for you, and he is a careful man. He has not wasted it on gowns for poor cousins. Judith is not even a cousin to you, other than through my marriage.'

I set my mouth. I did not care to be told that I could do

nothing. I picked up the silk. 'This gown is paid for from my own money?'

'Yes, indeed.'

'Why then can I not pay for another to be made for whom I choose?'

'That is why you are a ward,' said my aunt, taking the silk from me and folding it carefully before I creased it in my hands. 'You are not fit to manage your money. Left to you, Isabel, you would give it all away, to Judith, to the laundress and the stable boy and the pedlar with his broken combs and tatty ribbons.' She shook her head, exasperated. 'Your uncle has kept your money safe, and when you are married, it will be for your husband to manage.'

It seemed to me that I had precious little enjoyment of my fortune, and soon enough it would be Edmund's anyway.

'I'm sorry,' I said to Judith later when I had to tell her that there would be no new gown for her.

'Indeed I am very happy with this one.' She indicated my old gown, which her clever fingers were already re-stitching. 'How lucky I am that you are tall and I am not!' she said, with her sweet smile. 'If it had been the other way round, I would never have had anything so fine to wear.'

'You are too good,' I said, ashamed of the fact that I was always restless, always cross, while Judith, who had nothing, was always calm and sweet-tempered. 'Oh, Judith, I will miss you so!' I said impulsively.

'And I you.' She reached out and squeezed my hand. 'But as long as you are happy, Isabel, I will be too. I am sure that you will be. You could not ask for a better husband than Edmund Vavasour.'

I remember sniffing at that. I hadn't forgiven him for taking so long to negotiate the marriage. It did not seem to me that Edmund was over-eager to wed me.

'He is all a woman could want,' Judith went on. 'Comely, clever, courteous – and wealthy, of course!'

'You have him, then,' I said, still aggrieved at Edmund's failure to woo me anew.

'I wish that I could,' she said lightly, 'but Edmund only has eyes for you, Isabel. I am like the moon to your sun. As long as you are standing in front of him, he will not even see me.'

Of my wedding day itself, I remember little: motes of dust hanging lazily in the sunlight as it slanted through the chapel window; Edmund, pushing the ring onto my finger; the tightness of my lacing, the glow of my red skirts, the way they rustled against the floor. Fresh rushes had been laid in the great hall and were strewn with herbs. When we walked in for the feast it smelt sweet and welcoming.

But my wedding night, ah! That I remember. I lean on my stick in the great hall at Askerby, where it feels sickeningly strange and achingly familiar at the same time. I am not listening to Fiona and Philippa, who are having a snippy mother–daughter exchange behind me, or to George's ineffectual attempts to intervene. I am thinking about the great chamber at Crabbersett, how the sheets were scattered with rosemary and a fire was lit in the grate. I stood in my shift while Judith brushed and brushed my hair in a vain attempt to make it lie neat. She still had her bridelace tied to her arm.

'That is the best I can do,' she said, letting the brush fall at last. 'My arm is aching!'

I laughed and told her that she was released from her duties, but when she embraced me and said I looked beautiful, I clung to her for a long moment, perilously close to tears. Judith would always be my dear friend, but after that night when I would be married in truth to Edmund, nothing would be quite the same. I had hoped to take her with me to Askerby as my companion as we had planned, but my aunt did not think it was a good idea.

'Judith is fair, and you are not,' she said bluntly, 'and Edmund is a young man. Establish yourself as mistress first and make sure of your husband before you invite her to live with him.'

I was shocked. 'Judith would not seduce my husband!'

'I hope you are right and that we have taught her better than that,' my aunt said. 'I was thinking more about Edmund. You will learn to manage him, but you do not know him well yet.'

My aunt's warning was in my mind as I paced the chamber in my smock after Judith had left me alone. I remember the feel of the fine white linen brushing against my skin, the way my nerves fluttered. My aunt was right: what, truly, did I know of Edmund?

I had seen enough around the Manor farms to understand what was going to happen that night and in her usual blunt

way my aunt had made sure I knew what to expect. 'You will
get used to it,' she said. 'You may even find pleasure in it.'

So I wasn't nervous, or not exactly. But my heart was beating hard when Edmund came into the chamber, already
undressed, with a velvet gown over his nightgown. Adroitly he
dismissed his cheerful groomsmen.

'I thought you would be abed,' he said, unfastening the
velvet gown without haste.

'I have been to bed and slept and risen again waiting for
you,' I lied, as my breath shortened in spite of myself.

'I thought to give you time to prepare,' he said mildly.

'Prepare? What am I, a joint of meat to be dressed for your
pleasure?'

A smile touched his mouth. 'You do not need to do anything
to give me pleasure, Isabel. You need only be yourself.'

'Well, that will be no trouble to me,' I said, unsure how to
take his words.

'I know.' He came towards me, took my hands before I
could put them behind me. 'That is what I like about you. You
are just yourself. You do not pretend to be anyone you are not.'

I was puzzled by the idea. 'Who would do that?'

'Why, everyone. At court I pretend to be a man who knows
how to intrigue. I pretend I know just how to step, which way
to bend, to preserve my estate and keep the Queen benevolent.
Your uncle does not admit to the doubts and uncertainties that
plague all men. He pretends to be right about everything. Even
your little cousin Judith pretends to be meeker than she is. She
keeps her eyes downcast, but she misses nothing.'

'I do not know what you mean,' I said uncertainly, distracted by the feel of his thumbs rubbing over the backs of my hands.

'I know,' said Edmund, smiling. 'That is why I love you.' He said it as if it meant nothing, as if it scarcely needed to be said, and even though I was determined to stay aloof my fingers were twining around his as if they had a will of their own.

'My uncle said you were minded to choose a more obliging bride,' I said, and his smiled deepened.

'I do not want obliging. Strange as it may be, I want a maid who looks at me as if I am no better than a stable boy.'

'That is not how I look at you,' I said involuntarily.

'Is it not?' Edmund stuck his nose high in the air and looked fiercely down it in imitation of me. The worst thing was that I recognized myself and, in spite of myself, I laughed.

Edmund took the opportunity to move nearer. Flustered, I backed away until he had me pinned up against the great iron-bound chest where my aunt kept her best sheets. Only then did he release my hands to run his own up my arms. I could feel the warmth of his palms through the fine linen of my smock, and my blood began to boom in my ears.

'Lift your chin to me now,' he said, his voice low, but I was overwhelmed with shyness and could not raise my eyes from his throat.

'I cannot.' My voice was shamefully unsteady.

Edmund cupped my chin in his hand and lifted it for me. His eyes were very warm as they looked down into mine. Lowering his head, he touched his lips to mine, gently at first and then more firmly. His hands slid around me, pulled me close against him, and the hardness of his body was a shock that stopped the breath in my throat, but when his mouth left mine to drift persuasively down the curve of my neck, I shuddered with pleasure. Was this then what my aunt had meant?

'Oh . . .' I murmured and felt him smile against my shoulder where he had eased my smock aside.

'Oh?'

'I did not think it would feel like that,' I confessed.

'It will feel much better,' Edmund promised me, and taking my hand, he drew me over to the bed. 'Let me show you just how good it can feel.'

'Kate?'

George touches my arm and I start. For a moment I have forgotten them all, these strangers who stand in my hall, and talk as if they own it. I strain to remember more of Edmund, but he has gone, swallowed up into that chasm in my mind, leaving only the memory of thrumming pleasure.

'Kate, you're crying,' says George, appalled. 'Have you remembered something?'

'Oh, for heaven's sake, George,' says Philippa impatiently before I can stumble over an answer, 'leave the woman alone. Anyone would cry finding that they live in this gloomy house with a family like the Vavasours! Come on, why are we standing around in the hall, anyway?'

In spite of her brusque tone, I'm grateful to Philippa as I blot my cheeks with the heel of my hand. I don't want to talk about what I've remembered. I don't want to be told that I'm making it up, that my husband was called Michael. Not right now, when the memory of Edmund is so close, so dear.

'I think perhaps Kate should have a rest,' Fiona declares. She looks at her watch. 'Philippa, can you tell Jo to put lunch back until quarter past one? That'll give her time to lie down for an hour.'

There is nothing I want more than to be on my own right now, but there is something I need to do first. The dull throb of fear for my son has been a constant for the long weeks I have been in hospital, and I cannot lose myself in my memories of Edmund until I have found my child and seen for myself that he is safe. They insist that Felix is my son, and I am counting on the fact that the moment I see him my memory will come rushing back. How could it not, faced with my own child? But I'm very nervous. I want to see him, but at the same time I don't. I keep remembering how often I looked at the framed photograph of Felix in the hospital, how every time I thought: *That's not my son.*

I won't know until I am face to face with him.

'Where is Felix?' I ask.

There is a pause. I see the others exchange a look that I can't interpret. 'He's with Angie,' says Fiona after a moment. 'He'll be having lunch soon.'

'I'd like to see him.'

'I don't think that's a good idea,' Fiona says. She has made her plans and doesn't like to rearrange them. 'You look very tired. Why don't you lie down for a bit and meet him after lunch?'

'I don't want to lie down,' I say, although I'm exhausted. 'I want to see my son.'

Fiona folds her lips. She is used to giving orders and having them obeyed. She doesn't like objections, but after all, she is the one who keeps saying I am Felix's mother. 'If you insist,' she said after a moment. 'Philippa, perhaps you'd take Kate up to the nursery?'

Philippa looks as if she's about to protest, but in the end she just shrugs.

'All right. But there are a lot of stairs.'

There are. The flight of steps leading up from the great hall is wide and shallow, and I manage them easily enough, but still I have to stop and catch my breath at the top, holding onto the elaborately carved newel post.

Through an open doorway ahead of me I can see a bay window stepped up from the floor. The sun is slanting through the leaded panes and throwing a hatched pattern across the polished floorboards. It picks out the glow of a crimson cushion, its tassels glinting gold, and the light shifts very slightly. A subtle eddy in the air, the scent of gillyflowers drifting through the door, a ripple of a laugh that has barely faded . . . I'm not sure how I know, but there is someone just out of sight, and I hold my breath, waiting for them to cross the doorway, to catch sight of me and turn, and hold out their hands in delight: *There you are!*

'That's the long gallery.' Philippa has realized I am not

following her and retraces her steps impatiently. 'The visitors love it.'

'I thought I saw someone,' I say.

'I doubt it. The house is closed today.' She puts her head through the doorway and looks up and down. 'Nope. Empty. You must have imagined it.'

'Yes,' I say slowly. 'I must have done.'

Chapter Eleven

Philippa walks briskly along the corridor, and I limp after her. I keep glancing over my shoulder, as if I will catch a glimpse of whoever was waiting for me in the long gallery, as if I will see them beckoning me: *Where are you going? Come back!*

'Are you coming?' Philippa huffs out a sigh of irritation.

I make myself turn my back on the doorway and go on. 'Sorry,' I say. 'I'm a bit slow.'

The stairs to the other floors are steeper than the main staircase, and tucked away from the main rooms. The nursery, it turns out, is right at the top of the house, a relic of the days when children were handed over to the servants, who produced them properly scrubbed and polished at the appointed time.

'Were you exiled up here when you were little?' I ask Philippa as I pause for breath again in the turn of the stairs. My leg is aching badly, pain jabbing like red-hot pokers at my thigh, but I am not going to give up.

'Of course. The nursery has always been up here, so that's where we were.' Philippa turns to carry on up the stairs, ignoring the fact that I am still breathing heavily and badly in need of a rest. 'If you haven't already realized it, Ma and Pa both worship at the shrine of "the way things have always been done". The past is a religion at Askerby. You would never accept it before,' she says over her shoulder, 'but take it from me, it'll be much easier all round if you do.'

I grip the banister and push on my stick to haul myself up the next set of steps. I think about how envious Angie sounded of Philippa's childhood, how idyllic it had seemed to her watching from outside. Distant parents, banishment to a nursery and a worship of tradition don't seem very idyllic to me. 'It doesn't sound as if *you* accept it.'

'Oh, that's just me being contrary.' She hunches a shoulder, faintly defensive. 'I do find it suffocating sometimes, but Askerby is my home. I like knowing that the house has been here so long, and that so many traditions remain unchanged. I like being the Hon. Philippa Vavasour,' she says with a challenging look over her shoulder. 'I like thinking about how many daughters and sisters of earlier Lord Vavasours have lived here before me. Yes, I think we should change. I hate how we always have to pretend, how we can't say what we really think or feel because that's "not done", but at the same time, if you told me you wanted to divide the Hall into executive apartments or put a satellite dish on one of the towers, I would fight you all the way.'

Her vehemence catches me unawares. 'Hey,' I say, holding

up the hand that isn't clenched on the stick, 'it won't be anything to do with me.'

'But it will,' she says. 'Felix is the next Lord Vavasour, and what he thinks will be up to you. Whatever happens, I'll only ever be here on sufferance.'

There's no mistaking the bitterness in her voice now, but before I have time to reply, Philippa is marching down the corridor and brusquely opening a door at the end. I am still struggling to catch up when I hear her say: 'Angie, Kate's back.' And then, carelessly: 'Mummy's here, Felix.'

As I reach the door I see a small boy scrambling to his feet, his face alight with anticipation. Felix is four. I know this because I've been told. He has the Vavasour blue eyes and fair hair. It's obvious straight away that he is a bright, engaging child, but my disappointment at the sight of him is so acute that for a moment I can't breathe. I wanted so much for him to be the child I've been searching for, but he isn't.

He's not my boy. My hand trembles on my stick as I lean against the door frame, and I force myself to smile. Whatever I feel, I cannot hurt this little boy by refusing to acknowledge him. 'Hello, Felix,' I say.

Felix has started to run towards me, but at the sound of my voice he stops, and seems to look at me properly for the first time. 'You're not my mummy!' he says, outraged.

'Felix!' This from Angie, who has been playing on the floor with him and now scrambles to her feet.

'That's not my mummy,' says Felix stubbornly, and I am oddly relieved. At last here is someone who thinks as I do.

'Don't be silly, Felix.' Philippa manages to sound both sharp and bored at the same time. 'Of course it's Mummy.'

Felix's bottom lip is trembling but he stands his ground. He knows what he knows. 'No!'

'I'm so sorry.' Dismayed, Angie hurries to kneel beside him and puts her arms around him. 'He's just a little confused.'

'It's all right,' I say. 'I've been away a long time, and I look different.'

Felix's face is crumpling in distress. 'I want Mummy!' he cries, and when Angie tries to comfort him, he pulls away and hurtles across the room towards me. But he doesn't want to kiss me. He wants to punish me for not being the mother he's been waiting for.

'You're not Mummy!' he shouts at me, beating at my legs with his small fists and he is stronger than he realizes, or I am weaker than I do, because I stumble and almost fall. 'Go away!' he screams, his voice rising into hysteria. 'Go away, go away! You're not Mummy!'

'Oh, God!' Philippa rolls her eyes. 'I guess Ma was right after all. I hate it when that happens. It might be better to leave him for now.'

'I'm sorry,' I say, as Angie pulls Felix from me. She picks him up but he arches away, his face red and screwed up as he screams his fury and disappointment.

'Shh, now, sweetheart,' Angie croons to him. 'It's all right. Angie's here.' Leave him to me, she mouths over Felix's head.

'All right.' I'm shaken and not sorry to leave, although I feel guilty for walking away. But what can I do? I can't comfort

Felix when I'm not his mother. Felix knows that, and I know that. Why can't everyone else see it?

'Well, that was a disaster,' says Philippa, shutting the door on Felix's screams. 'At least Ma will be able to say "I told you so".' She gives me a cursory glance. 'Perhaps you'd better have that rest after all. You look done in.'

'Yes, I think I'll lie down for a bit,' I say. I need to be on my own. I'm in turmoil and my leg is hurting viciously.

Philippa glances at her watch. 'You've got an hour before lunch, but get going as soon as you hear the gong. Granny hates it when anyone's late.'

'I'm not that hungry,' I say. 'I might skip lunch.'

'Oh. Okay then. I'll tell Ma.' She nods briskly. 'I'll leave you to it.'

Obviously relieved at having got rid of me, she heads off down the corridor.

'Philippa?' I say, and she stops and turns impatiently.

'What?'

'Where's my room?'

My room is far away from the nursery, down a flight of stairs and along another corridor. I am somewhere in one of the wings of the house. I'm not sure what I expect, but it is not this pleasant, sunny room. There is a four-poster bed, with chintz bed hangings, and an old-fashioned dressing table with frothy skirts. A pale, deep-pile carpet and an antique table, polished to an intimidating shine. A massive mahogany wardrobe. A chest of drawers in the same polished wood. It is clearly a guest room; it smells of polish and clean linen, of old soap. It doesn't smell like *me*.

There is a scatter of jewellery on the dressing table, mostly earrings and beaten silver bangles, and an iPad on the bedside table. I know about iPads. Angie has one and I remember using it in hospital. Mine is charging. I flip it open and see that I have three messages. I slide my finger across the screen to unlock it, but it wants to know a password. With everything else I have lost, does it think I remember a password?

Now I really want to know what the messages say. Frustrated, I put the iPad down. It's the same with the phone I find on the mantelpiece. It seems I am very security conscious.

Several framed photographs stand on the dressing table, mostly of Felix as a baby and toddler, and there are a couple on the bedside table too. I pick them up and examine them. One I have seen before: it shows Michael and Felix and me on a beach somewhere. There is another one of Michael sitting in a pavement cafe. He looks relaxed, his arm thrown over the back of a chair, a glass of wine in front of him.

Sighing, I put the last frame down and stand, leaning on my stick and looking around the room, seeking some familiarity, some sense that this room really belongs to me. But all I get is that old sense of urgency: *Remember, remember*.

I limp over to the window. A deep window seat with cushions is built into the bay. When I kneel on it I can open one of the windows and look out over a swathe of grass to some trees, and behind them, to the moors that swell up towards the sky. Something stirs in my memory . . . *something* . . . but I can't grasp it. It shimmers and flashes out of sight, like a trout in a river; a glimpse of something that has gone before you can fix on it.

I wonder if it is another memory of Edmund? I hope so. I take out those that I have already, as if to polish them and turn them round in the sun, examine them from every angle. Every moment I remember of him is perfectly clear, and the truth of each hums in my bones. But none of them makes sense in this world I find myself in, where they call me Kate and tell me I belong.

A world where my child doesn't recognize me. Where my dog growls at me.

Am I Kate or am I Isabel?

Where is Edmund? And where is my son, whose name I don't know but of whose existence I am certain?

I feel precarious, balanced on the edge of something I don't understand. Carefully, I turn and sit on the window seat facing the room, my hands flat on the cushion. I am holding on. It feels as if the house is turning around me, circling me, wondering what I am doing here, and I blink, disorientated by the sense of unseen shadows shifting and plucking at the edge of my vision. And I think about the presence at the top of the stairs, the way I felt it had been waiting for me. *Where are you going?* it had demanded as I followed Philippa to find Felix. *Come back!*

The silence in the room is dense, watchful. All I can hear is my shallow breathing, the suck and sigh of it echoing in my ears. I want to ask, *Is there anybody there?* but I can see that there isn't. Of course there isn't. The room is empty. Still, I can't shake the conviction that there is a warning hovering in the trembling air.

The piping on the cushion is digging into my palms, and I make myself relax my hands. I must get a grip. I try to recall what Oliver Raine said. My memories as Isabel aren't real; they are snatches of experience that I have jumbled together and made into a story, that is all. But his theory doesn't seem so convincing now that I am back at Askerby, where I can sense the memories crowding the air, beckoning. They don't feel invented; they feel real, they feel *present*, so close that I can almost touch them.

Remember, remember.

'But I *can't* remember!' The words are wrenched out of me. They jar the silence and echo disturbingly in my head.

What is happening to me? I draw a shaky breath and make myself examine the situation carefully. I am Kate Vavasour, and I live at Askerby Hall. I jumped off the roof of this house and I cannot remember anything of my life before that. The only memories I have appear to belong to someone completely different, someone who lived at Askerby more than four hundred years ago. But I am imaginative and highly strung, I'm told. I might be making it all up.

Am I making Isabel up, or is she real? And if she is real, what does she want of me?

Remember.

My son. There is something I must do for my son. I have seen Felix, but I am not the mother he wants, and he is not the son I need. But I keep thinking about that awful scene with Felix, and I rub my chest where a niggling ache, a pebble, small and hard and uncomfortable, is lodged. Before I met him, he was just a face I didn't recognize in a photo. Now he is real. I keep seeing his face, the betrayal in the blue Vavasour eyes, the terror and fury as the small fists pounded me.

I don't remember him, I don't love him, not yet, but he is just a child, and my heart cracks to imagine what it is like for him to look at me and see not the mother he longs for but a stranger, an alien who looks right but feels wrong. I must find a way back to him, even if it means letting go of my longing for another child.

No, no, no! My head rings with a wild desolation. *No, I need to know that he is safe.* But I close my mind firmly to it. I press the heels of my hands to my eyes. I mustn't lose control. I mustn't tell anyone about the memories that I have. I must stay calm.

'I am Kate,' I say out loud. It doesn't feel true, so I say it again. 'I am *Kate.*'

Exhausted, I sleep all afternoon. That evening, there is a knock on my door, and when I call 'Come in', a fresh-faced girl carries in a tray and sets it by my bed. 'Lady Vavasour thought you might be tired,' she said. 'She asked the cook to send you an omelette so you didn't have to go downstairs tonight.'

I drag myself up against the pillows, knuckling my eyes. I have to admit that the last thing I feel like doing is eating with

Vavasours tonight. I'm not ready to face the family yet. ...nat was kind of her,' I say. 'Thank you.'

The omelette is delicious and I feel better for having eaten something, but after sleeping all afternoon I am restless that night. I lie in bed and watch the sky slowly deepen to violet and then to a dark blue spangled with blurry stars. I have left the window open, and I can smell the grass outside. The trees rustle and sigh in the light breeze that blows down from the moors, and the night is full of little chirrups and squeaks, of hoots and squeals and, once, a low cough.

It feels very late before I fall into a fitful sleep, and I'm troubled by a familiar sense of being dragged one way and then another, of hands reaching for me and not knowing if they want to pull me close or push me away. At one point I find myself blinking into the darkness with no idea of where I am. The night is dense, deep, but there is someone there, I can tell, stirring the darkness, slipping through the shadows. I am sure that I feel the brush of a hand against my cheek.

'Edmund?' I murmur, then wake properly, my heart jerking.

The silence is absolute, crushing. That is wrong, surely? Old houses creak and sigh and settle. Radiators tick, pipes gurgle, and beneath it all, the low hum of electricity and sleepers shifting and sighing. But in this room there is nothing. It is as if every sound has been sucked out of it until all that is left is the pulse pounding in my ears.

It takes me a very long time to work up the courage to switch on the bedside lamp. The harsh light makes me throw an arm over my eyes to shield myself from the horrifying conviction that everything in the room is jumping at me. When I lower it at last, I see that all is as it should be. The iPad is on the bedside table, the hairbrushes are on the chest, my skirt is slumped over the back of the chair where I threw it earlier, too tired to hang it up. There is nothing out of place, and yet everything seems alien and threatening. My eyes skitter from the chair to the curtains, from the chest to the door to the wardrobe, certain that each is bunched and ready to leap at me with its strangeness.

My son, I must find my son. It's not really a voice, more a vibration in the air, an urgency that lifts the hairs on the back of my neck and reaches deep inside me to twist and clench. *Find my son.*

Chapter Twelve

Used to hospital hours, I wake early, brushing away the bad dreams like cobwebs from my face. It takes me a few moments to remember where I am. Askerby. I look cautiously around the room that seemed so menacing last night. In the pearly light, it is stolid, still. Harmless.

As always when I wake up, I examine my memory: is there anything there? Images flicker and flutter just out of reach, but I can't grasp them. They feel closer than usual, that is all I can say. It is as if they are coming to the boil, slow bubbles rising, *almost* there, but not quite.

Pushing back the covers, I ease myself out of the bed and grope for my stick so that I can limp to the window. Outside, it is very early. The sun sends long, low shadows slanting across the garden like bars and in the stripes of light the grass shines silver with dew. The stillness is broken only by a rabbit loping across the lawn, but even that freezes, as if sensing my gaze, before darting into the shrubbery.

Beyond the trees, I see the moors soaring to the horizon, the morning sun turning their tops to gold. My heart lifts at the sight of the open hills, beckoning with promise. In spite of the jabbing pain – all those stairs yesterday were a mistake – I feel less vulnerable this morning, more determined. I can sense the memories creeping closer. It is like playing grandmother's footsteps. If I turn and look for them, they freeze. I need to catch them out, pretend that I'm not looking for them, and then whirl before they have a chance to vanish.

But at least they're there, ready to be snatched back if I am quick enough and clever enough. That makes me feel better. I am sick of waiting passively for my mind to fill in the missing pieces. There are things I can do. I can find out who I am, and what took me up the tower that day, what was so terrible that I threw myself off it. There is part of me that doesn't want to remember that, and another part that knows I won't be able to move on and change until I do.

But first I need to get better. Mary, the physio, has promised that we will start walking outside soon, but for the next few days I am confined to the house. She won't be pleased when she hears about all the stairs I climbed yesterday, but I had to do it. I had to see Felix for myself, and I could not send for him to be brought down to me as if he had been naughty. Besides, the thought of that terrible scene taking place in front of Fiona and the other Vavasours makes me cringe. Far better to have hauled myself up the stairs, even if my leg is on fire now.

You're not my mummy! The memory of his furious face bothers me. He is just a little boy, and he needs his mother. I feel terrible about not being the mother he wants, but I must try and make a relationship with him. I can't let Angie look after him forever, however devoted she is to him. Unless they are all lying to me, he is my son, whatever he and I feel. Inside my head, the need to find another son still beats insistently. I haven't forgotten that, I am yearning to remember him more clearly, but until I do, I must do what I can for Felix, the child who is lost in the here and now. I don't know how to help him, I just know that I will have to try.

But I can't face those steep stairs again, not yet. I should probably stay in my room today, but I am longing to explore further and to do something for myself. I think I could manage the main staircase, if I take it slowly. Mary is keen on setting goals. Today's will be to find the kitchen and make some breakfast.

I take a last yearning look at the moors, aglow in the morning light, before I turn back to my room. There's no use thinking about riding for a while, but perhaps in a week or so I will be able to make it to the stables and the quiet, comforting presence of the horses. That can be another goal. I could go and see Blanche, I start to think, only to catch myself on a barb of memory: Blanche will not be there, I realize with a sudden, sharp sense of loss. But there will be other horses.

I open the wardrobe, looking over my shoulder as if afraid someone will come in and catch me going through another woman's clothes. Are these really mine, these skirts in vaguely ethnic prints, these asymmetric tops? I pull out a baggy linen jacket, and the scent of orange blossom wraps itself around me.

My memory stirs: a face pressed into my neck, lips smiling into my skin. *I love the way you smell.* But no sooner has it come than it has gone again, leaving behind a sense of warmth, and nothing else.

I hold the linen to my nose, hoping the memory will resurface, but there is nothing. Disappointed, I put the jacket back, close the wardrobe doors and try the chest of drawers instead. I find jeans, a long-sleeved T-shirt, a soft hooded jacket. These clothes seem familiar. More like me, whoever "me" is. Getting into the jeans is a struggle and it hurts when I bend to put on the socks I have found in another drawer. I remember seeing some boots at the bottom of the wardrobe. My body protests when I pull them on, but they fit my feet so comfortably that this more than anything convinces me that these are my boots, my clothes, that this is my life, and I am, after all, Kate Vavasour.

If I am Kate, who is Isabel?

Remember, remember.

Everything takes so long now. Just getting dressed is a major exercise, and by the time I have finished, it is half past seven and I have to rest in the chair, breathing carefully through the pain.

The house is very quiet, quieter than it was at night. I wonder where everybody else is. Surely I am not the only one awake at this time of the morning? I don't even know where the rest of the family sleeps. It's easy to lose each other in a house this size, in pockets of silence and the shadowy turns of the stairs, or perhaps the Vavasours hide behind all those doors, each one closed like a turned back.

Just when I am feeling abandoned, I sense someone outside the door, and look up eagerly. Perhaps I have misjudged the Vavasours. Perhaps one of them – Fiona, maybe, who is always correct, or Philippa – has come to put her head round the door and ask if I'd like a cup of tea. I am longing for one, and not looking forward to the walk down the stairs, but I think I am probably more eager for company.

No knock comes. Instead, the silence deepens and I find myself staring at the door. Apprehension tickles between my shoulders. I'm certain I heard someone, but why are they just standing there?

'Hello?' I call. My voice sounds too high, not like mine at all.

There's no reply. Perhaps they thought I was sleeping and didn't want to disturb me? Or perhaps it was a practical joke? Except it's not very funny, and anyway, the Vavasours don't strike me as jokey types.

'Fine,' I say out loud. 'I'll get my own tea.'

I bite down hard on my lip as I lever myself out of the chair with my stick and make my way slowly over to the door, but when I get there, I find myself pausing, indecisive, my fingers on the handle. More than ever I am sure there is someone on the other side, but all at once I don't want to open the door.

I'm being pathetic. Am I going to cower in my room just because I don't know what is waiting for me on the other side of the door? Cross with myself, I snatch it open before I can change my mind, and see – nothing!

Then I hear it: a low growl, barely more than a vibration in the throat, and I look down to see the little dog, Pippin, lying with her nose on her paws, her eyes fixed on me. One corner of her mouth is quivering a warning and her hackles are alert, but I am so relieved to see a living creature that I laugh.

'Oh, Pippin, you frightened me!'

I can't bend very far, but I hold out my hand encouragingly. 'Have you been waiting for me? Come on, come and say hello.'

Pippin's growling deepens into a snarl and her lip curls up over her teeth.

'Is it the stick? Is that what you don't like?' Carefully, I rest it against the door frame but as I take a step towards her the dog snaps furiously at me, making me flinch back and stumble against the door, while she puts her tail between her legs and belts down the corridor in terror.

She's terrified? My heart is jerking in my throat and when I suck in a breath in fright, my ribs stab an agonizing protest. I hold my hand to them while I wait for my racing heart to slow, the tendons in my neck taut with the effort of not bursting into tears. I am ridiculously upset. Pippin is just a dog. She doesn't mean to hurt me, I know, but I can't seem to stop my lips trembling. Why is she so afraid of me? Anyone would think I was—

My mind jars to a halt, reverses to come at the idea again.

Anyone would think I was a ghost.

I cover my mouth with my fingers. My skin is warm. I can feel my breath, feel my heart beating. My leg aches and my ribs hurt, but my flesh is solid. I have bruised myself where I knocked my shoulder against the door as I recoiled from Pippin's attack in fright. I am real, I am alive. I am not dead.

Ghosts are insubstantial wraiths. They don't stumble against doors or long for a cup of tea. Of course I am not a ghost.

But what about those memories of my life as Isabel? What if she is somehow part of me, inside my head? I shiver, a fast, uncontrollable shudder down my spine, before I pull myself together. I'm being ridiculous. I don't believe in ghosts; at least, I don't think I do. Isn't Oliver Raine's suggestion that I have recreated a memory from a book I've read or a film I've seen a much more likely explanation?

Of course it is, I decide, relieved. Pippin is probably spooked by my altered appearance and the threatening stick. I probably smell different after those long weeks in hospital, too. I just need to give her time.

Steadier now, I take a good hold of my stick once more and set off in the same direction as Pippin. My stick makes a dull sound on the carpet runner as I limp along the corridor but otherwise the house is silent. At the top of the staircase I pause, one hand on my stick, the other on the elaborately carved finial. The air has grown taut, and I stand very still, straining to hear, while the silence condenses and grows thick and heavy, so heavy that it is an effort to breathe.

The door into the long gallery is closed this morning. It is finely carved, with a wrought-iron handle. *Turn it.* The idea shimmers in my head. *Turn it. Come in. Come in and see.*

I forget the fact that I am thirsty and want a cup of tea. Without conscious thought, I am at the door, taking hold of the handle, turning it.

As soon as I step into the long gallery, recognition settles over me like a sigh. Ah, yes, I do remember this. The gallery stretches the width of the house. On one side, ten bay windows overlook the courtyard and the gatehouse, five on either side of the great window above the front door. On the other the wooden panelling is hung with morose portraits of past Vavasours. Why have they moved the tapestries? I wonder. They were so beautiful, and more colourful than the paintings.

The room smells of old wood and beeswax and something elusive, something rich and lustrous, as if the years of dusting and polishing, of silks and velvets and leather shoes, of guttering candles and sunlight and warm bodies, are all pressed into the scent of the past.

The floorboards are dark and shiny with age, and the rubber base of my stick squeaks as I walk along the gallery. There is a humming in the air, or perhaps it is in me. A sense of waiting. Waiting for what?

Frowning slightly, I step up into one of the bay windows. It is as if opening the door to the gallery has cracked open something in my memory, too. I remember this room, I have stepped up into this bay before.

In the courtyard below, I see someone else at last. George is in a quilted jacket and riding boots. A riding helmet is tucked under his arm and he's studying a piece of paper – a letter? – in his other hand. Beside him, Angie leans in to point out a phrase, and George purses his lips. There is something intimate about the angle of her head, the way she stands so close to him. As I watch, George says something which makes Angie nod her head. Her shiny brown hair swings forward and she shakes it neatly back into place, and they both laugh.

I wriggle my shoulders, suddenly uncomfortable. I shouldn't be spying on them. I'm about to step back when I see them both turn as if to greet someone coming out of the door below me.

I lean closer into the window to see who it is, and just like that, memory slides into place, smooth as a well-oiled bolt.

I was leaning forward just like this while I waited eagerly for the carriage to bring Judith. Edmund had sent for her. It was his idea. He had business with the Council of the North and was sent for to York. He would be gone three weeks, a month perhaps, and he asked if I would like Judith to keep me company while he was gone. The elderly aunt who had helped me settle into running the house had died two months earlier, and Edmund feared that I might be lonely on my own. There was no question of me going with him, even if I had known how to go on in a city. For I was with child.

Four months it had been since my flowers had come down, and it had taken Edmund to make me realize what was happening with my own body.

He was delighted, but he had turned stern, forbidding me to do this or that as if I had suddenly become fragile. I loved my husband. My heart leapt every time he came into a room. I thrilled at the knowledge that I could look at him whenever I liked, that I could touch him whenever I wanted. Sometimes my eyes would rest on his mouth, on the angle of his jaw, or his hands, nicked and scarred in the way no courtier's should ever be, and my belly would clench in disbelief that I could be so lucky.

Together we rode out to the fields and woods, and I soon knew the folk in Askerby as well as I had done those in Crabbersett. We rubbed ears of wheat between our fingers and eyed the cattle to see how fat they grew. We chose a situation on firm, dry ground for a new malthouse. I was there when Edmund discussed the building of it with the joiner and I took the stick they were using to draw a plan in the dust, and suggested changes of my own. We planned to improve our stable and decided together when to wean a foal or cover a filly. We rode over to our neighbour's estate to inspect and buy his fine Turkoman stallion. In all things Edmund treated me as an equal, and I loved him for it.

But there were times, too, I admit, when Edmund baffled me. Times when he would retreat into silence and I did not know how to reach him. Then I would wish that I could talk to Judith. I missed her. She always understood.

I was not alone with a houseful of servants, but sometimes, yes, I was lonely. I had been fond of Edmund's aunt, who earned her place in the household by making everyone comfortable. When she died, I did my best to supervise the running of the house as she had done, but truth to tell I did not care overmuch if the silver was polished to a shine. As long as the horses were cared for and there was food on the table and clean linen, I was happy. I did not make my own cheese or hang over the cook. I had no special remedies or recipes. I did not mend my husband's shirts with my own hand. But the servants smiled as they went about their tasks, and if guests arrived there was always a good meal and good cheer to greet them.

Still, I missed having someone to tell how frustrated I was by the way the babe had taken me over. I was no longer just me. I was a vessel, carrying Edmund's heir. I was happy at the thought of a child, of course I was, but I felt trapped too, and I couldn't tell Edmund of my fear.

Judith would understand. She knew how I dreaded being bowed under the weight of a baby and unable to run. She knew how I feared the birth and how I feared ending up like my mother, bound to the bed, raving and thrashing at the unseen spirits that tormented her.

So I was wild for her to arrive. I had written straight away and Edmund had sent his coach, the one I never used, to bring her to me. I would have walked outside but I didn't want to miss her arrival, so I paced up and down the long gallery instead. When I heard the sound of carriage wheels I flew to the window and craned to see. Yes, it was Judith! I could see a servant helping her to step down from the carriage.

She stopped to shake out her skirts and look up at the facade of the Hall just as the sun burst out from behind a cloud. The brilliant light turned her face blank and I almost recoiled until I realized that it was but a trick of the light through the glass. When I peered closer, I saw that she looked her normal, sweet self.

Heedless of the babe I carried, I ran along the gallery to the stairs and down to the great hall. I burst in just as Judith was coming through the door. She was as neat as ever, her hair falling straight down her back and kept in place with a cap, her hands folded at her waist exactly as they had been when I had first seen her.

'Judith!' I flung my arms around her. 'Oh, Judith, I am so glad to see you! I have missed you so!'

Chapter Thirteen

Judith laughed as she disengaged herself from my embrace. 'Isabel, you have not changed at all! I thought to find you a grand lady, and here you are, running through the house like a country wench!'

'I fear they will never make a fine lady of me,' I said, cheerfully ignoring the subtle reprimand, and I tucked my hand into the crook of her arm. 'Let us go and be cosy. I cannot wait to hear news of everybody! Does my uncle still grumble with his gout? Is my aunt well? Is my cousin Lawrence still sulking at being called home? And what of Peg and Agnes?' I asked after the servants. 'How do they do?'

'Your aunt and uncle send greetings,' said Judith. 'They are looking to make a marriage for your cousin soon. The rest of the household go on well enough.'

It was nearly a year since I had seen Judith and I was more shy than I expected. She seemed so much more assured than I. Should I not be the one who had changed? Judith was a maid still while I was a wife and mistress of this great house. But I had never rid myself of the notion that somewhere a mistake had been made, and that sooner or later the world would line up to point a finger at me in disbelief and call me an imposter. She is but an unruly maid, they would say. She is not old enough to marry or be mistress of such a house.

Edmund laughed at me when I told him this, but I knew that if Judith had married instead of me, she would have assumed the running of the household without a moment's doubt. She would not have needed Edmund's aunt to show her how to go on.

The truth? My pleasure in seeing my friend was jumbled up with feeling inadequate and inexplicably chastened, and I found myself babbling to cover my discomfort.

I sent for wine and cakes from the kitchen, and Jennet, the little maidservant taken in from the poorhouse, brought them up to us in the parlour. Poor child, Jennet was not well favoured. She had a nose squashed up like a piglet's that made her breathe heavily through her mouth, and a club foot that meant she walked with a lurch that sent the wine slipping and sliding on the tray. I got up quickly and took it from her before the goblets tipped onto the floor.

'Thank you, Jennet.'

I could feel Judith looking at me as Jennet clumped away. 'What is it?' I asked, looking up from pouring the wine.

'Nothing,' she said, and her smile was back in place so quickly that if you did not know Judith as well as I did, you might have sworn that it had never slipped at all.

'No, tell me.'

'It's just . . .' Judith paused delicately. 'Well, I did not expect to see you behaving as servant rather than as mistress, that is all,' she said. 'You have no need to thank her or to take on her tasks.'

'I was just making sure the wine didn't fall,' I protested.

'You should not have her as a servant if she cannot be trusted to carry the wine,' Judith pointed out. 'As well have a dog and bark yourself.'

I was silent. I could not believe that rescuing the tray had been so wrong, but I felt foolish anyway.

'Oh, I do not mean to criticize, Isabel.' Judith leant forward in consternation and put a hand on my knee, and I remembered what Edmund had said about my face being too easy to read. 'Indeed, you must do whatever you think best. This is your house, and if your husband does not care for you to stand on your dignity, then who am I to say anything? I fear only that you let yourself be taken advantage of. You are so very trusting.'

Smiling, she sat back, evidently deciding that she had said enough. 'It is good to be here at last. May I take a cake?' She nibbled delicately at one. 'It is very good. I would use a little less saffron myself,' she said. 'I will give your cook a recipe of my own.'

She was so capable, I remember thinking enviously. Of course Judith would be able to make fine cakes while I, I went to the kitchen to steal scraps from the sugarloaf for my mare, and if the cook caught me she shooed me out as if I were a mere dab of a girl. Judith was right, it was time I tried for more dignity. I remember thinking that, too.

Lost in the memory, I have been standing in the bay window, my hand spread on the glass, but now I turn and look at the long gallery. It is very strange, this feeling of seeing the room as it is now overlaid with an image of how it was then. How is it possible that I can remember it so clearly?

Confabulation, Oliver Raine called it, a fantasy I am creating to account for the gaps in my memory. But these memories account for nothing. They make no sense at all. Instead, they confuse me even more. I shouldn't be able to remember a club-footed maid, a friend with a sweet face and subtle reprimand behind her smile, but I do.

To check, I retrieve my stick and walk along the gallery to open another door. This is where Jennet brought the cakes. I remember the fireplace and the window overlooking the garden. The room is still hung with tapestries, although they are so faded now you can barely see the figures. When Judith admired them, they were cheerfully coloured. Now they seem tired and grey. This is how the present seems to me, I realize, while the past is bright and clear.

There is a panel by the fireplace. *The Parlour*, it says, and it talks about the tapestries and the furnishings. Clearly this is one of the rooms open to the public, but it isn't one the Vavasours use. It has an empty, unlived-in feel to it. This is not how I remember it, with bright cushions on the chairs and carpets on the chests, with a jug of daisies on the windowsill, and

Edmund's dogs lying in front of the fire. It used to be a comfortable room, and I would sit here often with Edmund in the evening. The parlour was panelled by Edmund's father just before he died, and I remember the resiny tang of new wood that still lurked in the air.

It is long gone. The glowing wood is dark now and overlaid with centuries of smoke, and the room smells fusty and old. It is a museum, not a place to warm your backside in front of the fire, or play cards by candlelight.

I turn. The carved stone mantelpiece is the same, and clear as day, I see Judith running her finger along it. She didn't say anything, but a tiny crease appeared between her brows.

'The maids are busy at this time of year,' I said defensively.

'Dear Isabel, I am not criticizing. You have much to do here, and now that you are with child . . . well, perhaps I can be of help to you.'

What had we done then? I frown in an effort of memory. I think I must have shown her the house. I had been looking forward so much to Judith's arrival and I couldn't help feeling deflated, but I seem to remember she was lavish in her praise, so I must have recovered my spirits. I know I showed her the great chamber where I slept in the bed with Edmund. I remember how she gasped at her first sight of it.

I had never paid much attention to the chamber before. To me, it was a place of pleasure, a place where Edmund and I rode the beast of desire, a place of laughter and of love. I had barely noticed the intricately carved bedposts or the heavily embroidered curtains I insisted were tied back because I could not bear the thought of being shut in. I had eyes only for my husband.

But now I looked and saw it through Judith's eyes: the rich colours, the sumptuous tapestries covering the wainscot, the carved chests where I kept the fine gowns I hardly ever wore, being so much happier in my old frizado kirtle. There was a chair with embroidered cushions by the fire, and more cushions at the window where I sometimes sat and pouted at the rain when it was too wet to ride. And in the middle of the room, the great bed, hung with red silk, and covered with an embroidered coverlet.

Judith put a hand on it and pushed, testing the softness of the feather bed beneath. She fingered the curtains, rubbing the silk between her fingers, tracing the pattern of gold threads. 'Oh, Isabel,' she said, and there was a yearning in her voice I had never heard before. 'To think that this is all yours!'

'I am fortunate, I know,' I said.

'Fortunate indeed!' Judith laughed and bounced up on the bed and her eyes sparkled. It was as if we were girls again, and the momentary unease dissolved as I laughed with her. 'And I am fortunate to have you for a friend,' she said with a happy sigh. 'I can see I am going to be so comfortable here. I vow, if I could find a way to take your place I would,' she jested.

I laughed. 'You would not feel so envious if you had to spend the morning heaving over a chamber pot! Joan says the sickness will pass once the babe settles, but it has not happened yet.'

'Who is Joan?'

'She was Edmund's nurse, and lives at Askerby still. She is a wise woman with all manner of remedies,' I told Judith. Joan was a fat, motherly woman who treated Edmund as if he was barely breeched, and who liked to tell me tales of his childhood. For all her garrulous stories I had found her to be kind and wise indeed when anyone in the household fell sick of a rheum or a cough, and when Edmund had toothache, only Joan could help.

'Isabel!' On the bed, Judith's look of girlish mischief evaporated and she sounded shocked. 'You are not taking advice from a wise woman?' Her voice dropped to a horrified hush. 'What if she is a witch?'

'Joan is no witch,' I said scornfully.

'How do you know? These women conceal their true natures. Has she given you anything for the babe?'

I rolled my eyes in a way that would have had my aunt rapping my knuckles. 'A decoction to stay the vomiting, that is all.'

Judith jumped off the bed, all briskness. 'You must stop taking it at once. I will make you a remedy of my own. At least that way you can be sure that no harm is intended to the babe.'

'But I feel well,' I protested as she bustled over to me and put her arm around my waist.

'Better safe than sorry,' she said. 'I see it is as well I came,' she added with a smile. 'You do not need to concern yourself with anything, Isabel. I am here to look after you now.'

I have lunch on a tray in my room, and Fiona offers to send another up for supper, but I have had enough rest. I'm tired of thinking about Isabel and Judith and what those memories mean, tired of remembering how Pippin growled at me. I need distraction, company, some semblance of normality.

'I'd like to eat with you, if I may,' I say.

'Of course,' Fiona says pleasantly. 'I'll ask George to come and help you down the stairs. We usually gather for a drink in the yellow drawing room at six-thirty and eat a bit later.'

I don't like the idea of being escorted, but I got hopelessly lost this morning while I was looking for the kitchen. One of the guides found me in the end and made me sit down while she went to find Fiona, who promptly brought me back to my room and told me I should rest. I would have liked to see Felix again, but Fiona thinks he is still too upset after yesterday, and I feel duly chastened.

The yellow drawing room sounds very posh. 'Will I be okay as I am?'

Fiona's eyes rest for a crushing moment on my hoodie and jeans. 'We usually change, but you mustn't think you need to be formal.'

Oh. Clearly I *won't* be okay as I am.

I find another long skirt patterned in grey and purple and brown, the colours of the heather but washed out and mothy pale, and a short crocheted jumper. I don't have anything more formal in my wardrobe, anyway. If I've ever attended a hunt ball or any of the charity receptions Angie seems to organize, I must have borrowed a dress.

There are some cosmetics on the dressing table, so I am clearly not that minimalist. My face in the mirror is wan, and I pick up the blusher, but the brush feels awkward in my hand. I end up looking like one of those Russian dolls, with blobs of bright colour high on my cheeks which only exacerbate my pallor and the shadows under my eyes. It is not a good look and I rub them off with a tissue, settling in the end for just ruffling my short hair. It is growing back into a pixie cut. 'Very chic,' Angie assured me in hospital, although she was clearly being kind. I don't look chic, I look haunted.

My mind trips over the word, just as it did over *ghost*, and I swivel round on the dressing-table stool, unable to look at my reflection any longer. I have decided: for reasons best understood by Oliver Raine, no doubt, my mind has created an alter ego, but I am more determined than ever to keep those memories to myself. Sooner or later I must remember something of my real life, and then, presumably, I won't need Isabel's any longer. So when George asks me if I have remembered anything at all since my return to Askerby, I shake my head.

'Not yet.'

He offers me his arm, but I insist on walking myself. 'I'm supposed to be using my leg,' I tell him, but the truth is that I don't want to lean on him. I'm not sure why. He is a good-looking guy, and although his intellect clearly isn't sparkling, he seems nice enough, and he is very attentive to me, irritatingly so, in fact. He hovers around, ready to grab me at the slightest hesitation, until I want to snap at him to stop fussing.

Pippin trails us along the corridor. She was waiting outside again when George knocked, but this time I ignored her as she backed away, growling. 'I don't know what's got into her,' George says. 'She never used to be like this.'

'It's the stick,' I say firmly. 'I think it's confusing her. I'll leave her alone until she gets used to it.'

George tells me that the yellow drawing room is one of the rooms open to the public, but the Vavasours make a point of using it every day. 'One of the appeals of Askerby Hall is that it's a house that is still lived in,' he says. 'Of course we have private quarters, but we do use most of the rooms in the house, apart from those that we've tried to preserve with the original furniture, like the parlour and the great chamber.'

The yellow drawing room is not what you would call cosy. Three great chandeliers hang from the ceiling. Two sets of ornate sofas upholstered in a pale yellow face each other, divided by a large lacquered table. Various chairs with spindly gilt legs are dotted around, and framed family photographs are artfully posed on the highly polished side tables. The walls are papered with yellow chintz, and swagged and tasselled curtains frame the great windows. I can see that it's a beautiful room, but it's not one where you can loll around and put your feet up. I am hopelessly out of place in my vaguely boho outfit.

I am not the only one who thinks so. Margaret Vavasour is sitting on one of the sofas, and she looks me up and down with distaste when I come in with George. I remember seeing the photograph of her that Angie showed me, but it didn't convey the force of her presence. Her eyes may be sunken now, but their green is undimmed, and her back is as straight and her expression as imperious as when she was deb of the year. Like the room in which she sits, Margaret is beautiful but cold, and she makes no effort to disguise the contemptuous sideways twist of her mouth as she registers my skirt and crocheted jumper.

Like Fiona, Margaret is immaculately groomed. It might be June, but inside the house it is cool and Margaret is wearing a fawn cashmere twinset and a soft tweed skirt. A twist of pearls gleams at her throat and there are more pearls in her ears, and great jewels on fingers swollen and twisted with arthritis, the only part of her that concedes her age.

'Ah, here's Kate,' Jasper booms as George and I appear in the doorway. 'Come on in and I'll get you a drink.'

'Come and sit next to Granny,' George says, steering me over.

Granny. It's a cosy word that doesn't fit Margaret Vavasour. There's certainly nothing warm about the way she inclines her head. The other Vavasours are all watching anxiously. I wonder if I am usually as intimidated by her as the others seem to be.

I can't be sure, but I feel that I am not. So I ignore the chilliness of her greeting and make no apology for my appearance but bend instead to pat the dogs who push forward, oblivious to the glacial atmosphere. There are three black Labradors, one grey-muzzled and wheezing, and a golden retriever, all wagging their hindquarters and shoving wet noses into my hand. Only Pippin hangs back. She has followed us into the room and out of the corner of my eye I see that she is crouched by the door, ready to run if she has to, her ears flattened and her eyes fixed on me.

Jasper gives me a gin and tonic with a tired sliver of lemon floating in it. Is this what I like to drink? When I take a cautious sip I discover that the tonic is flat and warm.

'How are you feeling?' he asks me, when it is clear his mother is not going to acknowledge that I've been in hospital, but I notice that he glances at her first as if seeking permission to speak.

I would like to say that I feel overwhelmed and confused and very tired, but with Margaret's challenging gaze on me, I put up my chin and say that I am fine.

Chapter Fourteen

'They tell me you've lost your memory,' Margaret says in a cut-glass accent that belongs back in the forties.

Her dislike is a tangible thing. I can feel it poking and prodding at my clothes, my face, my accent.

I am determined not to let her discompose me, so I keep my voice level as I sip my tepid gin. 'Yes. I don't remember anything before I woke up in hospital.'

'Convenient.'

'*Mother . . .*' Joanna says in a low voice, and I glance at her.

George's mother came to visit me a couple of times in hospital, I remember, but she didn't make a great impression. She looks very like her brother, Jasper, with the same slightly frayed good looks, the same indecisive air. She has none of her mother's beauty or presence. There is discontent in the lines bracketed around her mouth, in the sullen downturn of her lips, that are so like Philippa's.

Margaret glares at her daughter. 'Why should we all dance

around Kate and pretend that she hasn't put us all to a great deal of trouble?'

'She's been in hospital,' says Jasper uncomfortably.

'Yes, and whose fault is that? If Kate chooses to jump off the roof, she should accept the consequences.' Margaret transfers her implacable gaze to me. 'I've got no patience with all this "understanding" we're supposed to do nowadays,' she says, her mouth twisting into a sneer at the word. 'We all grieve for Michael, but where would we be if we all tried to kill ourselves the moment we were sad? Do you think that we didn't lose people we loved in the war? That I don't still miss Ralph?' For the first time her voice quavers and I can hear that she is an old lady after all. 'He was my husband for twenty-two years, but I didn't jump off a roof to get some sympathy.'

There is an awkward silence. Oddly, I don't feel hurt by Margaret's attack. At least she is telling me how she feels rather than letting me grope around for a sense of who I am.

'Is that why I jumped?' I ask. 'Because I was distraught about Michael's death?' It just doesn't feel right to me, but what do I know? I don't remember Michael or how I felt. I don't remember standing on that roof and deciding that I couldn't go on. I only remember tumbling and terror and the ground opening up like a great maw to seize me.

'I can't think what else you had to be unhappy about.' Margaret lifts her glass to her lips and the huge emerald on her finger flashes. It reminds me of the way the house seemed to be sending me a message, and I look away. 'You have a healthy son, who will inherit the title and the estate when Jasper dies.

You have the support of the family and a beautiful home in which to live. You have no need to work. But no, that wasn't enough for you! You have to have a breakdown, and start gibbering about those bones that were dug up.'

'What bones?' I look at Fiona. 'What breakdown?'

But Margaret hasn't finished. 'Everybody falls over themselves because you're the grieving widow. Pah! There was a time when people had *courage*,' she says. 'We put up with what we couldn't change. We didn't fall apart the moment things didn't go our way. God knows what everything thinks of the Vavasours now,' she says. 'We used to be a family who knew how to behave!'

'What breakdown?' I ask again.

'I knew the moment Michael first brought you to Askerby that you were going to be trouble,' Margaret says. 'Sometimes I think it's just as well he died when he did.'

Fiona flinches.

'Mother!' Jasper protests into the shocked silence.

'Well, can you really see Kate as Lady Vavasour?' Margaret demands, waving her glass at me. 'She's got no idea of how to dress and no idea of how to behave, and we don't know anything about her family. She could be anybody. And now she's brought weakness of character into the Vavasour line, if not outright madness.'

'*Madness?*' This time the sharpness of my tone gets through to her. 'What was I doing?'

'I don't think this is a suitable topic of conversation,' Fiona starts, but I ignore her. I meet Margaret's cold green eyes.

'I want to know,' I say.

'You were gibbering about ghosts and all sorts of rubbish.'

'Ghosts?' It is like a breath on the back of my neck and my skin twitches in an instinctive shiver that I try to disguise by moving my shoulders restlessly. I look at the others. 'Nobody told me anything about this.'

'It's true, you were behaving a little erratically in the few weeks before you . . . fell,' says Fiona, 'but we hoped the accident would have cured you of all that. There seemed little point in dragging it up when you didn't remember it anyway. Losing your memory must be very difficult, but it does allow you to make a fresh start.'

'You had a bee in your bonnet about the body that was found under the Visitor Centre. We might as well tell her,' Philippa says when Jasper tries to shush her. 'She'll only ask someone else otherwise.' She turns back to me. 'When they dug the foundations for the Visitor Centre last year, they unearthed a load of old bones. There'd been a seventeenth-century build-ing there before, a dairy or something, so we knew it wasn't a modern body and we called in the archaeologists.'

Something is stirring in the back of my mind. I frown, trying to fix the images that are wavering: an excavator, its massive treads glutinous with mud; its bucket, lowered almost rever-ently; bones, stained brown with age; and a wave of horror enveloping me. Am I remembering, or imagining? It is so hard to tell.

Philippa waits for a moment, but when I say nothing, she goes on. 'It turns out the bones had been buried in a peaty

PAMELA HARTSHORNE

hollow that had preserved them. They've been taken away for forensic analysis now, but the archaeologists reckon they were at least four hundred years old. Of course, that tied in with the legend of Askerby's ghost, who's supposed to be a Tudor serving girl who got pregnant by some rapacious Lord Vavasour and committed suicide, and you latched onto that and decided that proved the ghost was a real person. You got a bit obsessed, to be honest, and kept insisting that the ghost wasn't a servant at all but an early Lady Vavasour.'

'Completely doolally,' Margaret puts in, just in case I've missed the point. 'There's no evidence for that whatsoever.'

'You did ask,' Philippa says defensively as I sit there, trying to take it all in.

'Why didn't anyone tell me about this before?' But that's not quite true, is it? Angie did tell me I'd been behaving 'strangely' when she came to see me in hospital. She said I wasn't myself, and that I was obsessed, but she didn't say anything about any bones.

'Well, like Ma says, we rather hoped you wouldn't remember what with everything else that's happened. Plus, it seemed a teeny bit tactless to draw the story to your attention again.'

'Why?'

Philippa glances at her parents and then back at me with a shrug. 'Because the ghost is supposed to haunt the tower. That's where she jumped.'

Pippin is waiting outside my door when I open it. She is there every day. She seems fascinated by me, but she fears me still. It has been four days now and I haven't been able to get close to her. Still, I try again, rubbing my thumb against my fingers in what I hope is an enticing manner.

'Good girl, Pippin. Come on, you're a good dog. I won't hurt you.'

I hold my breath as she wriggles forward on her belly. 'That's it,' I say encouragingly. 'Good girl.' She's getting closer and closer. 'Good dog,' I praise her, being very careful not to move, although my leg is protesting. It feels like a huge step when she touches her nose to my hand before losing her nerve and skittering away. I sigh.

'Come on then.' I know she will follow me. She watches as Mary examines my gait as I walk up and down the corridors. I know my way to the yellow drawing room and the kitchen and the dining room now, and she trails me, a small, distrustful shadow.

I am quickly bored by my routine but Mary isn't ready to let me go outside yet. 'A few more days,' she says. 'It's not like you haven't got masses of room to walk inside. Not many of my patients have their own long gallery!'

'I can't use the long gallery,' I grumble. 'I'll scare the visitors.'

'You're not short of a corridor or two either,' she says firmly. 'No going outside until I say so.'

I wonder what I did with myself all day. I do have a vague memory of Angie telling me that I spent some time researching the family history for a new display at the Visitor Centre, but I find no papers or notes in my room. Perhaps I put everything on the iPad?

I keep flipping open the cover in the hope that I will remember the password, but the screen just blinks infuriatingly back at me. Philippa told me Felix's birthday and Michael's, and I have tried various combinations, but when the iPad told me I was running out of chances I decided I should leave it for now. I'm still hoping my memory will come back, although there's little sign of it yet. However hard I strain to remember, it's like pummelling a dark, spongy wall. I can't break through it.

It would be helpful to have the notes I made before, but there's nothing to stop me from starting again, is there? I know there is a library in the Hall, lined with glass-fronted shelves; there must be a history in there somewhere.

I could look up Edmund Vavasour, I think. And whether he had a wife called Isabel.

I haven't 'remembered' anything more of her, but I have been thinking of her a lot. My memories, or fantasies, or whatever they are, of her life are jewel bright against the blank blackness of the rest of my mind. I think a lot about what Philippa said, about how obsessed I was by the Askerby ghost. The ghost who jumped from the tower just as I did. I long to talk to someone but I don't dare, especially not now I know that the entire family thought I was 'doolally'. I can't risk them thinking that again, but perhaps I can find out for myself if Edmund and Isabel were real people or just figments of my imagination. I will ask Jasper if I can use the library tonight.

But I have something more important to do first.

Last night there was a nasty little scene in the yellow draw-ing room. I'd told Fiona that I was still struggling with steep stairs and asked if Felix had to spend so much time in the nursery. I thought that perhaps Angie could bring him down to see me, but instead Fiona told her to bring him to the drawing room.

'He'll behave better if we're all here,' she said, when Angie ushered in a mutinous Felix. It was the only warning I had.

Told to sit next to his mother, Felix's face darkened, and his bottom lip jutted out. 'I won't! I don't want to. She's not my mummy!' he said, glaring at me.

I dug my fingernails into my palms. 'Please, don't force him,' I said to Angie, who was looking uncomfortable.

'Felix, stop being so silly,' Fiona said sharply, but he had burst into tears.

'I want Mummy!' he sobbed, and my heart cracked for him. 'Where's Mummy?'

'You're his mother,' Margaret snapped. 'Don't just sit there gormlessly. Do something!'

'I will do something,' I said levelly, 'but not here, with every-one watching him. Let him go,' I said to Fiona, who was trying to get hold of Felix. I wasn't sure if she wanted to hug him or wrestle him onto the sofa beside me. 'This isn't helping.'

Now I pause with my hand on the banister. My leg throbs at the prospect of the climb but I set my teeth. Bad leg or no, it is time Felix and I got to know each other.

I've dressed carefully, trying to decide which clothes look

the most worn and comfortable and will at least smell familiar to Felix. I chose jeans again in the end, with a T-shirt and a soft cardigan. I can't be sure, but they felt right when I put them on.

Angie opens the door to the nursery and can't quite hide the dismay that races over her face at the sight of me.

'I don't know if this is a good idea, Kate,' she says in a low voice, glancing over her shoulder at Felix. 'I can't bear the thought of him being hurt again.'

I'm conscious of a flash of irritation. What does she think I'm going to do to Felix? I shouldn't have to beg Angie for permission to see my own son, should I? But then I feel ashamed. Angie has been caring for Felix, making sure he is warm and fed and safe, while I have been denying that I am his mother. Which of us has more right to decide what he should have to do?

But I need to do this.

'Just half an hour,' I say, keeping my own voice level. 'I won't upset him, I promise.'

She doesn't like it, but in the end tells Felix that she is going to get some milk. 'I won't be long,' she says to him. 'Be a good boy for Angie.'

I know she doesn't want to leave Felix with me, but when it comes down to it, I am his mother. I don't want to have to pull rank, and I hope this isn't going to affect our friendship, but I can't talk to Felix with her hovering over me.

I try to offer a reassuring smile as she passes me with a dubious glance, and I wait until she has gone before slipping into the room without announcement.

I didn't really take in much of the nursery the day I came back from hospital, but now I see it's an airy attic room with dormer windows set into the roof. It's charming, I suppose, if you're a fan of Victorian attitudes and like the idea of shutting a child as far away from everybody else as possible. But Felix has toys and books and Angie's undivided attention. He is warm and clothed and well fed. Plenty of children would be grateful to live in such conditions.

Something to eat, clean water to drink, some schooling, is that so much to ask? The words echo in my head. My father. The memory wavers, solidifies. I have an impression of bone-crushing heat, the rasp of insects. I was sitting on the steps of a veranda of some kind. A paraffin lamp hissed into the dark and great moths blundered around it. My parents were sitting behind me and scraps of the conversation reached me, muffled by the soupy heat.

We can't make exceptions for her.

She's never going to fit in.

The people here have nothing, we have everything.

We should send her home. My mother will look after her.

The memory catches me unawares, like a blow beneath the ribs, a jab that snags the breath in my throat. I have been so focused on trying to remember something about Felix or my life at Askerby that I have forgotten I had a life before that. My parents: my father with a grey-flecked beard and an intent gaze, and my mother with her severely beautiful face, her long hair pulled back in a plait that hung down her back. I remember them now, in sturdy sandals and cheesecloth shirts, earnest and passionate but always somehow detached, as if they felt guilty about giving me love and attention unless every single child in the world could have the same.

And I, I did not deserve to be loved, I remember feeling that. There were so many desperate children out there; why should I be luckier than them? I had a roof over my head, I had food to eat, I had all the advantages that were an inescapable part of being a white, middle-class Westerner. I could not expect to be loved, too. That would be unfair. I understood that from a very early age.

I feel ridiculously shaky. After all this time waiting to remember something of myself, now it feels overwhelming. I don't know whether to be overjoyed at the chink in my memory, or dismayed at the lurking resentment I obviously still feel towards my parents. But this is good news: if my life up to now is a jigsaw puzzle missing most of its pieces, my parents are surely a corner piece, and who knows what other memories are waiting to push in after them? My mind is churning, and I need some time alone to sort out my thoughts, but I am in the nursery now, and Felix has seen me. I can't turn around and leave now.

I force the jostling emotions to the back of my mind and focus on the small boy in front of me. His expression has closed at the sight of me, and his eyes, those Vavasour blue eyes, are dark with suspicion.

'Hello, Felix,' I say.

His mouth tightens. 'You're not my mummy,' he says in the same bleak voice he used yesterday. No child should sound like that, and I feel a wash of guilt. If my fall from the tower hurt me, it damaged Felix more. If I could remember, I would know how to comfort him, but I don't. I can only be honest.

'I know,' I say. 'I look like her, but I don't seem right. I understand that.' I prop my stick against a chair and lower myself awkwardly to the floor beside him. My leg protests and I suck in a breath at the stab of pain, but I cannot have this conversation looming over him. When I am down, I settle my leg as comfortably as I can. I make no move to touch Felix.

He gives me a hard, suspicious look and returns to playing with his train, but I can tell that he is very aware of me.

'The thing is, Felix, I fell and hurt my head. I don't remember anything.'

He scowls, but he is listening.

'Do you remember what you had for supper last night?'

'Sausages,' he says grudgingly after a moment.

'Do you like sausages?'

Felix isn't sure where this is going. I can see him turning the question round in his head, trying to work out if it is a trick or not. 'Yes,' he says eventually.

'I don't know if I like sausages or not,' I say. 'I don't remember anything about my life before I was in hospital. I don't remember who I was or what I was doing. I don't remember you,' I tell him honestly. 'When you say I'm not your mummy, that's how it feels to me, too. So I won't make you say that I am. I know you feel that your real mummy has gone away and that I've taken her place, but I want her, too. I need you to help me find her again. Will you help me to do that?'

His small face is screwed up. He is perilously close to tears again, but he's holding on. He is brave, this boy of mine, if mine he is. He turns the wheels on his train. 'I don't know how,' he mutters.

'I don't know either,' I admit. 'Everyone else will tell you I'm your mummy, but you'll know and I'll know that isn't true until I can remember, and until I feel right to you. It's like a secret that only you and I know.' I'm not sure if Felix is following this or not, but he seems to be listening. 'We won't bother arguing with everybody, but we'll know the truth,' I tell him. 'That means that we don't need to pretend with each other, but we can be nice to each other, and we can get to know each other, like we've never met before. What do you think?'

I hope I don't sound too eager. Felix isn't sure and I don't blame him. If I am struggling to make sense of the world without a memory, how much more disturbing is it for a child to be faced with someone who looks like his mother but who feels all wrong?

But Felix is thinking about it; that is something. He takes his time, running the train absently over the carpet. 'Okay,' is all he says at last, and I realize that I have been holding my breath. It whooshes out of me, and I put a hand on the floor to steady myself. *Okay.* It isn't much, but for now it is enough.

Chapter Fifteen

Now what? It feels as though a big hurdle has been jumped, but I'm not sure what to do next. I glance around the nursery. There are lots of books, including a pile on the floor beside me.

'Do you like stories?'

Felix nods, still uncertain.

I pull a selection towards me and try to settle my leg into a more comfortable position. There is one about a steam engine called Frank, brightly coloured and appealing. I notice the train in Felix's hand. I show him the book. 'What about this one?'

A stricken expression flashes across his face. 'What is it?' I say, concerned. 'Don't you like this one?'

Another nod. His mouth is pressed together to stop it wobbling. A four-year-old shouldn't have to stop himself crying. 'Felix,' I say gently. 'Is this a book Mummy reads to you?'

He won't look at me, but his head bobs down and up.

'Do you want me to read something else?'

A long pause. 'You read it,' he whispers.

It feels as if a great fist has closed around my chest and is squeezing hard. Felix doesn't touch me, but when I open the book he moves a little closer so that he can look at the pictures, and as I read, my mind shimmers. I recall a place, sounds.

Michael, pulling a book out of a carrier bag. 'Look what I bought Felix! I loved this as a kid.'

Me laughing, flicking through the book. 'He's only six weeks old! I don't think he'll be reading for a while.'

'You're never too young for books. I'm going to read him to sleep.'

Michael – the same evening, or later? – with Felix propped in the crook of his arm, holding the book in his other hand, turning the pages awkwardly, making all the voices different, a squeaky one, a gruff one, while the baby looked up at him with opaque dark eyes.

Michael breaking off, a tic going beside his eye.

'What's the matter?' I said, catching a grimace.

'I've had a pig of a headache all day. Have you got any paracetamol?'

Me, popping pills out of the foil packet, putting my hand under the water to make sure it was cold before I filled the glass. Frowning. Something I didn't want to name was squirming queasily in my belly. 'You're getting a lot of these headaches,' I said as I gave Michael the glass. 'Perhaps you should go and see a doctor.'

'I can't bother the doctor with a headache,' he said, tossing back the capsules. 'I'll be fine.'

'Go on.' Felix's voice jerks me back to the present and my

hands tremble as I turn the page. The words dance sickeningly in front of my eyes and I blink slowly to focus.

Michael. *Michael.* At last. My throat is jammed with emotion: relief, love, grief. Michael, lanky and floppy-haired like Jasper, but with such warmth in his eyes. Michael with the swift smile that transformed his serious expression. How could I have forgotten him? And now that I have remembered him, how can he be gone?

'Why have you stopped reading?' Felix asks with an accusing look.

'I'm sorry, I . . .' I pull myself together with difficulty. How can I possibly explain to him? That squeezed feeling is crushing my ribs, and I struggle to breathe.

Tentatively I probe my mind, like feeling a sore tooth with a tongue. Is there anything else? How we met, the first time we kissed, the smell of his skin . . . ? But all I find is that fragment, poking brilliantly through the shrouds over my memory.

Michael. The thought of him is a dagger-bright shard of pain, but at least I remember him. I remember the intensity of feeling as I watched him read to our son, the dreadful premonition of what those headaches meant. But everything else – how we met, how we lived and how we loved, how he died – all that is gone.

I glance down at the small boy beside me, trying to connect him to the baby in my memory. There's still a block, but now that I have started to remember, the rest will come. I *will* remember, I vow. I am his mother, and together we will find our way back to how we were.

Taking a breath, I fix my eyes on the book once more. 'When Frank had puffed his way to the top of the hill . . .'

Angie comes back before the half-hour is up, 'just to see how you're getting on'. She has obviously been worrying about Felix and I can tell that she is surprised – or should that be disappointed? – when she sees him sitting quietly beside me.

Felix glances up as she comes in and offers her a wide smile but he doesn't move from my side, and I see Angie's face tighten just a little. I wonder if she has been expecting him to run to her, to choose her over me, and my elation at having remembered Michael and made some progress with Felix fades into a trickle of apprehension. Angie is my only friend, and I'm grateful to her for looking after Felix so well, but I can't help remembering how happy she was while I was safely away in hospital. I don't want her to resent me for coming home and trying to reconnect with my son.

But when I finish reading the story, Angie is all smiles. She claps her hands together. 'Wasn't that a lovely story Mummy read to you?' she says to Felix, who shoots me a glance of complicity. He is not going to tell her I'm not his mummy. He's going to stick to our agreement. We know the truth, even if nobody else does.

I smile encouragingly at him, and he jumps up to find another book. 'One more!'

'I think that's enough,' Angie says. 'Mummy can't sit like that any longer.'

It's true. My leg is agonizing, and when Angie helps me up

from the floor, only Felix's blue-eyed stare stops me from cursing at the pain. But it has been worth it. I still don't remember Felix, but I have made a connection with him, and it is strong enough to drown out the voice in my head which clamours: *No, not this one! This is not your child!* I don't try to kiss him goodbye, but I rest my hand briefly on the top of his head, feeling my palm twitch as if it remembers the springy softness of his hair.

'Maybe we could read another story tomorrow?' I suggest, but Felix is playing with his train and doesn't look up.

''Kay,' is all he says.

I leave Felix with Angie and begin the long trek back to my room. I turn the memory of Michael around and around, examining it from every angle. He is a vital piece of the puzzle that I am trying to put together. Now I have remembered my husband, and a little about my parents. Soon, surely, I will remember Felix too, and what I was doing just before I fell. I am recovering myself piece by piece, like a heavily pixelated picture that is slowly coming into focus. I am beginning to feel real after all, my existence more than just a smudgy reflection of Isabel's.

If our past didn't exist, we would need to invent it. Oliver Raine told me that. Holding onto the banister, I make my way carefully down the stairs from the nursery, trying to ignore the white glare of pain in my leg. What if Oliver is right, and those vivid memories of Isabel's life are simply some kind of transference? Perhaps now that I have remembered Michael, my subconscious will have no need to invent Edmund. Perhaps now I can recall something of my own childhood, I won't need to remember Isabel's. And now I have made a step to rebuilding a relationship with Felix, there will be no point in remembering a time when I bore another child.

No! No! The words flutter faintly at the back of my mind in frustration. *No, you know that's wrong! Felix isn't the son you're looking for. You know that he isn't. You need to find your son.*

The Hall opens to the public at eleven, so breakfast is eaten in the dining room before the notices are set out and the guides arrive, before the thickly twisted red ropes block off access to the Vavasours' private quarters. I can't help thinking it would be easier to have breakfast in the kitchen, to jam a piece of toast in the mouth while peering in the fridge for something to put in a sandwich, but that's not the way the Vavasours do things.

The dining room is certainly impressive, in a lugubrious kind of way. Vast and darkly panelled, it has a square bay window looking out over the knot garden. I can see neat box hedges and narrow gravel pathways, and I have a sudden, sharp sense of walking along them, talking earnestly to someone, but when I strain to see whose face it is, I get only the familiar blankness.

Ornate silverware sits on massive, carved sideboards, and the walls are hung with paintings in heavy gilt frames. Landscapes in murky greens and browns, and a number of portraits of nineteenth-century Vavasours with those disconcertingly realistic eyes that seem to follow you around the room. I sit facing the windows – because of course we all have a set place – and I was glad not to have to look at them at first, but now I almost think I'd prefer to look at the paintings instead. Then at least I wouldn't have the prickle between my shoulder blades, or the eerie conviction that at any moment one of them will reach out and clap a cold hand on my arm.

At a guess, the polished table could seat twenty. It sits squarely on an Eastern rug and high-backed chairs are ranged on either side. Three spectacularly ugly silver candelabra dominate the table. At breakfast a concession is made to informality, and we cluster at one end of the table, Jasper at its head. Margaret sits on his right, with George next to her and then Philippa. I'm on Jasper's left, next to Fiona and Joanna. This puts me directly opposite Margaret, and I have to eat with her contemptuous stare scraping over me.

When I suggest it might be easier to have breakfast in the kitchen, Margaret tuts extravagantly. 'Here she goes again, trying to change everything.'

I wonder what I tried to change before. 'I'm merely suggesting—'

'People like the fact that they're looking round a family home rather than a museum,' Fiona breaks in smoothly. 'The fact that we use almost all of the rooms here is part of what makes Askerby unique.'

'Felix is part of the family, and he doesn't eat in here,' I point out.

'You obviously don't remember what a messy eater Felix is,' Jasper says, a little tactlessly, I can't help thinking.

'No, I don't remember,' I say with a cool look.

'Felix is happy eating with Angie near the kitchen,' Fiona says firmly. 'With the best will in the world, he's only a little boy and this is an extremely valuable carpet.' She nods at the floor. 'Visitors don't want to see rubber mats or wipe-clean surfaces. They want to know that this has always been the dining room, and that the family still eat here as they have always done.'

If the visitors want a real sense of the Vavasours, they should visit the kitchen and see how they shut their children away, I reflect. I'm not paying attention, and I speak without thinking. 'It wasn't the dining room when it was first built,' I say, and they all pause in the middle of buttering their toast or stirring their coffee.

'What on earth are you talking about?' Margaret puts her cup sharply back in its saucer. 'Of course this was the dining room.'

But Edmund and I never ate in here. This was Edmund's closet, where he met his steward and his man of business, where he would talk politics with his neighbours and write letters and dispense justice. We kept to the old ways and ate in the great hall still, although after Judith arrived, we did use the parlour more, it is true.

I open my mouth to explain this, and only just manage to shut it in time. I can imagine how Margaret would react to *that*.

With an effort, I push the memories away. Haven't I decided that I don't need them now that I have remembered Michael? I must be more careful. I want to be normal, and sane, and not afraid that my in-laws will accuse me of being 'doolally' again. I can't gaily inform them of how I used to eat in the great hall with my husband and our servants and guests all together.

I meet Margaret's hard stare, and return it with a long, cool one of my own.

'I must have read it somewhere,' I say.

'Pity you can't remember something useful, instead of inaccurate rubbish.'

'Quite,' I say calmly as I pick up my knife and spread marmalade on my toast. I haven't told them I've remembered Michael. I don't feel like sharing him, not yet. I want to remember him as the man who loved me, not as the putative Lord Vavasour who didn't have the sense to find himself a suitable wife.

Margaret glares at me and there's another of those uncomfortable silences in which this family seems to specialize. I marvel again that Angie can find their life so alluring. Doesn't she feel the tension in the air? Can't she see how the Vavasours hold themselves apart from each other? It is as if the Hall has cast a spell on her, or perhaps it is her longing that blinds her, the yearning for George and a family and the security of knowing she never needs to leave home.

But who am I to judge? I cut my slice of toast in half, thinking about what it must have been like for Angie growing up in the lonely lodge with only her grandparents for company. No wonder she looked at the children living at the Hall and thought their life charmed.

The silence stretches and thins. I pick up my toast, but am afraid everyone will be able to hear me chewing, and I'm grateful when Jasper clears his throat and falls back on that old standby, the weather.

'Not a very nice day,' he says.

We glance with varying degrees of interest at the windows, where a steady, sullen rain is falling. So much for June. The dining room gets little enough sunlight as it is, and it is so dark outside that the lights are on.

'Try telling the dogs that,' says Fiona, gamely following Jasper's attempt at a diversion. 'They don't care about the weather. I hope you're not planning to go outside today, Kate,' she says, turning to me. 'You're looking very tired. I don't think you should overdo it.'

Without warning, another memory slides into place, and I pause with my toast still halfway to my mouth.

It's just a fragment. I don't remember what happened before or after, but it is very clear: Edmund, Judith and I were in the parlour. It was cold and wet, and Judith had ordered a servant to light the fire. Edmund was reading in the turned chair, his long legs stretched out to the hearth where his favourite hound lay sleeping, its flanks twitching as it dreamt. Judith didn't like the dog and had drawn her stool away from it. She was mending a smock, her stitches small and neat.

I couldn't settle. I was making an endless perambulation of the room, riding its boundaries as it were. I adjusted cushions, straightened the carpets on the chests, moved the flowers that drooped in the gloom, all the while sending yearning glances at the window, where the wind was hurling rain at the glass and making the panes rattle.

I didn't realize I was sighing until Edmund looked up from his book. 'It will not stop raining because you huff at it, Isabel,' he said with a sigh of his own. 'Why can you not sit quietly like Judith and occupy yourself some other way?'

'Yes, indeed, you should take care,' Judith said. 'You must not overtire yourself. You do not want to risk the babe.'

'How can I tire myself when I cannot go outside?' I snapped. 'I will not get tired walking around the parlour!'

'You might not, but you are tiring *us*,' said Edmund, exasperated. 'How do you expect Judith to concentrate on her stitching? I must have read the same page a dozen times now while you fret and fidget.'

'Very well, I will go and fidget elsewhere!' I flounced out of the parlour, banging the door behind me with a clatter of the latch. It was childish of me, but I felt childish. I wanted to get out. I could not bear to be cooped up all day.

More, I did not like the fact that Edmund and Judith were becoming allies. I wanted them to be friends, of course. I wanted Edmund to love Judith as I did, and I wanted Judith to see what a good husband Edmund was to me, but I did not want them to exchange looks and click their tongues against their teeth at me.

I stalked down the long gallery, my pantoufles slapping on the Turkey carpet, and swung round at the end, my skirts swishing furiously, to march back. I was on my third circuit when Edmund appeared. He didn't say anything at first, but paced by my side. Even though he seemed to be walking slowly, he had no trouble keeping up with me. After a while his quiet presence soothed me and I let out a long sigh.

'I'm sorry,' I said, tucking my hand into the crook of his elbow. He patted it with a smile.

'You don't like being penned in, I understand. Sometimes I think you are like a half-wild creature, Isabel, yearning for the woods and the moors. But, dearest, you must take care of yourself. Judith worries that you will become overwrought. She is afraid—' He broke off as if he feared he had said too much.

I stopped, dragging at his arm so that he had to stop too. 'What?' I demanded. 'What is Judith afraid of?'

'That you may resemble your mother more than you think.' Edmund spoke like a man picking his way through a thorn hedge. 'It is only because she cares for you,' he added quickly as my face darkened. 'She just wants you to be well.'

'I *am* well!' I cried, wrenching my hand from his arm in frustration and raising my fists to my temples as if I would beat myself. 'I am with child, not sick!'

'Of course,' he said soothingly, so soothingly that I nearly hauled out and beat *him* with my fists instead. 'But I am glad that Judith will be with you while I am in York. She will not let you do anything foolish.'

At the breakfast table, I lay down my toast with an unsteady hand. I remember it all so clearly. And now I remember what happened next too, how once Edmund had retired to his closet

I clattered back into the parlour. Judith was still sewing and for a moment I wanted to wrench the smock from her hand and fling it to the floor, to make her look at me and *see* me. *I am not a child!* I wanted to shout at her, even as I realized how childish I would seem if I did.

'What did you tell Edmund about my mother?' I demanded instead as she raised her brows in mild reproof at my noisy entrance.

'Why, only what your aunt told me.'

'What? What did she say?'

Judith's needle darted in and out of the fabric. 'Your mother was . . . excitable,' she said after a moment, having taken the time to find the right word. 'Her passions ran strong, your aunt said, just as yours do. When she discovered that she was with child again, she grew fearful and fretful and she would not be confined. Do you not remember?'

'I was but a child myself,' I said. I hugged my arms together and moved over to the fire for warmth. I did not like thinking about my mother. I remembered her only after my brother was born dead and she was strapped to the bed, her eyes bulging and rolling like a terrified horse, the whites glistening with fear in the stifling darkness.

Judith knew all this. She knew everything about me. She did not need me to tell her how I feared the madness that had consumed my mother, how I feared that I would share her fate, bound and screaming in the dark.

I had not told Edmund this, but he knew how I craved openness and light. One bright day he had taken me right up to the roof of the west tower. The light made me screw up my eyes, and the wind snatched at my hair. 'Turn,' he said, and I turned in a complete circle, slowly.

Far below, the estate stretched out in every direction. Behind were the moors, shifting endlessly in the light, rolling out to the horizon. Ahead, the village was no more than a scatter of humped roofs overseen by the church. There were woods and coppices, strip fields, the river. The track winding away to the bridge. I could see sheep dotting the moorland, cattle huddled together, chewing aimlessly. A small girl drove a gaggle of geese down a path to the pond.

'Everything you see is yours, Isabel,' Edmund had said, his hands warm on my shoulders. 'You are free here. You can ride as far as you will. You need never feel trapped at Askerby.'

Chapter Sixteen

Standing in the dark parlour, I remembered how my heart had swelled, how the light had poured into and around me. It was dazzling. I could feel it seeping into my skin, smoothing out my restless, prickly edges until I could breathe deep and serene. Edmund did not think I was mad. How fortunate I was to have a husband who understood me.

But he hadn't known about my mother. I had seen no need to tell him.

Now Judith had told him, would he start to watch me? Would he whisper to Judith not to agitate me? I remembered how she had hissed in a breath when I told her about the tower, how you could put your hands on the stones and lean out and see for miles and miles and feel everything bothersome lift and blow away in the clean air. When I looked at her in surprise, she had said she would be frightened; had I not been afeared of falling?

'Not I,' I'd said. 'When I'm up there, I feel almost as if I could fly.'

'Do not say such things.' Judith had shushed me, looking over her shoulder in case a servant might sprout from the skirting boards, perhaps. 'It makes you sound . . . fey.'

Mad. That was what she wanted to say. But I was not mad. I was just restless. Was that so hard to understand?

Judith laid her sewing aside and got to her feet. 'Isabel, there is no need to worry,' she said as she took both my hands. 'If only you will let us take good care of you.'

'I am not worried!' Pettishly, I pulled my hands away. 'I do not need to be cared for! I am not a child. I am not sick. I have told Edmund there is no call for him to worry, and do you not worry either, Judith.'

'We cannot help but worry about those we care for,' she chided me gently.

Did that mean I didn't care sufficiently for Edmund? I was not a worrier. I took life as it came, but now I fretted that I should be more concerned to show my love. Should I worry about Edmund at court? I could worry about vagabonds knocking him off his horse, about sly courtiers or the pox, but in the end, what good would it do? That way really did lie madness, I remember thinking.

'I wish you had not told Edmund about my mother, that is all,' I said after a minute, muffled. 'Now he will always be thinking I am about to run mad.'

'Isabel, Edmund is your husband. You should not hope to have secrets from him.'

'It is not a secret. It was just . . . something that happened. My mother was not always mad. It was only after her babe died and they would not let her out of that room.'

It was true. I did remember my mother then. Not as she was that last terrible time, but I had a flash of memory: my mother's laughter, her hand taking mine, running with me through the long, sweet grass.

Judith looked grave. 'Your aunt said that she was never steady. Her emotions ran up and down like fingers on a lute. Losing the babe merely pushed her over the edge into madness.'

I put my hands over my belly where my own child lay, all at once protective. 'Losing a babe would drive anyone to madness, I think.'

'Indeed,' said Judith. 'I fear you may be right.'

She smiled suddenly. 'But you are not going to lose your babe and you will not be mad,' she said. 'I will not let that happen. Come, stop sulking, Isabel. What will cheer you on this dull afternoon? Shall we make some merry music?'

And she was once more my dear friend, who knew just how to coax me out of the sullens and make me smile.

'Is there something wrong with your toast?' Margaret is talking to me, I realize belatedly, and I look down at my plate, where I have dropped the toast unawares. It looks brown and sticky and unappetizing. I pick up my knife but then am not sure what to do with it, so I set it down again.

'I . . . I'm not very hungry,' I say. I am still tangled up in memory. It is like waking from a deep sleep. I'm not sure what is real and what isn't. I wriggle my fingers, feeling the flex of tendons. I lay my other hand on the table, feeling the smooth, polished warmth of the wood. The studs in the chair upholstery are digging into my thighs. A flurry of wind spatters rain against the windows, drowning out for a moment the oppressive tick of the clock. This is real.

I lift my eyes. Margaret is regarding me with acute dislike. Jasper is looking anxious, Fiona studiedly neutral. Philippa is drinking coffee and gazing moodily out of the window. George has his head down and is applying himself to his breakfast, watched fixedly by one of the Labradors, who is hoping for a scrap of bacon, while Joanna fiddles nervously with her teaspoon. These people, these strangers, are real too. I am still having trouble thinking of them as my family, but I feel as trapped here as I did – no, as Isabel did – by the weather. I want to leave, but where can I go and what can I do until I remember more? And Felix. If he is my son, as everyone says he is, I cannot abandon him. I must try harder to make a connection with him, to remember. I can't move on until I do.

'Oh, good God, she's going doolally again—' Margaret says in disgust, and I realize I must be staring blankly.

'What were you thinking of doing today, Kate?' Fiona interrupts, ever quick to smooth out tensions.

Her question gives me time to recover myself. I badly want to drink some tea, but I am afraid my hand will be trembling, and that Margaret will comment on it. She'll think it's evidence that I'm going mad like my mother.

No, wait, my mother isn't mad. The mother I remember

screaming on the bed, the one who laughed and ran through the grass with me, that isn't my mother. That was Isabel's mother. *My* mother is in Africa. She isn't here when I need her. For a moment my throat tightens so painfully I can't speak, but I manage to draw a breath.

'I, er . . .' I struggle to anchor myself in the present. 'I thought I might have a look in the library,' I manage, acutely conscious of how long it has taken me to come up with a plausible answer. 'Angie told me that I was working on a display of family history. I was thinking I could get back to that. I need to do *something*.'

There is a tiny pause. 'Of course,' says Jasper heartily. 'Use whatever you can find there.'

'Do you know what I was looking at before . . . before the accident?' I'm not going to say that I jumped. I don't believe I did.

Again, an infinitesimal hesitation, a flicker of glances around the table. 'Not a clue,' Jasper says, sounding pleased to be so unhelpful. Fiona and Joanna shake their heads. Margaret and Philippa can't be bothered to listen.

'You were looking at the early history of the Vavasours,' George offers after a moment, looking up briefly from his sausage and bacon.

'What was the idea behind the display?' I ask him, but George's eyes slide back to his plate.

'You'd better talk to Angie about that. She deals with all the visitor stuff,' he says. 'She's awfully competent.'

Competent. It's a good word to describe Angie, but it's not very lover-like.

'All right, I'll ask her,' I say, wondering why they seem to be making such heavy weather of a simple question. 'I presume it was a history of the Hall. How long has it been open to the public?'

'Only since the mid-seventies,' Jasper says with an apologetic look at his mother. 'My father wouldn't hear of it, but when he died in 1971 . . . well, death duties, you know.'

'Ralph would have hated it,' Margaret says bitterly.

'George has done a marvellous job of generating new sources of income,' Joanna says loyally, before her mother can launch into a full-blown rant.

'Yes, I heard it's even been a movie set.' I jump in to help her. 'That must have been fun.'

It is as if I have thrown a brick through the window. The conversation, sluggish as it has been, stops dead, and the temperature drops. What have I said?

'*Film,*' says Margaret distinctly.

'I wouldn't call it fun.' George hurries in to head off another rant. 'It was a damned nuisance, but it paid good money.'

'And has brought in loads of new visitors,' Philippa puts in.

'It was very disruptive,' Fiona says.

'What was it called?' I ask. 'The movie?' I prompt when they all look at me.

Another exchange of glances. '*The Tower,*' says George.

Tower. The very word is enough to set something shrieking

and scrabbling at the back of my mind, and in spite of myself, I shrink into my seat, my mind swerving in panic.

'It was a horror film,' Philippa says clearly, a spark of malice in her face. 'It was based on the story of our ghost who, as you know, threw herself off the tower. You can see now why we didn't mention it before.'

'I think we should change the subject.' Fiona puts a stop to the conversation. 'Look at whatever you like in the library, Kate, but do call someone if you want to get something from the higher shelves. You're not steady enough to use a ladder yet.'

The library is lined with floor-to-ceiling shelves enclosed behind glass, each one stacked with leather-bound books. I have to squint to read the titles that are picked out in gilt on the spines: *Enshrined Hearts*, *Epistle to the Learned Nobilitie of England*, *Arcana Fairfaxiana* and various other Latin titles that mean nothing to me.

I can't see anything that says it's a handy history of the Vavasours, and I wonder where I started before. One tall book has *Askerby* in the title, and I need both hands to pull it down from the shelf. It is very old, and the smell of musty paper hits me like a blow when I open the book carefully. The print is hard to read – I can't distinguish an 'n' from a 'u', and the 's' looks like an 'f' – so I soon give up trying to decipher the text and look instead at the illustrations. One in particular catches my eye. It is an etching of a tomb, and shows a knight lying next to a lady. Their feet rest on small, carved dogs. The lady's face is plump and serene, the knight's is remote. He looks stern in his armour, but one gauntlet is off and the sight of their clasped hands makes my heart twist with a memory so sharp and sudden that I suck in a gasp.

Yes, I remember: I was in the parish church with Edmund. Perhaps it was after a service; perhaps Edmund had business with the parson. I don't recall. But we stood in the choir admiring the fine tomb of Sir Piers and his lady. Gently, I traced the fold of the Lady Anne's cold, stone gown. 'One of your fore-fathers?' I asked Edmund, and that half-smile I loved tugged at the corner of his mouth.

'I fear not. The Vavasours were but raggle-taggle mercers in York when Sir Piers sat in high estate here. We would not have presumed to look so high then!'

I touch the clasped stone hands. 'Once they were warm flesh and blood like us, and now, now they lie here in their dark tomb. Will it be the same for us?' I shivered, and Edmund took my hand.

'It is our lot,' he said, 'but at least they are together. It is touching, is it not, to see how close they lie? Let us have a fine tomb too, and I will hold your hand for eternity, and our grand-children and our grandchildren's grandchildren will look on us and smile to think of how much we loved each other.'

I have to blink away the tears as I touch the illustration in the book. Is this still part of my elaborate fantasy, or is there a tomb for Edmund and Isabel in the church? Surely that would be proof that I am not making it all up.

And if there is, what then?

I flick through the rest of the book, but I can't see any other double tombs. It doesn't mean it isn't there, though. When Mary lets me walk to the village, I will go, and I will see for myself.

And Michael, I remind myself guiltily. Michael may be buried there. I must ask.

I should be thinking about Michael, not about Edmund, but the two keep getting muddled in my mind. I just have that one memory of Michael to treasure, but there is so much more of Edmund to remember. Isabel's memories crowd into my head, as if jealous of the one tiny sliver of memory that ties me to the present, desperate to overwhelm it with clearer, more vivid images of a different life altogether.

I don't like the feeling of being pushed. Now that I have remembered Michael, I shouldn't need to invent a completely different life. For the rest of the day I concentrate fiercely on the present, and for a while it works. I am congratulating myself on my success at keeping Isabel at bay when I limp along to the landing and put my hand on the great carved finial at the top of the staircase, and a wave of horror washes over me. I snatch my arm back, my heart hammering in my throat.

I don't need to remember Isabel's life. I don't *want* to remember it. But I do.

Edmund was still away. It felt a very long time since he had kissed me farewell and I had stood with Judith, watching as he clicked his tongue, touched his horse with his spurs and cantered out through the gate, followed by his servant Richard.

The silence after they had gone had settled over the courtyard like a long sigh, and I was very glad of Judith beside me.

I missed Edmund. It was not an easy pregnancy, and I was queasy and sluggish and cold the whole time. Where once I would stride out at every opportunity and call for my horse, now I huddled by the fire, wrapped in Edmund's furred gown. Judith fussed over me, bringing me decoctions she assured me she had prepared with her own hands, but nothing seemed to help. The days and nights blurred into a fog. I forgot what day it was and my only sense of time was knowing it was too long until I could see Edmund again.

I had always been robust and I did not like feeling so listless and miserable. If this was what it was like to bear a child, I wanted no more of it. 'I am not sick,' I had told Edmund, but now it seemed that I was.

I thanked God for Judith. It is true I had been a careless housekeeper, but still, I had my duties, though even those I abandoned when my head swam and when my stomach squirmed and rolled and would never settle, no matter how often I held toasted bread steeped in strong vinegar to my nose or lay with a warm wormwood plaster on my stomach. Judith coaxed me to drink wine and chervil water, but it only made me feel worse, and one day when she was out of the room the thought of its sourness made my stomach rebel. I tipped it into the chamber pot and hoped the maidservant who took it away would not tell Judith I had spurned her remedy.

That afternoon I felt steadier. I even crept along to the

parlour by the long gallery, though Judith clucked and fussed. 'You are not well,' she told me. 'You should stay abed.'

'I have *been* abed,' I said fretfully. 'I cannot look at the bed hangings any more.'

Judith pursed her lips. 'It is a good sign that you are minded to be stubborn again, I suppose. Very well, mistress,' she said with mock subservience. 'Do seat yourself and I will send you some more remedy, since it seems to be working so well.'

She poked up the fire and I sank into the chair, looking around me with pleasure. The parlour was warm and welcoming. The wood was polished to a glow, the silverware gleamed. The cushions were precisely arranged. The carpets had been beaten, I could tell, and the tapestries aired. The scent of lavender hung in the air. There were no clumps of hair from Edmund's dogs gathering dust in the corners. There were no books discarded on the tables, no scattering of petals dropped from long-dead flowers as there usually were.

Quietly, unobtrusively, Judith had wrought a miracle, I realized. This was how the house should look, and I was ashamed of my own slatternly approach to housekeeping, comfortable though it made Edmund.

'Thank you, Judith,' I said, and she paused with her hand on the door to look over her shoulder. She did not pretend to misunderstand me.

'It is always a pleasure to help you, Isabel,' she said. 'Now, rest.'

'Will you not sit with me?'

'I must talk to the cook,' she said apologetically. 'I find there is great wastage of bread in the kitchen here. Every day there are trenchers left over which are given to the poor.'

'Oh, but so it has always been done at Askerby,' I protested, and Judith shook her head.

'Dear Isabel, the servants take advantage of your kindness. They do not get much past me, I do assure you. Do not worry about it. Now, are you warm enough?' She smiled as I nodded, vaguely troubled. 'I will send Bess up with the remedy forthwith.'

She bustled off, happy to be busy, I knew. I pulled the gown closer around me, finding comfort in the softness of the fur trimming. I should have been talking to the cook myself, although not to chide him for the extra bread he made. I had been neglecting my duties since I had been ill. In truth, I had neglected them since I came to Askerby as a bride. Edmund didn't concern himself with the servants. He just wanted things to be comfortable, like any man. Dealing with the house and the servants was women's work. My work. And it was time I did it, instead of leaving it to Judith to manage the house for me.

Chapter Seventeen

I rested my hand on my belly and I made a vow to my babe that I would be careless no more. I would be mistress in fact as well as in name. I would take pleasure in the making of cheese and the brewing of ale. I would learn to scrutinize the accounts, and order a feast fit for a nobleman. I would make sure the maidservants chased the last tumbling bundle of fluff out of the corners of the room and cleaned the windowpanes and I would ask Judith to teach me how to make remedies in the still room.

Fired with resolution, I sat up straighter in my chair, and when Bess came in bearing a goblet I even told myself that I would drink it.

'How do you do, Bess?' I asked. She was usually a sonsy, smiling lass, but she just mumbled an answer, stony faced, and set the goblet on the table beside me.

Now I came to think of it, it was not usually Bess's duty to fetch and carry. 'Where is Jennet?' I said, puzzled.

'Turned off, mistress.'

'Turned off?' I shook my head slightly. I could not be sure I had heard correctly. 'But . . . why?'

'Your orders, mistress.'

'Mine? No! I would not turn Jennet off.'

She shrugged. 'Mistress Judith said you said she was to go, so she went.'

When I demanded to know what she had done, Judith looked puzzled. 'But did you not want her to go?'

'Of course not! Why would I say such a thing?'

'She is a cripple,' Judith said, as if the answer was self-evident. 'She cannot work sufficiently. I was not surprised when you told me to send her away.'

I stared at Judith. '*I* told you to do that?'

'Why, yes. Do you not remember?'

'No.' A dull fear was building inside me. How could I not remember thinking such a thing? 'No, I don't remember.' I put a hand to my head, which was thudding suddenly. 'When was it? What did I say?'

'Why, I do not remember exactly,' Judith said. She picked up a cushion and plumped it before placing it, very carefully, back in position on the settle. 'But you were very clear, I assure you.'

'But you must have known I did not mean it!' Agitated, I got to my feet and paced around the chamber.

'Indeed I didn't.' Judith tutted when she saw that I had not drunk her remedy. 'Come, there is no need for all this fuss. It did you no honour to have such a creature in your house. There are many more servants where she came from.'

I felt as if I had never seen Judith before. 'Jennet has no

family, and you have turned her off without a recommenda-
tion.'

'*You* have turned her off,' she reminded me. 'I acted only on
your orders, Isabel. Now, drink your remedy.'

I struck the goblet from her hand. It smashed on the carpet,
spraying liquid everywhere. Judith's mouth dropped open and a
look raced over her face such as I had never seen before. I
thought for one terrible moment that it was excitement but
when she blinked and carefully composed her expression, I realized to my horror that it must have been fear. Judith, afraid of
me? I saw myself as she must see me, wild eyed, no memory,
and the parlour shrieked with the reminder of my poor, mad
mother. I drew a shuddering breath. I must be calm and controlled. But then I thought of little Jennet, of what would
happen to her, of what she must think of me. It was not to be
borne.

'Where has she gone?'

'I have no idea. The poorhouse, perhaps.' Her voice sharp-
ened as I turned for the door. 'Where are you going?'

'To find her.'

'Isabel, no! There is sickness in the village!'

'I care not,' I said. 'I did not send Jennet away. If I did, it
was in a delirium. I never meant that.' I drew the robe around
me. 'I am going to find Jennet and bring her back. She has a
place at Askerby as long as I am mistress here.'

Judith hurried after me. 'There is no need for you to go. If
you insist, we can send one of the other servants to fetch her.
Oh, what will Edmund say when he learns I let you go?'

Careless of my dishevelled appearance, I strode down the long gallery towards the stairs, with Judith almost running to keep pace with me. 'This is my duty,' I said. 'I will send no servant to go where I would not go myself.'

I was lashing myself for dropping the reins of the household, for falling so sick that I did not know what I was saying. In my haste, I didn't look where I was going, and when I got to the top of the stairs, I picked up the trailing gown too late.

I think that was what happened, anyway. I think I tripped. And I think Judith was trying to catch me, to pull me back. That must be why, for a split instant, I felt a hand at my back. But she wasn't pushing me. She was trying to save me.

All that went through my mind as I lost my balance and toppled forwards down the stairs. I flailed my arms, trying to catch hold of the banister, anything to help me regain my balance, but one foot landed on a step and skidded away from me, and before I could help myself I was falling, falling down, and then there was only blackness.

I look down the stairs to where I landed and I grimace, almost expecting to see myself lying in a crumpled heap at the bottom. I remember that sickening sensation of losing control, of knowing that there was no stopping what was about to happen. That feeling of falling, as if in slow motion, so that I had time to wish I could rewind time, to reverse my movements and stop at the point at which I could have swept the gown up, at which I could have changed everything.

But I did not. I fell, tumbling slowly in an ungainly cartwheel, and the only mercy is that I do not remember what happened after that.

Behind me comes a low growl, a warning vibration in the throat, and I turn. Pippin has followed me down the corridor as she usually does, and now she is backed against the wall, ears down and hackles up, her eyes bright with fear.

Under Mary's narrow-eyed supervision, I am allowed outside at last. My first walk is up and down the terrace above the knot garden, and I gulp at the fresh air. It is cool and clean and laced with the wildness of the moors. I look up at them, rolling tantalizingly up and away beyond the estate wall in the distance, and my longing to be there must be written on my face as Mary shakes her curly head at me.

'Don't even think about it,' she says with a mock glare. 'You'll get there, Kate, I promise, but not yet. You must be patient. Stay on the terrace for now, then you can walk along paths, but we need to be sure that you're completely steady before you can try walking on more uneven ground.'

So every day I make myself walk a little further, and I hate the fact that the smallest trip exhausts me. I spend a lot of time resting. I see Felix every day, too. That's another thing I hate: that I can't run around with him. I have to watch him running around with Angie and the dogs, or kicking a ball with George or Jasper. All I can do for now is read him a story.

Sometimes, though, he accompanies me on my walks. I am too slow for him, and he runs ahead with the Labradors while Pippin trails us at a wary distance. Felix loves the dogs, and teaches me how to distinguish one excitable black Labrador from another. Sheba has a grey muzzle, Felix shows me, and a barrelly waddle. Toto is all gleaming black coat and excitable muscle, and Molly, the golden retriever, is clumsy and willing.

The third Labrador is called Jago, according to Felix, and is George's dog. The other three are apparently happy to go with anyone who will take them for a walk.

'An' that's Pippin,' Felix tells me, pointing at her. 'She's a clever dog. She can do tricks.'

'Really? What does she do?'

'She can shake hands.'

'Do you think she'd shake hands with me?'

'No.' His small face closes, a door slammed, as he remembers. 'She only shakes hands for Mummy.'

We have never again discussed the fact that Felix doesn't believe I am his real mother, but he never calls me Mummy. I notice that. I am only ever 'you' or 'she', however hard Fiona tries to correct him. '*She* is the cat's mother, Felix,' she says irritably. 'Call Mummy Mummy.'

'Leave him,' I say. 'Felix and I have an agreement.'

'What agreement?'

'That's between Felix and me.'

I have breakfast and lunch with Felix as well, much to Fiona and Margaret's disapproval. I don't think Angie likes it much either. Although nothing is ever said, she prefers to have him to herself.

I submit to eating with the rest of the Vavasours in the evening. Meals in the ornate dining room are always ridiculously formal, and the Vavasours are rigidly polite to each other, except for Margaret who is rude to everyone. The Vavasours seem to think that this is a sign of her great character. ('Isn't she *marvellous*?') Margaret herself evidently believes that her great age, title or famous beauty, or possibly all three, entitle her to say whatever she wants, but I am appalled by the stream of spite that comes out of that still-beautiful face.

The extraordinary green eyes zoom in on the slightest blemish. Every meal is an ordeal as Margaret inspects her family critically, pointing out a spot on Philippa's chin, a rash on George's neck. Jasper is vilified if he has cut himself shaving, Fiona if she makes a crass mistake like wearing pearls instead of plain gold. Margaret spots instantly if you haven't washed your hair or ironed a T-shirt, and God help you if you put on an extra pound or two. Me, she despises. As she frequently informs me, I have no breeding. I think this means that I didn't go to public school. She loathes my short hair, deciding it is 'common', and my wardrobe disgusts her.

The only member of the family exempt from Margaret's special brand of invective is Felix, whom she adores uncritically. Felix, she claims, is the spitting image of his great-grandfather, the dashing Ralph Vavasour. He was a Spitfire pilot during the war, and I have heard many times already about his heroism. He was an extraordinarily handsome man. I have seen this for myself in the wedding photo that has pride of place on the piano in the yellow drawing room. Ralph and Margaret were married in 1949, and in spite of the fact that the photo is in black and white, Ralph seems to glow golden with heroic vigour, while Margaret clings to his arm looking like a fairy-tale princess, her arms full of orchids.

According to Margaret, Felix has the Vavasour golden hair, the Vavasour blue eyes, the perfect Vavasour features. My own contribution to his genetic make-up is passed over. Margaret doesn't care that Felix is quick to learn, or that his giggle is infectious. It doesn't matter to her that he is growing up to be open and loving and kind, that he loves dogs and books and trains and diggers. For her, it matters only that he looks the part of the next Lord Vavasour.

I wonder where it comes from, this need for physical perfection. It is as if anything less than beauty is revolting to her. She seems to have a morbid fear of the plain, or even the merely ordinary, which is why I am such an affront to her. I don't care about Margaret's opinion, though. I am waiting only to get stronger and to recover my memory, and then I will have to take Felix away from this place.

He needs to recognize me, too, I understand that, but I am certain that his memory of me is bound up with my memory of him: remembering will change everything. Then, I think, there will be no room in my head for Isabel, whose memories, real or invented, trouble me with an increasing urgency. I didn't mind so much when her life was happy, but her mood is darkening. The baby was lost, I know, although I cannot tell what happened in detail. The bone-deep sadness pressing against the back of my mind tells me everything I need to know.

There is something wrong with the house, I have decided. Something disquieting about the way the past seems to crowd

up behind me. I am constantly turning, expecting to see someone behind me, only to find myself staring at an empty doorway
or a smirking portrait. Walking along the long corridors, I have
the unpleasant sensation that someone is waiting, breathing,
behind each closed door.

At night, I lie awake, listening to sounds that might or
might not be soft footfalls. I find myself straining to listen at the
far edges of my hearing. Is that a whisper, or the breeze stirring
a curtain? The wind keening around the chimneys or a scream
echoing through the ages? It is as if the house is imprinted with
heat from bodies long gone, bodies that have left a warp in the
air, a tiny kink that throws every room very slightly out of kilter.

Isabel or no Isabel, this is not a good place for Felix to grow
up, of that I am sure. I am frustrated that I haven't remembered
more of my own life, but in the meantime, I push myself physically as far as I dare. There is nothing I can point to and say:
There is the danger, but a sense of foreboding is hunkered
down in the pit of my stomach and I can't shake the conviction
that I need to be able to take Felix by the hand and run if necessary.

Just when it seems that this June is going to be the dreariest on
record, the sun comes out. I never pull the curtains in my bedroom – I feel suffocated when they are closed – and I wake
early to a golden light pouring in through the window and a
swelling sense of possibility. Today, I decide, I am going to walk
as far as the stables. It is further than I have been before but it
will be worth the effort to be with horses again.

The dew is still deep when I let myself out of the house. Tiny diamond drops bead a cobweb that stretches between two bay trees. It trembles and glitters in the light, as fragile and exquisite as my memories of a life I should not be able to remember at all.

A life that I am not remembering any more, I tell myself sternly. It is several days since I recalled tumbling down the stairs and I am beginning to let myself believe that the whole episode, whatever it was, is over.

Outside, it is cooler than I thought, and I zip up my hoodie, pulling it closer around me as I take deep breaths of the clear, silvery air. It smells deliciously clean, of the new growth budding and unfurling all around me, green upon green. It feels good to be outside, away from the house with its sad, sly shadows and secretive sounds, where time seems to waver and voices trail off into a silence seething with words unsaid. I take a firmer grip of my stick and head for the stables.

I am almost there before I realize that nobody has told me the way.

The stables are large and well kept and I count four horses and an old pony in one, three hunters in the other. They are all subtly different from Blanche, but their blowy sighs, their huffs and whickers, are familiar. I greet them one by one, running my hand over their glossy necks, scratching under their forelocks and whispering foolishness in their twitchy ears as they dip their heads to find the treats in my palm. It is amazingly comforting to lean against their massive shoulders, to breathe in the smell of horse and leather, to feel the flex of powerful muscles as they shift their hooves in the straw, and my thoughts settle slowly, just as they always did when the stable was my first refuge.

When George finds me in there, my first instinct is to hide. I don't really want to talk to anyone and George is always a bit of an effort. He is nice enough, but a bit ponderous, and he makes heavy weather of conversations. I am surprised he hasn't married already. He is so traditional that I would have thought marriage to a nice girl who rode and liked Labradors would be the obvious next step, but now I come to think of it, George never mentions women. I wonder if he even notices Angie, sometimes. He is always faintly awkward with me. I can't decide if he is shy, if the whole situation around my accident and memory loss is too uncomfortable for him to deal with, or if he just disapproves of me.

But I don't want him to catch me skulking behind a horse, so I step out. 'Hello, George.'

'Kate!' George's blue eyes bulge in astonishment. 'What are you doing here?'

'I wanted to see the stables. I thought the horses might help me remember.' I reach up to pat the neck of the hunter which has been nibbling at my hoodie. 'It hasn't worked, has it? But it's lovely to see you again, anyway,' I tell it.

'But . . .' George is still goggling at me. 'But you're terrified of horses!'

'No, I'm not,' I start to protest, only to stop when I remember Philippa's incredulous face. *You? Riding?*

'You'd *never* have come in here before!'

I caress the hunter's handsome nose and feel his long lips questing hopefully for another treat. I can't imagine being frightened of him.

'Well, falling from the tower seems to have cured my phobia,' I say, ducking to step under the horse's head and out of the loose box. I'm not going to try to explain how much I remember of riding up on the moors. 'A bit drastic, but hey, if it works . . .'

George hates it when I mention my accident. Philippa is the only one who will acknowledge what happened. The rest of them would prefer to forget all about it. Ironic, really. They should try losing their memory and see how lost and lonely it makes them feel. They wouldn't be so keen to forget then.

Chapter Eighteen

Uncertain how to respond, George colours and his eyes bounce around the stable, avoiding mine, until I take pity on him and change the subject. 'Are you going for a ride?'

George goes positively pink with relief. 'I haven't got time today. I just stopped in to say hello to my girl here.' He runs an affectionate hand over the bay. 'This is Jinty.'

I can't help warming to him as the horse nuzzles his shoulder. It's hard to think badly of a man whose horse loves him. 'She's lovely,' I say with a smile.

George's flush deepens. 'Kate,' he begins, only to swing round as Angie's voice calls from the stable yard. 'George? Helloooo . . .'

A moment later, she appears in the stable. 'I thought I'd find you in here – oh!' Just for a second, her expression freezes at the sight of me, and then she smiles. 'Kate! Hello! Goodness, I never expected to see *you* in a stable.'

I'm getting a bit fed up of being told how much I dislike horses. I just can't imagine being scared of them.

'I thought I'd walk a bit further today, that's all.'

'You must be getting better if you've walked this far,' Angie says. 'Felix will be happy about that.' She sounds so delighted at the prospect that I decide I must have imagined her expression earlier. 'But you mustn't push yourself too far too soon, Kate. Felix is with Jo, by the way,' she adds with a little laugh. 'I haven't abandoned him!'

'I didn't think that you had,' I say, unable to keep the dryness from my voice. Sometimes Angie's devotion to Felix can be a bit cloying.

I glance between her and George. Whether I imagined her hesitation or not, it would be tactful to take myself out of the way. 'You were looking for George,' I prompt her.

'I just need a quick word.' She flashes me a grateful smile. 'The forestry contractors have been trying to track you down,' she tells him. 'They finally got hold of Lord Vavasour at the house, and I said I'd run down and pass on the message. They need a date for thinning the West Woods. When do you want them to start? If you're busy this morning I can ring them back,' she adds.

'You go on,' I say as George hesitates. 'I'm going to head back to the house now anyway.'

He frowns. 'I was going to offer you a lift. I've got my car here.'

My leg is aching and I'm wondering if I may have pushed myself too far already, so a lift would save me the walk back, but I find myself glancing at Angie. She doesn't say anything and she's still smiling brightly, but I'm sure she wants George to herself.

'I'll be fine,' I say. 'I'll leave you two to it.'

We've been heading out into the stable yard, and I pause in the doorway, blinking at the brightness after the dimness of the stable, just as Philippa rides in. Dismounting, she greets George and Angie in her usual brusque manner, and her eyebrows shoot up at the sight of me.

'Look who's here,' Angie says unnecessarily.

'It's amazing what falling off a tower can do for you,' I say before Philippa can exclaim at my fear of horses, and she grins.

'So it seems.'

'Perhaps Philippa could give Kate a lift back to the house?' Angie suggests.

She gets us all organized. I am to sit on a feed bin and rest my leg until Philippa is ready, while Angie and George head off to the estate office. 'You don't mind waiting, do you, Kate?'

I hate being so dependent on everyone, but what can I say? 'Of course not. If that's okay with Philippa?'

Philippa is unfastening the girth. 'Fine by me,' she says with a careless hunch of one shoulder.

'You know, I really can walk,' I say to her when Angie and George have gone and she has stabled her horse. 'You must have lots to do.' I'm not entirely sure what Philippa does, but she seems to spend a lot of time at the stables.

'Nothing that can't wait,' she grunts. 'I've had my orders from Angie, so I'd better do as I'm told.'

There is no mistaking the edge to her voice. 'I wouldn't have thought you took orders from anyone,' I say, carefully neutral. Philippa is the first Vavasour not to automatically describe Angie as 'marvellous'.

'Angie's done a great job of making herself indispensable,' Philippa says, digging around in her pockets for her car key. 'Beneath that helpful, super-super-nice exterior, Angie knows exactly what she's doing, if you ask me. And now we're all so used to Angie stepping in and sorting out any little problems that we've forgotten how to do anything ourselves. She's always down at the estate office. George might be estate manager in principle, but I reckon it's Angie who runs things down there.'

'I wondered if they might be . . .' I trail off suggestively. 'You know.'

'George and Angie?' Philippa gives a harsh bark of laughter. 'I don't think so!'

'Why not? I'd have thought they would have made a great couple.'

'I'm sure Angie would agree with you, but it's a very long way from the Lodge to the Hall.'

I wince at the dismissive note in Philippa's voice. I can't help thinking about Angie dressing up in her grandmother's shoes and pretending to be Lady Vavasour. *Thank you so much for coming.*

'Besides,' Philippa goes on, 'there's the little matter of George being in love with someone else.'

'*Really?*' It's news to me. I've never heard George mention another woman. I limp over to the Land Rover. 'Who?'

Philippa rolls her eyes as she opens the door for me. 'You, of course.'

'*Me?*' My jaw drops and I stare at her. 'No!'

'I thought you knew,' she says. 'You were always pretty good at picking up on signals.'

'It never crossed my mind!' I bite my lip. I wish I didn't know now. 'Why on earth would George be interested in me?' I ask when Philippa has helped me into the seat and jumped in herself. I'm a widow with a small son who doesn't belong in the country, and while I'm not plain, I'm not nearly as pretty as Angie, for instance.

Philippa doesn't pretend not to understand. She is bent over the steering wheel, poking the key into the lock. 'George was always jealous of Michael,' she says. 'Whatever Michael had, George wanted.'

I'm silent as she swings the Land Rover out of the stable yard and we go bowling up the avenue towards the Hall. I hope Philippa drives more cautiously on public roads. As it is, I have to hang onto the door and the engine is too loud for conversation, anyway. She squeals to a stop outside the gatehouse and yanks on the handbrake.

'Does Angie know?' I ask, and Philippa's mouth twists in a sardonic smile. She knows what I mean.

'I shouldn't be surprised,' she says. 'Angie knows all Askerby's secrets.'

*

I've walked too far. It is only when I drag myself up to my room that I realize how tired I am. Angie is right, I shouldn't try to push myself too hard too soon.

Shakily, I take off my boots and collapse onto the bed. I should really go and find Felix but I don't seem to be able to move. Exhaustion pins me to the mattress. I will just close my eyes for a moment.

My eyelids seem to clang shut, dislodging another memory from the impenetrable blankness in my brain. It spills free without warning, painfully vivid. I remember lying like this on a different bed in the great chamber, nailed down by misery. The loss of the babe felled me like a tree, and I, who had always been so restless, so quick, could now barely face the effort of opening my eyes.

There was a weight on my chest that made it hard to breathe, a pain in my belly, rawness around my heart. If it had not been for Judith I would never have got up at all. She dealt with everything. She brought me decoctions to help me sleep, and little dishes to tempt my appetite. She sat with me and bathed my face and brushed my hair. She held me and she told me to cry, but I dared not. If I let myself cry, I would let myself feel, and the pain would be too great to endure.

And she wrote to Edmund. She coaxed me as far as a chair by the window one day, but all I could do was sit, my hands limp in my lap. I was vacantly watching a fly beat frantically against the glass when I heard the click of the latch behind me. The effort of turning, of seeing who had come in, was too much, but something in the quality of the footsteps, firm on the wooden floor, did make me lift my head, and there was my husband, his blue eyes dark with sorrow.

'Isabel,' he said, crouching by my chair. 'Dearest wife.'

'Edmund.' I yearned for him, but guilt dragged at me, and I could not look at him straight. My mouth began to tremble. 'Edmund, I am so sorry. I am so, so sorry.'

'Hush now.' He plucked me up from the chair and carried me over to the window seat so that he could sit and cradle me on his lap like the child I had lost. 'Hush now, dear one.'

Now that I had started to cry, the tears came in torrents, and I shook with the great, wrenching sobs that tore from my throat as apology after apology tumbled from my lips.

'Isabel, it was not your fault. Judith told me it was an accident.'

'It *was* my fault,' I wept. 'I was running. I was thoughtless. Judith is right. I am too impetuous, too headstrong. Oh, Edmund, how I wish I had done as she advised! I am a bad, unruly wife. You should have chosen someone like Judith,' I told him, my eyes so swollen with tears I could scarcely see. 'Then you would not have had a moment's care.'

'Or a moment's joy,' Edmund said, twining his hand in my hair and kissing me softly. 'I do not want Judith,' he said. 'I want you.' His hand slid to cup my cheek, tilting it until I had no choice but to look up into his eyes. 'Only you, Isabel,' he said, and the warmth in his face smoothed like honey over the rawness inside me.

'Welcome back, Edmund.' Judith's quiet voice broke into

our absorption in each other. 'I am glad to see you. Shall I send for some wine?'

There was no telling whether she had heard what Edmund said, but still, there was a tiny, uncomfortable silence before Edmund lifted me to the cushions and got to his feet.

'Judith,' he said, and his voice was heartier than it would normally be as he went towards her with both hands outstretched. 'Judith, how can I thank you for the care you have given Isabel?'

She dipped a curtsey before taking his hands. 'You do not need to thank me, Edmund. Isabel is my friend. I care for her as for myself.'

'You are a good friend indeed,' Edmund said.

'Isabel will be well now that you are home.' She lowered her eyes. 'And it is time I thought about returning to Crabbersett, perhaps.'

'You cannot leave us!' I protested, shocked.

'You do not need me,' she said, 'and I fear some of my ways are not yours.'

'Not in any way that matters.' I hitched up my gown and went towards her. Edmund's return and the release of my tears had restored me to a sense of myself, and now the prospect of Judith leaving shocked me out of my lethargy. Only then did I realize just how much I had come to depend on her. 'I thought you would make your home with us, Judith. How would I have managed without you these past few weeks? Edmund, tell Judith that she must stay.'

There was a pause so tiny that afterwards I thought I must have imagined it, and then Edmund was smiling at Judith.

'No one will force you to do anything you do not want to do, Judith, but it would make Isabel happy if you would stay. You are welcome in my household for as long as you will.'

It seemed to me that his tone lacked a little warmth, so I seized Judith's hands between my own. 'Promise you won't go, Judith,' I begged her, and she smiled mistily and squeezed my fingers.

'Dear Isabel, of course I will stay,' she said. 'I will stay forever if that is what you want.'

'It is,' I said, grateful at having been able to persuade her so easily. 'That is exactly what I want.'

My hands are twisted in the covers as I lie on top of the bed. There is no use pretending any more that these memories are some weirdly vivid psychological phenomenon. Isabel is – was – real. Somehow her memories are lodged in my head, swamping out my own, and I can't get rid of them.

I am possessed.

I turn the idea around, inspecting it for flaws. It is illogical, completely irrational. I'd like to find a reason it can't be true, but there isn't one, or not that I can see. Oliver Raine may talk all he likes about transference and confabulation but I *know* these memories are real. They are inside me, part of me. The truth of them is seared into my mind.

What I don't know is what I am supposed to do about it.

What does Isabel want with me? What is it that she needs me to do?

Remember, remember.

I haven't remembered what she needs me to yet.

I am vaguely surprised at how easily I have accepted the notion of possession. Perhaps before I lost my memory I was the sort of person who believed in ghoulies and ghosties? I don't feel as though I was, but it's possible.

Oddly, the idea isn't as frightening as it should be. It's not as if she's making me *do* anything, I reason. My head is not spinning on my neck; I am not projectile vomiting or making weird googly eyes or talking in a sepulchral voice. Nobody need know that I remember things I shouldn't remember, that my memories belong to a woman who must have died over four hundred years ago.

What are you supposed to do when you're possessed? Exorcism is out; I have already decided that I can't tell anyone what's happening to me. If I try to explain about Isabel, they won't understand. They'll think I am making it up, that I'm losing it. I'm depressed, I'm stressed, I'm traumatized. I can hear all the explanations now. Or, worse, I'm unstable.

Say it: mad.

It would be so easy for the Vavasours to decide that I am not fit to look after Felix on my own. No, I must keep Isabel to myself.

So it's not frightening, but it is lonely, living with someone else in my head. For now I must keep my memories to myself, and carry on treading a precarious line between two identities, two realities.

You were supposed to die.

The memory of the press of malice, that voice flickering in my ear, that sense of hatred, makes me shudder. *That* is frightening. Which reality does it belong to? I am no longer sure. I cannot think of anyone who would want me dead – Edmund loved me, Judith was my dear friend – and the Vavasours might not approve of me, but they don't *hate* me . . . do they?

I wish Philippa hadn't told me how George feels about me. Now that I know, it is obvious, and his inarticulate devotion makes me very uncomfortable. I hope I never encouraged him. I feel awkward whenever I meet Angie, too. I am sure she cares for George more than she wants to admit. It must be horrible to see the one you love obsessed with someone else. I'd like to shake George and make him see Angie instead of me, but the last thing I want to do is acknowledge his feelings. I just have to hope that if I don't offer any encouragement, George will lose interest. When I've gone, it will be easier for everyone. Perhaps George will come to his senses then. In the meantime, all I can do is to keep building up my strength.

Mary is pleased with my progress. Once I can walk to the stables and back without collapsing, I extend my range. For now I am still confined to even surfaces, so I walk down the avenue, a little bit further every day: to a sweet chestnut, to a cattle grid, to a clump of cranesbill where the road curves.

Fiona likes to spend some time with Felix after breakfast, so

I go out once they are happily occupied. The summer mornings are fresh and the air smells rinsed, new. The grass grows thickly on either side of the road, bending under the weight of the dew. I walk as steadily as I can, and choose the next day's target before I turn back towards the house. Even on the softest of mornings the Hall crouches furtively against its backdrop of the moors, and the windows watch me, as if waiting for me to make a run for it. There is always a point when I wish I could just keep on walking, but Felix is there and I can't leave him alone. I have to go back, for now.

Now that I'm more mobile, there is no need for Angie to sleep at the Hall any longer. I feel bad when she moves back to the Lodge. I know how much she likes living at the Hall, but she only laughs when I stumble through an apology.

'Don't be silly! I've had a lovely time,' she says. 'I'm just glad you're better, Kate.'

It's not as if we don't see her still. She always seems to be at the Hall anyway, running up and down the stairs, popping into the kitchen with requests for Margaret, or bustling between the guides with a clipboard. Felix loves to see her. He squeals with laughter when she sweeps him up into a hug, and I try not to feel jealous of their closeness. I'm still not strong enough to pick him up.

I'm still not sure he'd let me.

After the stables, my next major goal is the car park and the Visitor Centre, which is set just off the avenue. The Visitor Centre is a stylish wooden building with a soaring roof and glass walls looking out towards the moors. The car park is screened from the avenue by discreet planting, and the first time I follow the road round and see the Visitor Centre, it feels like walking into a wall of sadness. I stop dead, one hand gripping my stick, the other pressed to my chest while I struggle to breathe through the waves of misery.

This is where they found the body. The memory, once so insubstantial, is clear now: the pile of bones, brown and stained; the excavator with its bucket lowered; the needle-fine rain. I can feel it still, and when I put my fingers to my face, my cheeks are wet. I am weeping.

You were obsessed. Philippa said that. She said I thought the bones belonged to an early Lady Vavasour. I insisted that the body so ignominiously dug up belonged to Isabel. I don't remember thinking that, but now that I am here, I can feel it. This is where Isabel was buried – but why here and not in the churchyard?

And as I stand there in the middle of the car park, oblivious to the cars around me, I am remembering once more.

Flying, soaring over Askerby and out to the moors. The breathless joy of being free. Edmund, Edmund should be here, I remember thinking that. *He should know how this feels.* But like a dream, the joy snaps in a blink into terror and I am falling, falling, ungainly and awkward. My skirts flopping over my face, suffocating me. I flail at them, but it is too late. I'm toppling and turning, over and under and round and round, and the terror blazes white around me and then there is nothing, a terrible blankness, that is all.

Chapter Nineteen

The beeping of a horn behind me jerks me into now, and I step aside, hastily knuckling the tears away. As I lift a hand in clumsy apology, the car slows and the driver's window slides down. It is Angie.

'You were miles away!' she tells me. 'You didn't hear the car even when I was right behind you.'

'Sorry. I was . . . thinking.' I summon a smile. 'Lucky you don't drive like Philippa!'

Angie laughs merrily. 'She's a terror on the roads, isn't she?' She looks round me. 'Where's Felix?'

I am instantly on the defence. I know Angie doesn't mean to, but she always makes me feel inadequate as a mother, as if I don't appreciate how lucky I am to have Felix. Perhaps, without a child of her own, that's how it seems to her.

'He's spending the morning with Fiona,' I say. However cool Fiona might be with me, there is no doubt that she adores her grandson and I know Felix loves her, too. He likes being with

her, and I think it's good for them to have a separate relationship. There is no reason for me to feel guilty at having some
time to myself. Still, I can hear a slight edge in my voice as I tell
Angie: 'He's fine.'

She doesn't seem to notice. 'Come in and have a coffee at
the Visitor Centre,' she says. 'It's ages since we sat down for a
proper chat.'

I hesitate. I'm repelled by the sadness of the place. I don't
think I want to go in. 'I should probably be getting back.'

'Oh, go on. You haven't made it to the Visitor Centre yet,
have you? You should have a look round. It might bring back
some memories.'

I can't tell her that is what I'm afraid of. On this sunny
morning, I have blundered into a dark and dangerous place,
and my head is jangling with alarm. I don't want to think about
the linen shroud wrapped over my face, about the cold earth
falling onto me, blocking out the sunlight forever. The air feels
jagged and precarious, and panic clogs my lungs, making my
breath choppy.

Angie's shrewd brown eyes rest on my face. 'You look as if
you could do with a sit-down, anyway,' she says.

I don't want to stay here, but Angie is right: I need a rest. So
I summon a smile and walk very carefully across to the Visitor
Centre while Angie parks her car neatly and gets out, retrieving
a box from the back seat and tucking it under her arm. 'Leaflets,' she says as she nods down at it.

The sick feeling that an unwary step could send me tumbling into terror only intensifies as I step into the centre. It has

been beautifully designed, and the feeling of light and space is striking after the secretive gloom of the Hall, but the smell of wet earth is almost suffocating.

Angie doesn't seem to notice. She leads me through the atrium, waving a cheery hello to the women behind the information desk, and past a gift shop stocking the usual array of flowery china, glossy cards, fridge magnets and tins of shortbread, to the cafe.

It should be inviting. It is bright and clean, with big windows looking out over the moors, and it hums with chatter and the chink of crockery.

Angie takes charge. 'You sit down,' she says. 'I'll get you a latte. What about a cake or a scone?' she adds temptingly.

There's no way I can force a cake past the horrifying sensation of earth crumbling in the back of my throat. 'Just coffee, please.'

'Oh, come on. They're really good here – and it's not like you need to watch your weight.' She wags a finger at me. 'You're still far too thin.'

'Really, coffee's fine.'

Breathing through my mouth to block out the smell of earth, I limp past the framed photos to find a table. There are stunning shots of the great hall, the long gallery, the parlour, the great chamber and the other rooms open to the public, interspersed with details of a carving or a tile, a flower from the walled garden and a face from a portrait that hangs in the great hall. My heart lurches into my throat when I read the label to one side: *Edmund, Lord Vavasour, d. 1697. Detail from portrait attributed to Sir Godfrey Kneller.*

But it's not Edmund. It doesn't look like Edmund and besides, Edmund could not possibly have lived until 1697. I'm not sure how I know this, but I do. This must be his son – no, his grandson. *My* grandson? I find myself thinking. I stare at the face intently, waiting for a spark of recognition, but there is nothing.

In spite of the smell, I am glad to rest my leg as I sink down at a table by one of the great windows. Through the glass I can see the moors rolling golden under the ever-changing sky. I can almost feel the wind that tatters the clouds and chases them to the horizon. It is a beautiful view.

That's why Edmund buried Isabel here, I realize. He laid her here where she could see the moors, where she wouldn't feel closed in, and I feel a sudden, fierce gladness at the idea. But what about the tomb he had promised, where we would hold hands for eternity?

And why does horror still seep through the walls of this bright, new building?

'Here we go. One latte.' I start as Angie sets a cup and saucer before me. 'Are you all right, Kate?' she asks, frowning in concern.

I muster a smile, although I suspect it's a ghastly one. 'I'm just tired, I think. You were right. I needed a rest.'

Angie settles opposite me. 'Are you sure that's all?' she asks, looking at me closely as she stirs her cappuccino. 'You're really pale.'

The temptation to talk to someone is overwhelming. Angie is my friend. I can tell her, surely, about what's happening to me? I moisten my lips.

'Kate?'

'It's just . . . do you smell anything funny in here?'

She sniffs the air. 'Coffee . . . cherry and almond scones . . . chocolate cake . . . What do you mean by "funny"?'

'Unpleasant.'

'I can't smell anything nasty. I hope there isn't a problem with the drains.'

'It doesn't smell like drains.'

'Then what?'

'It smells like a grave.'

'Oh, Kate.' Angie's face changes and she puts her cup down into its saucer. 'Oh, Kate,' she says sadly. 'Please, not again.'

I'm thrown by her reaction. 'What do you mean?'

She looks terribly worried. 'This is what happened before. They found a body when they dug the foundations here, and you were obsessed by it. You kept saying that it was someone called Isabel, or sometimes you said that it was Lady Vavasour, and that she should be buried in the churchyard. And sometimes you said that it was you.' She bites her lip. 'It was awful. You were in such a state. You kept wandering off to the moors. You'd just abandon Felix and leave him all on his own, or drift around the house as if you didn't even see anybody else. We were all at our wits' end.'

I swallow. 'I didn't realize it was that bad.'

'It was worst for Felix. It must have been terrifying for him, and he was so confused, poor little mite. Quite honestly, I'm not surprised he refused to recognize you when you first came home. You hadn't been rational for so long,' she says, and lets out a long sigh.

'The only silver lining to your fall was that you lost your memory,' she tells me. 'I know it's been hard for you, but we've all been praying that you don't remember everything. We were hoping that was the end of it, but if you start again about graves and ghosts and whatnot, I don't know what we'll do.'

I am twisting my cup between my hands, horrified to realize that I have been through all this before.

'It was a horrible, horrible time,' Angie says. 'Especially for Felix.'

'I'm sorry,' I say.

She hesitates. 'I know it wasn't your fault. You were having some kind of breakdown, I think, but please don't let it happen again, Kate. If you can feel yourself losing control, get help, but don't put Felix through that again. It's just not fair on him.'

I set my teeth. She has made her point. She cares far more for Felix than I do. I am a selfish mother who neglected her own child, while Angie was there to look after him. I don't like it, but who am I to say that she isn't right? She *was* there for Felix. She *has* kept him safe and happy. I should be grateful to her, not resentful. I make myself relax my jaw.

'I won't,' I say.

'So you're not getting any weird visions or hallucinating or anything like that?'

I can't tell her about Isabel now. Angie might be my friend, but she's not going to let Felix suffer again. She'll put him first. 'No,' I lie. 'Nothing like that. It's just the smell in here.'

'Perhaps the drugs you had affected your sense of smell?'

I cradle my coffee cup in my hands. 'I'm sure that's all it is.'

I glance around. Everyone else seems to be enjoying the bright room, laughing and chattering, oblivious to the stench of death and the dreadful drag of grief. Why can't anyone else feel it? I shiver in spite of the warmth of the cafe, and clutch my coffee cup tighter. I remind myself that I am alive, not buried in earth. I am as warm as I was when I lay with Edmund in the great bed, our limbs languidly tangled.

I remember pressing my lips to the warm, firm flesh of his shoulder. 'I want to do something for Judith,' I said. I don't remember when it was. It must have been some time after I lost the babe, because I was relaxed and contented. I stretched, sated, like a cat, against my husband.

'Give her a gown,' Edmund said sleepily.

'I have given her gowns,' I said. 'She deserves a greater gift than that.'

Wariness crept into Edmund's voice. 'What are you thinking of?'

'A husband.' I snuggled closer, delighted with my idea. 'I think we should find her a husband to comfort and delight her as you do me. Do you not have a neighbour in need of a wife? I do not want her to go too far.'

Edmund was silent for a moment. He had an arm around my bare shoulder and was toying absently with my hair. 'Judith does not come from a good family,' he said at last.

234

'She is related to me!'

'By marriage only,' he said. 'She is a connection of your uncle's wife, is she not?'

'I always think of her as my cousin,' I said a little sulkily. I did not like it when Edmund cast a damper on my good ideas. Sometimes he could be very careful.

'Thinking something does not make it so,' Edmund said. 'Your situation was very different from Judith's. You were an heiress. It was easy for you to snap me up.' He laughed as I pushed at him with the flats of my hands, but then sobered. 'It will not be so easy for Judith. Do not make promises you cannot keep.'

'But she is fair,' I protested. 'And she would be such a good wife. Think what a good housekeeper she is.'

'Men look for more than a fair face and an ability to dress meat,' Edmund said. 'I am sure Judith would be an excellent wife, but her birth counts against her, and I do not know anyone who would marry to disoblige his family and friends.'

I pouted. 'Well, perhaps we should let these gentlemen make up their own minds,' I said. I was sure that Judith's face and figure would be enough to tempt a man minded to wed. She could not look as high as a lord, but there must be members of the gentry who were not so proud. Of course, a first marriage must be carefully considered, but there had to be widowers who might marry to please themselves. 'Can we not invite some neighbours to dine so that at least Judith is seen to be accepted by us?'

'But who will keep my house if Judith weds?' Edmund teased, and I rolled on top of him, laughing as he tickled me.

'I will be a better housekeeper, I promise,' I said. 'I will miss Judith if she marries, but I just want her to be as happy as I am.'

Edmund's hand smoothed down my flank, and my skin warmed and tingled with pleasure at his touch. 'Are you sure Judith is capable of such happiness?' he asked thoughtfully, and I lifted my head in surprise.

'What do you mean?'

'She smiles, but she does not laugh as you do. She keeps her feelings locked away where no one can see them, while your every mood is writ large on your face.'

'That's just the way Judith is,' I said. 'She is quiet and sensible and modest. So has she always been.'

'Sometimes I wonder how well you really know her,' said Edmund, almost reluctantly.

I half smiled and shook my head, amazed that he could be so blind. 'I know her as well as I know myself, Edmund, and she deserves to be happy. I am sure there would be men who would be glad to have her to wife.'

And although Edmund was discouraging, I remained sure there would be someone for Judith. I said nothing at first, not wanting to disappoint her, but I made Edmund invite all his neighbours to a great feast. Of course, I made sure that they all knew that it was Judith who organized it all, and I was pleased when I saw how closely Sir Stephen Morley watched her. There was no mistaking the approval in his gaze, and I wanted to flounce over to Edmund and bid him watch how wrong he had been. Sir Stephen was a little stout, perhaps, but he had a kind smile and a nice little property that bordered Askerby. He was a widower with five children; it would be a good match for Judith.

But when I hinted at the prospect to Judith the next day, I was dismayed by her reaction. Her eyes filled with tears. 'If you want me to go, Isabel, why do you not just say so? I thought you wanted me to stay with you?'

'I do,' I said, alarmed. It was not like Judith to cry. 'I just thought you might like to have a home of your own. I just want you to be happy, Judith.'

'I *am* happy.' She dabbed at the edges of her eyes with her fingers. 'Askerby is such a fine house. I cannot imagine wanting to live anywhere else.'

'But . . . would you not like a husband of your own?'

'A fat widower with five children? Is that the best you think I can do?' I had never heard Judith sound so sharp before. Her words sliced at me like blades of summer grass: when you feel nothing at first and the sting comes later, when you realize you are bleeding.

'I am sorry,' I said stiffly. 'I was only trying to help.'

'I know what you were trying to do. You pity me and you think you will pick out a husband and toss him to me like one of your old gowns!'

'Judith, no!'

'I do not need any more of your charity, Isabel. It is enough that I owe you a roof over my head and food to eat.' And with that she slammed out of the chamber, Judith, who never slammed a door in her life, leaving me gaping after her.

'What should I do?' I asked Edmund that night.

'Leave well alone,' he said. 'Sometimes we don't want to be offered a chance. So it is with Judith, I think. As long as she is your poor relation, she can feel bitter in comfort. But give her the choice to wed and run a house of her own, and she cannot be resentful any more. It is easier to hate than to change.'

'Judith doesn't hate me!' I cried, distressed.

'Not you,' he amended, 'but her situation, yes, of course she hates that. What is there to love about being poor and dependent on another?'

I turned Edmund's words over in my mind. I hated the idea of Judith feeling bitter. She was always so sweet-tempered, so willing. And I realized I had been selfish to enjoy her company without thinking about what it might feel like for her. The next day I told her that I was sorry, although I did not say why.

'If Sir Stephen speaks to Edmund about you, Edmund will tell him that you are not minded to marry.'

'Thank you,' Judith said. She bit her lip. 'I am sorry if I seemed ungrateful. It is just that I . . . I am so happy here. I do not want to leave.'

There, I remember thinking, *Edmund was wrong. Of course Judith knows how to be happy.*

'Besides,' she said, 'you will need me now you are with child again.'

*

238

My vision clears, and I realize that Angie is still studying me with an anxious expression. 'Maybe you're pushing yourself too hard, Kate.'

As steadily as I can, I put down my cup and readjust to the present. 'I'm supposed to be walking a little further every day,' I tell her. 'My physio makes me set goals. Now I've done the Visitor Centre, I'm aiming for the Lodge, then the church, then the village.'

'Well, take it easy,' she says. 'At least if you get to the Lodge you can sit down with Babcia. Just be prepared for her to drift off in the middle of a conversation. She's getting very muddled now, poor thing.'

She's not the only one, I think, chewing my cheek.

Angie notices, of course. She reaches forward and lays her hand over mine. 'I'm your friend, Kate. You'd tell me if any-thing else was worrying you, wouldn't you?'

'Of course,' I say, but my eyes slide away from hers, out to the moors where I used to ride through the heather with Edmund. 'Of course I would.'

It is another week before I can walk as far as the Lodge, and I am looking forward to sitting down when I get there. Angie's grandmother, Dosia, is sprightly enough to open the door, and she smiles at the sight of me, although the dark filmy eyes are vague.

'I'm Kate,' I say. When I take her hand, it feels very fragile, tiny bird-like bones slipped into a bag of papery skin. 'Michael's wife.'

'Ah, Michael. Such a dear boy.' Her Polish accent is still unmistakable after more than seventy years. 'How is he?'

I hesitate. Why distress her unnecessarily? Perhaps if I remembered more of Michael myself, it would be harder, but as it is, it seems kinder simply to tell her that he is fine. 'He's sorry that he can't be here.'

Dosia leads me into the kitchen. 'I'm so sorry, my dear,' she says when she has filled the kettle with a trembling hand. 'What did you say your name was?'

'Kate. It doesn't matter if you don't remember me, Mrs Kaczka, really it doesn't.'

'Mrs Kaczka?' Her mouth turns down. 'That is very formal, I think. Please, call me Dosia. I am so old now, I am afraid I forget names.'

'I forget too,' I tell her. 'I had an accident. I don't remember anything about my life before.'

'Ah . . .' Dosia lets out a little sigh, and her eyes drift over my shoulder. 'Sometimes not remembering is a blessing, my dear. When you get to my age, there are many things you wish you could forget.'

She refuses my help in making the tea but she lets me carry the tray through to the sitting room. Like so many places at Askerby, this room is trapped in a different time, in this case the fifties. There is a maroon plastic suite with crocheted antimacassars. The gas fire is surrounded by shiny beige tiles, and the mantelpiece is crowded with knick-knacks and photographs in faded leather frames. It is dark in the shade of the woods, and even in the middle of a summer day Dosia has to switch on a lamp.

When she smiles, Dosia has a dimple exactly like Angie's, and old as she is, there is a warmth to her that makes me relax. I pour the tea and Dosia presses biscuits on me, lifting the plate with a shaky hand. I take two quickly so that she can put it down.

She tells me the story of how she came to Askerby. A bride at eighteen, she and her new husband Adam Kaczka escaped from Poland in 1938, soon after they were married. 'I was brought up on a country estate,' she says, a faraway expression in her faded dark eyes. 'Imagine what a shock London was to me, but we were grateful to be alive then. We all were.'

War seems very far from this quiet room under the moors where the clock ticks steadily. 'How did you get from London to Askerby?' I prompt her when she stops.

'Oh, that is another story! Adam was a pilot. He joined the RAF and flew Spitfires with Ralph.'

'Ralph Vavasour?'

Dosia nods, a reminiscent smile curving the corners of her mouth, and for a moment I glimpse the girl she must have been. 'Ralph and Adam, they were like twins. Both so handsome, both so brave.' She sighs and sets her cup shakily back in its saucer on the table beside her chair. 'They loved the war, you know. Some men are made for danger, and Adam and Ralph, ah, it was everything to them! The thrill of it, flying those planes, facing death every time they took off, the camaraderie . . . I don't think Adam, at least, ever wanted it to end,' she says wryly.

'It can't have been much fun for you, waiting for him to come home every night.'

'For me, no,' Dosia says. 'But for Adam and Ralph, they were living every day like it was their last. They were just boys,' she says sadly. 'After the war, it was hard for them. Nothing could live up to the excitement of flying into battle. Some people aren't made for a quiet, ordinary life.'

Chapter Twenty

I nibble at a biscuit and think of my parents, who apparently choose to live in desperate conditions in countries ravaged by war or famine or grinding poverty, who send their own child away rather than leave themselves. Perhaps they, too, fear the ordinary.

'But what about you?' I ask Dosia. 'What did you want?'

'In those days we didn't think about what we wanted. We thought about what we had to do to survive,' she says with gentle reproof. 'I had to leave my home, my family, my friends . . . no, quiet and ordinary had no fears for me.' The corners of her mouth lift in a little smile as she remembers.

'Were you in London during the Blitz?'

'For the first few weeks, but Ralph worried about me. He told Adam I could come to Askerby and I would be safe. He got leave and drove me up here. The Hall was requisitioned as a military hospital by then, but there was no one in the Lodge, he said.'

Her voice warms when she talks of Ralph. It was Ralph who worried about her, Ralph who made sure she was safe. I wonder what she really felt for him.

'And he left you here all on your own? Weren't you lonely?'

Dosia looks around the room as if remembering when she first saw it. 'I was happy to be here. There were no bombs falling on Askerby. I joined the Land Army. I did what I could. I was grateful.'

I am trying to imagine what it was like for her, a young woman far from home, left to manage on her own in this remote part of Yorkshire.

'Adam must have missed you,' I say, and she gives a crack of laughter.

'I don't think so. I think it suited Adam fine for me to be up here. I just cramped his style. I knew what they were doing – drinking and smoking and picking up girls. It was what they did when they weren't flying.' She shrugs tolerantly.

'Didn't you mind?'

'It was different then,' is all she says.

She lapses into silence, her mouth working, and I wonder if I have overtired her. I sit quietly for a while, but something about her story is pricking at me, a fingernail flicking at the edge of my mind. Have I heard it before? There is *something*, a memory trembling on the cusp.

'And after the war?' I ask.

'Ah, after the war, everything was different.' Dosia lifts her hands and lets them fall back into her lap. 'Adam and I had to learn to be married again. It was hard. Ralph got married, and his wife, well, she wanted him to spend time with her, not with his old friends.' Her voice has thinned. 'She didn't want us at the Lodge. Adam was too close, she thought. A bad influence on Ralph.'

That was Margaret, I think, but I don't want to interrupt her, not when the memory, whatever it is, seems so close.

'We had to leave Askerby and look for work,' Dosia goes on, lost in her own story. 'Adam didn't know how to do anything but fly. He grew up like Ralph, thinking he would inherit his father's estate. He never expected that he would have to work, and he didn't like being told what to do. He never lasted at a job. He'd lose his temper, or spend the afternoon drinking. I did whatever I could to earn enough to pay our rent, but it wasn't easy. Adam was a proud man and he turned bitter. Ralph tried to help us, but Adam hated having to be grateful.'

There! Grateful, it's something to do with being grateful . . . I almost remember why this story is familiar, but no, it is gone again. I bite back a sigh of frustration.

'How did you end up back at Askerby?'

Dosia's expression flickers strangely and she looks out of the window. 'I don't remember,' she says. She is lying, I am sure, but I have lied about my own memories, too.

'I have talked too much,' she says, and her voice thins. 'I am just a boring old woman, talking about the war. It is all so long ago.'

'It's fascinating.' I mean it, but she is plucking at the arms of her chair and I cast around for something that will divert her from whatever it is that is making her so anxious. 'Have you got any photographs from when you were young?'

Her face clears. 'Over there.' Her hand trembles as she points at an old-fashioned desk, and I struggle out of the chair to limp over and pick up a faded picture of a young girl with a round, smiling face, and carefully rolled hair. There is an appealing brightness and innocence to her, and I recognize the dimple that Angie has inherited.

'Is this you? You were so pretty!'

Dosia laughs at that and shakes her head. 'Oh, I was not so pretty,' she tells me, 'but prettier than I am now!'

I set the photo back in its place and pick up its neighbour. This one is in black and white, too. It is unmistakably Dosia again, wearing a full, flowery dress and a hat shaped like a petal. She is bending slightly, with her hands on the shoulders of a small boy, and smiling up at the camera. Beside her, a man with his hair slicked back in the style of the early fifties looks moodily at the camera.

'Is this your husband?'

That flicker again. 'Adam, yes.'

There is something odd about the little boy. At first I think that it is something to do with the picture or that the camera has shaken, but when I look more closely I see that his face is deformed, so skewed out of alignment that I cannot prevent a sharp intake of breath. His eyes are a strange downturned shape and set oddly in his face, but he is smiling widely.

'And is this your son?' I ask, my voice carefully neutral.

Dosia shrinks back into her chair. All at once she looks very frail and her eyes skitter around the room. 'That is Peter,' she whispers, in obvious distress. 'That poor boy. That poor, poor boy.'

I want to say that his disfigurement was not that bad, but clearly it was. I put the photo back and limp over to sit beside her. 'I'm so sorry,' I say. 'Is Peter still alive? Does he live with you and Angie?'

'Angie? Is she here?' She sounds fearful and her face is clouded with confusion. My heart cracks for her. I know what it is like to be lost in a world that doesn't make any sense.

'No, Angie's working,' I say calmly. 'She'll be back later.'

Dosia's mouth trembles. 'He was a good man,' she bursts out. 'He had a good heart.'

'Peter?'

'He deserved better.' Her rheumy eyes swim with tears and she puts her hand on my arm. It is as if a tiny bird has landed there, as fragile and as light. 'It's a secret,' she says, her voice quavering. 'You mustn't tell.'

I have no idea what the secret is, but I pat her hand reassuringly. 'I won't say anything,' I say.

'I don't want to leave.' She is leaning forward, her fingers scrabbling at my arm. 'Where would I go?'

'Nobody is going to make you go anywhere, Dosia,' I say, alarmed by her distress. 'You can stay here as long as you want, I promise.'

She sinks back into her chair. 'I won't tell,' she says. 'I won't say a word.'

*

I am still thinking about Peter Kaczka as I sit down to dinner that night. I wonder what it is like to grow up with a face that makes other people recoil. I had done it myself, I remember, ashamed. I couldn't help that small shock as my mind registered the abnormality. His features were so different that it was hard to process that he was just a little boy. The only thing I could recognize was his bright, happy smile.

'I see Kate is off with the fairies again.' Margaret's caustic voice scrapes through the air, and I jerk my attention back to the table. Margaret is sitting opposite me as usual, and I find myself comparing her still-beautiful face with Peter's grotesque one. *He had a good heart.* Dosia's words echo in my brain. The same cannot be said of Margaret. She and Peter are like some fable about beauty inside or out. In a fairy story, Margaret's inner ugliness would be exposed, and Peter's goodness would shine through, rewarding him with a handsome face to match his heart, but this is real life, and things don't happen the way they should. *He deserved better.*

'I'm sorry,' I say with a level look. 'I was thinking.'

'How are your walks going?' Jasper asks hurriedly before Margaret can frame a crushing retort.

'I'm getting further every day.' I pick up my knife and fork. We are having salmon tonight, with a herby cream sauce and new potatoes. There is something vaguely revolting about the pink flesh of the fish and I poke at it with my fork. 'I made it as far as the Lodge today. I met Dosia.'

Margaret's face twists with venom. 'She's still alive then?'

'Yes.' I refuse to let her needle me. 'She was telling me about the war and how she came to Askerby. It was fascinating.'

The air around the table tightens unmistakably, and although when I look up from my fish everyone is bent over their plates, I get the feeling that, inside, they are all frozen. 'What?' I ask, puzzled.

'Nothing.' Inevitably, it is Fiona who recovers first. 'Dosia is very old now. I've heard she's a bit gaga.'

'I wouldn't say that. She said that her husband was good friends with your father,' I add to Jasper and Joanna. I know it sounds like a challenge.

'Adam Kaczka, that old drunk,' Margaret sneers.

Joanna is pushing a potato around her plate. George looks uncomfortable. Philippa is concentrating on her salmon.

'They flew together during the war,' Jasper says. He sounds nervous, and his eyes flicker between his mother and his wife. 'The war brought all sorts of people together. I don't think they were friends, exactly.'

Margaret lifts her glass, and I see that her hand is shaking. 'I always said Ralph should get rid of both of them.'

Charming. I hope Angie never has to listen to the Vavasours talk about getting rid of her grandparents this way.

'Tomorrow I'm going to try to walk to the church,' I say. I don't want to listen to Margaret being vituperative about Angie any more. 'I could see it from the Lodge, so I don't think it will be that much further.'

'You'll be able to see Michael's grave.' Fiona sounds grateful for the change of subject.

'He's buried?' Why is this a surprise to me?

'No thanks to you.' As ever, Margaret is ready to attack. 'You would have it that Michael wanted to be cremated, but Vavasours have been buried here for generations.'

I frown. 'Surely Michael's wishes should have counted for more than tradition?'

'Yes, so you kept saying,' says Margaret.

I give up on the fish and put my knife and fork together. 'I obviously changed my mind.'

'I think you were too tired to fight it any more,' Philippa says unexpectedly. 'That, or you were being kind.'

'Kind?'

'Michael wasn't big on confrontation. He'd have hated to be the cause of a row, and you knew how much it meant to Ma and Pa.'

'I couldn't bear the thought of him not being here,' says Fiona stiffly. 'Jasper and I were very grateful when you agreed.'

I am glad to think that I am kind. My grandmother set great store by kindness. Unexpectedly, a picture jumps into my head: my grandmother, with her bright hedgehoggy eyes and her sturdy body like a bolster. I remember her pegging the washing out on the line, how the clothes would flap and snap in the wind. The memory jabs me like a finger poked under the ribs.

'What about Felix?' I ask. 'Does he understand that his father is dead?'

'He knows,' Fiona says. 'Whether he understands is a different matter. But we certainly talk about Michael with him. It's not a secret.'

So what *is* the secret? I wonder. What is it that makes the house seem as though it is leaning in, listening carefully for a word out of place? That freights the air with a nervous tension, as if the entire family is tiptoeing past a slumbering beast, braced for me to blunder into it?

Is it me? Am I the secret? Or is there something older at work here, something that seeps out of the wooden panelling and gathers in the corners of every room? Whatever it is, it makes the air dense and so heavy that it presses against my face and makes it hard to breathe sometimes. And it's not just here at the Hall. I think of Dosia cowering into her chair: *It's a secret. I won't tell.*

Outside, an unseasonable wind is picking up strength as it barrels down from the moors. It bullies the old windows and moans around the chimneys, seeking a crack in the old bricks, a way in. I tense, narrowing my eyes and angling my head to listen. Over the rattling and the whistling and the chink of cutlery on china, I am sure that I caught the end of a scream.

Askerby is a sturdy moorland village, with grey stone houses ribboning along the beck. It has a no-frills pub, popular with the walkers who head out over the moors, and is hanging onto a tiny post office cum general store. There is a pretentious spa hotel in secluded grounds on the outskirts of the village and the old vicarage has been turned into a chichi B&B.

The church of St Michael and All Angels stands on the edge of the village. Built of the same grey stone as the houses, its square tower is eerily familiar, and I pause with my hand on the lych gate, wondering if I remember it as Isabel or as Kate.

Somehow I don't think I am much of a churchgoer, but Isabel would have been many times.

I push Isabel out of my mind. I'm here to find Michael.

The sun is out today, but it's not that warm, and I am wearing a linen jacket over a T-shirt and jeans. I'm glad of the extra layer as I wander around the churchyard. A row of old yews blocks out the sunshine and the light is muted and vaguely oppressive. It is very quiet. The grass grows lushly over the graves. On either side of the path the headstones are ranged in neat rows, but some of the older ones are almost lost in the undergrowth, or hidden under the skirts of the overhanging trees.

I find Michael's grave easily. Its headstone is jarringly crisp against the weathered monuments around it, and stark in its simplicity: *Michael Vavasour. Dearly loved.*

I think about Michael reading to the baby in his arms, and I have to tip my head back to stop the tears. *Dearly loved.* I wish I remembered more of the ways I loved him, of how he loved me. I blink fiercely at the dense, dark yew that looms over the grave, and my mind stirs . . .

'Don't you want to invite your parents to the wedding?'

A pause. 'Your parents won't be there.'

'They'd have to come from Somalia. Yours would only need to get a train from Yorkshire. It's rather different.'

Michael's hand was moving rhythmically up and down my arm, his body warm. In the darkness I couldn't read his expression.

'Let's keep it just the two of us,' he said after a moment. 'It's

about the vows we make to each other. We don't need anyone
else there.'

'You know you're going to have to come to terms with your
family one day,' I said gently.

'Pot, meet kettle.'

'I have come to terms with my parents,' I insisted. 'I used to
resent them for always putting other children before me, but I
know now that's just the way they are. They're fired up about
injustice, and the unfairness of a world where so many people
have so little. They're doing what they can, and they couldn't
do that with a kid in tow. At least I had Gran. I used to feel
guilty about loving her so much more than I loved them, but
they didn't mind. They probably didn't even notice,' I added
after a moment.

'Come to terms with it, huh?'

I shifted restlessly. 'I'm trying. But you won't even try. You
never talk about your home or your family. If we're going to
get married, we should know everything about each other. I
think we should go to your parents for Christmas,' I decided.

How did I persuade him? I don't remember that. But I must
have done, because we drove up from London the day before
Christmas Eve. I didn't really have an image of Michael's parents in my head. Middle class, I thought, for sure, right wing
and conventional probably, and completely different from mine,
but I had no idea about Askerby. I just remember Michael driving up the avenue. I kept expecting an estate of executive
houses to appear, but the avenue curved and there was Askerby
Hall.

'Holy cow,' I said, gaping. 'Which bit do your parents live in?'

'All of it,' said Michael.

It wasn't a successful visit. Michael was tense and silent, while Margaret and his parents were appalled. They'd wanted him to marry someone with a headband and pearls who knew how things were done, not a girl with no sense of deference who had been brought up in the wilds of Africa and who looked them straight in the eye and refused to be intimidated.

I don't remember meeting Philippa or George or anyone else that time, although I suppose they must have been there. All I remember is driving out of the gate in silence. We didn't say a word until we had crossed the little bridge and then as if at a signal we both let out a breath.

'Thank God that's over!'

And then we looked at each other and laughed. God, yes, I remember how happy we were that we were leaving and that we were together.

Standing in front of Michael's grave, I press the heels of my hands to my eyes. I want to remember my husband, but each memory only reminds me of what I have lost, and of how much I still don't know.

Because if we hated Askerby so much, why had we come back? Why were Felix and I still here? And why had I jumped off the tower?

Chapter Twenty-one

Michael is buried next to his grandfather, Ralph, who has a grandiose marble slab marked with all his titles. I look down at it, remembering what Dosia told me about him: how brave and dashing and reckless he had been. *Some men are made for danger*. What had peace been like for Ralph? He married a great beauty, had children, lived out his days in his ancestral home. By any measure, his was a fortunate life, but I can't help wondering how often he hankered after the dangerous days and his friendship with Adam Kaczka.

I pull my jacket closer around me. It might be sunny in the village but there is something clammy about the shade in the churchyard. The air smells of damp earth and damp leaves, of sadness and regret.

I'm getting morbid. I pick my way between the graves. There are a lot of Vavasours, but the earliest headstones seem to date from the early nineteenth century. Did they have a clear-out of graves at the end of the eighteenth century or were people buried differently then? The branches of a horse chest-nut dip almost to the ground, and I duck underneath to brush the lichen from a headstone green with age. The carving is so worn now it is impossible to make out the name, but I think it might end in 'ur'. Vavasour? I trace the date with my finger: a one and a seven, what might be a six or an eight or a three . . . it's too late to be anybody I know, anyway.

Anybody I know? I straighten, cross with myself.

It has been a longer walk than I thought, and I lean on my stick more than I should as I head back to the front of the church and the porch. It is lined with yellowing notices about the flower-arranging rota, and lists of parish officials.

The heavy metal ring on the door squeaks as I twist it to step inside, where I'm met with that distinctively musty smell of English churches, a mixture of old hymn books and tattered kneelers and centuries of making-do and repair.

Inside the door is a table with black-and-white leaflets about the church, a pile of postcards that look as if the pictures were taken in the early sixties, and an honesty box. The display stand is more up to date. Photographs of a school in Uganda are pinned up; there seems to be some kind of link with the parish. I study the pictures of the smiling Ugandan children. They look very familiar, and an unexpected memory insinuates itself to the front of my brain: myself as a child in Africa, sitting on the steps of a school with children like these, watching mon-keys gibbering and squabbling in the trees.

Pleased to have another fragment of my past restored, I turn away and study the rest of the church. It feels very old. The silence seems congealed, faintly unpleasant. It muffles the thud of the rubber end of my stick as I make my way up the aisle of the nave and step into the chancel.

Past the choir stalls, in prime position on either side of the altar, are two tombs. On the right, a medieval knight and his lady recline side by side. Sir Piers and Lady Anne. I remember the engraving in the book, remember how once before I stood here with Edmund. I reach out and touch the clasped stone hands as I did then, and all at once the air seems to be humming warningly at me. I jerk around, obscurely certain that the church is watching me, tiptoeing closer to tap me on the shoulder. But of course, the walls are just where they are supposed to be.

This is ridiculous. My palms are damp, and I wipe the one that holds my stick on my jeans. My heart is trying to batter its way out of my chest. I stare at the altar as if challenging it to move.

Not there.

The words are in my head, but they seem to jangle in the silence, and I turn again to find myself staring at the tomb on the other side of the altar. Part of me wants to blunder back down the aisle in a panic, to burst out of the church into the sunlight and let the heavy wooden door slam to behind me, but another part is riveted on the painted effigy. The man lies alone, his hands pressed together in prayer. His doublet is blue, picked out in gold, and there is a magnificent ruff around his neck. His face is very sad.

My hand trembles as I reach out and run my finger over the

text carved on the edge of the tomb: *Hic iacet Edmund Vavasour*.

Edmund. The church spins sickeningly around me. 'Edmund,' I whisper. 'This cannot be.' My beloved cannot be dead. It cannot be that all that is left of him is this careworn effigy, not Edmund, whose blue eyes danced with humour, whose mouth seemed always about to curve into a smile.

Edmund, whose hands skimmed so skilfully over my body, who could make my senses sing with pleasure, make the world tilt and sigh when his lips curved against my skin.

Edmund, who lies here alone. The air aches with his absence and my vision blurs. The impossibility of him not being here hammers at me and my body curls up against the pain of it. My breath comes low and choppy, as if I am sucking in oxygen through a tangled bush of brambles.

He is gone. I will never be able to turn to him again, never rest my face against his throat, never feel his arms close warm and safe around me. I am adrift without him, flailing in darkness, not knowing which way is up. Without him nothing is safe, nothing is certain.

His tomb wavers through my tears. The knowledge that my husband is lying cold and lifeless and lonely there is lodged deep and bitter inside me like a stone. Why am I not there beside him? We should lie together, man and wife, as Edmund promised. We should be holding hands for eternity. That is what we wanted, not a lonely tomb and a forgotten grave overlooking the moor.

I press my hand over my mouth but I cannot hold back the

tears that course down my cheeks as I search the church with increasing desperation for some sign that Edmund does not lie completely alone. Perhaps the body under the Visitor Centre was not Isabel's. Perhaps she is nearby, not handfast, but close. But there is nothing: no wife, no child, no one. The closest I can find is a Ralph Vavasour who died in 1779.

'Edmund,' I whisper. 'Edmund, where are you?'

'Can I help you?'

So consumed am I by my grief and my longing for Edmund that I do not at first register that there is someone beside me, and the unexpected voice makes me gasp and stumble backwards. I find myself staring at a portly man with a dog collar and a luxuriant beard.

'Mrs Vavasour . . . Kate, if I may . . .' His voice is glutinously well modulated. It rolls around his mouth and comes out perfectly pitched for a sermon. 'I am so sorry to have given you a fright.'

'No, I'm sorry, . . .' Desperately, I try to wipe the tears from my cheeks. I feel horribly exposed, as if he has caught me with my knickers down, and I struggle to cloak myself in some composure. 'I'm sorry, I was just . . .'

'Thinking about your husband?'

'Yes,' I say, without looking at him. I concentrate on blotting a wet patch under my eye with my finger. 'Yes, I was.' It is the truth, but it is not what he means, I know that, and a wave of shame for the way I have let thoughts of Edmund swamp my grief for Michael crashes over me.

My cheeks burn with it, and he strokes his glossy white

beard in concern. 'There's no shame in grieving for the ones we love.'

Perhaps not, but what would he say if I told him I wasn't grieving for Michael but for a husband who died hundreds of years ago?

'You look very pale, Kate. Why don't you sit down for a moment?' He steers me over to a choir stall, and I sit obediently, too wretched to resist while he hurries off, muttering something about finding tissues in the vestry. Numb, I tip my head back against the carved wood and try not to think about Edmund, but my eyes fill once more.

The vicar comes back with a box of tissues. I take one to mop my face. 'I'm sorry,' I say. 'They may have told you that I've lost my memory. I'm afraid I don't remember your name.'

'Richard Rolland. We have met on many occasions at Askerby Hall when Lord and Lady Vavasour have been kind enough to invite me to dine,' he says, 'but of course I know you won't remember.' He caresses his beard, and I avert my eyes. There's something creepy about the way he strokes it, as if it were a cat. 'Lord and Lady Vavasour were very distressed by your terrible accident. I hope I was able to offer them some comfort. It has been a very difficult time for everybody.'

I can't imagine Fiona and Jasper being distressed, but I don't say so. 'The church feels very familiar,' I say after a moment, crumpling the damp tissue between my fingers. 'Did I come to services here?'

'Not that I am aware of,' he says, 'but you don't have to be a believer to find comfort here, my dear. All are welcome in the house of God.'

For a moment I am tempted to tell him how certain I am that the man lying in the tomb was my beloved husband, to confess that I am torn between two lives and grieving for two men. He is a priest. If Isabel is a spirit, he should know what to do.

But I don't feel as if I am possessed. I feel as if I am myself. I don't want to be prayed over or sprinkled with holy water or whatever it is he would do to exorcize her from my mind. I don't want to lose my memories of Edmund.

Besides, I'm not sure I trust the Reverend Rolland. Everything that comes out of his mouth sounds horribly rehearsed, as if he has been mentally flipping through a file of appropriate responses for priests. I don't like the eagerness in his voice when he talks about the Vavasours either. I can imagine him hurrying up to the Hall and talking to Jasper and Fiona, confiding his concern that I'm having some kind of a breakdown, offering to help with counselling.

He is watching me anxiously. 'You seem very sad.'

'I'm all right, really,' I say, looking around for something to do with the tissue, before putting it in the pocket of my jeans. 'It was just coming in here . . . it brought it all back to me.'

'Would you like to talk about it?' he offers solemnly. 'Even if you don't feel comfortable with prayer, it can help.'

'No.' My refusal comes out too brusque. 'I mean, thank you, but no.' Fumbling for my stick, I get back to my feet. I feel a fraud pretending to be grieving for Michael. I *did* grieve for him. I cried for him at his grave, but I didn't suffer the wrenching loss and loneliness that overwhelmed me at Edmund's tomb. I can't stand here and let Richard Rolland comfort me about Michael when I feel this way about Edmund. It is wrong.

I cast around for a way to change the subject, but everything comes back to Edmund. Limping to the tomb, I rest my hand on it as if it will connect me with him somehow. 'Do you know anything about Edmund Vavasour?' I ask Richard Rolland, and if my voice cracks as I say Edmund's name, I know he will put it down to my grief for Michael.

The vicar looks a little surprised by my question, but he follows gamely enough. 'Very little. He was a great benefactor of the church, I understand, but about the man himself?' He purses his lips, shakes his head. 'No, I'm afraid I don't.'

'He looks lonely here on his own,' I say. My fingers drift to the effigy's shoulder, as if I can will the stone to warm into life. 'Why wouldn't his wife be buried with him?' But even as I ask, the image of the excavator with its bucket lowered jangles in my mind, and I see the pitiful pile of bones in the mud.

'She may have remarried after his death, and be buried elsewhere.' Clearly the vicar is puzzled by my interest in the tomb, and just as clearly he is humouring me. 'Or she may have been buried under the floor here,' he suggests. 'The church interior was remodelled by a later Vavasour at the end of the eighteenth century, and these two tombs are the only survivals from an earlier period.'

He brightens as a thought occurs to him. 'But I believe an antiquarian did record the inscriptions on the grave slabs on the floor before it was replaced, and it's possible there may be some record of other family burials.'

'Really?' Absently, I wipe the last traces of tears from my face with the back of my wrist. 'Have you still got his notes in the church?'

'I'm afraid not. I only heard about them from my predecessor, who was very interested in the history of the Vavasours. He even wrote a pamphlet about them, but it was very dated and I'm not sure we have a copy of that either. I suspect all those kind of papers are at the Hall, but it must be many years since anyone has tackled them, so I've no idea if you'll be able to find anything useful.'

'I'll have a look.'

Richard Rolland insists on accompanying me back down the aisle to the porch.

'Can I ask you something, vicar?' I say, sliding a sideways look at his avuncular profile.

He beams. 'Please, call me Richard.'

'Richard,' I repeat obediently, 'do you know anything about the bones that were found when they began work on the new Visitor Centre?'

'Last year? Well, yes.' He glances at me in surprise. 'Do you remember that?'

'Sort of,' I say. 'I think I remember seeing them, anyway. Do you know what happened to them?'

Richard does more beard stroking while he thinks. 'As far as I know they're still in some laboratory. I think it was established that they were from a female but of considerable age, so there was no criminal investigation or anything. In fact, it's remarkable they survived at all. Presumably they're still doing various tests.'

'Why wouldn't she have been buried in a church?'

'I don't suppose we'll ever know that.'

'Could she have been murdered and her body hidden?'

'Well, it's possible,' Richard says. 'Or she might have committed suicide. Attitudes to suicides were very harsh in previous times,' he goes on, oblivious to the way every cell in my body is straining to shout: *No, no, no!* 'Certainly in the medieval and early modern period poor people who took their own lives were considered to be in league with the Devil and denied burial in consecrated ground.' He shakes his head. 'Tragic.'

He is keen to drive me back to the Hall – and no doubt to be invited in to lunch – but I am adamant that I will walk. 'I need to exercise my leg,' I tell him, even though it is aching already. I am desperate to be alone. I need to think.

I walk slowly back up the long avenue. The trees reach out for each other from either side, and the sunlight filters greenly through the leaves above my head. Last night's rain has left a sheen on the tarmac, and the grass is still beaded with silvery raindrops. It is a lush, tranquil scene. The horse chestnuts are heavy with candles and the great oaks stretch proudly above the grazing line. I wonder absently how old they are. That massive tree might have been an acorn, a tiny seedling perhaps, when Isabel and Edmund rode here. I look around me, eyes narrowed as I try to impose one scene over the other. There were more trees then, and the park was scrubbier, less manicured.

The house, though, that looks much the same, crouching behind the gatehouse wall, its towers poking up watchfully. As the avenue follows a graceful curve to end at the gatehouse, I find my eyes resting on the side of the tower. I can see the narrow window above the opening where filth from the garderobe emptied into the ditch below.

I wrinkle my nose at the memory of its stench. Still, it kept the smell away from the most important chambers. But the time I was stuck in there was very unpleasant.

I falter as the memory rolls into my head without warning.

It was a hot day, I remember that. The flies rose in a crowd from the hole when I opened the door, and I breathed through my mouth to avoid the worst of the smell. The garderobe was cramped, and although I could appreciate the convenience of it, I didn't care for the feeling of being shut in. It was not a place to linger, in any case. I had finished my business and straightened my skirts, but when I turned to open the door, it was jammed shut.

I rattled the latch, but it wouldn't lift. I tried it again and again, trying to close my mind to the stench and the flies and how small the garderobe was. There was barely room to turn around, and the heat was suffocating. I wanted to get out. I couldn't bear being closed in a small place. I beat on the door. 'Help!' I cried, feeling foolish, but better for the servants to snigger than to spend another moment in this tiny, foetid place. 'Help me!'

But no one could hear me. The garderobe was in the tower,

quiet and out of the way. The servants were busy about their business. I had told no one I was going there – why would I? I was quite alone, and I was trapped.

Chapter Twenty-two

The flies zoomed at me, their buzzing deafening, and the smell of the latrine wrapped itself around my face. I couldn't breathe, and a shameful panic began to build in me.

Frantically, I rattled at the lock again, and I began to scream, banging my fists against the door in such desperation that I did not hear Judith come running. 'Isabel! What is it?' she asked, the words tumbling breathlessly out of her as she pulled open the door so that I almost fell through it.

I slumped on the stone steps, gasping for air.

'Is it the babe?'

I shook my head and drew a shuddering breath. 'I couldn't open the door,' I said when I could speak. My heart was stuttering with relief at being out of the garderobe. 'The latch must be broken.'

Judith had closed the door on the smell, but now she lifted the latch experimentally. It clicked easily into place. 'It seems to work now.'

'I tell you, I couldn't open it!'

She frowned at my distress. 'It must have jammed. Perhaps the wood was swollen,' she suggested, although I could tell that she didn't believe it. No more did I. Wood does not swell and then shrink in a matter of moments.

'Come, let us go and walk in the garden,' she said. 'I know if I suggest that you sit still you will snap my head off, so we must do something to soothe your spirits, and I fear you are in no condition to go for a gallop on the moor, as I know you would wish.'

She was trying to humour me, I realized with a little shock. When had I turned so querulous? The babe was well advanced, but the need to be careful, to sit and walk carefully and to rein in my passions was hard indeed to bear. I was forbidden all immoderate exercise. I could not run or ride. Always I must be quiet and sedate. The moment I flung out a hand or raised my voice, Judith would lift her brows and look significantly at my belly. I did not want to lose another babe, she would remind me endlessly.

And it was true, I did not. I had vowed that this time I would not risk my child, so I submitted and muttered and was very bad-tempered. Judith made a syrup of tansy boiled up with sugar and insisted that I took a spoonful every day. Roasted apples with sugar would keep my body loose, she claimed, so I ate them dutifully every morning until I was sick of the taste of them.

I put a hand to my mouth, startled by how vividly I can

remember it. It is as if the appley, sour-sweet taste is still tingling on my palate.

I am remembering how I let Judith draw me outside to the garden, how I gulped at the sweetly scented air. Bees blundered through the lavender and the thyme, and the gravel crunched beneath our feet.

It was very peaceful but I couldn't stop thinking about the door to the garderobe, and how hard I had tried to open it. How had Judith been able to lift the latch so easily?

I felt a fool, but I had not been mistaken. The door would not open for me. I was sure of it. 'I don't understand how I could have been shut in,' I fretted, unable to concentrate on Judith's efforts to make conversation.

'Do not think of it,' she said, but the soothing note in her voice rasped on my nerves.

'How can I not think of it? I tell you, the door was locked!'

'Isabel,' she said wearily, 'there is no lock on that door.'

I put a hand to my head. I knew there was no lock, of course I did, but I was getting confused. 'It *felt* as if it was locked,' I amended. 'What if someone jammed the latch?'

'Who would do such a thing?'

'A prank, perhaps. They might not have realized that I was in there. They might have thought it was another servant.'

Even I could hear the desperation in my voice. Judith did not need to point out to me that the servants did not use the garderobe. They had a latrine in the yard beyond the kitchen.

Judith hesitated. She walked beside me, small and neat, her

eyes lowered, her hands folded at her waist. 'Isabel—' she began, and then stopped.

'What is it?'

'It is just . . . I fear for you sometimes,' she said in a burst of honesty. 'You are so violent in your passions, and you do not stop to think before you speak. *I* know that when you talk of pranks, they are just strange fancies common to a woman with child, but to anyone else you might seem . . .'

'Mad?'

She sighed. 'I just think you should be more careful about what you say, Isabel. Come,' she said, tucking a hand into the crook of my arm and putting on a smile. 'I am sure there is no need for concern, but let us say nothing to Edmund. We do not want to worry him, do we?'

The memories are rolling in like waves. They break in my head with shocking clarity, a relentless tide that surges up the blank beach of my memory only to be sucked back and return again and again, stronger and more detailed each time. Overwhelmed, I make it to my room and lean against the door, letting them wash over me. I lose my grip on the present and let them carry me back. I am lying on my bed in my room, but in my head I am still in the knot garden, the gravel knobbly beneath the thin soles of my slippers, Judith's hand reassuring in the crook of my arm. I can smell the herbs, hear the satisfied drone of the bees.

How could I have forgotten how fretful and uneasy I was then? I was happy to be pregnant again, but I found the enforced tranquillity very trying. I could not stride out the way I was used to any more, but lumbered along, burdened by the child growing inside me. I remember the dull ache in my back, and the way I had to cup my hands under my swollen belly for fear the weight of it would pull me over. The babe kicked and squirmed to be free.

'He is as restless as you,' Edmund said when he lay with his hand on my stomach and smiled to feel his son inside me.

And then, unbidden, another memory ripples below that one, and rises to the surface: Michael, his ear pressed to my belly. 'He's got hiccoughs!'

Remembering the look of awe and delight in those Vavasour blue eyes as he lifted his head to smile at me, pain rips through me so savagely that I catch my breath and fist a hand to my heart to stop it being wrenched right out of my chest. *Michael.* My eyes fill with tears again, just as they did then.

'I'm so happy,' I said, my fingers twined in his hair. I had never been loved like that before, never known the joy of loving back. We fitted together perfectly, and now we were having a child together. I could not believe that I could ever be happier than I was at that moment.

The two memories merge and blur. There is Edmund and there is Michael, two very different men, with the same dark blue eyes, the same ability to make me feel treasured, to make me shimmer with happiness, to send the blood dancing along my veins. They are different and they are the same – and they are both gone.

Loneliness crashes over me, and I lean back against the pillows and press my hands against my eyes. I have to stop crying. I have to be strong for my son. I have to do this on my own.

But I wasn't always happy. It's easy to forget that. After lunch with Felix and Angie, who continues to watch me with a worried expression that frays my nerves, I am tired but too consumed by memories to sit still. I wander around the house instead, mingling with the visitors, who crane their necks to admire the plasterwork ceiling that Edmund's father installed, and murmur respectfully about the age and beauty of the Hall. They point at the ornately carved and polished furniture, at the exquisite tapestries and the gleaming silver. They stand in the windows and ooh and aah at the gardens and wonder what it must be like to live in such a house, where the past seems to spangle with the dust motes in the sunlight slanting through the windows.

Or perhaps it is just me who feels as if those wavering fragments of the past might suddenly coalesce and take shape before my eyes? Perhaps the visitors don't keep turning their heads, expecting to see someone standing there in a kirtle and apron. Perhaps their ears aren't straining to hear a familiar shout or a laugh or the clatter of horses' hooves in the courtyard the way mine are.

I stand in the long gallery and feel the memories shimmering in the air around me. I remember how much I loved Edmund, yes, but as the birth approached, I was anxious and fearful, too. I longed for the baby to be born and to be free of the great weight that bore down on me, but I dreaded the birth itself. I couldn't stop thinking about my mother, of how she died pinioned in that dark room.

As my time drew near, Judith ordered the servants to prepare the chamber. They would close the shutters and build up the fire, even though it was high summer, and the heat was thick and soupy and the sweat made us change our smocks twice a day and sometimes more. I couldn't bear the thought of being shut up in the darkness. I would not be able to breathe.

'It is how it is done,' Judith said when I insisted I would not have it so. 'It is for your own good, Isabel – yours and the babe's. You have been so careful for so long now. You do not want to risk the child now.'

Of course I didn't, but as the babe kicked to be free, the thought of surrendering to that stifling room made it hard to breathe. I would go mad, like my mother. I was sure of it.

'You are not your mother.' Judith tried to soothe me, but the more she said it the more fearful I became. What if I *was* like my mother? According to my aunt, I was exactly like her, Judith herself had told me so. What if I too would end up screaming and wrestling with the bonds at my wrists?

My waters broke when I was walking with Judith in the long gallery, lumbering up and down like a great sow in farrow. 'It is time,' she said, and I dug my fingers into her arm as she helped me to my chamber.

'Judith,' I pleaded with her. 'Judith, do not let them close the shutters.'

'But Isabel—'

'Open the window. I want to be able to see the sky.'

'Isabel, you sleep with the shutters closed every night.'

'This is different.' I couldn't explain that at night I could get up if I wanted and open the shutters. I could go to the door and walk out. But giving birth, I would not be able to leave. I was trapped by the babe who would be born, by the women attending. Panic surged through me in waves. I did not want to die like my mother.

Remembering, I join a group of visitors who are shuffling into the great chamber. The curtains are partly drawn to keep the sun from damaging the fabrics, and it does not look so very different from the way it did that day. The guide recognizes me and smiles, but says nothing as I drift over to the bed. It is roped off now so that no one is tempted to finger the fabrics or test the softness of the mattress as Judith once did.

The midwife pursed her lips and muttered when I told her I wanted air. It was dangerous, she said, and would be a risk to the child. She told Judith that my husband should rule me, but Edmund knew me in a way they never could.

'She will do better if she can breathe,' he told Judith, who told the midwife, who eyed me askance and muttered some more. She would tell everyone that I had lost my reason, but I didn't care, not then. Grumbling, she bade one of the maids bring her fresh butter and smeared it over her hands while I was made to lie on the bed, a pillow under my head and another under my buttocks, my knees spread and my heels braced against a board.

I gritted my teeth and thought of my husband and the child that was to be born, and how, once we were free of each other,

I would be able to walk and ride again. I wanted the babe, yes, but I longed to feel myself again, too.

But first I had to endure the birth. The fire was stoked higher and the older women of the household gathered around, patting my shoulder comfortingly and doling out cheery advice that I barely heard. The midwife snapped out orders, sending maids running for sweet almond oil or mugwort boiled to a syrup with white wine and sugar, for a poached egg when she learnt I had not eaten, and some cinnamon water. I ate what I was told, swallowed when a spoon was put to my mouth, until the pains started in earnest and I lost track of the hours.

My body took me over, and did what it would with me, tugging and twisting and wrenching until I yelled: hoarse, guttural screams that must have made Edmund wince as he paced in his closet. But I had no thought for him then. I was an animal, bellowing and grunting and sweating, and my world narrowed until there was just me and the thing inside me that was desperate to get out.

When my son slithered into the world at last, I was too weary and battered to feel anything for him. The love and wonder I had hoped for and expected were lost in a grey fog of exhaustion. The midwife put him to my breast, but the effort of holding him was almost too much. I felt disconnected from the bloody, squalling creature on me and I was glad when the women took him away to clean him and swaddle him, while my belly was anointed with oil of St John's wort and I was swathed in linen. They lay warm cloths on my breasts and forbade me to sleep. Instead I was given a warm gruel, spicy and sweet, to drink, and some bread and butter to eat.

Edmund was allowed to come in then and inspect his son. He peered into the cradle and touched a finger to the baby's cheek. 'He is a fine boy,' he said to me. 'What say you to Christopher for a name? After my father?'

'As you wish.' I was still sore and too tired to care by then. Where was the elation I had been told I would feel?

'Christopher.' Edmund gazed proudly down at his son. 'It is too big a name for such a small child. We will call him Kit for short.' He turned to me. 'You have done well, wife.'

'I am glad you are pleased,' I said, but I sounded so disgruntled that Edmund came to sit on the edge of the bed.

'Was it very bad?' he asked, a smile lurking in his eyes.

I sighed. 'They tell me it is our lot as women to suffer. We have our grandmother Eve to thank for that.' Or so Judith had told me. As an unmarried woman she had no place in the birthing chamber, but she had tiptoed in to see me with the gruel the midwife had ordered. 'Still, it is over now. I will sleep for a week, I think.'

'As long as you are well,' Edmund said. He leant forward to kiss my mouth gently. 'I will leave you to rest, sweeting.'

He got to his feet, and I caught at his doublet as I realized that he was going to leave me alone, and the fears that had been banished by the pain of birthing bubbled back. 'Edmund, you won't let them bind me, will you? Whatever happens?'

'No, I won't let that happen.' Edmund laid a cool hand on

my forehead. 'Sleep now, my bird. No one will bind you, I promise.'

I slept at last and when I woke, Edmund had kept his word. The chamber was full of sunshine and my mind was clear. I was not tormented by visions or raving, and a deep thankfulness coursed through me.

Still, the lying-in was not a success. I remember that the ladies from thereabout came to sit with me, but they were scandalized by the cool chamber and the windows left open to let in the soft summer air. For thirty days I had to lie there, and I was quickly bored. The women all clucked at my restlessness and told me that I should enjoy the peace, but I couldn't wait to be up and outside again. I was soon sick of drinking wine and eating cakes and listening to my neighbours complain of their husbands and servants. Judith told me to shush when I grumbled. She said they would think me strange if I did not try harder to be like them, but I was wild to leave the chamber, wild to get out of this house and to run free once more.

Chapter Twenty-three

In the great chamber, I am aware of the people around me, of the murmur of lowered voices, but I am in the past too, remembering how glad I had been to be left alone one day. I can still feel the weight of the bedcovers as I pushed them back and got out of bed. Today the floorboards are smooth and polished with age, but then there was rush matting beneath my bare feet. I went over to the window and lifted my face to the sun.

Still wrapped in the memory of that day, I cross to the window as I did once before and look out over the knot garden to the park beyond and the moors where they rise in rolling, golden glory up to the sky. I remember wishing I could run out, out through the sweet summer grass and down to the river, where it paused at a bend under the trees, silvery and still, before it rippled onwards. I wonder if it is still there.

The water there was deep and so clear that you could see every pebble, and sometimes you would catch the flash of a trout turning, the glint of its scales in the sunlight. I leant at the window, just as I am doing now, and imagined sitting there with Edmund, just the two of us, letting the water cool my swollen feet.

A sound from the cradle made me look round. It wasn't a cry, more like a small animal snuffling, and suddenly curious, I went over. My son was looking up at me with dark, serious eyes, and I had the strangest sense of the world tipping. It was as if I had never seen him before, as if he had suddenly appeared in the cradle. He was real, I remember thinking. He was not something kicking inside me. He was a child.

My child.

'Oh.' It was all that I said. I wanted to say, 'Oh, it is *you*,' but that would have made no sense. It was like meeting an old friend unexpectedly, that same feeling of surprise and recognition.

I knew Judith would tell me to leave him in his cradle where he was well swaddled and safe, but I picked him up and held him against my shoulder. I could feel his whiffly breath on my neck, feel the warm weight of him. He was more solid than I expected, more real.

I still wanted to go out, but now, I realized, I wanted to take him with me. If Edmund and I sat by the river we would be incomplete without him. As he squirmed in his swaddling against me, I lifted him away from me a little so that I could look at him properly. His face was scrunched up, his mouth a tiny pucker, his eyes dark and intent as he stared back at me.

'Kit.' I tried out the name and it felt right in my mouth. 'Kit. My son.'

And then it came, the feeling I had been missing until then. It settled over me like a soft blanket, pouring like liquid sunlight along my veins.

Love.

I remember it so clearly that I turn and look again for the cradle, but it is long gone, replaced by a heavily carved chest. My throat is tight, the yearning for my son so intense that for a moment I cannot breathe with it.

'Are you all right, Mrs Vavasour?' the guide murmurs at my elbow. 'You're very white. Do you need to sit down?'

'No, I'm . . . I'm fine,' I manage. 'I'll just . . .' I make a vague gesture, unable to think about what it is I will just do, knowing only that I must find my child. 'I was just going,' I say feebly.

I feel her curious eyes on my back as I take a firmer grip of my stick and limp to the door. Outside the chamber, I look around vaguely. My mind is full of Kit. This is what I have been trying to remember for so long. I must find him, I must see that he is safe.

The stairs are full of tourists coming up from the great hall below. I turn and lift the scarlet rope that marks off the private areas of the house and replace it behind me, catching the surprised looks of a couple just reaching the top of the stairs. With my stick and my short hair and my faded jeans I probably don't look like the kind of person they expect to see living in a house like this. I smile at them, too delighted to have remembered my son at last to mind when they only look disapprovingly back at me. I am going to the nursery to find Kit.

I am halfway up the stairs when I realize that his face is beginning to blur in my mind again, and I clutch onto the wide banister in a panic. No! No, I cannot forget him again! But his features are fading inexorably and in my mind I see another baby, another boy. In my memory, I am holding him away from me so that I can inspect him, but he isn't swaddled as Kit had been. He is wearing a soft white Babygro and his tiny hands are flexing and grasping at something only he can see.

Michael's voice, thick with emotion. 'I think we should call him Felix and hope that one day he is as happy as we are.'

And me, nearly as weepy as Michael. 'Felix. I like that. Yes, let's call him that.'

My own voice rings in my head and the rush of relief at remembering Felix at last is so great that my knees actually buckle and I have to grope to sit down on the stairs, my stick clattering down beside me. I drop my head onto my knees, my eyes stinging with emotion while love for two different children churns and swirls through me. I can feel Isabel's yearning for Kit tugging at my head, but I won't give in. I hold firmly onto the image of Felix and now that they have started, the memories come barrelling in, taking my breath away.

Felix, his first gummy smile.

Felix smeared in puree, rubbing his hands through his hair.

Lifting Felix to smell his nappy, handing him to Michael: 'It's your turn.'

Felix shrieking with laughter as he tumbled between us in bed.

Felix, blue eyes dark and puzzled, watching a coffin being lowered into the ground.

I cover my face with my hands and weep. I am crying for all the times I have forgotten until now, for Michael and the happiness that turned out to be so short, for Felix, left all alone while I lay in hospital, and for Isabel, whose son is lost. It is not Kit playing with a toy train in the nursery, it is Felix. My son, not hers.

I haven't forgotten Kit, but for the first time I realize that I am not Isabel. She is in my head, but she is not me. Real or imaginary, I will have to decide what to do about her, but for now Felix comes first. I want to rush in and grab him to me, to hold him tight and breathe in his Felix smell, to cover him with kisses and promise never to go away again. But I know that would just frighten him. So I blow my nose and knuckle the tears from my cheeks. I retrieve my stick and haul myself to my feet, and I make myself walk quite slowly up the rest of the stairs and along to the nursery, where Fiona told me she and Felix would wait for me after walking the dogs.

Felix looks up when I go in. I wonder if he will see how I have changed, if he will somehow know that his mother is back, but the Vavasour eyes are wary still. Felix has looked up too many times in the hope of seeing me to let himself believe I am me again just yet.

'Hello,' I say, amazed at how normal my voice sounds.

Felix grabs a book and runs over to me. 'Story!'

'Felix!' Fiona chides. She is big on manners. 'What do you say?'

'Story, please.'

'I'll read you a story,' I agree, although my smile wobbles a little when I see that it is the book Michael bought for him again. 'Let's sit on the sofa.'

Felix scrambles up beside me on the nursery sofa and sits with his legs sticking straight out ahead of him. As always, he keeps a little distance between us. I long to hug him to me, but I make myself open the book instead and start to read.

As I read, Felix looks at the pictures and turns the pages for me. He knows the story off by heart and knows exactly when to reach out and turn the page over. He inches a little closer and I feel his warmth. Gradually, he lets himself lean against me until at last he is pressed into my side. I lift my arm, very casually, and put it around him so that he can shift into a more comfortable position. He doesn't stiffen or protest, and I feel my heart settle into a slow, steady beat. I cannot kiss him or cuddle him yet, but he is my son once more, and with my arm encircling his small, sturdy body, with his warm weight against me, for now that is enough.

The relief of having remembered Felix is enormous. The most important part of me has been restored and it feels like a blessing, but it's hard knowing that he distrusts me still. He has been hurt, my boy. He knows I am not complete, not yet. Does he sense the otherness in me? When he looks at me, does he see Isabel? I think about what Angie told me, about how terrified he was, and I ache with guilt. She is right: I cannot put him through that again.

The iPad is still lying on the table beside my bed. I haven't tried to get into it since my abortive attempts earlier. I sit on the window seat and hold its sleek shape on my lap, thinking, and then I open it up, sweep across the screen to unlock it and wait for the password prompt to appear. Kit was born on 7 August 1598. Without letting myself think about it, I type in: Kit07081598 and the screen miraculously clears.

So I have been through all this before.

I am looking at an array of icons against a blue background. According to the little red circle in the corner of one of them, I have over a thousand emails waiting for me, but when I open them up, most are junk. It seems as if I was taking my research into the family history seriously, as several messages are concerned with Vavasour genealogy. A couple of emails from friends in London of the 'we-must-try-to-meet-up-this-year' variety; I get the impression that we exchange a message once a year or so, and that they are unlikely to have missed me yet.

There's a message from my father, telling me the Vavasours have finally managed to get in touch with them and have told them that I am out of danger. They are relieved to hear it and hope that I am back on my feet soon. They are sorry that I have had such a bad time, losing my husband and then having such a terrible accident, but at least I am not struggling to survive in the desperate conditions they see every day. When things look bleak, I must never forget how very fortunate I am.

They won't be coming back to see me. There are too many other lives to save where they are. Michael's family will look after me, they know, but they are thinking of me and send their fondest love.

I close the message. Fondest love. I think about Felix. Unstoppered at last, my love for my son is welling up inside me, filling me up and making me whole again. There is nothing I would not do to keep him safe. I cannot imagine hearing that he was in hospital and not clawing my way to his side if necessary. If I had to choose between my son and a thousand strangers, I would not hesitate. Does that make me selfish? Is that why my parents cannot love me?

I almost wish I had left the password unguessed, the messages unread, but as I scan through the inbox there is one more email that catches my eye. *Greetings from LA*, it says in the subject line. It is from a Matt Chandler.

I open it up.

Kate,

We agreed it would be easier if we weren't in touch, didn't we? Has it been easier for you? If I'm honest, I haven't found it easy at all. I can't tell you how many times I've sat down to send you a message, just to say that I'm thinking of you and Felix and hoping that you're doing OK. It seemed to me that was what a friend would do, but friends also keep their promises, and I said that I wouldn't contact you.

But I'm breaking that promise now, because sometimes life sends you a message that you just can't ignore. The success of The Tower *took everyone by surprise – me most of all! – and now they're talking about a sequel which is to be called, after much deliberation,* The Return: Tower II *(hey, don't blame me, I had nothing to do with it). Anyway, I've been hired to write another script, same premise, same setting.*

I want to come back, Kate. I want to rent a cottage in Askerby for a few months – it'll be easier to write there, and I can't help thinking that it'll be easier to be in the same country as you, too. I want you to know that I don't expect anything to change. You made your decision and I will always respect that, but I hope that we can be friends as we were before. I miss being friends with you. I miss you.

If you really think it would make things too difficult for you, tell me, and I'll go write somewhere else, but I hope you won't. I'd like to see you again.

Your friend

Matt

I read the message through three times. I'm not sure how I feel: unsettled, uneasy, uncertain, guilty. Who is this Matt? Why has no one told me about him? *We agreed it would be easier . . . you made your decision*: it sounds as if I had a relationship with this stranger. I shift uncomfortably on the window seat. How could I have *done* that? I was bereft when Michael died, I have remembered that. It doesn't sound as if it took me long to recover. Am I the kind of woman who will drop her grief like a discarded jacket and move on to someone else?

But there is a tiny glow inside me too, a seeping warmth. Someone has missed me. Someone has been thinking of me. I have a friend.

'Matt Chandler?' Angie regards me with dismay when I ask her if the name means anything to her. 'Please tell me he hasn't been in touch with you!'

'I found an email from him,' I admit. 'I managed to get into my iPad.' I hope she won't ask how I remembered the password, and she doesn't. She is too busy looking worried.

'Oh, Lord, I was afraid this would happen!'

It is a warm evening and we are sitting in the Lodge garden. I asked Angie if she would like a drink at the pub but she said it was 'a bit rough'. She had a bottle in the fridge, she said. 'I'll come and pick you up to save you the walk.'

You can't see the moors from the garden, but I am just glad to be out of Askerby Hall. Too much has happened today. My head is churning with Felix and Kit, my memories overlapping with Isabel's. Now that I have remembered Felix, Isabel's power over me seems more of a threat, but what can I do? Felix is more important to me than ever and I don't dare let the Vavasours get the idea that there is anything wrong with me. I am longing to talk to someone about it, but I know how Angie will react. Ever since that day in the cafe, she has been watching me for signs of an imminent breakdown. She is my friend, she says, but when it comes to Isabel, I know I can't trust her.

Now it seems I have another friend. I want to know more about Matt before I reply to his message, though. Angie's reaction is hardly encouraging. She sits back in the garden chair and regards me with a little frown. She looks very pretty in a demure print dress, while I am in jeans and a T-shirt. There is no sun in the garden at this hour, and I'm glad of the jumper with the sleeves that come down over my hands. A tiny hole is unravelling near the hem and I try to poke the threads back through before it gets any bigger.

'Who is he?' I ask her.

She sighs. 'Last year we let the Hall out as a location for a low-budget film.'

'*The Tower*,' I say slowly, remembering what Philippa and George had told me.

'Yes. Between you and me, it was a load of tosh and a huge hassle, but it turned out to be an unexpected success and I have to admit it's brought a lot of new visitors here. We're even planning a new display in the Visitor Centre.' Angie seems to realize that she is getting off the point, because she picks up her wine. 'Well, anyway, Matt Chandler was the scriptwriter, and you used to spend a lot of time with him.'

'What are you saying, Angie? That I had an affair with him?'

She spreads her hands. 'You said you felt really guilty about sleeping with him. Michael hadn't been dead that long. I blame Matt,' Angie says firmly. 'He was all over Felix, always hanging around, making you laugh.'

Making me laugh. When was the last time I laughed? The

atmosphere in the Hall is deadening. There is no laughter, no teasing, no warmth.

There are only shadows. And secrets.

Chapter Twenty-four

'Why didn't anyone tell me about this?'

'Frankly, we were all glad that you'd forgotten him. Matt Chandler was bad for you, Kate,' Angie says. 'You weren't yourself even before they dug up those wretched bones. He changed everything, and you couldn't seem to see that it was all going to end badly. I mean, the guy's from Hollywood. He wasn't going to hang around in Askerby, was he? And of course he didn't. You were miserable when he left, and the next thing we knew, you were obsessing about bones, and we know what happened after that . . . If you ask me, he's to blame for everything. We all tried to warn you, but you wouldn't listen.'

All? I turn my glass on the arm of the chair. 'The Vavasours knew about him?'

'You didn't make a secret of it. I met you once when you were walking with him and Felix. You weren't touching, and it's not like you sprang apart when you saw me or anything, but you were all lit up.' Angie sounds baffled as she remembers.

'He was really casual, just said he would see you around and ruffled Felix's hair, but I saw the way you looked at him.'

I shift uneasily. I don't like the idea that everyone was watching me and tutting about what a fool I was making of myself.

'You were obsessed by him,' Angie tells me, shaking her head at the memory.

Obsessed. That word again. I was obsessed by the bones. Obsessed by Matt Chandler.

Obsessed or possessed?

'I don't know how you could have forgotten Michael so easily,' Angie is saying sadly. 'I know it had been two years, but Michael was *so* lovely and Matt Chandler . . . He wasn't even attractive!'

I'm not sure I agree. I googled him, of course, after I read his message, and I found a photo of him at some award ceremony. Matt Chandler doesn't look anything like Michael. In the picture he looks faintly crumpled. He's dark, with a big nose and glasses. Angie's right, he's no looker, but there's a humour and an intelligence in his face that is far more attractive than the classical Vavasour features. I can quite see how I might have been attracted to him, but Angie has made my relationship with him sound so sordid.

I chew my thumbnail uncertainly. Of course, I had gathered from his email that Matt was more than the friend he claimed to be, but still, I'm disappointed. I don't like the idea of being in sexual thrall to a man I had only just met, of being obsessed, of being a fool. The warmth that has been glowing in the pit of my stomach since reading his message is rapidly cooling to an ashy grey.

'In his email, he said he was just a friend,' I say.

'Well, he would say that, wouldn't he?'

'I just wish I remembered what it was all about.' I drink my wine, frustrated. I'm sick of learning about my life at second hand. It's like hearing about a stranger who has nothing to do with me. 'Maybe I needed a friend then.'

Angie looks hurt. 'You had me.'

'Okay, maybe I needed *another* friend,' I amend, managing a smile. 'Or maybe I was lonely.'

'How could you be lonely living at the Hall with the Vavasours?'

I can't believe she doesn't understand. 'A crowd is the loneliest place to be. It's not the same as being with somebody special. Don't you ever get lonely, Angie?'

'What do you mean?'

'Come on, you're young, you're pretty . . .'

'Oh.' Her face clears as she realizes what I am driving at. 'I don't believe in sleeping around,' she says primly.

Unlike me, apparently.

'I'm saving myself for the right man.'

'George?' I hear myself ask, and she looks away.

'Is it obvious?'

'No, it's just . . . you spend so much time together.' I am awkward. I have made a mistake. I know I only said it because I was irritated. 'I'm sorry, I shouldn't have said anything.'

'I did think at one time we might be about to get together,'

Angie says, her expression wistful. 'There was a point when I'm sure George was beginning to think of me as more than just his assistant. It was as if he suddenly *saw* me, you know? But then you came back with Michael,' she finishes flatly. She doesn't look at me. 'He's in love with you.'

'You know there's nothing in it, don't you, Angie?'

'Why not? George is handsome and kind and he loves Felix. And he belongs at Askerby. You could have everything.'

Everything Angie wants.

'I can't believe you would just throw all that away,' she says bitterly.

'There's nothing to throw away, Angie. George doesn't love me. I don't think he even knows me.' I think about what Philippa said: *Whatever Michael had, George wanted.* 'It's been such a strange time,' I say, 'but I'm getting stronger every day. As soon as I'm better I'll be leaving Askerby.'

I would have thought she'd be delighted to be left alone with George, but instead she looks appalled. 'Do Lord and Lady Vavasour know?'

'I don't know. Surely they don't expect me to stay forever?'

'But Felix is Lord Vavasour's heir!'

'He's also my son,' I say with a hint of impatience. 'And there's no way I'm leaving him here.'

'What will you do for money?'

'What everyone else does – work.'

Angie straightens. 'Has your memory come back?'

'Not about that, no, but so many other memories are coming back that I'm sure it will soon.'

'I didn't realize you were starting to remember so much,' she says slowly.

'It's still only bits – Michael, Felix, sometimes bits of my childhood. It's like trying to put together a great jigsaw puzzle.' I try to explain. 'When I remember something, I have to work out where it belongs. I can slot in a piece here, a piece there, but I can't join any of it up yet. And everything since Michael's death is pretty much a blank. I've got no memory of anything that happened last year or why I went up that tower.'

'Perhaps that's just as well,' Angie says. 'You were very depressed after Matt Chandler left. I wouldn't try to remember if I were you.'

'You think I jumped because of *Matt Chandler*?'

'That's why I really think you should ignore his email.'

I'm silent, trying to process what she's told me. Could I really have been so obsessed by the American that I tried to kill myself? Everything in me screams that it's not true. I had Felix. I wouldn't have left him, not unless I had a mental illness.

Not unless I was mad.

What if I *was* mad?

Angie thinks I was obsessed. It's a small step to madness from there.

'How will you work if you can't remember what you did before?' Angie has returned to the prospect of me leaving.

'There'll be something I can do. Work in a shop. Cleaning.' I have gathered from Jo, the cook at Askerby, that cooking is not one of my skills, so that's out. 'I could be a waitress.'

'They all sound very bad for your leg.'

The fact that this is true doesn't make it any less annoying. 'I don't know,' I say irritably. 'I'll get something.'

'I can't believe you're really thinking about leaving Askerby,' Angie says. 'After everything the Vavasours have done for you!'

'I'm grateful to them, of course, but I've got to have my own life. You work, Angie. I thought you of all people would understand.'

'I don't understand,' she says. 'I don't understand how you could even think about taking Felix away from everyone who loves him. He belongs here.' Her voice thickens. 'And I'd miss him so much,' she says, fishing out a tissue and blowing her nose.

'Well, I'm not going to do anything immediately,' I say awkwardly. 'I'll have to wait until I'm a bit stronger anyway, and I keep hoping more of my memory will come back. But I can't hang around forever, Angie. Felix will be going to nursery school in the village in September. I'll go mad if I don't have something to do.'

I wince at my choice of the word 'mad', but Angie doesn't seem to notice.

'Why don't you go back to working on the history exhibition for the Visitor Centre?' she says eagerly. 'I'm sure if you were busier, you'd be happier.' Perhaps she's hoping that will be enough to distract me from leaving. 'Now that you've got into your iPad, you must be able to get at all the notes you made before.'

I have found various notes, in fact, but it doesn't seem to me that I had got very far. I had drawn up a family tree but I couldn't go further back than Edmund Vavasour, who died in 1697. I couldn't link him to my Edmund. There was no mention of Isabel, no mention of Kit. If it wasn't for the vividness of my memories I would wonder if they were real or not.

I know what Oliver Raine would say.

'It looks as if I was thinking of a display about the war and the post-war period,' I tell Angie. 'That might be interesting to follow up. Your grandmother was telling me about being here during the war. She must have a lot of memories of the forties and fifties.'

Angie pulls a face. After her determination to get me thinking about the displays once more, her enthusiasm seems to have waned very quickly. 'I'm not sure how reliable they'd be. Babcia's getting so confused nowadays.'

I said hello to Dosia when I arrived and she seemed happy to see me, but Angie didn't suggest that she join us for a drink. She said something sharp to her grandmother in Polish – or perhaps it just sounded sharp because I didn't understand – and Dosia nodded, but I saw that her hands were trembling.

'She's happy watching television,' Angie said as she handed me a glass to take out into the garden and pulled the bottle of wine from the fridge, so I didn't insist, although I was sorry not to talk more to Dosia and there was still so much of her story that I wanted to know.

'How did your grandparents end up back at Askerby?' I ask Angie now. 'Dosia told me they moved around a bit after the war. Didn't they want to stay here?'

'Oh, I think so. My grandfather flew with Ralph Vavasour

in the RAF, and by all accounts they kept up their hard-living, hard-drinking lifestyle after the war too, but when Ralph married Lady Margaret, that all stopped.'

'She didn't want to play second fiddle to Ralph's friends, I'll bet,' I say, but Angie looks disapproving. She doesn't like it when I criticize the Vavasours.

'It wasn't appropriate for Lord Vavasour to be carrying on like that, not now that he was married. I think she hoped that, with Adam out of the way, her husband would settle down.'

'But they came back eventually.'

'Because Ralph felt sorry for them. It was hard for my grandfather to have no estate of his own. Before the war, in Poland, he was a count. He never expected to have to work for his living.'

I'm surprised. You'd think Dosia would have mentioned if she was a countess. 'Dosia didn't tell me that.'

'Didn't she? It's true,' Angie says. Her eyes rest on the vegetable patch, where the summer cabbages have gone to seed. 'We weren't always confined to a little lodge. If circumstances had been different, I could have grown up in a big house, too.' She smiles ruefully. 'Funny how things turn out. But my grandfather was bitter about his lost inheritance. He hated being dependent on his friends, and he took to drinking heavily – vodka, of course. I don't know what he and Babcia would have done if Ralph hadn't let them come back here.'

I sip my wine thoughtfully, thinking about Adam and Dosia and how hard it must have been for Adam to see Ralph enjoying the life that should have been his, too. 'It must have been hard for Dosia too,' I say, 'especially when she had a child.' I hesitate. 'I saw a photo of Peter.'

'He was born like that.' Angie is matter-of-fact. 'Nowadays it's called facial deformity syndrome but back then he was just a freak. I don't think he ever left the estate.'

'Was he your father?'

'God, no. I don't think he would have had much success with the ladies, do you?' Angie's voice is light, but the casual cruelty of it makes me grimace. She doesn't notice. She's telling me about her father, Marek, born about five years after Peter. 'Dad was always wild,' she says. 'He took after my grandfather but of course he didn't have a war as an outlet for his reckless- ness. Instead he got a local girl into trouble and they got married, as they still did in those days, but it wasn't a success. My mother took off when I was still a toddler.'

I start to say that I'm sorry, but Angie brushes my sympathy aside. 'It's not a big tragedy. I don't even remember her. Dad and I moved back into the Lodge, which was fine by me. After he was killed on his bike a few years later, my grandparents brought me up, and since my grandfather died, it's just been Babcia and me.'

It's a sad story. I wonder how much her mother's abandon- ment has affected Angie. Is that why she is so good at looking after everybody, and so reluctant to leave the only home she has ever known?

'Tough on you,' I say quietly, but Angie only shrugs.

'At least I got to grow up at Askerby. If my mother had taken me with her, who knows what dump I'd have ended up

in?' She shudders extravagantly. 'I can't believe you'd even consider doing the same to Felix,' she adds with a sidelong look.
'Here he's got a whole estate to run around in. You'll be lucky
if you can even afford a garden.'

I'm not going to rise to that one. 'What happened to Peter?'

'He died when I was eleven.'

'So you remember him?'

'Yes.' Something shifts in her eyes, something I can't identify
but that for some reason makes me look over my shoulder.
There is no one there. 'Yes, I do.'

Angie offers to drive me back when we've finished the bottle,
but it's still warm and I opt to walk. 'I'll make the most of the
long summer evenings while we've got them.'

The moors are glowing gold in the slanting sunshine as I
head back across the parkland. I wish I could be up there on a
horse, riding free – or is it Isabel who wishes that? I hardly
know any more.

The grass in the park is already yellowing and tired by the
middle of July, and everything looks as if it could do with a
good tidy. Even the cows who watch me pass with vacant eyes
seem faintly raggedy. The hedgerows are clogged with brambles
and dead seed heads, and the cow parsley that once stood tall
is now slumped and smothered by sticky willy. Every now and
then, I swipe at the tangled mess with my stick.

It is very quiet. During the day, the estate is thronging with
visitors, but they are all gone now and Askerby seems to be
catching its breath. I take my time, not eager to step back into

the cold embrace of the Hall which waits at the other side of the park. I can't shake the notion that it is watching me, its windows fixed on my dawdling approach, glass gleaming black and malicious in the evening light.

I am being fanciful. I stop and take another cross swipe at the thronging weeds with my stick, only to gasp in fright as a pheasant explodes out of the hedge in a whirr of wings. My heart is jumping wildly, and I pat my chest to calm it. It was just a bird, but my nerves are jangling, just as they did when the old woman stepped into my path as I rode back to the Hall one day.

Edmund was away in York, and I had slipped out before Judith could scold me about riding alone. My husband might tease me that I was a poor housekeeper, but he admitted that I was a fine farmer. I liked to ride with him to check on our fields and woods, to see that the hedges were well made and the sheep growing fat, that the corn grew high and the cows were calving as they should, but if he was absent with other duties, as he often was, I would go alone.

I knew every nook and cranny of Askerby: where the cattle huddled to shelter from the rain, the bend in the river where Edmund taught me to tickle for trout, every dip and curve of the track as it wound its way up onto the moors where the sheep summered. I was proud of my orchard where I grew apples and damsons and quinces, and in spring I planted the seeds in the vegetable garden with my own hands, loving the crumbly feel of the soil between my fingers. At harvest time, I held the golden grains in my hand and oversaw the sorting and weighing of corn. I inspected the coppices and bound the wounds of man and animal alike. As long as I was outside, I was fearless and happy.

But when my mare reared as the woman seemed to appear out of nowhere like a creature from the stories Judith read in the evenings, yes, there was a moment when I was afraid.

Chapter Twenty-five

Fear streaked through me, only to vanish as I recognized her. This was no magical creature. This was Eliza Wood, the lackwit. Bent and twisted as an old tree, she eked out a living on the outskirts of the village, and although folk avoided her where they could, most knew that she was harmless enough. She mumbled and muttered to herself as she hobbled past, and her pale, filmy eyes were vacant. I was cross with myself for being startled by such a creature.

'What do you want?' I said, more irritated with myself than with her. Blanche was snorting and sidling in agitation, and most of my attention was on trying to calm her.

Eliza shuffled closer and took hold of my saddle. 'For you,' she whispered, holding up a twist of paper, and I took it without thinking.

'What is this?'

She snorted and snuffled into her hand. 'Hemlock,' she said, her mouth stretched in a grotesquely toothless smile, and a sly look swam behind the pale eyes.

'Hemlock! What do I want with hemlock?' I demanded, more unnerved by her than I wanted to admit.

'Eliza asks no questions. She does as she is asked.'

'Well, I do not want it!'

'But you asked for it, mistress,' she whined. 'You sent for me and asked me to prepare a poison in secret, so here it is. You promised me a penny.'

'I? No!'

'A penny, you said.' Her eyes darted from side to side. 'A penny for poison.'

'But I . . .' I stared at her uneasily.

This was not the first time I had forgotten a conversation. Ever since getting stuck in the garderobe I had been aware of Judith gently reminding me about things I had done or said that I seemed to have wiped from my memory. Just little things. 'It matters not,' she always said. Since Kit's birth it had been happening more often, not every day or even every week, but often enough for me to have a queasy feeling in the pit of my belly.

'You are a mother now,' Judith said. 'You have much to think about. What does it matter if you forget that you told the maid to bring a caudle for the babe? She will take it away again. Do not worry about it.'

But I did worry about it. After Kit was born, I dutifully drank broth made with comfrey and knotgrass; I took spoonfuls of peony seeds powdered into a posset; it seemed for a while as if every dish was flavoured with verbena. I did every-thing that I was told and as a result I suffered no fevers, but ever since, my head had been fuzzy, and I felt sometimes as if I were suffocating. Edmund and Judith both told me this would pass, that now that my babe was born my body was adjusting itself once more and that all would be well, but the longer I felt blurry and tired, the more anxious I became.

And now this! Surely, *surely*, I could not have forgotten talking to Eliza? And about poison!

'I asked you for nothing,' I said, hating the tremor in my voice. 'Why would I need poison? Begone with you!'

Eliza wouldn't let go of my saddle. 'A penny,' she insisted. The slyness deepened into cunning. 'A penny for my trouble, that is what you promised.'

The emptiness in her eyes disturbed me, and my mare side-stepped, fretful. In the end I tossed the old woman a penny as the only way to get rid of her, and she caught it in one gnarled hand. 'Be off with you now,' I said firmly, and she vanished into the trees as silently as she had come.

I was left holding the twist of paper. I made to throw it away and then stopped. What if it was indeed poison? Very cautiously, I opened the paper and sniffed at the seeds inside. They had a musty, micey smell. I was no expert in the still room but it seemed like hemlock to me. Shuddering, I emptied the seeds onto the ground and tucked the paper into my sleeve.

Edgy and unsettled, I rode slowly home. 'I have never spoken to her before,' I said when I told Judith what had hap-pened. 'I haven't!'

'I believe you, Isabel,' she said soothingly. 'Of course you haven't.'

'Then why would she say that I had? Why give me poison?'

'They say she is a witch.' Judith lowered her voice and looked over her shoulder before leaning closer. 'I heard she mildewed John Aske's corn when he refused to give her a loaf. And that she bewitched Mary Kirk's boy Tom, who is like to die.'

'A witch? No!' I said. 'But she is very strange. I think she must be . . .' As always, I faltered at the word, but Judith had no such scruples.

'Mad? I daresay she is.' She shivered. 'I would have been sore afraid if I had met her. You should not go out alone, Isabel,' she chided me. 'Indeed you should not. You see what may happen.'

'She did not hurt me.' But the encounter had left me with a sense of disquiet. I pulled out the twist of paper. It still had some seeds clinging to it, and I did not want to leave it where some child might find it. 'What shall I do with this?'

'Burn it,' Judith advised, but it was a warm day and there was no fire yet burning in the grate. 'Give it to me,' she said. 'I will take it to the kitchen and burn it for you.'

Remembering that day, I stand by the hedgerow, my hand still fisted against my heart, and unease uncoils within me anew. The sun has slid behind the trees, and as if at a signal, the warmth is leached from the air. A shiver prickles its way down my spine. In the distance, the house is watching me and I could swear it is smirking.

*

305

The closer I get, the more my sense of foreboding deepens. It is as if the house is sending out invisible tendrils that are coiling around me, drawing me in so that it can devour me. Part of me wants to turn and run in panic, but I can't. My son is in there.

Where is my son? That isn't me, that's Isabel. She wants Kit, not Felix. Why is she searching for him so desperately? Something terrible is going to happen – *has* happened – and I need to try to stop it. But how can I change the past?

Find him. They're not words, more a sense of urgency, of desperation.

If I can find what happened to Kit, will Isabel leave me alone? I test the question in my mind. There's no answer – did I really think there would be? – just that press of need again. *Find him.*

I let myself in at the side door, into the boot room with its pervasive smell of dried dog food and damp leather. Battered waxed jackets hang on one side of the room above a line of green wellies and riding boots. Little curls of dried mud from their treads are scattered over the floor like fat worms, like slugs.

The Labradors come to greet me, blundering into each other. It is not enough for them to wag their tails. Their whole back halves swing from side to side in their pleasure at the sight of me. Molly searches around for a present and brings me an oven glove. It is impossible not to feel warmed by their welcome. There cannot be anything wrong with a house where these dogs live in such simple happiness.

Then I catch sight of Pippin watching from the doorway, her lip lifted in a snarl, and I swallow. I think the wrongness is in the house, but she thinks it is in me.

Perhaps she is right.

I settle the dogs down and push through them. Pippin backs away as I leave the boot room and head up the back stairs to the private quarters, but she follows me at a distance. I can hear the television in Margaret's sitting room. She'll be in there, her mouth twisting with contempt, but her eyes fixed on the screen. In spite of complaining endlessly about what rubbish it is, she loves to watch television and criticize everyone she sees.

Find him. Felix should be asleep, but I need to see him. I may not be able to find Isabel's son, but I can make sure that my own is safe. But an impulse I can't explain makes me turn away from the private wing when I get to the top of the stairs and head for the great chamber instead.

The rooms that are open to the public are still and shadowy. The visitors have gone, the lights are off. Here above the main staircase, the air is thick and seems to hum at a pitch just beyond hearing. I push open the door to the great chamber. In the fading light I can make out the huge bulk of the bed.

The chamber smells of old wood, old fabrics. Like the parlour, this is a dead room, set aside for tourists to gawp at, to marvel at how quaint and old and crooked the past is. How dark and inconvenient. How smelly and uncomfortable. But I don't remember it like that. I remember laughter, a zest for life. I remember warmth and certainty. I remember colour and smell and taste and texture. The darkness, the shadows, belong in the present; it is the past that is bright and clear.

When I lay in that bed, the curtains were richly embroidered and the sheets made of fine linen. They were packed in chests with lavender and rose petals, and the smell of summer hung in the air.

Edmund was still away and I was on my own. Perhaps it was just a day or two after I had met Eliza. I'm not sure now, but it was a hot night, I do remember that. I missed Edmund. The bed felt lopsided without him, and I tossed and turned, unable to settle. The feather bolster was lumpy, and I was sure I could feel the rough wool under-mattress through the linen sheet, and the feather bed beneath me.

I pushed the coverlet off, and then pulled it over me once more. I lay on one side, and then the other. I stretched across Edmund's side of the bed, and then wriggled back to my own. The head sheet covering the pillow was all twisted and tangled by then, and in exasperation, I thrust my hand under the pillow to turn it over and beat it into a more comfortable shape before I smoothed out the sheet.

My fingers brushed against something that crackled. Puzzled, I groped for it and drew it out. I could feel that it was a small twist of paper and my heart started to thud painfully. It was too dark to see, but I did not want to light a candle. I knew what it was.

It was the twist of hemlock.

The hemlock I had scattered on the ground, the paper I gave to Judith to burn. I remembered doing it.

How could it be in my bed? I sat bolt upright, turning the
paper in the dark. I was frightened. Had poor, mad Eliza crept
into the house to leave it for me? But why would she give me
poison? And how would she have known where I slept?

The memory of her sly, mad eyes made my scalp shrink and
my flesh prickle. I didn't like the idea of her in my house. What
if she found Kit? The thought of those hands reaching for him
made me throw back the covers and get out of bed, possessed
by an urgency I could not explain. I had to see him, right then.
In my nightgown, I felt my way to the door and up to the nursery, where the nurse, Meg, snored in the truckle bed. Kit lay
safely swaddled in his cradle. In the dim light, I could barely
make him out. I had to lay my hand on him to feel his chest lift
and fall, to know that he was breathing. I sighed with relief,
and tiptoed to the door.

Very carefully, so as not to wake him or Meg, I closed the
door and eased the latch into place. I turned to go back to my
chamber and nearly screamed as a figure loomed out of the
darkness.

'Isabel!' It was Judith's voice, and my knees buckled with
relief. 'What are you doing creeping around in the dark?' she
whispered.

I could have asked her the same, but my heart was still battering with shock. 'I had to see Kit.'

'I heard a noise,' she said. She came closer, and as my eyes
adjusted to the dark, I could see that it was her, small and neat
and tidy even in the middle of the night. 'I did not think to find
you here. What is the matter?'

'I think Eliza Wood may have been in the house,' I said urgently, and her hands flew to her mouth.

'The witch?'

I drew her away from Kit's chamber. 'I found something in my bed,' I said, my voice still lowered. 'Come and see.'

Judith hesitated. 'Isabel, do you feel quite well? You are behaving most strangely.'

'I will have to show you or you won't believe me,' I said impatiently. The house was so familiar to me by then that it was easy to find my way, Judith following reluctantly in my wake.

In my chamber I used the tinderbox to light a candle. A breeze through the open window sent the flame swooping and a grotesque shadow span around the room, over Judith's worried face. Sheltering it with my hand, I carried the candle over to the bed where the twist of paper lay where I had cast it aside in my panic to get to Kit.

'See!' I said, pointing.

Judith looked at the paper, and then at me. 'The paper?' she said carefully, and even though there were just the two of us in the chamber, I lowered my voice further.

'It is hemlock.'

Judith sucked in a gasp of fright. 'Hemlock? Dear God, Isabel, why do you have poison?'

'Eliza put it there.'

Even in the darkness I could see her horrified expression. 'What are you doing with the witch?'

'Nothing!' Something about her reaction felt wrong, and

apprehension tickled my spine. 'I told you, she surprised me while I was riding.'

'When was this?'

'The other day. You must remember,' I said, and the disquiet deepened when she just stared at me. 'I told you,' I insisted. 'She would give me the hemlock and I gave her a penny to let me go. Then I emptied the seeds but brought the paper home for safety and you said you would burn it. You did!' I said with rising desperation as she slowly shook her head.

I snatched up the paper. 'You burnt it,' I said.

'Then why is it here?' Judith asked gently.

'I . . . don't know.' I put a hand to my head, suddenly uncertain. I could not have imagined the whole incident, but why would Judith lie to me?

'Let me see.' Judith held out her hand, and I put the paper in it. As I had done before, had I not? She untwisted the paper and bent to sniff very cautiously, just as I had done on my horse. Aghast, she lifted her head. 'This is hemlock!'

'I told you it was.'

'Isabel . . . what are you planning?'

'I tell you, nothing!' I was near tears. I didn't understand what was happening. 'I found it under my pillow.'

'I thought Eliza gave it to you?'

'That was before. I got rid of the seeds and you burnt the paper.'

'And now it has appeared again in your bed?'

'I know how it sounds.' I shook my head, dull with confusion and fatigue. 'There must be an explanation.'

'There is,' Judith said firmly. 'You are tired and distracted by the baby.'

She put the paper down, took the candle from me and set it on the chest. Come, get back into bed,' she urged me, turning back the coverlets and patting the mattress, and for want of anything better to do, I climbed obediently between the sheets. 'You haven't been sleeping well, you told me that much, and you have been forgetful lately, it must be said. But that will all change as soon as Edmund comes home,' she said reassuringly. 'In the meantime, we must get rid of the hemlock. It is too dangerous to have lying around.' She picked up the paper with its deadly twist of seeds. 'Shall I take it for you?'

'No,' I said. 'I'll get rid of it myself.'

'Well, if you are sure.' Judith put the paper back on the chest. 'What if . . .' She started to turn away and then stopped. 'Oh, do not mind me.'

'What if what?'

'What if you forget tomorrow, and one of the servants finds it?'

'I will not forget. I want to see this thing in full light,' I said grimly. 'Put it in the box,' I told her. 'I will throw it away tomorrow.'

'Very well,' she said, obviously reluctant. She hesitated again. 'Do not say anything to Edmund, Isabel. You know how he worries for you. And I will say nothing either,' she promised. 'It will be our secret.'

Chapter Twenty-six

It is six weeks since I left hospital, and Oliver Raine comes out to assess me. I am nervous about seeing him. I remember his shrewd eyes and the easy way he manages silence, how when you talk to him you end up saying things you didn't mean to say at all.

He asks where I would like to talk. I'd really prefer to be outside, but the spell of fine weather has blown away on a gusty wind that is bossing the tops of the trees around and splattering rain against the windows. Besides, my leg still isn't up to walking far. I opt for the Vavasours' private sitting room instead.

Fiona has a gracious exchange with Oliver, makes sure that we have tea and biscuits and then leaves us to it. I perch uneasily on the edge of a chintz-covered armchair. I don't like this room. It is not that everything is immaculate or just so – there are old newspapers lying on the sofas and copies of *Country Life* and *Horse and Hound* open on the ottoman, the Persian carpet on the floor is faded and some of the chair covers are on the shabby side – but there is an oppressive tastefulness to everything that always makes me feel prickly and obscurely resentful. Apart from one or two books and some recent photographs, almost everything in the room has been inherited. The furniture is antique, the pictures painted by ancestors or collected by some long-dead Vavasour. Nothing so naff as a television mars the restrained beauty of the décor. I and my stick are the only jarring notes.

Oliver picks up on my discomfort. 'Are you sure you wouldn't like to talk somewhere else?'

'No, this is fine,' I say, and take my tea from the tray. No pottery mugs in here; tea is always served in porcelain cups and saucers.

I can see that Oliver doesn't believe me, but he sips his own tea and looks around him. 'This is a beautiful house,' he says mildly.

'Yes,' I say, but with just enough hesitation to make him raise his brows.

'You don't think so?'

'It's not that. It's so old . . . of course it's beautiful.' I twist my cup in its saucer, wondering how to explain the feeling I have that the house is crouched and secretive, that the past drags at the air and blurs the light. That I can only breathe properly when I am outside. My good leg starts to jiggle and I force it to stop. 'I just don't find it very welcoming,' I say feebly.

'The house or the Vavasours?'

'The house, mainly.' I don't find the Vavasours welcoming

either, but it doesn't seem tactful to say that to the man they are paying to help me. 'I don't know why I'm still here,' I say in frustration. 'I clearly don't belong. Surely I must have been able to earn my own living and support Felix by myself? But now I can't remember anything to do with work, so until I do remember or learn to do something new, and my leg is better, I feel trapped. Perhaps that's why I don't like the house very much.'

'Well, let's talk about what you've remembered,' Oliver says, leaning forward to put his cup and saucer on the ottoman. 'Lady Vavasour tells me that some of your memory has come back.'

'Yes. I remember Michael and Felix and coming here for a visit once. And I remember a few things from my childhood, but it's all so patchy,' I say with renewed frustration. 'Flashes of memory that I can't put together properly. Like, I remember Michael reading Felix a story, but not how we met, or how he died. And nothing about the time I've been living here, or what I was doing up that bloody tower.'

I don't tell him the other memories I have had, of meeting Eliza and finding the twist of hemlock beneath my pillow. It was just a piece of paper, but whenever I think of it, I feel cold and foreboding roils queasily in my belly.

'It's possible that you may never remember what happened immediately before your fall,' Oliver says. 'As for the other memories, there's no reason to think they won't come back eventually the way the others have done. Do you have any sense of what has triggered the memories you *have* had?'

I force my mind away from the twist of hemlock and think

back. 'Not really . . . sometimes it's because I'm doing something that I did before, like reading Felix a story, but often they just come. One moment my mind's blank, and the next the memory is there. It's weird. They're not coming in any order either. Seeing giraffes as a child, then walking along a beach with Michael, then my grandmother, then being in some bar in Madrid and laughing . . . Most of the time, they don't make sense at all.'

'We like to think of our lives as unrolling in a clear chronological order, but unfortunately our minds don't work like that,' Oliver says. 'Your brain has a filing system but it doesn't seem to be one that you recognize.'

He pauses. 'What about the dreams you were having in hospital?' he says casually, so casually that I know this is what he has been building up to all along. 'Have you had any more?'

My good leg starts to judder again. I want to lie, to laugh and say: *No, I've forgotten all about them*, but the words clog in my throat. Oliver waits patiently. There's something about his steady gaze that makes me certain he will know the truth. My eyes slide away from his.

'One or two,' I manage after too long.

'Are they the same as before?'

'They're different every time, but I'm the same. Isabel.'

Another pause. 'Why don't you want to talk about them, Kate?'

'Because I'm afraid you'll think I'm mad.' The words burst out of me before I'm aware of them, and I bite fiercely down on my lip, still unable to meet his gaze.

Oliver doesn't seem shocked. 'Mad is a strong word,' is all he says.

'Okay, insane . . . crazy . . . bonkers . . . take your pick!' My cheeks are burning with humiliation. Why have I started this? I don't want to talk about it, but now that I've begun, I know Oliver won't let it go.

'You don't strike me as irrational,' Oliver says mildly.

'It doesn't seem weird to you that I can remember a life lived over four hundred years ago? They're not dreams! I'm *remembering*!' My voice rises, rattling out of control, and I force myself to stop and breathe. 'They're memories,' I say more calmly. 'They come when I'm wide awake, and I know that they're not real, they *can't* be real, but at the same time, they *are*. I can't explain how vivid they are.' My hands have bunched into fists and I relax them, deliberately flexing my fingers. 'It's not like I think I'm regressing or going back in time or anything like that. I'm aware of where I am the whole time. It's just like remembering anything else.'

Oliver steeples his fingers, rests his mouth on them as he studies me. 'So the dreams . . . memories . . . aren't frightening in themselves?'

'No,' I say, but I don't sound that certain.

'But you're afraid, anyway?'

'I'm not *afraid*, exactly . . .'

'How do they make you feel?'

I think about Edmund, his mouth hot on my skin, the way he smiled when he drew me to him. I think about holding Kit, laughing with Judith. 'They're happy memories, most of them.

317

But sometimes I feel sad, remembering. I had a miscarriage . . .' My voice starts to crack at that, and I hurry on. 'But mostly I feel urgent . . . as if there's something I need to do, something about my son.' I stop, helpless to explain.

'About Felix?'

'About Kit.'

'Kit is the son you remember in this other life?'

'You see, I told you it sounds mad,' I say defensively.

'It certainly sounds disturbing,' says Oliver, 'but as you've said, you're aware that these are memories that don't seem to make sense.'

I moisten my lips. 'I don't want you to tell Fiona or Jasper about this!'

'I'm not going to do that. There's a little matter called patient confidentiality.'

'So they can't have me sectioned?'

Oliver stops steepling his fingers and leans forward, concerned. 'Kate, is that what you're afraid of?'

'I don't want to be shut up.' My voice wavers. Is it me who's afraid, or is it Isabel? 'I have to be here for Felix.'

'Why would the Vavasours want to section you?'

I think about Felix. Fiona and Jasper want him to grow up at Askerby. How far would they go to make sure that happens?

'If they knew I had these extra memories, they might think it made me an unfit mother.' Great, now I sound paranoid.

Oliver sits back. He looks almost stern. 'Kate, as far as I can tell, you're functioning perfectly normally for someone who's undergone a severe trauma. You're making a good physical recovery, and you're lucid and intelligent. You don't remember everything, but you've regained some key memories and you're working on rebuilding your relationship with your son. All those are very positive signs.'

'But what about the dreams?'

He tips his head from side to side thoughtfully. 'They're more interesting, I agree. Strictly speaking, they're not dreams, as you're awake. From what you've told me, they seem to be a kind of reverie.'

'Like a daydream?'

'If you like. Your mind has created an alternate world that seems perfectly coherent, a world that functions at a subconscious level. How are you getting on with Felix?'

I'm a bit thrown by the sudden question. 'It was . . . difficult . . . at first, but we're spending more time together now. He's starting school in the village in September. Fiona and Jasper aren't keen, but I think it's better for him to have a normal routine.'

'So you remembered him?'

'Not immediately, and not everything, but yes, I know he's my son.' I take a breath. 'But he doesn't recognize me.' I tell Oliver how Felix and I agreed to pretend at first. 'I don't know now if that was a mistake. He's happy to spend time with me, but he never calls me Mummy, never. I haven't managed to convince him yet that I really am the mother he remembers.'

Just as I haven't managed to convince Pippin. The little dog is fascinated by me, and follows me around, but if I try to get close, she bares her teeth at me. Nobody can understand it, but I do. She's frightened of me.

Or she's frightened of Isabel.

I don't tell Oliver this.

He has gone back to steepling his fingers. 'Perhaps your concern about your connection with Felix is finding expression somehow in imagining another mother and child,' he suggests. 'Your "memories" could be a way of distancing yourself from a problem that feels too painful or too difficult to deal with otherwise.'

I think about that. It does seem to make a kind of sense. I hope it makes sense, anyway. I wonder about that twist of hemlock and the dull fear that knocked in my throat.

'So if I'm dreaming about being afraid in the past, it's because I'm afraid of something now?'

'Possibly. What are you afraid of in your dreams?'

'Of going mad,' I say slowly.

Oliver doesn't say anything. He doesn't need to. It does make sense.

'And I've got this horrible sense that something's going to happen,' I go on, my fingers twisting in my lap. 'Something terrible, and I should be able to stop it, but I can't remember what it is. I'm scared, but I don't know why.'

'It's frightening facing the future when you've lost so much of the past,' Oliver says reassuringly. 'Feeling scared of what's to come is perfectly understandable, but you're doing well, Kate,' he tells me. 'You're a lot stronger and more resilient than you think you are. How are you physically?'

Without meaning to, I rub my leg. 'Better.' I'm not sorry to change the subject. 'I'm doing my exercises. Every day I try to walk a bit further. I'm allowed to walk on grass now. 'I'm not up to long hikes yet, but I'm getting there.'

'Don't overdo it.'

'That's what everyone says. I'm being careful.'

I *am* being careful, but I am frustrated with how long it is taking, too. The truth is, I am often bored. Angie thinks it's a good sign and that it means I'm feeling better, and I am certainly stronger. I don't have to rest quite so much and going up and down stairs isn't enough to exhaust me now. Slowly, my body is healing just as the doctors said it would, but until all my memories come back, there is a limit to what I can do. I am stuck, marking time. I can't go forward until I can look back and see what brought me to where I am now.

I spend a lot of time with Felix. Now that I can walk on grass, we have explored more of the estate. It was Felix who took me to the river during the hot spell. The dogs came with us, as they usually do, the Labradors and Molly bounding ahead, Pippin trailing suspiciously.

The becks tumble down off the moors and gather quickly into the River Aske. There is a special place where the water ripples silver over the rocks and bends into a pool with a matching curve of sandy beach. The river there is shaded by overhanging trees and hidden behind a tangle of undergrowth. Scenting the water, the Labradors crashed through it and down the riverbank, and Felix followed. I could hear shrieking and splashing while I was still trying to catch up. When I got closer,

I could see a faint path, but if you didn't know just where to pick your way through the trees and scramble down the bank, you would never know the pool was there at all.

At the top of the bank, I glanced back at Pippin. 'Are you coming?' I asked her, but she just dropped to her haunches and flattened her ears at me.

'Suit yourself,' I said, and ducked under a branch, and that's when I remembered that I knew this place. I had been there many times before.

It is different now – the trees are different, the pool is deeper, the riverbank is steeper – but I knew that I had once pulled off my stockings and hoisted up my skirts to paddle there, while Edmund lounged on the grass, his hands beneath his head and his shirt untied. I don't remember exactly when it was – before Kit was born, perhaps – but I do remember looking down at my toes and marvelling at how strange my feet seemed as the sunlight fractured and rocked over them with the movement of the water. I called to Edmund to look, but he said he was too hot and too lazy to move, so I waded out with my hands cupped full of the cool water and sprinkled it over him.

'Marry, my lady, you will pay for that!' Edmund's hand shot out and grabbed my ankle, tippling me over onto him. Quick as a cat, he rolled me beneath him so that I lay pressed into the grass, pinioned beneath his lean, hard body. 'How shall I punish you?' He pretended to growl, but though he narrowed his blue eyes fiercely, I could see how merrily they danced.

'I am not afraid of you,' I said pertly. 'You are too hot and too lazy to do anything, are you not?' The next moment I was squealing with laughter as he tickled me until I begged, gasping, for mercy.

'I am never too hot for you, Isabel,' he said.

The memory is a fierce ache inside me every time I come to the river. Edmund's hands deft at the laces of my bodice, his mouth hot on the curve of my neck. Our bodies shaking with laughter, then stilling as our eyes met, coming together in a sweet rhythm that left us both shaken again and clinging to each other while the tremors passed. Every moment of that hot afternoon is inscribed on my memory: the sweaty, sticky tangle of our limbs, the smell of the grass that was imprinted on my skin afterwards, the ragged sound of our breath, the tickle of a fly investigating my nose. I was so sated and content I could barely summon the energy to wave it away.

'Let that be a lesson to you, madam wife,' Edmund said, easing himself off me at last to flop onto his back beside me, and it ended as it had begun, with laughter.

Oliver tells the Vavasours that I am making good progress, and arranges to come back in another six weeks. I am grateful to him for not mentioning my 'reverie' to them, but I wonder if he would have been so sanguine if I had told him just how much Isabel dominates my thoughts.

Find my son. Remember.

I drift through the old rooms that I remember being new, searching for Kit, hoping for a sign that will tell me where he is and what Isabel wants me to do. The visitors talk in hushed voices as if the Hall is a church, oblivious to the way the air hums with the babble of voices long fallen silent. In the great chamber I stand by the bed, my head tipped to one side as I strain to catch an elusive memory above the shrill of danger. I wish I had some way of connecting directly with the past. There is still so much I don't remember, so much I need to remember.

The fabrics in the room are dull with age, their colours leached by centuries of sunlight and scrubbing. On the bed, the coverlet is made of a yellowing ivory silk embroidered with tiny flowers. The hangings are a heavy green and gilt, and the pelmet linking the four bedposts is fringed with gold tassels. They are old, but they are not what they were. The bed is the same, though. I recognize the carvings, and the feather bed still perches atop the mattress. Absently, I test its springiness by pressing on the cover, just as Judith did when she first came to Askerby. It is stiff and unyielding now, instead of the inviting luxuriousness that I remember.

Chapter Twenty-seven

'Excuse me.' Lost in my thoughts, I don't at first realize that the sharp voice is addressing me. '*Excuse* me,' comes again, more firmly, and I look round. A woman is glaring at me. She is lean and whippy, with short, grey hair and a thin face.

'Yes?' I say in surprise.

'Can't you read the notice?' She points at the little plaque on the end of the bed. 'It *says* "Do Not Touch".'

Over her shoulder I see the guide realize what is happening and get up from her seat to rescue me, but I lift a hand to say that I will deal with it myself.

'So it does,' I say. 'I'm sorry.'

'It's not me you should be apologizing to,' she says, unmollified. 'What do you think Lord and Lady Vavasour would think if they could see you poking at these lovely old fabrics? How long would they survive if everybody was like you and touched whatever they wanted? We should respect the past,' she tells me sternly.

Is she right? I wonder as I apologize meekly and slip out. Will the past crumble if we handle it? Maybe we need to take a proper hold of it, and look it straight in the face. If we always accord the past a respectful distance, how will we ever discover the truth of it?

I send Matt Chandler a brief email, explaining that I have had an accident and lost my memory. I tell him that if he comes to Askerby, I won't remember him, but I don't tell him not to come. This is partly wilfulness: not only did Angie tell me to ignore Matt's email, she told George, and George has told Fiona and Jasper, and all are adamant that I have nothing to do with Matt Chandler again.

'Why on earth did you tell George that I'd heard from Matt?' I ask Angie.

'I thought he should know,' she says, not even looking embarrassed.

'It's nothing to do with him!'

'The Vavasours have a right to know if you're thinking of taking Felix away.'

'For God's sake, it's just an email from a friend! It's not as if I'm planning to run away with him. I don't even remember him! And anyway,' I say, too cross to think about what I'm saying, 'I'd have thought you would be delighted at the idea of me seeing this Matt again. George would soon forget me if I'm not here.'

'George isn't like that. He's loyal.'

'I think you're wrong, anyway,' I say. 'He's never said

anything to me about how he feels – *if* he feels anything for me.'

'Because he's thoughtful. He's giving you time to get over Michael's death.'

'If I slept with Matt Chandler, I obviously got over that some time ago,' I say tartly, and Angie's expression stills.

'I think it would be better if you forgot about that.'

I am irritated by her insistence that everybody else knows what's best for me. I don't remember everything, no, but I am not a child. I can make my own decisions. So no, I won't do as they say and tell Matt not to come.

And I admit, it is curiosity as well as bolshiness that makes me respond to him. Askerby is a self-absorbed world. There are the visitors and social events, and the Vavasours put on a fine show of being involved in the community, but the truth is that they're not really interested in anything else that goes on in the world. As August passes, I feel increasingly trapped here (or is it Isabel who feels that?), and it's one of the reasons I insist on sending Felix to the village school over Fiona and Jasper's objections. They want him to go to a private school in York, and offer to pay the fees ('It's got a wonderful reputation') but it seems to me ridiculous to drive all that way every day just because they're afraid Felix will pick up a Yorkshire accent. They don't say this is why, but I know it is true, for all they dress it up in an insistence on the importance of education and opportunity.

'He's only four,' I remind them. 'We don't need to worry about his A-level results just yet. It's more important that he learns how to get on with other kids,' I say. 'It's too isolated here. We're incredibly lucky to have a school in the village at all. We should support it, and not just by handing out prizes at sports day.'

When September comes, I am vindicated by the fact that Felix loves school, and is eager to see his new friends every morning. Walking to and from school soon becomes part of our routine. I can do it easily now, and on the way back I often drop in at the Lodge to say hello to Dosia.

The rest of the day drags, if I am honest. There is no cooking to do, no housework, and once Felix is at school, I have all day to myself. I should be grateful I have life so easy, I know, but I can't ride and I can't remember enough to work, and I'm going slowly—

I catch up my thoughts before I think 'mad'. Is that all Isabel's memories are? A sign that I don't have enough to do? Is sitting around feeling frustrated at everything I still can't remember really the limit of my capabilities? No wonder I'm getting maudlin. I need a job, I decide, and I think again about what Angie said about getting back to work on the family history. It would be a start.

I haven't found much of interest in the books in the library, and after some prodding, Jasper produces an archive of family papers. When I open the first of the boxes, I am appalled. Letters, diaries, old photographs, bills, newspaper cuttings, scrapbooks and diaries are all jumbled in together.

My first task is to sort them into date order. Joanna volunteers to help me. I haven't spent much time with her before, but

I am glad of the company as much as anything else. I don't feel Isabel so strongly when there is someone else there, and Joanna keeps that terrible sense of urgency at bay.

Our hands are soon filthy. 'I can't believe nobody's done this before,' I say, gingerly opening a letter to a nineteenth-century Vavasour. It turned out to be a sad letter from an Elizabeth Vavasour, writing about the death of her son in Brazil, of all places. *You see that we are in the dark about everything, except the one terrible fact that we have lost our dear Horace.* My throat constricted with sadness when I read her brave attempts to find consolation in the fact that he had died in the arms of a friend so far from home. 'I thought a family like this would be interested in its own history.'

'We know our history,' Joanna says. 'It's in every guidebook.'

'Yes, and it sounds like it was written in the thirties,' I say, making a face. 'It's horribly dated.' I have read the guidebook that sells for £3.50 in the Visitor Centre in search of clues for Kit, but I have learnt nothing I don't already know. The history makes much of Edmund's grandfather, a merchant who made a fortune in York and turned his son into a gentleman, but Edmund himself only gets a mention for his tomb, and the story jumps briskly on to the eighteenth century, when the second son of one of the Lord Vavasours rediscovered his ancestor's mercantile spirit and travelled out to India with the East India Company. Other than that, the Vavasours are remarkable for their lack of ambition. Perhaps most of them were content to stay safely tucked away from stirring events at Askerby. Or perhaps they were afraid to leave.

'We've got the facts,' Joanna says with a shrug. 'They don't need to be changed. We know the truth.'

It's a Monday and the house is closed to visitors, so we're in the library. I pull a scrapbook out of the box and turn the pages carefully. On the verge of crumbling into dust, dried flowers are pressed between its pages, along with ticket stubs, poems painstakingly copied out and illustrated, and a mass of newspaper cuttings: births, marriages and deaths of people who must have meant something to the compiler of the scrapbook, book reviews, a letter about a swarm of bees attacking a man in Regent Street, a report on a lecture at the Royal Institution on *Dogs and the Problems Connected to Them*.

I wonder if the lecturer covered the problem of a dog that thinks you're a ghost. Pippin hasn't come into the library, but I know she will be lurking outside, waiting to see where I go next.

I close the scrapbook. Intriguing as it is, it is not the kind of material I am imagining for the new display. 'Don't you think it would be interesting to include more everyday stuff in the display? Not just the official history, but other people who have lived and worked on the estate over the years.'

Joanna looks wary. 'What do you mean?'

'Well, I was thinking about someone like Dosia,' I say. 'How many years has she been at the Lodge? She must have seen so many changes. And there must be other people in the village who can give a different perspective on the history.'

'I thought you were doing a family history?' Joanna says abruptly.

'I was thinking of it more like a history of Askerby,' I say. 'It's not just the Vavasours who live here.'

Joanna doesn't like the idea. She wants a neat family tree with portraits. She thinks that all people want to know is which Lord Vavasour died when, and the name of the son who succeeded him. The more she tries to discourage me from including 'ordinary' people, the more determined I am to make them part of the display.

The next day, when I have dropped Felix at school, I knock at the Lodge door and ask Dosia if she has any photographs.

'Of course, of course!' Some days Dosia tires easily and drifts off in the middle of a conversation, but she is sprightly today, and her face is bright with pleasure. She takes me over to the old writing desk by her chair. Her hands are unsteady and I help her unlock the desk and lower the table. The desk is stuffed with papers, leaflets, newspaper cuttings, bills, postcards and letters from the days when people still wrote them. I recognize the thin blue airmail paper that my parents used to use when they wrote to me, and another sliver of memory slides into place.

'There should be an envelope . . .' Dosia clicks her tongue as she hunts slowly through the desk, but eventually she gives a triumphant exclamation and I help her pull out a tatty brown envelope that is, indeed, stuffed with photographs when I peer inside.

We shake the contents onto the dining table that is pushed against the wall. Most of the pictures are in black and white, but there are some faded shots from the seventies and eighties where the colour has leached and blurred.

We look through the photos together. Dosia's fragile hands shake as she picks each one up and examines it, but she smiles as she remembers. She shows me her two sons dressed in cowboy costumes, pointing guns at the camera, and another picture with their hair slicked back, tidy in jumpers, ties, and long socks and shorts. They look glum, as if they're about to go to church.

'This is Marek.' She touches his face gently and sighs. 'And this is Peter.' Peter's strange features are unmistakable but I don't like to say so.

'Marek was Angie's father?'

'That's right.' We find some photos of Angie, with Marek as a toddler, a serious little girl, her blonde hair clipped back, and another when she was a teenager, and in every one she is startlingly neat.

I laugh as I point this out to Dosia, who studies her granddaughter. 'Yes,' she agrees after a moment. 'She was always careful.'

'It doesn't look as if she was a rebellious teenager,' I say. I wonder if I was?

Dosia shakes her head and her hand trembles as she lays down the photographs. 'Angie always knew what she wanted.'

I pick up the photo of the two boys again. Marek has an edgy look to him, as if at any moment he might explode into a roaring temper. He looks just like his father. In contrast, Peter is fair. Marek scowls at the camera; Peter always seems to be smiling. He must have got his sunny nature from Dosia. Adam looks morose in every photo except for the one we find at the bottom of the pile.

'Oh, this is a great picture!' I exclaim. It shows two young men in flying gear. Their arms are slung around each other's neck and they are wearing identical cocky grins. I recognize Ralph Vavasour at once, but have to do a double take for Adam, who is unrecognizable from the sullen man who looms in the photos with his wife and children.

'That was taken during the war,' Dosia says.

'Your husband was a very good-looking man.'

Her eyes are on the photo. 'Oh, yes, Ralph was always so handsome.' Her voice wavers reminiscently and a smile warms her face. 'Like a golden god.'

I hesitate. Is she more confused than she seems? But with his dark, brooding looks, there's no way Adam Kaczka could ever have been described as golden. She must have misheard me.

'I meant Adam,' I say carefully, pointing at him.

'Ah, Adam . . .' Dosia's smile fades. 'Yes, he was handsome, too.' There is a bleak undercurrent to the frail voice.

I think about golden, glittering Ralph Vavasour, driving Dosia up to Askerby. Why didn't Adam go with them? He was a good-looking man, but he was always going to be over-shadowed by Ralph's dazzling charm. It was Ralph who worried about Dosia, Ralph who wanted her to be safe at Askerby. And who could blame Dosia, finding herself alone in a strange country in the middle of a war, for being swept off her feet by a hero?

Did she and Ralph have an affair?

Dosia wasn't beautiful like Margaret, but there is a sweetness to her that Margaret clearly never had. The photos of her give a sense of warmth. She is always smiling, and the children lean trustingly into her. One lovely picture shows her in a garden, her hand shielding her eyes against the sun, smiling directly at the camera.

'I like this one. It's you, isn't it?'

'Yes, it was taken out in the garden right there.' Her gaze drifts to the window. 'Ralph brought a camera one day. He was so bossy! Stand here, stand there, look at the camera! He used to take lots of pictures but then he got married . . .' She falls silent, remembering. 'Well, it was a long time ago.'

Her expression is so unguarded and so sad that I feel as if I have stumbled on a private moment, and I make a show of looking through the other pictures. I find one of more children, sitting in the garden, drinking juice and squinting at the camera. It always seems to be sunny, but perhaps that was the only time the camera came out.

'Who is this?' I ask after a moment, pointing at a fair boy. He reminds me of Felix.

Dosia peers at it. 'Is it Michael?' she says. 'Such a dear boy.'

'I don't think it can be Michael,' I say. These children look as if they belong to a more distant time. 'Could it be Jasper?'

Something crosses her face, so fleeting that I can't catch it. 'Perhaps. Jasper and Joanna, they came to play sometimes, when Margaret wasn't there. Joanna and Marek were the same age.'

'Really? Which one is Joanna?'

When Dosia points, I don't recognize Joanna at all in the bright, laughing child hanging around Marek's neck. 'Joanna loved Marek,' Dosia says. 'I always wondered if the two of them might . . . well, Margaret wouldn't have had it, I know, but Joanna found someone even more unsuitable after Marek married Doreen.' She sighs. 'Two unhappy marriages instead of one happy unsuitable one. But who's to say Marek and Joanna would have been happy? You never can tell.'

'No.' I think of Margaret and Ralph's wedding photo, the fairy-tale glamour of it. 'No, you never can.'

I can't help it; my eyes keep going back to Peter. His face is strange, yes, but once your eye adjusts to the skewed features, it is his smile you see instead. Is it possible he is Ralph's son? He has fair hair, but then so did Dosia. It doesn't mean anything. Trying to appear casual, I sift through the photos again, wondering if there are any that might show the colour of his eyes.

I think I am being discreet, but Dosia is sharper than she seems. 'Peter . . . he had a good heart,' she says when I stop at one picture of him, 'but nobody looked past his face to see it.'

'And yet we're always told that appearances are deceiving,' I say. 'Why do we never believe it?'

Dosia looks down at Peter. 'We see what we want to see.'

If Ralph and Dosia had an affair, no wonder Adam took to drink, I think. It must have seemed as if Ralph had everything, even Adam's wife. But why then would he have come back to Askerby? Unless he didn't have a choice?

'Poor Peter,' Dosia says sadly. 'Poor boy. It wasn't fair. It wasn't his fault.'

I am longing to ask Dosia how it happened and how she felt, but if it is a secret, it is hers to tell or not tell. It would not be kind to trick it out of her, or take advantage of her age and confusion.

Besides, how would I know if she was telling the truth? How would *she* know what the truth is now? I remember what Oliver Raine told me: how even the most vivid of memories can turn out to be false. The photos Dosia is looking through seem incontrovertible: we can say that Marek was in the garden at the same time as Jasper and Joanna and Peter, but what brought them there, how they felt, what happened afterwards, all that is lost now, or so filtered through their individual memories and overwritten by later memories that the truth can never be told.

Dosia's photos are like my memories. They are just moments preserved in time, captured because somebody happened to have a camera. But why this moment and not the next, or the one before? They lie jumbled on the table just as the memories jumble in my head, apparently unconnected. I want to gather them up, find the missing pictures, and put them all in a clear order. Then, I think, I will be able to make sense of everything. But perhaps I want the impossible? Perhaps no one can ever make sense of it all? All we can do is work with what we have, and fill in the gaps as best we can. I will never remember absolutely everything of my life, I realize. If I did, my head would simply explode. So I will have to carry on picking my way between the memories that belong to me, and those that seem to belong to Isabel.

'Dosia, may I take some of these photos to copy?' I ask, remembering my task. 'I will take great care and bring them back. I'd like to include some in an exhibition so that people can see what life at Askerby was like after the war. This one, for instance,' I say, pulling out a photo of children on bicycles in front of the Hall. 'Or this one.' It is one of Peter when he was the gamekeeper, a job that kept him out of the way of gasps and pointing fingers.

'You want to put up a photo of Peter?' There is an odd note in Dosia's voice.

'He belonged to Askerby, too.'

Dosia looks out of the window, to the place where Ralph Vavasour once made her stand to have her photo taken. 'Yes, you're right, he did.'

Chapter Twenty-eight

I think about Dosia and Ralph as I walk back up the avenue. I am sure that I am right about them having an affair. It explains the unacknowledged tension between the Hall and the Lodge, and that feeling I have that behind the polished facade presented to the public lies something out of true.

Did Margaret know? Is that why she is so bitter? She talks about Ralph all the time, but she wouldn't be the first woman to turn her husband into a saint after he has died, to sweep all the hurt and humiliation under the carpet and pretend that her marriage was everything she had wanted it to be.

We know our history. Wasn't that what Joanna said? But the Vavasours only know what they want to know. For them, all that matters is the Hall and that it is safely passed from father to son. For the Vavasours, it's not about feelings, it's about show. They're not interested in the unmarried daughter pasting snippets from the outside world they will never experience into a scrapbook or a heartbroken mother writing news of a son's death.

Or a man in love with his best friend's wife.

Did Adam know? Was it betrayal that wiped that blazing grin from his face, not the anticlimax of peace? I wonder what it was like for Dosia when Peter was born, and whether his terrible disfigurement had seemed like a punishment for adultery. *It wasn't fair. It wasn't his fault.* Did she feel guilty, or did she love him all the more because of whose son he was?

I imagine her playing with him, the way I used to play with Kit.

No, wait . . . My steps slow. That's wrong. I should be thinking about playing with *Felix*. But I can't help it, it is Kit I remember.

My Kit. I used to play with him in the nursery while Meg looked on jealously. She would much rather I stuck to my business of being the lady of the house, so that she could keep Kit all to herself, and we had an unspoken rivalry for his attention. He was such a dear child, plump and gurgly and giggly, with Edmund's blue eyes. I loved to be there when Meg unswaddled him to wash him and change his soiled clouts. He had little rolls of fat around his wrists, and at his neck, and when I blew kisses on his stomach he would squeal with laughter and kick his legs in delight. He liked me to carry him around the nursery making clip-clop noises and jolting him as if we were trotting.

'Look how he loves to ride, Meg!' I would cry gaily. 'Your

pappa will buy you a pony and we will take you up onto the moors with us, sweeting.'

Meg would shake her head and tut and tuck in the corners of her mouth disapprovingly, but many times I saw her tickle him and give him a kiss when she thought no one was looking. I think she loved Kit nearly as much as I did.

Kit. My son. I ache for him and for Edmund with a savage, bone-deep need, and my steps falter as loneliness and longing sweep over me like a great, rolling wave and I actually stagger under the force of it. The tears are burning in my throat. I have to stop and press the back of my hand against my mouth while I struggle free of Isabel's grief and yearning and remind myself that I am Kate, that my son is playing happily at school in the village. I know where he is, that he is safe.

The temptation to head back to the school, to burst into his classroom and hold him tight, is so strong that I am on the point of turning before I remember that Felix would push me away. As far as he is concerned, I am still a stranger masquerading as his mother. It probably wouldn't go down very well with the teachers either. They can't have parents interrupting classes to grab their children and reassure themselves that they are alive. I can just imagine the phone call to Fiona: *Felix's mother seems a little overwrought.*

I cannot hold him yet, but at least I can be with him and know that he is safe. It is Isabel who is searching so desperately for her son. She needs to know what happened to him. I will have to look harder in the archive. He was Edmund's son. If he survived infancy and grew to adulthood, he would have been Lord Vavasour.

I strain for a memory of Kit as a boy, or grown up, but all I have are images of him as a baby, grabbing at my cap with his fat little hands, bumping his head against mine as he learns how to kiss. A slow dread is stealing through me, trickling icily in my gut. What if Kit never grew up? There were so many ways a child could die then: the pox, a fever, a fall.

No, it cannot be! Not Kit, not my son.

I struggle to disentangle my thoughts from Isabel's. I must think clearly. There must be something somewhere in the records about him. There *must* be.

I won't let myself consider that there will be nothing to find because Isabel and Kit never existed. I don't want to believe that, out of everything I could have remembered, all I retained was a memory of Edmund's tomb and that I have created a whole world around it.

It is easier to believe that Isabel's spirit is part of me, some-how. It should be more frightening, but instead it feels true.

'Kate?'

Deep in thought, I have only vaguely registered that someone has been walking towards me down the avenue. Most visitors take the path that leads from the car park to the Hall and it's rare to encounter anyone heading into the village on foot.

When I hear my name, my heart plunges. I'm wrapped up in my memories of Kit and Edmund; I don't want to leave the past to deal with the present, but the man has stopped, and he knows my name. I can't walk past the way I wish I could.

Biting my lip, I look up, but the face is blurred behind my tears. Desperately, I blink them away and look again. The man is dark and solid rather than tall. He has big features balanced by horn-rimmed glasses, and a humorous face. There is something familiar about him, and my breath stumbles.

'Kate,' he says again on a breath, and then stops as if unsure what to say next. 'You don't know who I am, right? Crap, this is awkward.' He blows out a sigh and drags a hand through his hair, knocking his glasses askew. He straightens them. 'I guess I should introduce myself? I'm Matt Chandler.'

He holds out a hand, and after a moment's hesitation, I take it. A tiny tingle of recognition zips up my arm and vanishes.

Matt Chandler. I know who he is now. I have seen his face before.

'I know,' I say, moistening my lips. 'I looked you up on Google when I read your email, but I'm sorry, I don't remember you.' I don't, but there is a very faint buzz under my skin, as if my body does.

There is a tiny pause. 'It must have been weird to get an email from a total stranger,' Matt says at last, and I smile a little, thinking about my jumbled memories and the driving need I feel to find a child who was born over four hundred years ago.

'Everything's been weird lately,' I tell him.

'I can't imagine what it's been like for you, Kate. I just wish I'd known.' He lifts his hands helplessly and lets them drop.

'There's so much I want to say to you, but the hell if I know where to start!'

I have been studying him furtively. He has a nice mouth, thin-lipped but mobile, and there are creases in his cheeks as if he smiles a lot. His handshake was warm and firm, and the thought that his hands have been on my flesh sets up a fine vibration deep inside me. He is a stranger who knows me intimately. He knows how I taste, how I feel. He knows me better than I know myself.

I clear my throat. 'I didn't know what to say when I wrote to you. I wasn't sure if you would come or not.'

'When you told me you'd been in an accident, I couldn't not come,' Matt says. 'I've rented a cottage in the village, and got here last night.' He jerks his head in the direction of the Hall behind him. 'I went straight up to try to see you this morning, but you'd gone out. I got Lady Vavasour instead, who told me that it would be "unhelpful" if I contacted you again.' He mimics Fiona's voice with uncanny accuracy, and the corner of his mouth quirks in a smile that for one jolting moment looks so like Edmund's that I suck in a sharp breath. 'I've had warmer welcomes digging a pizza out of the freezer.'

I bite my lip. 'I'm sorry.'

I'm not sure how I feel about being confronted with Matt Chandler in the flesh, but I didn't tell him *not* to come. 'We should probably talk,' I say, 'but not at the Hall. Why don't we meet later, when Felix is in bed?'

We agree to meet at the pub in the village that night. It does not go down well with the Vavasours when I tell them over dinner what I'm doing.

'That bloody American! Why does he want to come around stirring things up again?' Jasper demands, and Fiona's lips thin.

'I do think it would be most unwise if you got involved with that man again, Kate,' she says.

'It was stupid to get involved with him in the first place,' Margaret snaps.

'I'm not a prisoner here, am I?'

'Of course not.'

'I'm not asking permission,' I say coldly. 'I'm doing you the courtesy of telling you that I'm going out and may not be back until later.'

Outside, it is raining, a thin, seeping rain. I'm not looking forward to the walk down to the village. I'll be soaked. I can't wait to be able to drive again, but Mary keeps telling me I need to be patient a little while longer, so for now I'm still dependent on others.

I turn to George. If nothing else, here is an opportunity to convince him that I'm just not available. 'George, would you give me a lift to the pub?'

But he won't meet my eyes. 'I'm not going to encourage you to make a fool of yourself again, Kate,' he says.

So much for being in love with me. He doesn't love me enough to help me.

In the end, Philippa pushes her chair back. 'I'll take her,' she says roughly.

'How do you stand it?' I ask her in the car.

She shrugs. 'They love Felix. They don't want you to meet someone else and take him away from Askerby.'

'I can't live like this forever, Philippa. You need to help them understand that. Of course, Felix will always be their grandson and I'll bring him for visits, but we need to have a normal life, too.'

'Normal?' Philippa makes that barking sound that I now realize is a laugh. 'What's that?'

Matt jumps to his feet when he sees me hesitate just inside the pub door, and his face blazes with an expression that both startles and warms me. For a moment I think he is going to rush over and sweep me into a hug, but he just beckons cheerfully. 'Come on over, I've got us the best table.'

He gestures ironically to the table wedged in the corner of the bar by the fireplace. The Vavasour Arms has yet to be bought up and transformed into a gastropub. People come for the beer, not the food. It serves chicken and chips, scampi and chips or steak pie and chips, and a vegetarian lasagne. That's it. The décor is basic, too, with tired old hunting prints and a worn floral carpet. A wooden bench runs around the walls, with square, scarred tables ranged at various intervals, and a selection of round stools if you fancy some company, although most of the locals are happy to sit side by side with a pint on the table in front of them.

It's Monday, so it's quiet. There are three men leaning at the bar. They nod politely as I pass. I'm sure they know who I am, and that news of my visit to the pub will flash around the village, but I refuse to feel guilty. I am allowed to have a drink.

Even so, I hesitate when I get to Matt. There's an awkward moment when I wonder how to greet him. Do we kiss, or shake hands, or what? Matt solves the problem by waving me to the wooden bench. 'Sit down,' he says. 'I'll get you a drink.'

Evidently he knows what I like better than I do, because he returns with half a Guinness, opaque and dark beneath its head of creamy foam. I look at the glass he sets before me in surprise. 'Is this what I drink?'

'You used to.' Matt rubs his head ruefully. 'Sorry, I should have asked. I think I know you, but I don't. Do you want something else, Kate?'

I take a sip and lick the foam off my lip. The mellow, malty taste is instantly familiar. Clearly I do like it. 'This is fine,' I say.

After a moment, he takes the stool opposite me. He is compact and dark, with an interesting, intelligent face. He is not good-looking, certainly not in comparison to the golden Vavasours, but there is something very attractive about him all the same, something to do with the acute eyes gleaming behind his glasses, I think, or with the humorous expression that means you don't really notice the big nose or the way his hair is receding at his temples.

He has a pint of lager on the table. 'English beer is an acquired taste,' he says when he sees me looking at his glass. A faint smile touches his mouth. The mouth that has kissed mine, that has pressed hot against my skin. I shift on the wooden bench. 'You used to give me a hard time about not drinking real beer.'

'Oh, so I'm a beer snob?' I say lightly. 'Good to know.'

I wrench my eyes from his mouth, and look at the table instead, but then I'm looking at the fingers wrapped around his glass and that is just as bad. Flustered, I take another sip of my Guinness. I drink wine with Angie, gin and tonic with the Vavasours, but the Guinness tastes right here. It feels more like me.

'How are you, Kate?' Matt asks after a while. 'I mean, really?'

I open my mouth to tell him that I'm fine, but something else comes out instead. 'I'm struggling,' I hear myself say.

He nods. 'I've been trying to imagine what it must be like to lose your memory. How do you know who you are if you haven't got a past?'

'You don't.' It's easier if I don't look at him at all. 'It's scary,' I say, turning my glass between my hands. 'Like you're naked and everyone else is wearing clothes. They all know things about me that I don't.' I'm vaguely surprised that I'm talking to him like this when to all intents and purposes I've just met him, but it feels comfortable. It feels as though I know him already. As, clearly, I do. 'But I've started to remember some things, and every little memory that slots into place helps me to remember who I am.'

Comfortable as I am talking to Matt, I decide not to tell him about the memories that don't belong to me at all. I'm not ready to trust him that far. Not yet.

'But you don't remember anything about me?' He sounds disappointed.

'No, when I got your email, I asked my friend about you. She told me we met when you were making a movie at the Hall last year.'

Matt nods. 'I wrote the screenplay. If you're looking for an upside to losing your memory, forgetting you've seen *The Tower* would be a good place to start,' he adds drily. 'But we've all gotta pay the bills, right? I can't say it ended up the most artistic movie ever made, and the critics duly slammed it, but it's been one of the surprise hits of the year, so none of us are bitching and moaning too much about the reviews.'

I like listening to him. He has one of those American accents that make you think of swing seats on a porch or syrup falling slowly from a spoon: easy, warm, relaxed, with an undercurrent of laughter that buffs away your jagged edges and leaves you ready to smile.

I understand again why I might have been attracted to him. I shift again on the bench. 'So . . . we were friends?'

'Yeah . . .' He says it on a long breath that hums with things left unsaid. 'We got on well. I can't say why. We just did.'

Something shimmers between us. I think it might be a memory, of warmth, of connection, but the harder I try to haul it to the front of my mind, the faster the feeling evaporates. Whatever it is, it is tightening the air and shortening my breath, and I'm aware of my pulse thudding in my ears.

There's another silence. I turn my glass on its mat, very carefully.

'Matt,' I say, lifting my eyes at last. 'Will you do something for me?'

'Anything,' he says without hesitation, and I can't help comparing him with George, sullenly refusing to meet my eyes.

'Will you tell me what I'm like? *Really* like? Don't be polite,' I add when he hesitates. 'If I'm a bitch or lazy or whiny, I want to know. I need the truth.'

Chapter Twenty-nine

Matt nods his head slowly as if he understands, and he takes
his time answering. He turns one of the beer mats round and
round on the table while he thinks. Tap, tap, turn. Tap, tap,
turn. It ought to be annoying, but I find it strangely soothing.

'You're tough,' he says at last. 'I think that's what I noticed
most about you at first. You've been through a lot. You talked
about growing up in Africa. Do you remember that at all?

'Just fragments. A hot night, insects, monkeys in the trees,
that kind of thing. I know my parents are still there, but I don't
remember much about them.'

'They work for NGOs, have done for years, and they're passionate about the need to help people. Good for them,' Matt
says, 'but from everything you've ever told me, they only care
about people in the abstract. They're not interested in individu-
als, least of all their own daughter. They sent you back to
school in the UK because they felt guilty about giving you special attention. Better to pack you off out of sight so they could

concentrate on all the starving children who just wanted food, not love.'

Abruptly, Matt slams the mat onto the table with the flat of his hand, making me jump. 'Sorry,' he says, shaking his head. 'It makes me mad just to think about it.'

'I had an email from them,' I say, thinking that if I had told him so much about my childhood, we must have been a lot closer than Angie made out. She had made Matt sound like a pseudo-celebrity taking advantage of my vulnerability, someone I had slaked my sexual frustration on rather than a friend I had talked to. 'They told me to remember how lucky I was to have enough to eat and access to medical attention. Which is true, of course, but not really what I wanted to hear.'

'That sounds right.' The humorous quirk of his mouth has flattened into a straight line. 'You put a good face on it,' he says. 'You used to spend holidays with your grandmother, and you said being moved around from country to country when you were younger made you very self-sufficient, but being sent away by your parents has to scar a child.'

I make a face. I don't like that idea. It's too close to vulnerable and obsessive and highly strung and all the other things I've been led to believe I am. 'I'm scarred?'

'No, scarred is the wrong word.' He tips his head from side to side, thinking. 'Independent is better. You've got a certain way of setting your chin, like you know you're going to have to deal with everything by yourself. It always gets me here,' he says, thumping his chest lightly with his fist. 'So yes, tough, independent, a bit combative, maybe. Stubborn as all hell.

'You're a great person, Kate,' he says seriously. 'Funny, generous, loyal, kind, sharp. And brave,' he adds. 'When I met you, you'd been badly wounded by Michael's death. Not broken, but, yeah, wounded deep inside. You said you felt like a bit of you had gone away and for a while you were rudderless without him. But you were coping. You had Felix, so you had to, you said. You kept your chin up, you let yourself laugh at my jokes. You were thinking about moving on.'

'With you?'

'No, not with me,' he says levelly.

I take a breath. 'But we had an affair, didn't we?'

Matt's eyes narrow. He doesn't answer immediately, but cups his hands around his beer and studies it as if it has the answer to a very difficult question. 'We were friends,' he says at last. 'We still *are* friends, I hope, or at least can be again.'

My cheeks are prickling with heat. 'So we didn't . . . ?'

'Once.' He lets out a long breath and rubs a hand furiously over his hair. 'Yes, once. It was a mistake. It just . . . happened.'

'Oh.' I chew my lip. It doesn't sound like the sordid obsession Angie had hinted at, and if it had been a one-night stand, why were the Vavasours so concerned about it?

'Kate, you don't need to feel bad, I promise you. Yes, we got carried away once, and you felt terrible about it, and I'm sorry about that. I think you felt you'd betrayed Michael, but from everything you told me, Michael was one of the good guys. He'd have understood that you were lonely and needed some comfort.'

'Is that all it was?' I hear myself ask. I'm looking at his

hands and I'm thinking about Edmund's hands, and there's a muddled tide of warmth rising inside me.

'For you, yes. I always knew that.'

'And for you?'

A smile lifts the corner of his mouth. 'It was different for me.' He looks up from his beer and the eyes behind his glasses are very steady. 'I was in love with you and I still am.'

I open my mouth but I can't think of anything to say, so I shut it again.

'I know, it must be weird to hear that from a stranger, and I don't want you to think I'm a crazy stalker guy, but that's the way it is. It's kind of ironic,' Matt goes on after a moment. 'I was always Mr No Commitment, Mr No Time For All That Crap, but when I met you . . . I could see that you were sad, but trying so hard not to show it, and that was it for me. We just . . . clicked,' he says.

'We just used to talk,' he insists, as if I don't believe him. 'Felix was with us most of the time. He's a great kid, and he was part of what we had. There wasn't any hiding or pretending. We were just friends. We had a connection, sure, but we never acted on it, you because you were still grieving for Michael, and me because . . . well, the same reason, I guess. I knew how you felt about him.'

'But then we did?' I prompt him when he seems to have stopped again.

'We'd arranged to meet for a drink one night. We only had a few more days' shooting and then we were all flying back to the States so it was kind of a goodbye. We met in the pub in the village, where everybody else was drinking. It wasn't a secret. But you were angry that night. Lady Margaret had you all riled up about something, and you were in a funny mood – combative, fiery. And when we left, it was dark outside, and I thought I might never see you again . . .' He pauses. 'You let me kiss you in the car park, in the shadows, where no one could see us, and you kissed me back. And when I asked if you'd come back to my room with me, you said yes.'

He has told this whole story without looking at me, but now he turns and I see that his jaw is tense. 'It was pretty amazing, Kate. You said so too, but afterwards, I know you felt guilty, as if you'd committed adultery. So I didn't try to make you stay. I let you go. I didn't want you to feel uncomfortable, and we agreed that it would be better if we forgot it ever happened.' He slides me a sidelong look. 'Of course, I didn't think you'd take it literally,' he adds drily.

I can't help it. I laugh.

'Listen, Kate.' He puts out a hand as if to touch me, but pulls it back to his glass. 'I don't know what you told anyone else, or what anyone else has told you, but there were just two of us in that room that night. Nobody else knows what it was like. It wasn't a sordid affair. You don't need to feel guilty or ashamed or anything. You were just taking some comfort from a friend, that's all. Don't let anyone tell you any different, okay?'

'Okay,' I say. 'Thanks, Matt.' I pause. 'Still, I must have been sad when you left,' I venture, and he gives me a quizzical look.

'I guess, but you had plans. You were talking about moving to York or Leeds and getting a job. You certainly weren't ready to commit yourself to a new relationship, especially not with a guy who lived in LA.'

'So you didn't think I was likely to do anything stupid because you'd gone?'

'Like what?'

'Like throw myself off the tower? Didn't they tell you?' I ask when he stares at me in horror. 'How do you think I lost my memory?'

'You . . . the tower . . .' Matt is stuttering in shock. 'Jesus Christ, Kate, I thought you had a motor accident. What the hell were you doing up the tower?'

'That's the thing – I don't remember. The general consensus seems to be that I jumped off because you'd gone.'

'No way.' Matt doesn't hesitate for a second. 'There is *no way* you would have done that, Kate. Even if you had felt that way about me, which you didn't, you would never have left Felix.'

Ever since I woke up in hospital, the thought that I might have tried to kill myself has been dragging at me, a terrible weight of guilt and disbelief, but the absolute certainty in Matt's voice cuts it loose at last. Knowing that he doesn't believe it either brings such a rush of relief that I can't help smiling at him, and I lift a hand to my neck to feel the bunched muscles there starting to unknot.

'That's what I think, too.'

'But how did it happen? I've been up on that tower. Half the goddam movie was about characters being thrown off the roof, and there's no way you could trip accidentally.'

It is on the tip of my tongue to tell him that I know, that I remember being up there with Edmund, but I stop myself just in time. I picture the stout walls, the crenellations that were built for decoration rather than defence. No archer ever knelt on the broad stone step and fired arrows at an approaching enemy. Those battlements were for show only.

I remember standing on that step, Edmund behind me. The stones came up to my waist, and I set my hands flat on them so that I could lean out through the gap. I wasn't afraid of heights, not then.

'I don't know,' I say. 'I can't remember. The doctors say it's unlikely that I ever will. Apparently it's quite common for the brain to wipe out the events immediately before a severe trauma.'

'But if you didn't jump and you didn't trip . . . ?' Matt trails off and I look back at him. He is only voicing the suspicion that has been unfurling slowly in my head and that I can't now dislodge, incredible as it seems. I am sure that I didn't jump, that I *wouldn't* jump. But if I didn't, and it wasn't an accident, then what is left?

I'm not ready to say the unthinkable out loud, that someone pushed me, but I remember drifting in and out of consciousness at the hospital, that sense of people beside me, leaning over me.

It would have been better if she'd died.
You were supposed to die.

I have assumed it was a dream, a hallucination, but maybe it wasn't. Maybe somebody wanted to kill me.

Maybe they still do.

But who would want to? It seems incredible. I know the Vavasours don't want me to take Felix away, but *murder*? Surely they wouldn't go that far? I think about Fiona, always cool, always correct. Jasper with the tic that jumps anxiously under his eye. Joanna, fretful and nervous. Philippa, bored and surly. Shy, stolid, handsome George. I don't see any of them pushing me. Margaret might be glad to see me gone, but even if she would go as far as murder, she's not physically capable of it.

They don't care for me, but they don't hate me . . . do they?

Matt is watching my face. His voice lowers. 'Jesus, Kate, do you really think someone tried to *kill* you?'

It sounds so melodramatic that I shake myself. We're getting carried away. Matt writes stories for a living. Of course he's going to think the unthinkable. This is absurd. 'No,' I say with a half-laugh, but it isn't quite as sure as it should have been. 'No, of course I don't. There must be another explanation.'

Matt has rented a car, and he drives me back to the Hall. By tacit agreement, we had another drink and changed the subject. He told me about the script he was writing, and entertained me with stories against himself when he saw he could make me laugh again. Sitting in that tatty pub with a stranger, I was more relaxed that I could remember being since I woke up in the hospital bed.

But now the Hall squats in the darkness, like an enormous

toad, and I can picture a great tongue flickering out to grab me and gobble me up. I am far too fanciful tonight. It's just a house, but still, I don't want to get out of the car and go in.

Matt pulls on the handbrake but leaves the engine idling. In the dim light from the dashboard, I am acutely aware of him, and when he undoes his seat belt and turns towards me, every cell in my body fires up with a mixture of fear and excitement and anticipation while my heart knocks unevenly in my chest.

'Come and see my cottage tomorrow,' he says. 'Bring Felix. I'd like to see him again.'

I don't even think of hesitating. 'All right. We'll come after school. We can have tea. You're in Yorkshire now,' I tell him as he tries unsuccessfully to hide his look of dismay. 'Of course it has to be tea.'

Matt laughs and gets out so that he can help me from the car and hand me my stick. I don't really need it now, but I take it just in case. Now I'm glad of something to hold when Matt reaches out and just touches my cheek. His thumb is slightly rough, and I am sure I can feel every line, every tiny dip and nick of it, as it grazes my skin.

'Everything's shit,' he says. 'You've had a terrible accident, and you're hurting and you don't remember me, and I haven't written a word since I got here, but I'm happier now than I've been all year. I just wish I could have been here for you when you needed me, Kate.'

I smile at him as he drops his hand. 'You're here now,' I say.

*

The dogs greet me, moaning with pleasure, when I let myself in the side door. Molly brings me a shoe, and I thank her, trying to keep my balance as they bump their sturdy bodies against me and their tails whack against my bad leg. Pippin is in her basket. She lifts her head to watch, but when I look her way, she growls a warning, deep in her throat. She isn't ready to trust me yet.

It's not that late and there are still lights on in the private quarters. I can hear the sound of the television as I pass the snug, but I don't stop and go in. I don't want to talk to the Vavasours now, not with my ridiculous suspicions curdling my mind, but when I head for the stairs George looms out of the shadows, making me swallow a scream.

'George! You gave me a fright!' I accuse him, my hand at my throat, where my heart is still battering.

'You're back then?' His voice is bleary, and I realize that George, shy, stolid George, has been drinking.

'Of course I'm back,' I say, irritated. 'What did you think, that I was going to run off and leave Felix behind?'

'Oh, yes, you'll always come back for *Felix*. You'd do anything for *him*, wouldn't you?'

I don't understand the bitterness in George's voice and I don't like it. 'Yes, I would,' I say evenly. 'He's my child and that's what mothers do.'

George makes a sound that is half snort, half sob, so loud that it makes him sway dangerously on his feet. 'I don't know what you see in that Yank, anyway,' he slurs. 'He's a Jew, you know.'

'At least he's not a drunk,' I say coldly. 'You've got no right to tell me who I can and can't see, George.'

'What if I want the right?' To my horror, he stumbles to his knees. 'Marry me, Kate, you know I love you.'

'Get up, George, for God's sake!' I could gladly clout him around the ear with my stick. 'You're being ridiculous! There's no question of me marrying you.'

George lurches to his feet and bumps back against the wall, dislodging a painting, which tilts alarmingly sideways. It's hard to tell in the shadows, but I think it is a rather fine landscape by a seventeenth-century Dutch painter. 'Why not?' he demands as I push past him and straighten the picture.

'Because I don't love you, and even if I did, I would make you a terrible wife.'

'No, you wouldn't! You'd be perfect!' His voice drops enticingly. 'You could stay at Askerby. I'd look after Felix. A boy needs a father.'

'You didn't have one,' I point out, perhaps cruelly, 'and anyway, Felix has a father. Nobody is going to replace Michael.'

George's face hardens. 'You were going to replace him with that Yank before.'

Before, I might have hesitated, wondering if it were true, but Matt has told me what happened, and I believe him. 'I wasn't, and I'm not.' I take a deep breath. 'George, I'm not the woman for you. If you thought about it, you'd realize that I am right. You need someone who loves Askerby as much as you do. Someone who belongs here.'

'What are you talking about?' He is swaying on his feet and

I bite my lip, realizing I should never have started this. But perhaps it wouldn't be a bad thing to put Angie in his mind?

'Forget about me,' I say. 'Look around you for someone you can build a real relationship with at Askerby.'

'Like who? There's only Philippa, and she's practically my sister, quite apart from batting for the other team.'

'There's Angie.'

'*Angie?*' George cracks an incredulous laugh. 'Angie's the *help*,' he says, clearly only just stopping himself from calling her a servant.

'Her grandfather was a count,' I say, and he snorts.

'That horrible old drunk!' he says, apparently unaware of the irony of his own slurred speech. 'I doubt it very much! Besides, you never saw her uncle. The guy was a *freak*,' says George. 'Michael was the only one who would talk to him. He practically had two heads. Do you think we want genes like that in this family?'

I eye him with distaste and lean forward to drill a finger into his chest. I am sorely tempted to tell him my theory that Peter was Ralph Vavasour's son, but even if I am right, that is not my secret to tell. 'Don't you ever, ever say anything like that again,' I spit at him. 'Peter Kaczka had a happy nature and a good heart. If you ask me, his are exactly the genes this family needs.'

Chapter Thirty

'What's up with George?' Philippa has wandered into the library to find Joanna and me opening another archive box. It's an unpleasant, blustery day and the wind is throwing petulant handfuls of rain at the windows. 'He's like a bear with a very, very bad headache this morning.'

'I think he had too much to drink last night.' Joanna's gaze flickers to me, and Philippa follows her aunt's glance.

'Oh, so it's your fault, Kate. Did you give him the push?'

'I don't want to discuss it.' I'm in a bad mood. I couldn't sleep last night. There was too much going round and round in my head: my suspicions about an affair between Dosia and Ralph Vavasour, Matt Chandler, Kit, George, the memory of that malevolent whisper in my ear: *You were supposed to die.* The images tumbled and span together, bumping into each other and muddling up until I saw Dosia holding Kit, Matt with his mouth pressed to Angie's throat, George advancing towards me on the tower, and I had to jerk myself out of my exhausted doze. I don't believe any of the Vavasours caused my accident, of course I don't. I just can't think of another explanation yet.

Matt's arrival has unsettled me, too. He has come from the outside, like a sailor back from the sea, bringing a whiff of the ocean, a sense of the world beyond the moors. Now the Hall feels even more claustrophobic than it did before. I am longing to leave, but where can I go? I have looked at my finances, and it appears that I have just under four hundred pounds to my name. I know my parents would say that for some people that is an unimaginable fortune, but it doesn't seem a lot to bring up a child. Effectively, I am living entirely on the Vavasours' charity. I will give myself until Christmas, I decide, and then I will find a job, any job. There must be child support that I can claim, and housing benefit, perhaps, until I am settled. I will manage, somehow.

But I can't go anywhere until I remember. It is not lack of money that keeps me here, it is my lack of memory. I need to remember, that is clear in my mind, but the more I strain to fill in the blanks of the months leading up to my fall, the denser and more resistant my memory becomes.

All in all, I am tired and out of sorts, and in no mood for Philippa's needling. She is sitting on the library desk, kicking her heels against the old wood and ignoring Joanna's pointed frown.

'So, how did you get on with Hollywood last night?' she asks me, and I bang down the cardboard lid of the box.

'His name's Matt, and I don't want to discuss that either.'

'Ooh, touchy, touchy!'

'Are you here to help or just get in the way?'

She gazes moodily out at the driving rain. 'I'll help.'

Once she gets into it, Philippa is surprisingly efficient and less likely to get distracted by a photograph or by reading out a snippet from a letter, but even she stops when Joanna unearths an old photograph album.

'Oh, look, it's Daddy during the war,' Joanna exclaims.

Sure enough, there is Ralph Vavasour looking dashing in his pilot's uniform. There is one of him leaning against a car with Adam Kaczka. They both have cigarettes in their hands and are smiling their devil-may-care smiles. The bond between them leaps out of the photo: it is the friendship you notice first, and then the friends.

'That's Angie's grandfather,' I say, and Philippa looks curiously over Joanna's shoulder.

'Adam? God, I'd never have recognized him. I used to be terrified of him when I was little,' she tells me. 'He was always drunk and shouting in Polish.'

I notice there are no photos of Dosia, but perhaps that's not surprising.

Joanna turns the pages of the album. Each is divided from the next by a gossamer-fine sheet of waxed paper, and the photographs are stuck in with corners. More pictures of Ralph, and then there is Margaret standing next to him at a party. She is wearing long evening gloves, holds a cigarette holder in her hand, and the boat-shaped neckline of her gown shows off her clavicles to perfection. Her smile is wide, her eyes huge and luminous. She looks like Vivien Leigh or one of those other impossibly glamorous movie stars, too flawless to be real, her lipstick perfectly glossed to catch the light.

'She was stunning, wasn't she?' Joanna's voice holds a kind of awed pride as she studies her mother. There is Margaret skiing in Gstaad, Margaret shooting in the Highlands, Margaret sitting on a yacht on the Riviera, always surrounded by other beautiful people. It is as if nothing plain or ordinary could be allowed into the charmed circle that surrounded her.

And here is the famous wedding shot, the fairy-tale ending to Margaret's glorious progress through the social scene. 'Were they as happy as they look here?' I ask Joanna.

Joanna looks troubled as she closes the album. 'Things were different in those days. More private. They weren't all over each the way couples are nowadays.'

'Don't look at me,' says Philippa with a shrug.

For some reason I find myself blushing. Were Michael and I 'all over each other'? Or, worse, Matt and I? But no, Matt said we were just friends.

Apart from that one time. The time I'm not sure I want to remember, but can't stop thinking about. *What was it like? How did I feel? Where did he touch me?*

Philippa digs out another album, of Joanna and Jasper as children, and flicks through it while I carry on unpacking the archive box. I can see the photos out of the corner of my eye. Jasper and Joanna look stiff and unhappy in most of them, and I remember the picture of Joanna hanging around Marek's neck and laughing. I am on the verge of telling her about it and the other photos of Dosia's that I have put aside to scan for the display when I am distracted by pulling a leather-bound book out of the box.

'It's a diary,' I say, opening the book and squinting at the closely handwritten lines. 'I wonder what the date is – oh!' A folded sheet pressed between the pages has fallen out and I put down the diary to open it carefully.

The paper is very fragile, and covered in what look like tiny squares and cramped black ink marks.

'What is it?' asks Joanna, intrigued, and Philippa closes the photo album so that she can see, too.

'I'm not sure.' I hold the sheet at different angles to see if that makes it any clearer. 'Something about funeral monuments?'

'I wonder if it's the plan of the church floor before it was repaved in the eighteenth century?' Joanna says suddenly.

'It could be.' I am excited. 'The vicar told me something about a plan drawn up by an antiquarian. Maybe this is it?'

Together we pore over the sheet. Once we know what we're looking for, it's easier to decipher the spidery writing. Our helpful antiquarian recorded the position of all the gravestones inside the church, together with the names and dates of birth and death that were still legible in the eighteenth century. Some of them go back a long way.

'Look, here's one for 1569!' Joanna points and then squints at the text. 'Rad something Vavasour?'

'Ralph Vavasour,' I say without thinking.

Philippa looks at me in astonishment. 'How do you work that out?'

'Ralph was *Radulphus* in Latin.' I have no idea where the words come from. Ralph was Edmund's grandfather, I know that.

'I didn't know you knew Latin.'

Nor did I. 'It must be one of those things I've forgotten I know,' I say weakly.

I lean back over the plan. 'Can you see a Christopher Vavasour anywhere?'

'Christopher?' Philippa is still regarding me curiously. 'Who's he?'

'I think he was Edmund's son,' I say, preoccupied with searching for Kit's grave.

'And who might Edmund be?'

I hesitate. 'His tomb's in the church,' I say after a moment, my eyes not quite meeting hers. 'I've been, er, doing some research on him, and I think I read somewhere he had a son.'

Joanna is moving her finger over the plan, trying to work out dates. 'Here's another early one – 1604. Oh, could it be Edmund's wife? *Uxor Edmundi* . . . *uxor* is wife, isn't it?'

'Yes, but . . .' I open my mouth to say that Edmund's wife was buried under the Visitor Centre, but Joanna is still deciphering.

'It's hard to read . . . looks like a "j" . . . and is that a "d"?'

Philippa nudges Joanna aside to have a closer look. 'Judith, looks like,' she says. The name seems to explode in the silence of the library and hits me square in the belly, driving the air from my lungs.

'Judith?' I echo sharply when I have caught my breath. 'Judith wasn't Edmund's wife!'

They both look up, surprised by my vehemence. 'There must be some mistake!' I say. 'Let me see!'

The tiny lettering dances in front of my eyes, and I squeeze them shut to steady myself before I can look to where Joanna's finger is still pointing. It looks enormous against the miniature print, a giant's finger thrust onto the page. At first I can't see anything but that in grotesque detail, where she has chewed the skin by her nail, the creases across the joint, the ragged cuticle, but at last I can focus on the letters, and no matter how hard I look at them, I can't make them say anything other than 'Judith'. There is no way it can possibly be mistaken for 'Isabel'.

And anyway, you know where Isabel was buried, a voice inside my head reminds me. *She wasn't buried in the church because she committed suicide, didn't she?*

But Judith, Edmund's wife? 'No, that's all wrong,' I say, dry-mouthed as I back away from the table, shaking my head furiously. 'That's not right. Edmund wasn't married to Judith.'

Philippa and Joanna exchange a look. 'How do you know?' Philippa asks. 'I thought we didn't have any evidence about his wife.'

'We do!' My voice rises in spite of myself and I wave a hand wildly in the direction of the Visitor Centre. 'We found her *bones*!'

'Kate, we don't know who that was,' Joanna says, carefully reasonable.

'I'm telling you, it was Isabel! Edmund's wife!'

Another look passes between them. 'Uh-oh,' Philippa says with a wary glance at me. 'This is what you were like before your accident. You kept banging on about those bones. You were completely batty about them.'

I stare at them in mute frustration, remembering too late that Angie has told me they have been through all this before. I know that if I tell them how clearly I remember Isabel's life they will decide that I am crazy; if I don't, they will conclude that I am crazy anyway. My head is pounding: sharp, jarring blows that make my eyes twitch. In desperation I press the heels of my hands to them, and memory slams into my mind like another brutal hammer blow.

I remember sinking onto a stool with my hands just like this, pressed hard against my eyelids. My head was roaring with pain, and the rustle of approaching skirts scraped at my nerves.

'Isabel?' Judith's voice was low with concern. 'Isabel, dearest, what troubles you?' She placed a tender hand on my shoulder. 'Is it the headache again?'

'I cannot think,' I muttered between my teeth. 'I feel as if my head is about to break into little pieces.'

'Come, lie down. I will bring a rose cake to bind to your head. It will take away the pain.'

I stood unresisting as Judith gently unpinned my skirt and sleeves, and loosened my laces so that she could draw my bodice off, and when I was down to my smock, she bade me lie on the bed while she went to fetch the cake she made with pressed rose petals.

Boom, boom, boom went my head. It had been like that ever since Edmund had been summoned to court. I longed for him to come home but scorned to write and say that I needed him. So I wrote news of the bees, of the honey we had collected from the hives in the orchard, and of the wool that was baled up and ready to be sent down the river to York. I told him I had had to poultice one of the palfreys and asked if he would send two pounds of starch and some good Gascony wine from London. I told him that his son was growing well, but I did not tell him that I was sore afraid, that at times the darkness span in my head and roared in my ears, and made me forget what I had said or done.

Judith sent for the physician, who diagnosed an excess of heat in my brain. He squirted beet juice up my nostrils with a syringe to purge my head, a horrible process that left me coughing and streaming and gasping, and prescribed a diet of warm, moist foods to balance my humours. The chaplain urged me to private meditation and prayer, and I did try, but my mind kept wandering, and although Judith sat with me for many hours and read the Scriptures, nothing could distract me from the rushing in my head.

'I saw Eliza again today,' I told Judith as she was binding pieces of rose cake to my head. The sweet scent of the petals was cloying and the cake felt lumpy and uncomfortable at my temples but I submitted because it was churlish to reject the remedies she made so carefully for me.

Judith clicked her tongue in disapproval. 'You should not speak to her,' she chided me. 'She will ill-wish you if you do not take care.'

'I only wanted to know how she got into the house.' I moved my head restlessly on the pillow.

'Eliza has not been here,' Judith said soothingly as she tied the last binding and stepped back. 'Who would let her in?'

'I don't know, but she was here.' I lowered my voice to a whisper, even though there were no servants nearby. 'She left more hemlock for me, here in the chamber. I found it on the pillow this morning.'

It was the first thing I had seen when I woke that morning. A simple twist of paper, but at the sight of it I had felt ice pool in my belly, and pain jabbed in my head. I had to get out, to ride up onto the moors where I could breathe properly and where the darkly whirling thoughts would clear and settle. Up on the moors, I knew that I must act and not just scuttle away from Eliza in fear, so I had ridden down to the village to confront her in her cottage.

Inside, it was damp and dim, and the smoke hanging sullenly in the air stung my eyes. Eliza was hunched on a stool counting something – coins? – that she whisked out of sight when she saw me stooping in her doorway.

'Good morrow to you, mistress,' she said, and the slyness curdling her voice made my shoulders twitch. 'What do you here?'

I could just make out the gleam of her eyes. A sour stench coiled into my nose and I was glad that I could not see what was trampled into the mud floor. Breathing through my nose, I demanded to know why she dared to come to my house, but Eliza whined and cringed and denied it again and again.

Judith frowned when she heard what I had done. 'If it was not Eliza, then it must have been one of the servants. Where is the hemlock now? Did you throw it away?'

'I put it in the box,' I said, looking at the cedar box that sat on the chest. I struggled to sit up but Judith put a hand on my chest and pushed me gently back against the pillows. 'Do you stay there. I will fetch it.'

I lay back and closed my eyes, and when I opened them Judith was standing with her back to me, looking into the box, her spine straight and very still.

'You see?' I said.

Slowly, Judith turned. She carried the box over to the bed and opened it. It was empty.

'Someone must have taken it,' I said, but my mouth was dry. A fear I didn't want to name was drumming at the back of my mind.

'Isabel.' Judith's voice was very gentle, her face creased with pity. 'Isabel, do you think it is possible that you imagined it?'

The fear was beating harder, louder. I couldn't hear anything above its pounding: *mad, mad, mad*. I shrank back against the pillows and stared up at my friend.

'Judith,' I whispered. 'Help me.'

'You have the headache, that is all,' she said, squeezing my hand. 'It is a cross that must be thankfully borne if it increases your devotion. This afternoon we will pray together, and if God wills, the pain will cease. But for now, I will bring you some posset ale and you may sleep for a while.'

She let go of my hand. Glancing at the table as she made to

leave, she picked up the letter I had written to Edmund the day before. 'Is this for your husband? Shall I send for the carter to take it to London?'

'Bid him hurry,' I said. I plucked at the coverlet. 'How much longer will the Queen keep Edmund at court? I wish he could come home.'

'It will not be long, surely,' Judith said. 'And you must be sure that you are well before he comes home, so rest you there, and I will fetch that ale.'

Chapter Thirty-one

'Hey, buddy, remember me?' Matt greets Felix with delight when he opens the door.

Felix obviously isn't sure, but equally obviously doesn't want to admit it, so Matt gives him a prompt. 'Remember we made a movie at Askerby Hall last year?'

'Yes . . .' Felix's face is pulled together with concentration. I can tell that he is longing to remember, really remember. I know the feeling.

'And we gave you your own director's chair with "Felix" written on the back?'

It is still in the nursery. Felix is on firmer ground now. 'Yes!' He nods importantly. 'I remember.'

I wish I could be reminded as easily.

Matt holds the door open wide. 'Come in. I'm all set to have a go at making tea.'

It is a nice cottage, plain but warm and well equipped, and it has been recently refurbished so that it feels bright and new.

The ground floor would fit into a corner of the long gallery, but the air feels lighter here. It doesn't have that shadowy sheen that I have become almost used to at the Hall. The cottage is old, too, but it doesn't have the same precarious atmosphere of secrets and shut doors, of feeling that an unwary step will send you tumbling through time. At the Hall, the wall between my life and Isabel's is rubbed so thin that I can't distinguish between the two and our memories muddle and merge, but sitting in the cottage kitchen I feel as if I have found an anchor to real life, a certainty to hold onto: here I can be Kate without Isabel's memories clamouring urgently in my head.

Ever since finding the record of Judith being buried in the church as Edmund's wife, I have been fretful and churning with anxiety. What if I have all this wrong? Memories are notoriously unreliable, Oliver Raine has told me that. Time and again, research has shown that the most vivid of memories bears little resemblance to reality. The brain picks pieces out of a kind of pick'n'mix selection box of memories and puts them together with a seasoning of invention and a hefty dollop of wishful thinking, he says. So even if I am willing to accept the fact that I am haunted by the spirit of a woman who has been dead for four centuries, there is no reason to suppose that her memories are truer than those of anybody else.

What if Judith *was* Edmund's wife, and Isabel a servant, just like legend says? What if she was obsessed by her master, and I am remembering her dreams rather than her life? I gnaw at my thumb while I force myself to consider this. Perhaps Isabel had an affair with Edmund. Those memories of making love by the river might be true, while believing herself to be his wife was but a fantasy. Little pity was given to a serving girl who fell pregnant, even if the child was fathered by her master. Isabel might have faced the choice of being turned off to become a vagrant or of killing herself and her child. It would explain why she is buried ignominiously in the grounds of the estate instead of in the churchyard, as befitted Lady Vavasour.

Suicides were denied burial in consecrated ground. I remember Reverend Rolland's sombre tones, and everything in me rises up as if in a great shout: *NO!* Isabel would not have jumped off the tower, I am sure of it. Lady Vavasour or serving girl, she would not have killed her child or herself. It is impossible that she would have done such a thing.

Unless she was mad.

I remember how muddled I – she – was about things. *Was* it possible? Is that why she can't rest?

Perhaps that is why there is no sign of Kit in the records. Perhaps he was just a servant's brat. Perhaps he never lived at all.

No! No, no, no! My head rings with the conviction that I am wrong. Kit was no phantom child. He was flesh and blood, warm, *real.*

I *remember* how much I loved him, and how I feared for him. I hated being weak, but Judith's words that day gave me courage. I had to be well before Edmund came home, and I had to be well for my son. I did not want Kit to grow up fearing madness as I had done.

So I forced myself out of bed, and pinched my cheeks to

give them some colour. I ignored my spinning head and dragged myself up to the nursery. Kit was in his cradle, blue eyes alert, and when I bent over and saw him smile up at me, the rigid fear inside me melted away.

'Unswaddle him,' I said to Meg, who pursed her lips, but couldn't prevent her expression from softening as she undid his swaddling bands and pulled off his shirt. She lay him on the coverlet on the table and he squealed with pleasure as he kicked and flailed and grabbed his toes, and she watched jealously while I cooed over him. His eyes were clear, his belly plump and there were sweet rolls of fat at his wrists and ankles. He was a sturdy baby, happy and healthy, and I swore to myself that I would keep him so.

'Who is my pretty boykin?' I tickled his tummy and made him shriek with laughter, and when I glanced at Meg, I caught a smile on her severe face.

'He looks well,' I said.

As soon as she saw me looking, she tucked her smile away. 'You would not have thought so last night,' she said dourly. 'He was somewhat wayward then, crying and wailing.' She shook her head at Kit. 'And look at him now!'

'Has he a tooth growing?'

'Aye, mayhap. He was drooling.'

'Perhaps Judith could make an ointment for you to rub on his gums?' I offered. 'She made one with daisy roots that helped my Lord Vavasour when he had the toothache.'

Meg bridled. She liked Judith even less than she liked me. 'I have my own recipe, my lady. I will use that.'

'As you wish.' I knew better than to try to convince Meg to do anything she didn't want to. I was not a very stern mistress, but I knew that Meg would do anything for Kit.

'Meg,' I said impulsively. 'If anything should happen to me . . .'

She scowled. 'Nothing is going to happen to you, my lady.'

'But if it should . . . you would have a care of Kit, would you not?'

Meg folded her lips in a grim line. 'Doubt not of it, mistress.'

'Thank you,' I said, heartfelt. 'Thank you, Meg.'

'Ask your mom if you can have a cookie.'

I look up to see Felix holding a big tin of biscuits. 'Can I have a cookie?' he asks obediently. He doesn't add 'Mummy', but shoots me a complicit glance. It is the one he uses to remind me that he is only pretending that I am his mother, and every time the thought that he still doesn't recognize me plummets through me like a stone. I don't know how to persuade him that now I am only pretending to pretend.

'You can have two,' I say, holding up two fingers. 'But no more. Say thank you,' I add automatically as Felix puts the tin on the floor and squats down to burrow through it.

Matt places a mug of tea on the table in front of me. '*Voilà!*' he says with a flourish. 'Who says I don't know how to boil water?'

I take a sip. It is so strong it makes my eyes water. 'That's

Yorkshire tea, all right,' I say. 'Consider yourself a master tea maker.'

My attempt at jollity doesn't fool Matt. 'You seem pre-occupied,' he tells me. Pulling out a chair, he sits opposite me. 'Are you worrying about what we discussed last night?'

'No . . . yes . . . no, not really.' I cradle the mug in my hands. 'I just wish I could *remember*. Not just you, everything. It feels like I'm on a track and my wheels are spinning but I can't get anywhere until I know what happened last year.'

'It must be tough,' Matt says sympathetically. He tries his own tea and pulls an exaggerated face. 'Bleuch! How can you drink this stuff?'

He's trying to lighten the atmosphere, and I laugh oblig-ingly. 'It's an acquired taste.' There is no point in fretting endlessly about Isabel, I decide. I will find Kit if I can, but it is Felix who matters more. Somehow I need to convince him that I am his mother again, but in the meantime I must pull myself together before Matt, too, starts to think that I am obsessive and depressed.

A large board is propped up against the dresser behind Matt. It is covered in differently coloured Post-it notes, each one covered with scribbles. 'What's that?'

He glances over his shoulder to see what I am looking at. 'Oh, that's my story board. What you see there is plotting in action. It's not a pretty sight, is it?'

'What's your story about?'

'It's pretty much a rerun of what happened before.' He tips back in his chair and bends down to filch a biscuit from the tin that is still on the floor being rearranged by Felix. 'In the first movie I had a character who lived in a house with a truly uncanny resemblance to Askerby Hall who got haunted; cue much screaming and special effects. This time the house has been rebuilt as luxury holiday apartments and I've got a group of guys who think it's a good idea to rent it for a class reunion.'

'And one of them gets haunted?'

'You got it. Cue more screaming and special effects.' He grins at me. 'That's the fun and games. I'm still trying to work out how it ends, though.'

A bit like me and Isabel.

I toy with my mug. 'So it's a ghost story?'

'Ghost story, horror, comedy, all in the great tradition of *Ghostbusters*,' he says with mock grandiloquence.

Felix is happily counting out biscuits onto the tiled floor. Matt doesn't seem to mind.

'I suppose you don't believe in ghosts,' I say.

'Sure I do.' He says it so easily that my mouth drops open and I stare at him. 'Why wouldn't I?' he asks, lifting his brows at my surprise.

'I don't know . . . I just assumed that your movies were poking fun at the supernatural.'

'They do, I guess, but that doesn't mean I don't think ghosts exist. I keep forgetting you don't remember,' Matt says, brushing biscuit crumbs off the table. 'I came to Askerby years ago, when I was travelling around England with a girl. We were bowled over by the place, and it was a beautiful day, so we thought we'd climb the tower and look at the view. The lady at the ticket desk said it was pretty special.'

'It is,' I say. I'm looking into my mug, but I am remembering Edmund's hands on my shoulders, the way I had to narrow my eyes against the wind. The flash of sunlight on the river, the moors rolling breathlessly away into the distance and my chest expanding with happiness.

'So we set off up those stairs,' Matt goes on. 'We were talking and laughing at first, but as we got near the top we both fell silent. It's a long climb in an enclosed space and you think you're going to climb round and round for ever, so I thought it was claustrophobia at first, but it was more than that. The air in there was clammy and there was this terrible feeling of – I don't know – urgency, I guess. I started to feel panicky. It's hard to describe what it felt like,' he confides, 'but it gave me the heebie-jeebies. Jess – my girlfriend – said later that she felt exactly the same, but neither of us wanted to suggest turning round and going back down.

'I couldn't wait to get out of that staircase and onto the roof,' Matt tells me, 'but the moment we did, we were hit by this wave of sadness, grief, misery, fear. It was like it just rolled over us, a wash of cold terror, like you could *touch* it. It was horrible.'

He grimaces at the memory. 'I don't mind telling you, I was shit scared. I'd never felt anything like it before. Jess could feel it too. She grabbed my hand and started babbling that she didn't like it, she wanted to go, but she didn't want to go back down the spiral staircase. In the end, we decided the stairs were less scary than the roof, so we bolted back down and were both white as sheets when we got to the bottom, where it was a perfectly nice sunny day and nobody else seemed to have noticed anything wrong at all.'

'Were there other people up on the roof when you were there?'

'A few. They clearly didn't feel it, or there's no way they could have stood there calmly looking at the view.' Matt's shoulders twitch at the memory. 'But when I mentioned it to one of the volunteer guides, she said we weren't the first visitors to feel it, and she told us the legend about the servant who jumped off the tower.'

I open my mouth to say that it wasn't a servant, it was Isabel, but I shut it again. Since seeing the evidence of Judith's grave, I am not sure any more.

'That was my inspiration for *The Tower*,' Matt says. 'It was a straight drama to begin with, but over the years I changed it, and when I pitched the idea to a producer, he suggested throwing a few laughs in as well, and because I'm not the kind of guy who suffers for his art, I rewrote the script. It might seem like I think ghosts are a load of fun, but I've never forgotten how it felt up that tower, and I sure wasn't laughing then.'

I glance at Felix but he's still absorbed in counting biscuits. I'm remembering how the Vavasours claimed that Matt encouraged what they called my 'obsession'. 'Did I use to talk about seeing ghosts before?'

Matt's brows shoot up. 'No. Why? Are you seeing them now?'

I hesitate. I am so tempted to tell him about my memories as Isabel. It would be good to talk to someone about them, and I don't think he'll scoff. Out of the corner of my eye, I catch sight of Felix stealing a look at me before sneaking another biscuit, and I wag a warning finger at him. This isn't the time.

'No,' I say to Matt, and it is the truth. I haven't *seen* anything. It is all in my head. 'Sometimes the atmosphere at the Hall is a bit unsettling, but that's probably me.'

'Okay.' Matt doesn't look as if he believes me. 'Well, I recommend staying away from the tower.'

I shudder at the thought of it. 'I think I learnt that lesson,' I say, rubbing my leg ruefully, and he slaps his forehead.

'Shit! I wasn't thinking. Sorry, Kate, you don't need me telling you about the tower.'

'It's all right. Things are weird enough for me at the moment without going near that tower. I'm happy to give it a wide berth. In fact, if I never go up it again, it'll be soon enough for me.'

With some help from Philippa, Joanna and I work our way through all the archive boxes and end up with five piles of documents divided into centuries, from the seventeenth to the twenty-first. The pile for the nineteenth century is by far the biggest. The Victorian Vavasours were clearly fascinated by their own history, fortunately for us, as most of what we know of earlier Vavasours comes from them.

There is some fascinating material from the first half of the twentieth century, too, but after Margaret and Ralph's fairy-tale wedding in 1949 it is as if all interest in recording the family history stops. Since then, they have only looked back, not forwards. They have preserved what history they have, yes, but they haven't made any of their own.

Thanks largely to an unmarried Vavasour daughter who went through all the family papers in the 1860s, I have been able to draw up a line of descent which will be central to the display in the Visitor Centre. Edmund's grandfather, Ralph Vavasour, merchant of York, is right at the top, and Felix at the bottom, with a direct line linking the two. The title has not always descended from father to first son; sometimes an eldest son dies or is killed, and sometimes the line jumps a generation, as it will from Jasper to Felix, but it is direct. Most families can only trace their history directly for three or four generations before the line breaks, ending in childlessness or premature death or – worse – a family of daughters, but the Vavasours have beaten the odds, and look proudly back on an unbroken line of male heirs.

There is only one link missing. I haven't found Kit. A dotted line connects an Edmund Vavasour who died in 1697 to my Edmund. *Isabel's* Edmund, I correct myself quickly. Edmund died in 1613, when he would have been in his forties, I calculate. It is just possible, I suppose, that the later Edmund might have been his son, but it is very unlikely. That is what I tell myself, anyway. There is a Lord Vavasour missing. His name might not be Christopher, I know, but it might be. It might be.

I haven't given up hope of finding him yet. Isabel won't let me. *Find him. Find him. Remember.*

Chapter Thirty-two

Joanna tells me that there is a scanner in the estate office, so I gather together a selection of photos and other material from the archives and various albums and put them in a folder with the ones I have borrowed from Dosia. The estate office is a bit further than the stables but not as far as the village, so I can walk there easily, although I'm not sorry to be able to rest my leg when I get there.

George greets me coldly. We have been rigidly polite to each other ever since the night he got drunk and asked me to marry him. It makes for an uncomfortable atmosphere sometimes but the last thing I want to do is offer him any encouragement. I am hoping that in spite of everything he may start to see Angie in a new light, although why she would want someone who can talk about 'bad genes' is beyond me. If I am right about Dosia and Ralph, Peter's genes were as much Vavasour as Kaczka, but I don't know for sure and I can't say anything. It is Dosia's secret, not mine.

Angie is briskly elegant today in a black trouser suit. She is much smarter than George in his cords and fraying cuffs, and I marvel again at his casual dismissal of her as 'the help'. It seems to me that she is brighter, more competent and certainly better dressed than any of the Vavasours. George would be lucky to have her.

When I explain that I am here about the displays, George passes me on to Angie. If she has picked up on the frigid atmosphere between George and me, she doesn't comment on it, but happily clears a desk so that I can spread out the A4 sheets showing what I've done of the family tree so far.

'These show the line of direct descent between fathers and sons, or sometimes grandsons,' I tell her. 'I've included wives where I can, so it isn't too male heavy, but we don't always know their names.' I haven't put Judith's name next to Edmund's. I still think there must be some kind of mistake. I don't want to believe it is true.

'Wow, this looks great,' Angie says. 'You've done so much work.'

'Most of it was done by Sophia Vavasour,' I admit. 'She never married and seems to have devoted her life to the family history. We found her notes, and she'd done a lot of digging in the parish registers, and there was apparently a family bible which recorded all the names that seems to have completely disappeared. It's a shame, as it must have had so much information about other members of the family, too. They don't seem to have been very interested in their daughters.'

'That's how the estate has survived intact,' Angie says,

unconcerned. 'It's been passed down from father to eldest surviving son, and hasn't had to be broken up to support the
younger sons.'

'Primogeniture.' I look at the family tree without enthusiasm. 'It seems so unfair.'

Angie shrugs. 'You might not like it as a system, but it's
going to work in Felix's favour. Askerby will be his some day.'

'I'm not sure that will be good for him.' Frowning, I
straighten from the desk. 'I wish there was some way to disinherit him.'

'*Disinherit* Felix?' Her head comes up and she stares at me
in astonishment. 'Are you crazy? What on earth would you
want to do that for?'

'It just seems so unfair, Angie.' I try to explain. 'Even the
royal family have moved on from a boys-only approach! Felix
should make his own way in the world, not be chained to this
place all his life. If anything, it should go to Philippa when
Jasper eventually dies.'

'Philippa?' Angie says scornfully. 'What good would that
do? Philippa's a lesbian.' She makes no attempt to hide her distaste.

I remember that George hinted at the same thing. I have no
idea if they're right or not, and I don't see that it matters,
anyway. 'So?'

'So she won't have children, will she?'

'She can do what she likes. The point is that she can make
her own choice, not be bypassed because of some law set up in
the Middle Ages.'

Angie's mouth is tight with disapproval. 'If you're going to change the laws of inheritance to include women, strictly speaking George should inherit. Joanna is older than Lord Vavasour.'

'Fine by me,' I say, gathering up the sheets of paper.

All at once the air is precarious, as if it is shimmering with fumes that will explode at the slightest flick: an ill-chosen word, a careless intonation. I don't want to fight with Angie, so I fold my lips, concentrate on pulling out the other items I've found for the display. I've put together snippets from diaries and letters, a menu for a grand dinner at the beginning of the nine-teenth century, sepia photographs from the Victorian era, some of the portraits that still hang in the Hall, and various other images that I think together make for a varied and interesting display.

'What do you think of these?' I ask Angie, laying them out on the desk and moving the conversation to what I hope will be safer ground.

'They're great,' she says in a warm voice, and I am relieved the awkward moment has passed. 'Really colourful and engag-ing. I like this one.' She points at a sepia photograph of a Victorian Lady Vavasour playing with her dog.

'Yes, I like that, too. And this one.' There's another photo-graph of an Edwardian family picnic, where the dogs also feature. One looks very like Pippin, and the sight of it gives me a little pang.

Angie moves on to the wartime display. I have included one of the photos of Ralph and Adam in their RAF uniform, but I have found other pictures, too, of the Land Army and the Hall being used as a hospital. I've scanned a poster from 1942 and some quirky newspaper clippings. I think it looks pretty good.

I'm conscious that the material from the post-war period is thinner. I started with Ralph and Margaret's wedding picture from 1950, as that seemed to mark the real start of the new era. I lay out Dosia's photos and the ones I have taken from the Vavasour albums. There's one of Michael and Felix that I like; Jasper and Fiona's wedding; Joanna on a horse; George and Jasper with guns and Labradors.

Angie's eye skims approvingly over them all until she comes to the photo of Peter Kaczka with the baby pheasants. She taps it with a polished pink fingertip. 'Why on earth have you included this one?'

'It's a good picture,' I say mildly. 'It shows the estate isn't just about the Vavasours.'

'I don't think you should use it. It gives the wrong impression.'

I stare at her. 'What do you mean?'

'You know what I mean, Kate.' Angie pulls the photo out and hands it firmly back to me. 'It's nice of you to think of it, but nothing you can do changes what Peter looked like. It'll make people . . . uncomfortable.'

'That's their problem, isn't it?' That edginess is back in the air, but this time I don't feel like backing down. 'It wasn't Peter's fault that he didn't look like everyone else. He had a place at Askerby just like them.'

'Only thanks to the generosity of the Vavasours.' There's a little tic going at the corner of Angie's mouth, and her dimple has quite disappeared. 'Peter had somewhere to live and a job, and if you think Adam was able to support his family all those years without help, you've obviously never lived with an alcoholic. I never knew that Lord Vavasour – the old Lord Vavasour – was supporting us all those years until Babcia let it slip last year, but I don't think we can repay them by associating Askerby with someone like Peter. I don't think Lord and Lady Vavasour would like it, and frankly, I don't think Babcia would want people staring at his picture and thinking of him as a freak.'

I'm puzzled now. It doesn't sound as if Angie has any suspicion that Peter might have been Ralph Vavasour's son, and if anyone were to suspect, surely it would be Angie? So perhaps I am wrong about that.

'Dosia did say that she liked the idea of using Peter's photo,' I say, reluctant to give up on it just yet. It's a great picture, and even if he wasn't Ralph Vavasour's son, he lived and worked at Askerby: why shouldn't he be shown to have been part of its history?

But Angie isn't having it. 'Babcia's confused,' she says with finality. 'If you asked her again today, she'd say something different. Forget the photo, Kate,' she says. 'It'll only make trouble.'

What trouble? For whom? And why? Frustrated, I look down at Peter's smile. There is something here that I don't understand.

Briskly, Angie gathers up the other photos and makes a neat pile. 'Shall I get these scanned for you?' The dimple is back.

'You've done a great job, Kate. George is going to be so pleased.'

Remember, remember. The constant drumming in my head is getting louder and more insistent with every day that passes. It's like a terrible kind of tinnitus. Sometimes I can barely hear above the urgent hum, and I find myself frowning and leaning forward in concentration if I have to listen. At night I lie in bed and feel my blood beat and boom: *Find him. Find Kit. Remember.*

'You look tired.' Matt has fallen into the habit of meeting Felix and me at the school gates and walking slowly back to the Hall with us along the riverbank. He says that walking is good for the creative process. He says it gives the ideas tumbling around in his head time to rearrange themselves and settle.

I'm not sure if that's true or not, but Felix and I both look forward to our walks together, and if Matt can't make it for some reason the way home seems longer and duller somehow. Felix doesn't even try to hide his disappointment then. I have to be bright and cheery and remind him that Matt is busy and isn't obliged to spend any time with us, but the truth is, I know how he feels.

The last thing I want is to feel dependent on anyone, least of all someone who is to all intents and purposes a stranger, and one whose stay in Yorkshire is only ever going to be temporary at that. I can't help thinking about what Angie said when she first told me about Matt: *The guy's from Hollywood. He wasn't going to hang around in Askerby, was he?* Still, I feel safe with

Matt in a way I can't explain. He's in Askerby, but he's not of it. He doesn't belong here, and he is a reassuring reminder that there is a bigger world out there, one that doesn't centre around the old Hall with its watchful windows and scurrying shadows.

It is a soft, still autumn day, with hazy sunshine and gnats drifting in clouds over the river, tiny specks that catch the light. The warmth in the air is shot through with the rich, mellow, composty scent of damp earth and dry leaves and rotting fruit. Felix is running ahead with the dogs, who have quickly cottoned on to the new routine of afternoon walks.

As ever, Pippin trails behind, stubbornly suspicious. She remembered Matt. The first time he called to her, she fawned over his shoes, wriggling with pleasure and turning submissively onto her back so that he could scratch her tummy. I admit it: I was jealous. I thought I might take advantage of her guard being down and get close to her, but the moment I stepped towards Matt she sprang onto her feet, hackles up, and growled at me.

'What the—?' Matt stared from Pippin to me and back. 'What's got into Pippin?'

I sighed. 'It's a long story.'

Now I study Matt under my lashes, wondering how much he will believe, how much I dare tell him. He's right. I am tired. My face doesn't come as a shock when I look in the mirror now, but there is still a bruised look around my eyes, and I am far too thin. My body is all jutting bones and sharp angles.

'I haven't been sleeping well,' I tell him.

'Is your leg still painful?'

'It's all right.' I brush the pain aside. I am used to it now, used to the way an unwary movement can make it sink its hot teeth into my leg. 'It's not that. It's more . . .' The temptation to confide in him is a tangible thing, rising in me and pushing the words out of my throat before I realize I have succumbed. 'I'm frightened.' The relief of saying it, of admitting it to myself, is so huge that I feel light-headed.

'Frightened?' Matt's brows snap together and he stops to face me. 'What of?'

'That's the thing, I don't really know.' My eyes rest on Felix, who is buzzing in circles with his arms outstretched while Molly leaps and barks around him. She's unsure of the game but willing to have a go, anyway.

I'm carrying Felix's coat, and I concentrate on folding it carefully over my arm. 'I don't know if it's something in the house or something in me, or maybe it's both—' I flounder to a halt. 'I'm not making sense, am I?'

'Tell me,' says Matt. 'Tell me from the beginning.'

So I do. I tell him everything I remember since waking up in hospital as we walk along the riverside path, brambles and collapsing bracken catching at our legs, while Felix jumps in puddles and the dogs quarter the grass, jaunty tails wagging, uncaring of anything but the scents in their noses, and Pippin hangs back warily.

Matt listens as if what I have to say is normal. He doesn't exclaim or interrupt, he just nods his head or gives me a little prompt – 'Go on,' 'And then?' – when I lose my nerve and falter.

He waits until I have told him about the hemlock, and how much I feared I might be losing my mind. And how much I fear now that I may be losing it again.

'So you're possessed?' he says when I have stumbled to the end. He says it the same way he might ask if I had flu, with concern but not disbelief. Thank God, not disbelief.

I let out a breath on an embarrassed half-laugh. 'Yes.' It is such a relief to say it out loud that I say it again. 'Yes. I've tried convincing myself that it's just a way of coping with the trauma, like Oliver suggested, but the memories are too coherent, and they're too real. Confabulation, or whatever he called it, might explain one memory, but not a sequence like this, and anyway why would I invent a memory set in Elizabethan times? It doesn't make sense. But being possessed sounds even crazier, I know.'

'Not to me,' Matt says. He has been walking with his head down, his hands stuffed into the pockets of his jeans, but now he glances up. 'Did you know I was with you when they dug up the body under the Visitor Centre?'

'No,' I say slowly. 'No one told me that.'

'We were having a walk, like today. It's what we used to do, walk and talk.'

'Devils that we are,' I say with a lift of my brows, and he grins, a fast smile that cracks his face and sharpens the air.

'Always,' he agrees. 'We'd finished shooting and it was just before I was due to go back to LA. We were being very grown up about it, but it made conversation sticky. There was so much

I wanted to say to you, and so much I thought you really didn't want to hear.

'Anyway,' he says, moving a bramble aside so that I can pass, 'I guess we were both glad of the distraction. It had started to rain, and we were heading back to the Hall. Felix was fascinated by the diggers, and he insisted we went that way every day. But that day the excavator had stopped and there were a lot of people standing round, looking as if they didn't know what to do.

'You know what it's like when everyone's looking down a hole – you gotta look, too. So we did. There wasn't much to see. Someone said they'd dug up a body and when I knew what I was looking for I could just see a few old bones. Could have been a bear for all I knew, but you took one look and fainted dead away. If I hadn't been standing right beside you, we'd have been picking you out of the mud,' Matt says. 'As it was, by the time I'd carried you over to one of those portable cabins the contractors used as an office, you were coming round. You said all you remembered was terror, like a blanket dropped over your head, but then the feeling had gone. You were embarrassed about it.'

He pauses and glances at me again. 'You really don't remember any of that?'

I shake my head. 'Nope, nothing.'

'Well, if I had to guess, I'd say that's when Isabel got into your head.'

I think about it. I suppose it does make sense. 'But why me?' I have a childish urge to stamp my feet. Haven't I had enough to deal with, losing Michael and surviving a terrible accident? Why do I have to be haunted, too? I want to concentrate on Felix and getting better. I don't want to be terribly afraid for a child who isn't mine or to have my mind taken over by a woman who died hundreds of years ago. 'Why not anyone else who was there? Philippa must have seen the bones, and Angie, and Fiona . . . all sorts of women . . . and none of them are haunted,' I say with a touch of sullenness. 'Why pick on me?'

'Maybe you're particularly susceptible or sensitive,' Matt suggests. 'Or maybe you're the one who has most in common with Isabel.'

'Oh, yeah, right. She's been dead over four hundred years, and I live in the twenty-first century. We're like twins.'

Matt ignores my sarcastic tone. 'You both had husbands you loved very much, and young sons you would do anything for,' he points out. 'You were bereft when Michael died,' he says evenly. 'Everybody knew that. Maybe that made you vulnerable.'

'Maybe.' I can see Felix hopping impatiently up ahead and I start walking again. 'I just wish I could remember what she wants me to do. Why can't she rest?'

Chapter Thirty-three

'Because she's never been properly laid to rest,' Matt says, as if the answer is obvious. 'She killed herself, for whatever reason, so she can't find peace until she's resolved whatever trauma drove her to take her own life. I researched it when I was writing the script for *The Tower*. Nobody in Tudor times had any sympathy for suicides. Those who gave in to despair were believed to have succumbed to the Devil, and their spirits were supposed to return to haunt the living. They used to drive an iron-tipped stake through the hearts of the corpses to stop them walking again. I know,' he says, seeing my horrified expression. 'Pretty gruesome, right? It wasn't what you'd call a compassionate age.'

I push that image aside. 'That is *if* Isabel killed herself,' I say. 'I just don't believe it.'

'You told me she was worried about losing her mind.' Matt is choosing his words with care. 'Isn't it possible that she did?'

I can feel my bottom lip jutting out mutinously. 'What

makes you so certain that's what happened?' I counter after a moment.

'Because you were up that tower, too,' Matt reminds me.

My hand creeps to my mouth as I realize what he is saying. I have been so convinced that I didn't jump from the tower, I have even come to suspect that someone must have pushed me, although I can't think of anyone who would do such a thing. But what if I *did* jump? What if Isabel made me jump? I remember how confused she was, how her memories seemed so out of kilter with everyone else's. What if that confusion was the beginning of a madness that drove her up the tower to try to fly off? What if she took over my body as well as my mind? What if she still could?

I chew at my bottom lip. 'What do you think I should do, Matt? Should I try to get her bones reburied next to Edmund's?' I have no idea how I would go about arranging such a thing, but it must be possible.

He doesn't answer immediately. 'Do you think that's what Isabel wants?'

No. The denial rings so loudly in my head that it's hard to believe that Matt can't hear it. And why am I pretending? I know what Isabel wants.

'She wants me to find Kit,' I say. 'She wants me to remember, but I *can't!*' I clutch Felix's coat to me. 'She won't leave me alone. She's always in my head now. I'm afraid I'm going mad, just like her.' I draw a shaky breath. 'She wants me to do something, but I don't know what, and I don't know if I'm frightened because she is, or if I'm frightened because I'm talking about a woman who died four hundred years ago and seems to be communicating with me as if that's somehow normal.'

Felix has seen that we have stopped again and runs back impatiently. 'Come *on*!' he cries.

We are following the river, round past the beach where Edmund pulled me down into the long grass, past the track which leads up to the moors, a track I have ridden a thousand times, it seems to me. And now the path turns off and Askerby Hall comes into view. Matt asks if I feel safe there, and I hesitate. To me the house feels untrustworthy. It is fixed into the landscape, but inside there is a wrongness that coats the air with an invisible sheen. It comes and goes, like a flickering light bulb that steadies the moment you reach towards it. Nobody else seems to notice it, certainly not the visitors who flock to the Hall every day, craning their necks to admire the intricate carvings, gasping at the magnificence of the long gallery, nudging each other when they spy the family photographs nestling between the heirlooms.

It is a strange life, half on show, half hidden behind the scenes. I can see the interest in the visitors' eyes as they watch us step over the twisted red ropes or walk through doors marked *Private*. Do they imagine us behind the closed doors? Do they picture us living an idyllic life rooted in the security of generation after generation owning the house and land? They don't know about the silences at the table, punctuated by awkward gobbets of conversation, or the slice and stab of Margaret's cruel remarks.

I try to explain this to Matt. 'It's not that I feel unsafe, exactly, but the more I remember, the more repellent the house seems. Sometimes I think about running away, but it's as if something won't let me go. I'd thought I would leave after Christmas, and find somewhere just for Felix and me, but now, I don't think I could, no matter how much I wanted to. I can make it as far as the village, but if I left the estate . . . it's crazy, but I'm convinced that something would happen to me. The car would slide off the road, a tree would fall, *something*. If it was just me, I would risk it, but I can't go without Felix and I can't take the chance of him being hurt. I can't explain how I know, but I can't leave Askerby until I've done what I have to do here.'

'And you've no idea what it is you need to do?'

I do, of course I do, but I've been trying not to think of it. 'I thought at first it would just be a question of finding Kit in the records, but now I think it might be something to do with the tower.'

Dread uncurls in my stomach just saying the word. Every time I approach the Hall now, the tower leers at me. I imagine it leaning down like a great lizard, flickering out a long tongue, licking horror over me. My head spins and a great roaring fills my ears, and once again I am falling, falling. A stifling darkness rolls over me and my throat closes and I can't breathe, I can't *breathe*.

'Kate.' Matt puts out a hand and for a strange disembodied moment I see myself as if looking at a stranger, eyes huge and haunted in a chalk-white face, gulping for air. 'Kate,' he says again, snapping his fingers in front of me. 'Kate, look at me.'

His words reach me through a fog of fear but I manage to focus on his face. He is looking straight into my eyes, and behind his glasses, his own are very steady.

'That's good,' he says calmly, and his hand is firm and warm under my arm. 'You're having a panic attack. Just think about breathing slowly. In, out, in, out. That's it. Attagirl.'

I slow my tattered breathing while I do as he says and focus on him. It is the first time I have let myself look at him so directly, and I am seeing him in extraordinary detail. How strange that the line of his mouth, the creases edging his eyes, that roughness on his jaw, should already be so familiar. And while I am still trying to sort out my breath, a new memory slams into me, sharp as a slap: his hands racing over me, warm and urgent; arching beneath them, clamouring to be touched harder, deeper, everywhere; the delicious slide of skin on skin; that mouth, oh God, that mouth . . .

Shaken, appalled, I step back out of his grasp. 'I'm sorry,' I say breathlessly. 'Sorry, I . . . sorry.'

'Hey, it's okay.' I can feel Matt's worried gaze on my face, but I can't look at him.

The blood is pulsing beneath my skin, pushing a warm wash of colour up my neck and into my cheeks. I will it to subside but it only throbs harder. I am furious with myself. Of all the times to remember that night! I am careening crazily between horror, humiliation and lust. I can't find my balance. Giddy and a bit sick, I clutch my stick so hard my knuckles show white.

'Kate, this isn't good,' Matt says. 'I think you need help.

What if this is what happened before? If Isabel was somehow responsible for you being up on the tower in the first place, what's to stop her doing it again?'

'What sort of help? Is there a helpline you can ring if you think you might be haunted?'

Matt isn't impressed by my facetiousness. 'I'm serious, Kate. You don't want to mess with this. You've nearly died once. It's time to call in the Church. There must be a priest in the village.'

'The vicar.' I think of Reverend Rolland, the disturbing way he strokes his beard. I cannot imagine confiding in him. I am sure that he would go straight to Fiona and Jasper, no matter what confidences priests are supposed to keep. He adores the Vavasours and is always angling for invitations to lunch at the Hall.

'I can't talk to him,' I say, and when Matt raises sceptical brows: 'I *can't*. He's big pals with Jasper and Fiona. If they get wind of the fact that I'm talking about being haunted, I know they'll use it against me. They'll say I'm an unfit mother or something. They'd love that,' I say bitterly. 'They want Felix to stay at Askerby, at least until they can pack him off to boarding school. Forget the fact that Michael was wretched there, that's what Vavasours do. "It didn't do me any harm," Jasper says, but you only have to look at him to know that it did! They'll do anything to stop me taking Felix away.'

'If Isabel pushes you off the tower again, they'll be able to do whatever they like,' Matt says brutally. 'You need to stop this somehow, Kate, before it all gets out of control.'

*

I lie on my bed, my hands over my face. I am trying to think of Kit, trying to remember what it is Isabel wants me to remember, but all I can think about is that night I spent with Matt. The memory rolls through me in wave after breathless wave of lust. I remember the piercing pleasure of flesh on flesh, the easy way he coaxed heat through the blur of grief and sent it soaring into a flame that burnt away thought, memory, everything but the feel of him, the touch of him. I let myself slip, spin out over the edge and fly off into a dazzle of sensation. I let myself forget Michael.

Afterwards, I cried. I couldn't forgive myself for that. It would have been so much easier if sex with Matt had been terrible, but I couldn't pretend that. Our bodies had locked together perfectly, clicking into place like a language that is suddenly understood, and it felt like a betrayal.

Matt knew. He told me he understood. 'You're not ready,' he said. 'I know that. You don't have to feel bad about it, Kate.'

I am ready now. Perhaps I had to forget them both before I could remember clearly but Matt is right: Michael would not have minded. He would have wanted me to be happy. The realization unlocks something inside me like a sigh, and I lower my hands. I have a sense of the future. It might be with Matt, it might not, but I have been released. I can move forward now.

Or I could if I were not still tied to Askerby by Isabel's desperation. I sit up and rub my hair. It is growing longer now. Soon I will look like my old self again.

Find Kit. That is all I need to do now. After that, Isabel can rest, and I can go. I can start to forget all over again. I tell myself that it is only the past that needs to be set right. Now that I am looking to the future, I don't think about the present, or that voice I thought I heard in hospital: *You were supposed to die.*

The scanned images for the display have gone off to the printer, and now I'm waiting for poster-sized drafts to come back. In the meantime, I am making a catalogue of the papers to cover my search for Kit. I don't want the Vavasours to know just why I am so dedicated to their archive. If they get the idea that I am obsessed with looking for someone long dead, they will use it against me. They don't like the fact that I see Matt so often. He is not welcome at the Hall, they have made that very clear.

I say nothing, but I won't give up my friendship with him. Since remembering the night we spent together I have felt acutely self-conscious when I am with him, but Matt doesn't seem to notice and we still walk together almost every day. Walking and talking isn't much, but for me it is a lifeline, my link to the outside world and to a future where I might be able to do other things: go to a bar, visit an exhibition, see a movie, simple things that presumably I used to take for granted and that now seem unutterably remote.

I will do them again, I promise myself, but first I must find Kit.

I have ploughed through a history written by the local vicar in the fifties, a dry account of when the first Lord Vavasour was given his title and estates in the late fifteenth century. A fortified keep once stood here, until Edmund's father knocked it down and built the Hall instead. I remember how its windows flashed and glittered, the raw smell of new wood. It wasn't a beautiful old house then. It was new and ostentatious, flaunting the family's wealth, caring nothing for heritage or tradition. It was all about showing off. If Edmund's father were here today, he would raze the Hall to the ground and erect something extraordinary in steel and glass.

The vicar doesn't mention Kit. He assumes that the Edmund Vavasour who died in 1697 was Edmund's son.

Find him, Isabel urges me. *Find Kit.*

I am working my way through the other papers now, reading more carefully the letters, diaries and books that we just skimmed through before.

I find Kit at last on a foggy Monday morning. Outside, the mist is thick and grey and smothers everything, and you can't see more than a few feet. I was glad of Jasper's offer to drive Felix to school. The light is so dense that I have to switch on every lamp in the library. It is very quiet. There are no visitors on a Monday; the walls of books create an effective sound barrier on the noisiest of days; and the fog absorbs any sounds from outside.

I curl up in one of the leather chairs near the window and open a packet of letters from an Emily Vavasour to her sister Sophia in 1867. As always, it takes me a little while to get my eye in, but when I do, her handwriting isn't too hard to read. Emily, it seems, was on an extended visit to cousins in London, and she wrote to her studious sister details that she thought might interest her about the people she had met and the places she had seen.

And then, when I least expect it, the name Christopher jumps out at me. She wrote:

> *I have seen a great many people of one sort or*
> *another. Last night we dined with Mr and Mrs Russell.*
> *Mr Russell is a great antiquarian and was most*
> *interested to hear about your book. He told me all about*
> *one of his ancestors, Sir John Russell, who kept a diary*
> *that Mr Russell says is extremely interesting for its*
> *observations about daily life at the time. Mr Russell*
> *was eager to show me an excerpt dated 1652 relating to*
> *the funeral of Christopher, Lord Vavasour, that he had*
> *just been reading about, as he was much struck by the*
> *coincidence of meeting me and he wondered if we were*
> *the same family. I wished you had been there as you*
> *would have been able to answer him so much more*
> *intelligently than I did, but I send you an account here*
> *as well as I remember it.*

My hands are beginning to shake. Could this be it? Could I have found Kit at last? I smooth out the letter on my knee with hands that aren't quite steady and read on:

> *Sir John described his great grief and affliction at the*
> *death of his friend Christopher Vavasour. It seems that*
> *he (Lord Vavasour) died of what was thought to be the*

plague and was interred in London rather than at his
estate. According to Sir John, Lord Christopher's son,
Edmund, was also much afflicted and gave his father a
funeral suitable to his quality. The description of the
procession and of the mourning rings and gloves was so
interesting. Mr Russell told me that Sir John writes
later of seeing the funerary stone erected by Lord
Christopher's son and widow that he says marked the
great affection and esteem in which he was held. What
do you think of that, my dear Sophia? If it is of interest
to your history, Mr Russell would be glad to send
you a copy of the whole extract as it relates to Lord
Christopher, but as your book has already been printed
I daresay it may be too late to change it?

Christopher. *Kit.*

My hands are shaking. I turn the letter over, but there is no
more about Mr Russell or Sir John. Emily moves on to news of
their brother and an unenthusiastic description of his betrothed.
Clearly she feels she has indulged Sophia's interest enough.

Could it be? 1652 . . . I am trying to calculate in my head.
Kit was born in 1598, which would make him fifty-four when
he died. He lived, and he loved. He had a wife, a son, a friend
who grieved for him. My throat closes.

'Kit,' I whisper, and Emily's writing blurs as the world rocks
around me with a mixture of remembered loss and relief. I have
found Kit at last.

Now, perhaps, Isabel can rest. I will ask the Vavasours if her bones can be buried in the church next to Edmund, and then, surely, she will let me go?

Chapter Thirty-four

I can't wait to tell Matt. 'I've found Kit!' I gabble the story of Emily's letter down the phone to him. He probably doesn't understand what on earth I'm talking about, but I am too elated to slow down. 'You know what this means, don't you? I don't need to call in a priest. I'm free of Isabel now.'

'Are you sure?' I can hear him frowning dubiously, and I pat myself all over as if to prove to myself that Isabel has really gone.

'I'm sure. She wanted me to find Kit and I have.' I am fizzing with relief. It is only now that I realize how Isabel's memories have oppressed me. The constant insistence on remembering has worn away at me, rubbing at my sense of self until it is frayed, but now that it has gone, I'm not quite sure what to do with myself. Cut loose without warning, I feel as if I could easily float away if I don't grab at something, and I curl my fingers more tightly around the phone.

'Then that's great.' Matt's voice is warm in my ear. 'It's good to hear you sounding so upbeat again, Kate.'

'I'm so happy,' I tell him. 'It's like this great weight has been lifted off me and I can move on. It feels wonderful.'

I have been released, and a whole world of opportunities is about to unfurl in front of me. How long is it since I felt anything like this giddy exhilaration? Not since I stood on top of the tower with Edmund, I think, and then I shake myself. I am supposed to be losing Isabel's memories now. She can't have any more use for me now that I have found Kit for her . . . can she?

The thought of the tower punctures my elation, a pin stabbed into a balloon. Not everything is resolved, I remember. There is still the blank square in the centre of my mind, the void where the memory of what caused my fall lies, and the giddiness whooshes out of me as I realize what I have to do. It isn't over, not yet. I don't want to remember what happened on the tower roof, but I must.

'What is it?' asks Matt when I fall silent.

'I'm thinking about the tower,' I say slowly. 'I still don't know what happened up there.'

'You said the doctors warned you that you might never remember what happened immediately before the accident.'

'I know. It just feels that this is the last piece of the puzzle. What was I doing up there?'

'What happened to moving on?'

'I need to know, Matt. I need to remember, and I think the only way to do that is to go back up there myself.'

There's a silence at the other end of the phone. 'I really don't think that's a good idea,' Matt says at last. 'You might not know *why*, but you know *what* happened last time you climbed the tower. Don't do this, Kate,' he says, but there is resignation in his voice, as if he knows it's pointless arguing. He sighs. 'You're like the character who knows there's an axe murderer on the loose and waits until she's alone in the house before she investigates the noise in the dark cellar.'

I bridle. 'I'm not that stupid, Matt. I wasn't thinking of going up alone. I don't think I'd dare, to be honest.' I hesitate. 'Actually, I was wondering if you would come with me,' I say. 'Would you mind?'

There's a long pause and, too late, I remember Matt's telling me about climbing the tower before and the horror and grief he sensed up there.

'It doesn't matter if you don't want to,' I say hastily, but he interrupts me.

'No, if you're going to do this, I'll come,' he says. 'But I'd feel better if a priest came with us as well.'

'Isabel's not the problem now,' I say confidently. '*I'm* the problem. I've got this one block left, and I have to get past it somehow. I don't think a priest is going to help. I'd rather it was just the two of us.'

Matt is reluctant, but he agrees in the end. We arrange that he will pick Felix up from school and drive him back to the Hall, which will give him an excuse to be here if necessary.

'But be very careful, Kate,' Matt says. 'Promise me you won't do anything silly.'

'I won't.'

'Tell me you won't even *think* of going up there alone.'

'I promise,' I say.

The day drags. By the early afternoon, the fog has heaved itself off the ground and the sun is doing its best to burn through, but it is no more than a fierce white circle in the sky. The light is luminous, uncanny. It trembles with anticipation, although that may be me projecting. I am restless all day.

Now that I have made up my mind to face the tower, I am longing to get it over with it. One last hurdle and I will be free. That's how it feels, anyway. All I need is to understand what happened, and then I'll be able to leave Askerby. Felix and I will go to York, I think, or Leeds. Somewhere I can get a job. I won't be able to afford much. There will be no ancestral portraits hanging on the wall, no crested silver cutlery, no long gallery to run in on rainy days, but there will be no shadows either, no oppressive sense of the past pressing down on everything.

For the first time in ages, I think of my parents in Africa. They would say that we will be lucky to have shelter at all. A flat, however small, will have a roof. It will have running water and electricity. It will be enough.

The house doesn't like my plans for the future. I can feel it. The air is jagged one minute, smothering the next. Inside, my earlier happiness has crumbled and I am edgy and uneasy. I can't settle. I keep going outside, even though I know it is too early for school to be out. At least outside I can breathe. I shield my eyes from the sun and crane my neck to look up at the tower.

It looms above me, and I can almost hear it taunting me: *Dare you know the truth?* My heart bangs in my chest. I wish Matt would come. We'll climb the tower together and at the top I will hold onto him and I will remember. I wish it was over, though. I know I need to do it, but I am frightened of what awaits me up there.

The sound of tyres on gravel makes me turn sharply, only to almost stumble over Pippin, who has followed me outside, and her hackles rise as she backs away from me.

'Pippin, it's me,' I say, part pleading, part exasperated, but she only growls.

Sighing, I turn back to the car that is parking neatly to one side. To my disappointment, it's not Matt. It's Angie.

She raises her brows at me as she hops out from behind the steering wheel. 'What on earth are you doing out here, Kate?' she asks, reaching back into the car to pull out a pair of boots and a plastic folder. 'You must be freezing.'

Now that she mentions it, I am cold. I hug my arms together self-consciously. 'I'm . . . waiting,' I say.

Angie looks at her watch. 'Are you going to collect Felix from school?'

'Not today. Matt's picking him up.'

'Oh. I see.' As always, Angie's face goes carefully blank whenever Matt's name is mentioned, and there's an awkward pause.

'Whose boots are those?' I ask to change the subject.

'Lord Vavasour's. He asked if I could get them re-heeled for him. I need to discuss possible menus for the guide dogs reception at the end of November with Lady Vavasour, so I thought I'd drop the boots off at the same time.' She pushes the car door shut with her hip and heads for the door, her feet crunching on the gravel. 'Are you coming in?'

'Not just yet.' My eyes have gone back to the tower. It's beckoning me, drawing me in.

Angie follows my gaze and stops. 'Kate? You're not thinking of going up there, are you?'

'It's the only way I'm going to remember,' I say. 'I feel it.'

'I don't think that's a good idea.' Her arms full of boots, Angie regards me worriedly. She's wearing trousers and a pale pink shirt with a padded gilet, and even on a day like this when the mist leaches all the colour from the world, her hair looks shiny and her eyes bright. 'I really don't.'

'I have to, Angie. Otherwise how am I ever going to know what happened?'

'Kate, stop this,' she says in exasperation, coming over to me. 'You don't *need* to know. All that matters is that you survived, surely? Just be grateful for that. Don't let yourself be sucked into all that stupid ghost nonsense again. Forget the tower. Stay down here and welcome Felix back from school and get on with your life without this constant looking over your shoulder. The past doesn't matter.'

'But it does,' I say, frustrated. 'Angie, don't you see? I *can't* get on with my life until I remember what happened.'

She isn't going to be convinced. 'And how do you think

Felix will feel when he comes home to find that you're not here, you're up the tower?'

'I won't go until he gets back . . . unless . . .' I hesitate. 'Unless you'd come with me now?'

'Oh, no,' she says, backing away.

'Please, Angie. Felix won't be back yet. There's plenty of time to go up the tower, see what's up there, hope to remember, and come down again, all before school's out.'

All at once I am wild to have it over and done with. Wouldn't it be better to have been up and down the tower before Matt brings Felix back? If I wait, I will have to make sure Felix is with someone I trust before Matt and I can climb the tower, and the day will be eking away. If I go with Angie, I will be able to keep my promise to Matt and still be able to face my fears before he gets here. And Matt has his own fears of the tower. I can spare him that, at least.

'Matt made me promise that I wouldn't go up on my own, but I'd be okay with you.'

The more I think about it, the more I want Angie to agree. I've hardly spent any time with her since Matt arrived. It isn't deliberate, it's just the way things have worked out. I was miffed by how firmly she dismissed the idea of including Peter Kaczka in the display, and I daresay she was miffed by my refusal to take her advice about Matt. I know, too, that she doesn't like Matt, but she is still Angie, cheery and capable, and she is not a Vavasour. I have brushed aside my suspicions of them by now. Those menacing words – *You were supposed to die* – must have been part of some hallucination. Still, I don't want to climb the tower with any of them, just in case I am wrong.

Angie sighs. 'I thought you were over all this.'

'I will be over it,' I say. 'All I need is to go up the tower, and then if I don't remember, I'll never think about it again. I promise. What time are you meeting Fiona?'

'We didn't agree a time,' she says slowly. 'I was hoping to catch her now.'

'How long is it going to take us? Quarter of an hour? Twenty minutes? You'll have plenty of time to return Jasper's boots and talk menus with Fiona afterwards. Please, Angie,' I say again.

Angie stands her ground. 'Kate,' she says seriously, clutching the boots to her gilet. 'Kate, I'm begging you not to do this. For Felix's sake, if nothing else.'

'I'm *doing* it for Felix.' I'm impatient. Why won't she understand? 'I can't be myself again unless I remember what I was doing up there before I jumped. *If* I jumped. Isn't it better for Felix if I remember who I am?'

'It's better for him if you stay right here on the ground,' Angie says, and I lift my shoulders in defeat.

'All right, I'll wait for Matt.'

'Matt?' she says sharply.

'He said he'd go up with me.'

'What about Felix? You're not thinking of taking him up, are you?'

'Of course not,' I snap back at her. Her apprehension is catching. 'I'll make sure he's safe, don't worry.'

Angie's lips tighten. 'You're determined to go through with it, then?'

'I can't explain. I just know that I have to.'

She looks up at the tower, and then at me, and she lets out a long, complicated sigh. 'All right,' she says almost to herself. 'Better me than Matt, I suppose. I'll go with you.'

I am too relieved at the thought of being able to get the whole business over with as soon as possible to wonder what she means by that. 'Thank you, Angie.'

'Let me just put these back in the car.'

She stores the boots and the folder away and turns to me, squaring her shoulders as she contemplates the tower. 'Let's get it over with,' she says. 'Do you need your stick?'

I decide it'll just get in the way on the stairs. 'I'll manage without it,' I say.

We go back inside to the great hall and along to the bottom of the stone stairs that spiral to the top of the tower. I have fallen silent. The thought of climbing up them is shrinking my flesh against my bones, and a cold hand grips my entrails as terror pops its head over my shoulder and leers in my face once more. *The tower?* it seems to say. *Come on up, I'm waiting for you.*

I put my foot on the bottom step and stop. My mouth is dry, my heart thundering against my ribs. 'I . . . I don't think I can do it after all,' I whisper.

'Then let's go back,' Angie says promptly.

Coward.

'No.' I change my mind and press my hand against the wall.

If I go back at this stage, I'll lose my nerve, and I might not try again. 'No, let's do it now.'

The staircase is very narrow, and the stone steps are worn smooth and slippery with age. The walls are roughly plastered and whitewashed, and punctuated by a few narrow windows that let in a meagre light. I keep one hand flat on the wall as I climb with Angie behind me. My heart is thudding against my ribs, and dread lies cold and queasy in my stomach. I'm very glad Angie is with me.

'So you're back with Matt?' she says after a while, from below me.

'I'm not exactly *with* him,' I begin, and then stop. What is the point of pretending? 'Yes. I don't know what will happen, but . . . I like him, Angie,' I say simply.

'You know George is talking about going to New Zealand?'

'George?' I stop and stare down at her. 'What on earth for?'

'To get over you.'

'That's crazy,' I say. 'He'll forget about me once I've gone.'

'That's what I think, too,' Angie says in an odd voice.

We pass the landing where the garderobe used to be. I remember the overpowering stench, the roughness of the wooden door beneath my fists as I beat at it to be let out.

I'm out of breath and my leg is aching when we finally emerge up onto the flat roof of the tower. I'm wishing I had fetched my stick after all, but it feels good to breathe the fresh air after the staleness of the staircase.

The sun is still blocked by the fog, but it is surprising how far you can see now. I turn slowly. Narrowing my eyes to blind myself to the roads, the pylons and the wind farm in the distance, I can imagine it is still as it was when Edmund brought me up here and told me I was free. It is as if I can still feel his hands on my shoulders, and longing for him constricts my throat.

Edmund, Edmund, where are you?

I open my eyes properly. We are standing on panels of smooth lead sheeting jointed with hammered ridges and dotted with capped vents like little mushrooms. They slope from the centre of the tower roof to the edge, where a stone step leads up to the crenellated wall. I can see the gap between the stones where I leant that day, but Edmund isn't here now. There is nothing here, but even as I think that, danger starts to shriek in my head, and I stand very still.

'What is it?' I'm too intent to wonder about the strained note in Angie's voice. 'Have you remembered something?' she demands, and I nod. Because it is as if a veil is being ripped from my mind.

I see myself running up the staircase after Judith, my heart pounding. 'Come quick!' she had cried. 'Eliza has Kit in the tower!'

I did not stop to question her. The thought of my child in those gnarled hands, being ogled by those vacant eyes, made my blood turn to ice. I picked up my skirts and ran after Judith. When we burst onto the roof, and I saw Kit lying bemused but unhurt on the coverlet from his cradle, I was so relieved that I bent almost double, the breath whooping from my lungs, and a hand at the stitch in my side.

Judith darted over to pick him up. 'The Lord be thanked!' she said.

'Indeed.' I straighten with difficulty, still breathing heavily. 'Where is Eliza?'

'Perhaps she flew away like you once wished to do,' Judith suggests. There is something strange in her voice, but I can't place it. 'A witch can do whatever she likes, can she not?'

'I shall have her banished from the village,' I said furiously. Now that the intensity of relief had passed, anger coursed through me. 'She has threatened my son. I do not care that she is poor or lacking in wits. I shall have her whipped!'

'You cannot have her banished for being mad,' said Judith reasonably, 'for then you would need to banish yourself.'

I was not really listening. I was looking at Kit and thinking about how glad I was to see him. 'Banish myself? Why would I do such a thing?'

'Because you, too, are mad, Isabel,' she said. 'Quite, quite mad.'

My smile faltered. 'Judith?'

'Why else did you come running up here like a madwoman?'

'You told me Eliza had taken Kit!'

'Did I? She is but a poor, foolish old woman. Why would she do such a thing?'

'I do not know.' I looked at Judith's face. It was as if a hand had passed over it, wiping away the familiar meekness and leaving behind an expression that glittered with malice. She was Judith, but not Judith, and something terrible uncurled inside me. Was it me or was it her who had changed? Was she mad, or was I?

'Give me Kit,' I said.

'I think not.'

Judith jumped up onto the stone step. She was too close to the battlements with Kit. My heart was banging against my ribs. 'Judith, what are you doing? What has happened?'

'Your husband is coming home,' she said.

Edmund. Thank God. My face lit up at the thought of him. Edmund would make sense of all this. He would tell Judith to stop behaving so oddly. Everything would be well once Edmund was home.

A thought struck me. 'Why did he write to you and not to me?'

'Oh, did you not know? Edmund and I have been corresponding.'

'What about?'

'Why, about you, dear Isabel, and how worried we both are. I wrote to him to tell him how strangely you have been behaving. I told him not to worry, but of course he does. Still, I did not expect him to return quite so soon.' She clicked her tongue, exasperated.

My head felt like a dandelion gone to seed: my thoughts would scatter at the slightest puff. All I could think was that she held Kit too close to the edge of the tower, and that the friend I had loved like no other had become a stranger. A stranger holding Kit. I was desperate to snatch him from her, but something about the glitter in her eyes told me to stand very still.

My mouth was dust dry. 'Judith, I do not understand,' I said.

'I know,' she said. 'You understand nothing, Isabel. You never have. You are such a simple, trusting fool. You believe everything you are told. No wonder Edmund is worried about your behaviour.'

'What do you mean? What behaviour?'

'How you forget the simplest things. The poison you bought from Eliza.'

'I bought nothing from her!'

'But who will believe that when she told everyone about the penny you gave her?' Judith laughs, and the sound makes my skin shrink. 'I gave her a penny, too, if she played her part, and she did it well, did she not? She earned her tuppence!'

'Edmund will believe it,' I said, my voice shaking.

'Will he? When I tell him how you lost your reason and carried Kit up the tower? How close you came to throwing him to his death?'

She swung Kit towards the battlements, and dread pooled cold and black in my stomach. 'Judith, stop this now.'

'Who knows what would have happened if I had not come to find you?' she said, as if I had not spoken. She put her head on one side, considering. 'Yes, that is what I will tell Edmund when he returns.'

'He will believe me,' I said. I knew that it was true.

'But you will not be here,' she said, almost gently.

I shook my head. I didn't understand what was happening. Nothing of what Judith was saying made any sense. 'Of course I will,' I said. 'Where would I go?'

'That is indeed the question,' said Judith, and she chuckled. 'You, Isabel, are going to fly, just like you always said you wanted to. Don't you remember? Edmund brought you up here. You told me how it felt with his hands on you, telling you that everything you saw was yours. But for you that didn't matter, did it? All you cared about was the fact that Edmund was there and you felt free. You felt as if you could fly, you said. Well, now is your chance.'

She jerked her head towards the battlements. 'Fly, Isabel,' she said, with a smile that struck a chill right down to my bones. 'If you can,' she added. 'And if you cannot, then you will have to die, won't you?'

Chapter Thirty-five

Die. My hand went to my throat at the word. I had been afraid
that I was losing my reason but now I saw the truth. It was not
I. It was Judith who was mad.

'Judith, what has happened to you?' I whispered.

'Nothing has happened,' she said, almost surprised. 'I am as
I have always been. I know what I want and I have been pre-
pared to wait for it. Oh, how I have waited!' she said, jiggling
Kit reflectively.

I thought about making a leap for him, but she was too far
away, and too close to the edge. How could I be sure that this
stranger who looked like Judith and sounded like Judith would
not drop him?

'What is it that you want?' I asked. My mind was blurry
still and the impossibility of what I was hearing was beating at
me. I wanted to lower my head and shake it like a cow ridding
itself of flies, but I didn't dare take my eyes off Judith.

'What do I want? Why, that is simple,' she said. 'I want to

be you, Isabel. I want to be Lady Vavasour, with your fortune and your doting husband and your fine house and your darling child. Years and years I have spent pretending to be pleased for you. Years of being sweet and helpful, of being *grateful* to you.' She spat out the word. 'It was always so easy for you, Isabel. You had wealth and I had *nothing*.'

'It was not fair, I know,' I said, trying to keep my voice steady. I had to stand very still, as I would with a frightened horse. 'I did not care that you were poor, Judith.'

'No, *you* did not care, but *I* did! Who would look at me, only ever the poor connection?'

Too late I remember Edmund. *Do you think Judith is capable of happiness?* 'I did not know you were so unhappy.'

'Of course you didn't,' Judith said contemptuously. 'You know nothing.'

I was shaking, unable to comprehend the hatred that spilt out of her. This had to be a nightmare, I remember thinking that. I had to be asleep in my bed. What else could it be when my dearest friend had turned into this woman with bitter eyes and a venomously twisted mouth?

'You could have been happy if you had chosen to be,' I said. 'You did not have to want my life. You could have been happy with your own.'

'What opportunity have *I* ever had for happiness?'

'My aunt and uncle gave you a home, I gave you friendship. Stephen Morley would have wed you,' I said, but that only made her pace faster. 'You could have had a husband and a home of your own.'

'Pah, that fat squire! Why would I settle for him when I could have Edmund?'

'Edmund?' I stared at her, my heart beating horribly in my throat.

'I took one look at him when he stood in the great hall at Crabbersett that day, and I wanted him,' Judith said. 'But he only ever had eyes for you. He never even saw me.' Her whole face convulsed with bitterness. 'Why not? I am beautiful, am I not? I am more beautiful than you,' she said, 'but he saw only you.'

Bafflement threaded her voice. I looked at her, at the golden hair and pale, perfect features, and I realized that her beauty was that of a frosty morning, hard and cold and repellent. I had always thought of her as beautiful, but I had projected onto her the warmth I wanted to see. What other mistakes had I made?

'He saw only your inheritance,' Judith said, as I realized she must have said many times to herself to justify the way Edmund's eyes passed over her.

'No.' That I knew to be untrue. 'Perhaps the fact that I was an heiress brought him to Crabbersett in the first place, but he cares nothing for that. He loves me.'

'He will learn to love me instead.'

'No.' I shook my head, sure of that at least. 'No, he would never love you.'

'Well, it will be enough that he marries me,' she said carelessly. 'He will need a mother for poor motherless Kit, abandoned by you in your madness.'

In spite of my resolve to stay calm, I was trembling. 'I would never abandon my son. Edmund knows that.'

Judith only smiled and stepped nearer to the battlements, and my heart froze mid-beat. She held Kit over the edge, and sensing the danger, he started to cry. 'Judith, stop this,' I managed, but my mouth was so dry I could hardly get out the words. 'He is just a babe.'

'Would you do anything to save him, Isabel?'

'Anything. I will give you anything you want if you will just bring him back to safety.'

'Then jump,' she said.

Perhaps I should have realized that was coming. I had been a fool about so much, and I was a fool about that, too. But I could not believe what I had heard.

'Jump,' she said again. 'I am tired of waiting. It is my turn now. I will be distraught when Edmund comes back, and we will comfort each other.' She tilted her head to one side, imagining the scene. 'I will take your place at last, Isabel. *I* will be Lady Vavasour then, and when I have a son of my own, perhaps poor Kit will inherit his mother's madness?'

'Judith,' I whispered, terrified. 'I must be mad indeed to think you are saying such things.'

'I have been giving you wormwood to confuse you for years.' She laughed at her cleverness. 'Why do you think all those remedies were so bitter? But you are such a trusting soul, Isabel! You even believed you had tripped when I pushed you down the stairs that day!' Then the wild laugh dropped from her face like a stone, and she was once more bright-eyed and deadly serious. She held Kit back out over the edge. 'Now, jump, or I will drop your precious child.'

'No!' The cry was torn from my throat and I leapt up onto the stone. 'Judith, no!'

'Jump,' she said, implacable.

'Edmund,' I stutter, my mind scrabbling frantically for a way out. 'If you drop Kit, you will never have him. I will tell him what you did.'

Judith was unimpressed. 'But who will he believe, you who have killed his son, or me, who has been running his house, sending him letters while you never reply to his?'

'I have never seen them,' I said slowly. 'He does not reply to mine.'

'If you had ever troubled yourself with the running of your household then you would have known that your letters were never sent, and that Edmund's to you went straight onto the fire once I had read them. But no, you must ride out and run wild, and this is your reward,' she said triumphantly. 'The neighbours will not be surprised, not after they saw how strange you were at your lying-in.

'Besides,' she said. 'Kit would still be dead. I would not have to see you happy. That would be something. Now,' she went on briskly, 'my arms are getting quite tired holding the child. I may just drop him anyway.'

'No.' This time I could barely manage more than a whimper.

Judith nodded at the gap in the battlements. 'Up you get then. It is simple – Kit dies or you do.'

'Judith, I thought we were friends.' I could not believe that it had come to this. I could not comprehend what she was saying.

'You wanted a friend so you saw one,' she said. 'But I hated you right from the start. Who do you think told on you when you rode out with Edmund that day? I watched your uncle beat you afterwards and I pretended to cry, but I had to hide my smile in my sleeve.'

'I would have given you anything,' I said dully.

'Oh yes, new gowns for Judith, a bed of my own, anything I asked for, and I had to be so grateful. I didn't want your gowns,' she said, 'I wanted your life, and I shall have it. They won't even be able to bury you in the churchyard, I'm afraid,' she added with a sly smile. 'The Devil has been whispering in your ear and you are about to give in to temptation.' Her voice hardened. 'Now, jump.'

She let Kit slip in her hands, and he screamed anew.

'Jump,' she said again. 'Jump now, Isabel, or I swear I will drop him.'

What could I do? What could I *do*? I put my hands on the battlements, one on either side to support myself, and I lifted a foot up. There was a rushing and a roaring in my ears: the wind tugging at my gown, terror chuckling in my head, and Kit, wailing in Judith's arms.

Meg, I remembered. Meg would care for him. But he had to live. And if he were to live, it seemed I had to die.

'Go on,' Judith said in a hard voice.

'Do you promise me you will not drop him?' My own voice was reedy with shock. It sounded as though it belonged to someone else.

'Edmund needs a son for me to care for,' she said, considering. 'If you are both gone, who knows what he might take it into his head to do? So, yes, for now I need Kit. When you are dead, at least he has a chance of life, so let that be a comfort to you. Now,' she said, 'enough discussion. Kit will never be safe as long as you are alive, so jump. Do it now, Isabel.'

I looked at my son for the last time. 'Kit, dear one, stay safe, live long.'

Swallowing hard, I lifted my other foot up to stand between the battlements. I was shaking as if with an ague, and the ground below tilted horrifyingly up to meet me. I couldn't look down. Ahead I could see the moors rolling up and away, and with an odd detached part of my mind I thought of riding up there with my husband, of laughing as the breeze snatched at my hat, of being certain that I was the happiest of women.

'Edmund,' I whispered. 'Edmund, forgive me,' and I stepped out into nothing.

Then I was flying at last, spinning, tumbling, not elegantly but awkwardly, my heavy skirts flapping, and all I felt was disbelief that this was really happening. I could not end that way, I remember thinking that. No, I was dreaming, and I would wake with Edmund beside me and Kit in his cradle, and my dear friend Judith in the next chamber. I had time to think all of that as stone walls and green fields and the sky lurched around me, and then the ground rushed up to grab me and there was a great white flash and then nothing.

My hands are crossed at my throat in horror. 'Oh my God, oh my God, it was *Judith*!' I feel sick and giddy, as if I am falling still. Staggering over to the stone step, I sink down onto it and drop my head between my knees. My mind is ringing with shock, and that blazing, brilliant flash burns still behind my eyes. I can't seem to catch my breath. My chest heaves but I can't suck in enough air, so I am gasping and gulping in panic.

Slow, slow down, I tell myself. Breathe in, breathe out. Slow.

Gradually, the dreadful tightness around my chest eases, and my galloping heart slows, although an echo of its fearful hoof beats still thuds in my ears. When I lift my head from my knees at last, I realize that I am crying and I swipe at my cheeks with the back of my hand. 'Isabel,' I murmur. 'Oh, Isabel.'

Her last terrible moments are playing on a hideous loop inside my head and I'm not sure how long I sit there staring blankly ahead before some quality in the silence brings me back to the present. My eyes focus on a dark figure outlined against the strange colourless sun. I can't make out its features, and my heart jerks as I scramble instinctively to my feet. 'Judith!'

Then she moves and I see who it is. 'Oh . . . Angie, thank God!' I sit shakily once more, patting my pounding heart back into place. 'Jesus, I've just remembered something terrifying . . .' I trail off because I am remembering something else, too. I'm remembering being up on the roof another time. It's not Isabel's memory, it's mine.

'You were here, too,' I tell Angie slowly. 'I remember you.'

She lets out a long, long sigh. 'I was afraid you would. I *begged* you not to come up here, but you wouldn't listen, would you? You never *listen*.'

'But—' I stop. My memories are getting muddled. Angie was there, I remember that, but she kept merging into Judith. I remember the jolt of terror when she bent to kiss my cheek in hospital. *I'm your friend*, she said.

Just as Judith had been Isabel's friend.

I have been so terrified by what happened to Isabel that I haven't realized that there is a new and very different danger right in front of me.

'Was it you?' I ask. My tongue feels too big for my mouth and I can hardly get the words out. 'Did you push me?'

'No, I didn't push you. You jumped all by yourself.' Oddly relaxed, Angie wanders over to the gap in the battlements where Isabel once stood. 'Right here,' she says, pointing, and turns back to face me. 'I didn't know what was going on at first. You made me come up here with you that day. You'd been acting strangely ever since those bones were discovered. We all thought you were having a breakdown, so when you insisted on coming up here, I thought I should probably play along. I didn't know what you were going to do, though. I swear I didn't.'

I moisten my lips carefully. 'So what happened?'

'You were babbling about somebody called Kit and a woman called Eliza, but I couldn't follow most of it. Then when we got here, you started going on and on about a Judith,' she tells me. 'It was crazy. You kept jumping up on the step there, and then you got up on the battlements.'

I had been reliving Isabel's life, and her death, I realize. That time, though, I survived the terrible fall, and I have only been remembering. I am not 'strange' or 'mad' now. Now I know exactly what happened.

'It was *really* creepy,' Angie says. 'I tried to talk to you, but I couldn't get through, and then . . .' Her voice cracks a little and she spreads her hands. 'And then you . . . you jumped. One minute you were there and the next you were gone.'

Gone. I remember tumbling through the air, the terror and the disbelief.

'Why didn't you say anything before?'

'I thought you were dead,' she says. 'No one saw me come up, and no one saw me go down, so there didn't seem any point in saying anything. I did have a few bad moments when I realized you'd survived,' she confesses, 'but then you lost your memory, and I realized that even if you did remember, nobody would believe you, especially after you'd been behaving so weirdly.'

And now? I think. Who would believe me now?

The roof feels very cold all of a sudden. I'm glad I'm sitting down. I am still horrified by Isabel's death and I have been jolted from that into an equally horrifying present. There is a buzzing, high and white, in my head, and my mind is slipping and sliding, scrabbling desperately for a grip. I can hardly comprehend what Angie is telling me so calmly.

'I don't understand. If you were here, if you saw me about to jump, why didn't you stop me?'

Her eyes slide away from mine. 'You don't know what it was like before then. You were like some crazy person, Kate, rambling on and on about the past the whole time. I tried to talk to you about the effect you were having on Felix, we all did, but you wouldn't listen. It was like you'd been taken over or something.'

'But that's exactly what had happened,' I say bitterly. 'I was possessed by Isabel, so possessed that I relived her life, and then I relived her death, and you didn't lift a finger to stop me.'

'Possessed?' Angie sounds irritated rather than guilty. 'You weren't *possessed*!'

'Then how do you explain the fact that I jumped at all?'

'You were upset when the American left, and instead of getting a grip, you let yourself go,' she says. 'You worked yourself into a breakdown but if anyone suggested that you talk to someone, oh no! You weren't going to do that. You weren't depressed, and you didn't need help. Admitting you were depressed would be much too ordinary for you, wouldn't it, Kate?'

I'm shaken by the dislike in her voice. Were all those protestations of friendship a lie? Has Angie hated me all along?

'Whatever you thought, you didn't have to let me jump,' I say as levelly as I can. I don't want her to know how upset I am. How frightened.

'It wasn't like that.' Angie twists her hands fretfully together. 'It all happened so fast. You've got to remember that I was terrified, and keeping as far away from you as possible. I didn't know what you were going to do.'

'So you just stood there and let it happen?'

'All right, yes, I did!' Goaded, she shouts before struggling to get herself back under control. 'You've got no idea how difficult you'd been,' she said more calmly. 'Poor darling Felix was frightened and confused, and everyone else was worried sick. It wasn't like you were being a good mother. It wasn't like you were *happy*.' Her voice thickens with resentment in spite of herself. 'You had Felix, you had a home at Askerby, you had everything I've ever wanted, but did you appreciate it? No! You have to get involved with Americans, and you talk about leaving and you start carrying on about dead people and . . . I don't know . . . when you got up there on the battlements, I just thought how much easier it would be if you just jumped and put us all out of our misery.' She swallows. 'I didn't push you, Kate, but yes, I wished you would jump and then you did.' She lifts her face from her hands, and her expression is half dazed, as if remembering that moment of disbelief. 'I couldn't believe it.'

I can't help myself. 'I thought we were friends,' I say bleakly. Just as Isabel thought Judith was her friend.

'You had *everything*,' Angie says in reply. 'Ever since I can remember, I've longed to be a Vavasour, to be part of the family and to live at the Hall. It's not like I wouldn't belong,' she says. 'My grandfather was a *count*, but nobody ever wanted to know that. I was just the girl at the Lodge, good old reliable Angie.' Her mouth twists.

I find myself wanting to reassure her that it isn't how the Vavasours think of her, but I can't. That is exactly what they think.

'When I was little girl I wanted to marry Michael so I could be Lady Vavasour,' she goes on after a moment, 'but Michael always had such funny ideas, it wouldn't have worked. Anyway, I preferred George. We've got so much in common, more than he knows,' she says, her face softening. 'I dreamt of marrying him, of having a family to fill up the Hall, and we'd look after Askerby together. We'd have made a great team. I didn't mind not being Lady Vavasour if I could have George and stay at Askerby. I made a point of being around to help him in the estate office. I was there for whatever he needed. I was sure he would look at me one day and *see* me, and realize that we were meant to be together.'

'And did he?'

Her gaze grows distant. 'I thought so. We were clearing up after a Christmas party for the estate workers in the old Visitor Centre, just the two of us. Someone had put up some mistletoe from the West Woods, and he kissed me.' Lost in the memory of that moment, Angie smiles, and I feel a pang of pity for her. 'We ended up making love right there in the Visitor Centre,' she tells me. 'It was my first time, but I didn't regret it. I wanted it to be George. I wanted him to know that he was special, that it was only ever going to be him.'

She presses her clenched fists to her chest, remembering that moment. 'I was so happy afterwards. I was so sure that was it, and we'd be together forever.'

Poor Angie, so desperate for a place in George's life that she could mistake a drunken fumble at a Christmas party for true love.

The almost exalted expression in her face fades. 'But the very next day Michael came back for Christmas, and he brought you, and George took one look at you and wanted you instead,' she says dully. 'He told me what had happened had been a mistake. He even apologized.'

'Oh, Angie.' In spite of knowing that she let me jump, I am desperately sorry for her.

'He said he hoped we could both forget about it.' Her mouth trembles. 'How could I forget it when he was there every day?'

'I'm sorry,' I say. 'You know I never encouraged George, don't you, Angie? Not once.'

She doesn't seem to hear me. 'I hoped that he would forget about you after you left, but he never kissed me again, and then Michael got sick and you came back and that was that. You even had a baby,' she says bitterly. 'You had *no idea* how lucky you were.'

'Michael died,' I remind her.

'You've still got Felix. I love him.'

'I know you do,' I say carefully. 'You're brilliant with kids, Angie. You should have some of your own.'

Her face contorts. 'How is that ever going to happen while you're around?'

'I'll leave.'

'But then you'll take Felix away, and I don't think I could bear that. I couldn't love him more if he was mine, and I know he loves me, too.'

'Yes, he does.' I feel sick. Angie sounds so reasonable.

'So you see, when you jumped, I was horrified, but there was a bit of me that was glad, too,' she confides. 'As I ran down the tower, I was already thinking about Felix, and George, and how we could comfort each other and be a little family. Four-year-olds forget pretty quickly, and I'd been more of a mother to him than you had those past few weeks. I didn't think it would be too long before he was calling me Mummy. I mean, he won't even call you Mummy now, will he?' she says with a glint of malice. 'I've noticed that. I'm sure it wouldn't take him long to forget you altogether and think of me as his mother.'

My fingers curl into fists. Take my place with Felix? Over my dead body, I think, and then I catch myself. My dead body was exactly what Angie was counting on. My pity for her evaporates. I'm sorry that she has been deluded by her dreams about George, but she is not having Felix.

'How disappointing for you that I survived,' I manage through clenched teeth.

Angie doesn't even bother to deny it. 'You were supposed to die, but you didn't. You came back to Askerby and you're living here again, and George is in love with you again and you don't even *care*!' She gestures wildly in frustration. 'It's so *unfair*. And now George is talking about going to New Zealand. Everything's gone wrong, and it's all your fault! *Now* what am I supposed to do?'

Chapter Thirty-six

'I don't know,' I say, 'but let's talk about it downstairs, where it's warm.' As we've been talking, the air has chilled and the fog has drifted down from the moors to blanket the gardens in a ghostly blur.

Angie frowns. 'We can't go back now, Kate,' she says.

'Yes, we can.' With an effort I keep my voice even. 'We can sort this out.'

'No.' She shakes her head so that her hair swings. 'It's too late for that. Everything's spoilt now.'

'Angie, you said you didn't push me and I believe you. No one's going to arrest you for attempted manslaughter.'

'You'd tell the Vavasours what happened, and they would send me away.'

I try to laugh. 'They'd never get rid of you, Angie. They rely on you too much.'

'For errands, perhaps,' she says bitterly, 'but George will still be gone. He won't stay if you're here.'

'Then I'll go,' I say, surreptitiously calculating how long it would take me to get to the stairs. Unfortunately, Angie is standing between me and them, and I am so slow. I can't run properly on my leg. The only thing to do is to wait until somebody comes. Until then I will pretend that we are having a normal conversation and that the glitter in her eyes doesn't freeze the marrow in my bones.

'But you'll take Felix with you.'

'Yes.' I'm not going to lie about that. 'I'll take Felix, but you and George can make a relationship on your own, if that's what you really want. You're a pretty woman, Angie,' I add cajolingly. 'You could make him want you.'

I sound like a pimp. Maybe it isn't fair to play on her delusions, but I am afraid. Afraid for myself and afraid for Felix if she gets her way. Angie might love him, but there is a hollowness inside her that I can only now see. Behind that mask of cheerful competence is an absence of empathy that means she can watch a friend jump to her death and think only of what it means for her. I don't want Felix brought up by a woman like that. I don't want him brought up by anyone but me.

For a moment I think that she has heard me. She looks straight at me, and I can see her thinking about it, twisting her hands together obsessively as her mind ticks away at the possibilities.

She has a choice. She can step back now and accept that her idea of using Felix to create a Vavasour family all for herself is nothing more than a fantasy. She can face the truth and choose to make a family of her own in the real world, with a man who will treat her to more than a quick shag after a Christmas party, away from Askerby.

Or she can choose a dream based on yearning and wishful thinking and envy. And death. Mine.

'No,' she decides at last. 'George wouldn't leave Askerby if Felix was all alone. He'd stay and help, and he'd need me to look after Felix. I'd be there for both of them.'

She has considered her options, and her best bet is for me to die.

I struggle to my feet, ignoring the white heat of pain in my leg. I am not going to sit meekly here and discuss my death.

'I'm not going to jump, Angie,' I say, unable to prevent the breathless waver in my voice. 'It's different this time. I've remembered what happened, but I'm not possessed. I'm not going to make things easy for you. If you want me to die, you're going to have to push me off yourself.'

I am betting that Angie isn't capable of murder . . . but what if I'm wrong?

Her face crumples. 'I don't want to kill you! I just want a family! Is that so much to ask?'

'No,' I say. 'But you can't have mine. You can't have Felix.'

'But George won't look at me unless he needs me to look after Felix,' she says, as if that is entirely reasonable. 'Even if he loved me, he's afraid I might have a freak baby like Peter.' She makes a sound that is halfway between a sob and a laugh as she paces between me and the stairwell. 'It's ironic, really.'

'Because Peter was Ralph Vavasour's son, and George is related to him, too?'

She spins round. 'You know?'

'I guessed,' I say. 'I wondered if Ralph and your grand-mother might have had an affair.'

'You think you're so clever, don't you? No, Babcia wasn't Peter's mother.'

'Then who was?'

'Why, Lady Margaret, of course.'

I gape at her. '*Margaret?*'

'*Yes!*' Angie's smile is eerily normal and I blink, disorientated by the sudden conviction that I am not really standing on top of the tower discussing whether or not Angie is prepared to kill me. 'You have no idea, do you?'

My mind is racing. I feel as if I have missed a turn and am backtracking frantically, desperate to catch up. 'Peter was Margaret and Ralph's son?'

'Got it in one! Babcia told me all about it one day when she was confused, but she was sworn to secrecy if she wanted to stay at the Lodge, so she gets very anxious if you try to ask her about it. I think it's best that nobody else knows, don't you? The Vavasours wouldn't like the truth getting out.'

I am hardly listening. 'Margaret and Ralph *gave their son away?*'

'Well, you couldn't have the next Lord Vavasour looking like that, could you? They were both so beautiful, it must have been quite a shock to them,' Angie says reflectively. 'Of course, the doctor and the midwife knew the truth, but in those days it was easier to hush things up. They gave out that the baby had died, and Ralph took Peter to his old friends Adam and Dosia.

442

They were living in some dump in Leeds, apparently. Adam was drinking, they had no money . . . they were in no position to refuse. And Babcia thought, I think, that if they could come back to Askerby, everything would be all right. Adam and Ralph could resume their friendship and Adam would stop drinking.

'Of course, it didn't work out like that. The last thing Margaret wanted was a permanent reminder of her ugly child, but what could she do? When it was clear that there were going to be no more good old days, Adam took to blackmail like a duck to water, and he never had to work again. Ralph kept paying out until he died, and then Adam extracted a promise from Margaret that he and Dosia had the use of the Lodge for as long as they lived.

'Meanwhile, Ralph and Margaret kept trying for a baby who didn't look like he belonged in a circus.' Angie recounts the story coolly, cruelly. 'It took them a little while. First they had Joanna, who was a girl and no good to them, but at last Jasper was born, and after that they never touched each other again. It's an edifying little story, isn't it?'

'It's horrible,' I say. 'But it sounds as if Peter ended up with a kinder mother than his own would have been.'

'Oh, Peter, he didn't care about anything except his stupid pheasants,' Angie says dismissively. 'He never said boo to a goose. He wouldn't have wanted to be Lord Vavasour. Can you imagine his portrait hanging on the wall?' She laughs, a high, wild laugh that sends a convulsive shudder down my spine. 'It was better for everybody when he died. It's better if he's just forgotten, and he nearly was, until you came along wanting to include him in your display, like a genetic slip was something to be proud of!'

How is it possible that I have never sensed the wrongness in Angie before? I cannot believe what I am hearing. *It's better if he's just forgotten.* 'Why would you want to be part of a family that could just give away a child who doesn't look the way they want him to look?' I ask her in disbelief.

'Because of Askerby.' Angie looks at me as uncomprehendingly, just as I must be looking at her. She gazes over the battlements to the gatehouse below. 'I love every stone of this house, I know every picture. Nobody knows Askerby the way I do,' she says fiercely. '*Nobody.* This is my *home.* Why does nobody understand that? But I'll never be part of it unless George marries me.'

My stomach twists nervously. My leg is jangling with pain, but I am afraid that sitting down again will put me at a disadvantage if I need to run after all.

'There are other families to be part of,' I say. 'Other places to love.'

But Angie isn't listening. 'I could tell him about Peter,' she says, and I'm not sure if she's talking to me or to herself. 'George knows I'd never tell anyone else the truth. The bad genes are on his side, and anyway, we'd have Felix. I'm sure he'd be a good father. We'd be such a lovely family.' She turns on me suddenly. 'Much better than *you*,' she adds with a resentful look.

I'm not having that. In spite of my fear, I put up my chin. 'I'm Felix's mother. Nobody is going to be better than me.'

She shakes her head. 'You're a bad mother, Kate. You jumped off the tower here and left Felix all alone. You forgot all about him. All that time you were lying in hospital, who was looking after him? I was! I'm the one who picked Felix up when he fell over. I'm the one who kissed his scraped knee better. I put him to bed and fed him and read him stories while you, you didn't even recognize him! You've been too lost in some past to bother about your own son,' she says contemptuously.

'Look at you today! You couldn't even be bothered to pick him up from school or wait to see him when he got home. You were too busy wanting to get up here and find out about your precious past. Well, now you know. You chose the past, and I choose Felix.'

There is just enough truth in her words to make me wince, but there is no point in claiming that it was not my fault, that I didn't choose to be possessed by Isabel. Maybe at some level I did. Maybe in my grief for Michael I refused to let go of the past, just as Angie says.

'I begged you to leave things be,' she reminds me. 'I *begged* you not to come up here today, didn't I? I didn't want to come, but you made me. You remember that, don't you?'

'Yes, I do.' She's right, I asked her to come. '*Please, Angie,*' I said. This is my fault.

'If you had just listened to me, none of this would have happened,' she tells me, her eyes bright and accusing. 'But maybe it is just as well.' She lets out a long sigh. 'George will go away if I don't do something and at least this way I've got a chance. There's only one problem.' She looks at me. 'You.'

She has crossed some threshold. She could have stepped back, but she has surrendered instead to the void inside her, to the hungry hole that demands a child, a family, a place with the Vavasours. She is committed now. I can see it in her empty eyes.

'So . . . what can I do?' Angie spreads her hands, inviting me to help solve her problem. 'I don't suppose you'd like to jump again?' She smiles at me, looking so normal that the breath stops in my throat.

'No.' I back away until I come up against the step. 'No, it won't work this time, Angie. I haven't been behaving strangely.'

'I think you have. Talking about disinheriting Felix, obsessing about some old tomb. Oh yes, Joanna and Philippa told George you were up to your old tricks again. And then, of course, I'll be able to tell them that you sat in the cafe and said you could smell a grave. It doesn't get stranger than that.'

'It's not the same. I didn't know what I was doing last time,' I say, 'but this time, I do. No one will believe it if I fall now. If anything happens to me, they'll know you're responsible.'

'Why should they? Did anyone see us come up here together?'

'Matt knows I was coming up the tower,' I say.

Angie dismisses Matt with a wave of her hand. 'Who cares what he thinks? Anyway, he doesn't know I'm up here with you, does he? He won't be able to prove anything, and I'll be there to console George.'

446

'He didn't want to be consoled last time,' I point out, and Angie's lips thin.

'Because you survived. That won't happen this time. I'll make sure you go over where there are no trees to break your fall.'

I watch in horror as she jumps up onto the platform and walks around the walls, peering over between the gaps in the battlements so that she can choose the best spot. 'Here, I think,' she decides at last. 'Flat onto the gravel.'

'They won't believe it.' Carefully, I edge around so that I have a clear run to the stairs. If only I had my phone with me. But I wasn't meaning to come up the tower when I met Angie. I was waiting for Matt.

Longing for him gusts through me. I can picture him so clearly: the alert eyes, the smile that hovers around his mouth. He is sensible, self-deprecating, *sane*. When he comes, I will tell him I am ready to leave this place, with its sour secrets and centuries of bitterness and betrayal.

But first I have to get past Angie. She has jumped down from the step and is eyeing me with a calculating, predatory look that slows my heart to a painful thud. Is this how a rabbit feels, skewered in headlights, or a vole, sensing too late the owl poised overhead for a dive?

'Oh, they'll believe me,' she says. 'They'll believe me because they'll want to.' She taps her fingers thoughtfully against her mouth. 'I'll tell them you lured me up here,' she decides. 'I may as well use your own story, after all. You've been obsessing about those bones again, so I'll say you thought you were the ghost, and that I was the poor Judith who you were shouting about before. Ah, you see!' she exclaims as my expression changes. 'It's true, isn't it?'

She shouldn't have reminded me about Judith. That was a mistake, I think, as something implacable settles hard inside me. The memory of Judith holding Kit runs through me clear and cold. She threatened to hurt my son. This time, Judith isn't going to win.

'Well, we'd better get on with it.' Angie rubs her hands together, all practicality. She sees my gaze flicker to the stairs, and steps quickly into my way. 'Don't make this hard on yourself, Kate. You'll never get there before me with that peg leg of yours.'

'I can try,' I say, knowing I won't make it.

'Then I'll catch you and push you down,' she says. 'You can break your neck. It's all the same to me.'

'You won't be able to explain that away as suicide.' I am oddly calm.

'True. Another fall would be more poetic, but at least you'd be *gone*.' Without warning, she lunges at me on the last word and I stumble back, my bad leg buckling. I cry out as I fall, and Angie is on top of me. It is like being attacked by a wild animal. There is no reasoning with her, no rules. I am fighting for my life. I am fighting for Kit, and for Felix.

I am unprepared for how fast and powerful she is. I'm trying to beat her off with my hands, but she gets her knee on my chest, right where my ribs were broken, and the pain is a bright dazzle behind my eyes. I can't think about it, though, I can't pass out. I have to stay alive.

There is a great red roaring in my head as I scrabble desperately for a hold, but the panels on the tower roof are smooth and my heels skid over them. I manage to grab onto one of the vents, but Angie is straightening and hauling me up. I can't believe how strong she is. The vent slips from my damp grasp and my fingers scrape over the panels as Angie drags me towards the edge.

I have no breath to scream but I do my best to make myself heavy, and kick and scratch at her when she bends for a better grip.

'Bitch!' Angie draws back her arm and delivers a slap to my face that makes my head jerk to one side.

'Angie, for God's sake! Stop this!' I gasp, beating at her, but she won't stop.

'This is all your fault,' she mutters. 'You always have to spoil everything.' And she kicks my bad leg.

Agony blossoms so violently that it blots out everything for a few seconds. When I come round, I am too close to the wall. Terror gives me the strength to break free and I start to crawl away.

'Come back here!' Furious, Angie pounces on me and grabs at my arm and twists it behind my back so that I sob with the pain of it.

'Angie, please!' I try as she yanks me up and back against the parapet. I am perilously close to the gap now. 'We can stop this.'

'No,' she pants. For an instant sadness races over her face, regret for the path not taken, but then it is gone. 'No, it's too late now.'

'You're not having Felix – *argh!*' I can't prevent the howl as she hits me again in the ribs. She knows exactly where to hurt me. My yell almost smothers the sound of tyres on the gravel below, but I hear the clunk of a car door closing. Hope energizes me. 'Matt! Matt!' I scream, before Angie drags me down out of sight and claps her palm over my face.

Did he hear me? It's so high up here, but he'll be looking for me, won't he?

Angie is punching at me one-handed, but the thought of Matt has given me strength and I grab hold of her hair and pull it as hard as I can. The neat, shiny bob is wildly dishevelled now.

She grunts in pain, swearing under her breath as she gets her knee back on my stomach and beats at me with her vicious hand, but I am fighting not just for myself but for Isabel, who could not risk fighting Judith with Kit in danger. I can feel her remembered rage swelling in my head. She knows now that Judith didn't win in the end, that Kit survived and Edmund was buried alone. Judith might have been mistress in name, but I know in my bones – or perhaps it is Isabel who knows – that she had no joy of it.

Angie's palm is clamped over my face, smothering me, but I summon another burst of energy to bite her hand. She yelps and snatches it away, which allows me to draw breath for another scream, and I scramble up as best I can. We're right over by the gap again, scratching and scrabbling at each other, swearing, sobbing for breath.

'Matt!' I manage desperately, but it is Angie who risks a glance below, and she laughs triumphantly.

'It's not Matt, it's George! Looks like your hero isn't coming after all!' And then she starts screaming, too. 'George! George! Help me! She's trying to kill me!'

Does she really believe there's a way out of this? I can't spare the energy to contradict her or to see how George reacts. Having summoned him, Angie cannot afford to have me still here on top of the tower by the time he gets up the stairs to rescue her. She redoubles her efforts, but I have Isabel's strength inside me. We are not going to give in now, but still, I am tiring as Angie's blows rain down on me, and pain hammers at me. She manages to drag me up and back to the gap, and is shoving at me, forcing me down into it when George bursts out of the stairwell.

'Kate! Angie!' He bends over, heaving for breath, just as I did when I ran up those stairs to reach Kit. 'What the hell is going on?'

I can't speak. I don't dare take my attention from Angie. She is debating whether to give me one last shove and send me over anyway. I can feel it, feel her hands tense, but at the last minute she must realize that her only chance with George would go with me. Changing tactic, she lets me slump back onto the tower roof, where I curl up against the pain, whooping for breath.

'George! Thank God!' she cries, and stumbles over towards him. 'I think Kate's gone mad!'

'What the—?' George staggers a little as she throws herself at him.

'She attacked me!'

'What? Why?'

'She's had another breakdown,' Angie says breathlessly, but George is already putting her to one side and hurrying over to me.

'Kate! My God, Kate, what's happened to you?'

Angie's face convulses. 'George! *She* went for *me*!'

George isn't listening. He's patting his pockets for his phone, handing it back to her without looking at her. 'Kate's hurt. Call an ambulance.'

Over his shoulder, I see Angie take the phone instinctively. She stands looking at it in her hand for a long moment.

'For God's sake, Angie, call 999!' George snaps while I am still desperately trying to suck in a breath. 'Kate needs help!'

'Kate,' she repeats, quite quietly at first. 'Kate, Kate, Kate!' Her voice rises to a shriek. 'I'm sick of it!' And she pulls back her arm and throws the phone over the parapet as hard as she can.

George watches it go, open-mouthed. 'Angie! What's got into you?'

'She doesn't love you, you know,' she says to him. 'She's going away. You don't need to go to New Zealand. We can be happy here without her.' Her smile is somehow grotesque in her battered face. It is the first time I have ever seen her look less than immaculate. I have got in some scratches and slaps of my own and her hair is a mess, but more disturbing by far is the shining insanity in her eyes.

'I know,' George says roughly. 'It's not about Kate. I just need to get away from Askerby for a while.'

'But . . . you can't!' The last vestige of colour drains from her face. 'You can't leave me!'

George looks uneasy. 'You'll be fine, Angie. I'm sure the new estate manager will find a job for you, and if not there'll always be work for you at the Hall.'

A job. Not a family, not a home, not a place to belong.

I see the moment when Angie realizes that it's over, the moment her dream is kicked out from beneath her. George will not marry her. Felix will not be hers. I will not die.

Instead I will know what she did, or rather, what she didn't do. I will tell the Vavasours and they will shun her. She'll have to leave Askerby.

I'd die if I had to leave.

The thought spreads across her face like a drop of ink in water, colouring everything. All she has ever wanted, knocked out of her grasp and shattered.

Desperately, I drag myself up. 'George,' I rasp. 'Stop her!'

But he doesn't understand. He doesn't see her walk dreamily over to the parapet. Half blinded by pain, I throw myself towards her. 'Angie, no!' I try to cry but it comes out as barely more than a whisper.

She is too quick for me. I clutch hold of the edge of her quilted gilet, but already she is climbing up into the gap, while George is still frozen in place.

'Angie, don't!' I plead, scrabbling for a better grip. 'We'll work something out. It'll be fine.'

I don't think she hears me. She looks down almost reflectively. 'I won't leave,' she says to the air. 'This is where I belong. This is where I'm going to stay.'

Then she spreads her arms and steps out into the misty air, leaving the gilet hanging limp and empty in my hands.

Chapter Thirty-seven

Helpless, I slide back down to the lead panels, while George looks blankly around him. 'I have to get help,' he says at last, his voice raw with shock.

'Matt's coming,' I manage. I don't suppose I sound any better. I am still clutching Angie's gilet and shuddering with reaction. 'I don't want Felix to see . . . to see . . .' I can't finish.

I don't want him to see Angie's body. She had picked out that spot for me, where there were no trees to break her fall. She is lying on the gravel in front of the Hall where she never belonged.

'No. God. No.' He rubs a hand over his face. 'Can you move?'

'I'm . . . not sure.' Now that the danger is over, the pain is raging and darkness flickers at the edges of my consciousness. I lay my head back against the parapet. 'You go. Get help. Stop Matt.'

I think I may pass out then. The next thing I know, I am

lying on the roof of the tower and Matt is bending over me, his face ravaged. 'Kate. Jesus, Kate,' he keeps saying, over and over again. He strips off his jacket and tucks it around me, and I clutch gratefully at it. I am so cold I cannot imagine ever being warm again. It should be dark, I think, but the sun hasn't yet given up its struggle to break through the mist, and as a result the light is curiously bright and blank and blurred all at the same time.

'I'm okay.' My voice scrapes in my throat and my lips are so dry it is hard to get the words out. 'Felix?'

'Felix is fine. George stopped me at the gatehouse and told me what had happened. I took Felix to the Lodge, and Fiona is looking after him. George has called the police and they're sending an air ambulance.'

'Is Angie . . . ?'

Matt shakes his head, grim-faced. 'The air ambulance is for you. I don't think we can get you down those tower steps.'

'I'm—' A scream as I try to move my leg cuts off my attempt to assure him that I am fine.

'That's what I thought,' Matt says.

There isn't room to land the helicopter on the tower roof, so a paramedic is lowered with a stretcher. Matt holds my hand as I am strapped on.

'You're going to be okay,' he says, and I believe him.

The paramedic tells me jokes to distract me from the fact that I am dangling in mid-air as we are winched up to the helicopter. The door is barely closed before the chopper lifts and swings away into the eerie light. Below, through the glass panel,

I see Askerby Hall grow smaller and smaller, and Matt, a tiny, lonely figure on top of the tower, watching me go through the mist.

They keep me in hospital overnight for observation, but I am only badly bruised and shocked. I am fine until Matt arrives, and then, to my shame, I burst into tears. He spends the night by my bed, and I fall asleep at last holding his hand. He is still there when I wake in the morning.

He drives me back to Askerby. I think of the last time I drove that road with Fiona and Jasper, and when we crest the hill, I remember again how wet Isabel was when she rode to Askerby for the first time with Edmund after her wedding. This time, though, it doesn't feel like my memory.

I try to explain it to Matt. 'It's as if Isabel isn't part of me any more. I can remember, but it's like a film I've seen now, not like something that happened to *me*.'

'Maybe now you know what happened to her, and to her son, she can rest at last,' he says. 'She doesn't need you any more.'

'I hope so.'

Just like before, we turn in past the Lodge and I think about Angie, growing up there on the boundary of the estate, dreaming about living in the big house, about belonging. We drive up the avenue, around the curve in the road, and there is the gate-house again and, beyond it, the Hall. Matt stops the car outside the great carved doorway and I look up at the house through the windscreen. I don't see the darkness now, I see the warm

PAMELA HARTSHORNE

brickwork. The windows are no longer watchful, they are just old, and while the tower makes me wince at the memory, it doesn't seem to be reaching for me. It is just a house.

I can't help my eyes going to the patch of gravel where Angie must have landed. It has been brushed over, the police tape removed. There is no trace that she was ever there at all. She is part of Askerby's past now.

I am frowning slightly until I realize what is missing. 'Where are all the visitors?'

'The house is closed today. "Due to unforeseen circumstances."' Matt hooks his fingers in the air. 'Even the Vavasours couldn't carry on as if it was business as usual today.' He glances at me. 'Ready?'

'Yes.' I take a deep breath. I remember it all now. I can face anything.

Matt helps me out of his car. I wince as I move my battered leg around but I am distracted by the door opening. Felix stands there, framed in the carved doorway, his expression alight with anticipation. He stops at the sight of me, as if he is uncertain, and I brace myself for the guard to drop over his eyes, but then he hurtles towards me, down the steps and across the gravel.

'Mummy!' he cries, throwing his arms around my thighs. 'Mummy!'

His small sturdy body knocks me off balance and back against Matt's car. My ribs shriek in protest, but never has a pain been more welcome. I wrap my arms around my son and press his head against my stomach. 'Felix.' My throat is so tight, it is all I can say. 'Felix.'

I look over his head at Matt, who smiles and nods down at my feet. Pippin has followed Felix and is squirming and pawing at my ankles, wagging her tail, whimpering with joy. 'It's over,' he says softly. 'Welcome home.'

Angie's death has hit the Vavasours hard, harder than I expected, and George most of all. I tell them the truth in the end. It seems to me there have been enough secrets and evasions.

'I didn't know,' George says dully. 'I had no idea she thought of me as anything other than a boss.'

'Didn't you?' I ask. 'Angie seemed to think that you and she were on the verge of getting it together before Michael and I came back to live here.'

A flush deepens the ruddiness in his cheeks. 'Once. When we'd had too much to drink one night. But it didn't mean anything,' he says. 'I never really thought of her that way.'

That was the problem, I think.

'It meant something to Angie,' I say. 'All she ever wanted was to belong here. She wanted to be part of a family.' I look at Margaret. 'Even one that thinks nothing of getting rid of an inconvenient child.'

Two spots of hectic colour burn in Margaret's cheeks. 'What would you have done if you had given birth to a *monster*?' she demands. 'Things were different in those days. If the child had been obviously mentally disabled, we could have changed the entail, but there was no sign of that.'

'He just wasn't pretty enough for you,' I say coldly.

'It was all Ralph's fault,' she spits out. 'He was supposed to take it away, not bring it back. We told everyone my baby had been stillborn, but it was always *there*! That vile man, Adam Kaczka, he never let me forget it! We had to pay and pay and *pay*! Ralph was besotted with that Polish woman. "We owe her," he kept saying. Anyone could see that she was in love with him. That's why she wanted to come back here. Ralph said she swore not to tell the truth, but I might have known she would babble in the end.'

'She kept your secret a long time,' I say. 'She's ninety-five, and she gets confused. It wasn't hard for Angie to work out the truth.'

Margaret's mouth works. Her lipstick, I see, is bleeding into her upper lip. 'Ralph blamed me,' she said. 'He wanted an heir, and I gave him one. There was nothing wrong with Jasper or Joanna, but he could never forget the first child. Once Jasper was born, he couldn't bring himself to touch me.' Her eyes are dark with memory. 'But I didn't complain. I knew my duty. I did what I had to do. If Ralph wanted that . . . that *thing* . . . as his heir, he could have said, couldn't he?'

She's right, I think. Ralph didn't have to hide Peter away. He didn't have to fall in with Margaret's plan. Had it, in the end, been no more for him than an excuse to get Dosia back to Askerby?

Margaret is eighty-seven. She is not going to be punished. What would they charge her with? Being unfeeling? I suspect the Vavasours are not the only family who have got rid of unwanted children, one way or another.

Fiona is staring at Margaret. 'How have you lived with yourself all these years? If I could have Michael back for five minutes, I would do it. I can't imagine giving my son away . . . !'

'You've done all right, haven't you?' Margaret snaps. 'You've been happy to be Lady Vavasour, and Askerby is still here, isn't it? It still has its traditions, the way it always has. The family is here, and the Hall will be passed on to the next generation and then the next. *That's* how I live with myself. It is the family that matters, not the individual. But you,' she says, fixing me with her cold green glare, 'you care nothing about the Vavasours. You don't care about Askerby. All you care about is Felix.'

'That's right,' I say. I'm not going to be ashamed about that. 'Felix is always going to be my priority.'

'What will happen to Askerby when Jasper dies?'

Jasper shifts uneasily in his chair. 'Felix will inherit Askerby, of course.'

'That will be Felix's decision to make,' I say. 'For now, he's just a little boy. He doesn't need to be burdened with the expectations of the Vavasours just yet.'

'So you're taking him away?' Fiona's mouth trembles. Felix is all she has of Michael now, I remember.

'We'll come back,' I say. 'You'll see Felix for holidays, for visits. But for now we need to make a life of our own. When he's older, he can decide for himself whether he wants to take on Askerby or not.'

Fiona nods, swallows. 'And you? Are you going to America?'

'I don't know,' I say. 'I'm not ready to make that kind of decision yet.' First, I need to remember what it's like to live an ordinary life. Now that my memory has come back, I can work, and Matt will be here for another few months . . . 'We'll see,' I say.

I worry about what will happen to Dosia now, but Jasper and Fiona are paying for a carer to look after her. When I go to see her, I'm not sure if she will really understand what happened to her granddaughter, but it turns out that she knows more than we think. She is not confused about Angie, much as she might wish to be. *Sometimes not remembering is a blessing*: that was what she said to me when I first went to see her.

I take Dosia's fragile hand. 'I'm so sorry about Angie,' I say, and she sighs tremulously.

'Poor Angelika,' she says sadly. 'How was she ever going to be happy? She never understood that you can't always have everything you want.' Dosia sighs again and shakes her old head. 'I blame myself,' she says. 'Her mother abandoned her, her father died, she had nothing but this Lodge and her old grandmother . . . perhaps if I hadn't wanted to stay here so much, she would have found something else she wanted besides the house she could never have and a family who would never accept her.'

'She could have been happy with what she had,' I say, remembering what Isabel said to Judith. 'Yes, it must have been hard to be abandoned by her mother, but Peter was rejected by his, too.'

'He didn't know that,' Dosia points out.

'He spent his life with a terrible disfigurement, but in all the photos I've seen of him, he was smiling,' I say, and she nods, a wavery bob of her head, and taps her frail heart.

'He was the child of my heart,' she tells me, her eyes filling with tears.

'He was lucky to have you as a mother,' I say. 'He must have known that.'

'I loved him,' she agrees. 'Not just for himself, but because he was Ralph's. Adam never forgave me for agreeing to the deception, but how could I not take the baby? What would have happened to him otherwise? But Marek, he was Adam's son. He never understood why Peter was so special to me.'

'And Ralph?' I ask. 'Did he know his son?'

'Ralph did his duty.' Dosia lets out a long, regretful breath. 'He was Lord Vavasour. He did what was expected of him. You know, we never slept together, not once.'

She looks so sad that I squeeze her hand. 'But you loved him, anyway.'

'Yes.' Her old face softens. 'Yes, I loved him. He wanted us to go away, but I said no. How could we do that to Margaret, to Adam? To Marek and Joanna and Jasper? And to Peter most of all. What would have happened to him without us? Our families were more important than what we felt for each other.'

Dosia falls silent, and I wonder if she is sleeping, but she is thinking. 'That was something Angelika never understood,' she says. 'She thought a family was a thing you can have. Poor child.' Her voice quavers with sadness. 'She didn't understand that a family isn't something you're entitled to. It's about what you do, and who you care for, and what you're prepared to give.'

George is still going to New Zealand. He is shocked by Angie's death but he isn't grieving for her. He says he needs a change and to do something for himself, and I think he is right. Philippa is going to manage Askerby in his stead. Margaret hates the idea, of course – a woman managing the estate! Whoever heard of such a thing? – but I think Philippa is looking forward to it.

'Like love,' I say.

'Yes, like love.' Dosia nods. 'Angelika didn't know how to give. She only knew how to envy and to want.' She looks at me with her wise old eyes. 'But you, you have love to give, I think?'

I smile. 'I am lucky. I have a son.' I look down at Pippin, who has settled with her head resting possessively on my foot so that she will know the instant I move. 'And a dog!'

'And a lover?' She laughs at my expression. 'You young people, you think you invented sex. Remember,' she says, 'love isn't just about giving. Sometimes it's about taking, too, and sometimes that is harder to do. I wouldn't take it from Ralph,' she remembers sadly. 'I thought it was wrong. We chose to put our families first, and that was the right thing to do, yes, but now he is dead and I am old and alone, and I cannot help sometimes thinking about what it would have been like if I had been brave enough to accept being loved by him, if I had been brave enough to change, to take a second chance. I wonder if our families could have changed with us.'

Dosia sighs, a long, wistful sigh. 'So remember, dear child,' she says to me. 'Remember to look forward. Remember to take as well as to give. Promise me that if you have the chance to love again, you will take it.'

I think about Michael and how much I loved him, and then I think about Matt, about how safe and settled I feel knowing that he is there. There is so much that we haven't discussed, so much that is still uncertain, but I know how my heart swells at the thought of him. I know how he makes me laugh, and how Felix shouts with pleasure at the sight of him, and how the touch of his hand makes my blood hum, low and insistent.

I smile at Dosia. 'I'll remember,' I say. 'I promise.'

We lay Isabel to rest on a blustery spring day. I have persuaded the Vavasours to have the bones DNA-tested at last, and once you get past all the scientific humming and hawing, there seems little doubt that the bones found under the Visitor Centre belong to an ancestor. Fiona and Jasper are still hoping that Felix and I won't move too far away. They have made arrangements to have Edmund's tomb opened, and Reverend Rolland holds a special service in the church at Askerby.

Standing next to Matt, holding Felix by the hand, I watch as Isabel's bones are laid carefully over Edmund's coffin and the tomb is resealed. I let the words of the service roll over me and I remember the times when she was happy: lying next to Edmund, strumming with the pleasure of his touch; laughing with her son; riding over the golden moors with the wind in her hair. Her bones are here, but her spirit is riding on and on towards the horizon with Edmund beside her. A new plaque sits ready to be attached to the tomb. It is my gift to her, in thanks for letting me share the happiness of her life.

In memory of Edmund Vavasour and
his beloved wife, Isabel, and of their son,
Christopher Vavasour. *Requiescant in pace*.

Rest in peace.

Acknowledgements

Writing the story is only the first step in making a book. I am grateful, as always, for the support of my editor, Louise Buckley, of Wayne Brookes and of the whole team at Pan Macmillan, who take my words and turn them into a real book. In particular, I would like to mention the copy editor for *House of Shadows*, Mary Chamberlain, who sorted out my muddled dates and tidied up my original manuscript with awesome efficiency.

Special thanks are due to Julia Pokora for advice on Polish, and Antonella Gramola Sands on Latin; to Ailsa Mainman, who knows people who know about old bones; and most especially to Mary Abbott, who was so helpful about Kate's medical care and physiotherapy, and who scratched her head to make the treatment fit the needs of the story. Thank you, Mary: you get to be the best of physios in fiction, as in real life! Needless to say, any mistakes on any subject are all of my own making.

I'd like to take the opportunity to thank, too, all the new

friends and readers I have made through my Facebook page, www.facebook.com/PamelaHartshorneAuthor. Their enthusiasm for my books and general encouragement means more than they can possibly know.

extracts reading groups
competitions books new
discounts extracts
extracts
competitions extracts discounts
books
new events
events books
extracts new reading groups
new titles reading groups
interviews
events extracts
discounts
new books events
events new
discounts extracts discounts
www.panmacmillan.com
extracts events reading groups
competitions books extracts new
reading groups
events
reading groups
books
interviews new books extracts